fruitcake

RABBIT HOUSE PRESS
Versailles, KY 40383

Published in the United States of America by Rabbit House Press, December 2023.

For inquiries about author appearances and/or volume orders contact us at rabbithousepress.com.

ISBN: 979-8-9871928-8-7

Editor: Erin Chandler
Cover design: Carrie Dyer
Interior design & formatting: Brooke Lee

fruitcake

MARK DANIEL COMPTON

RABBIT
HOUSE
PRESS
rabbithousepress.com

Chapter One

As locals drove past the Dixon Southern Baptist Church, they could not help but notice the colorful black woman climbing the stairs of what everybody in town knew was an all-white congregation. Lula May Dixon did not look as if she had been born in the nineteen thirties, she was much too agile for anyone to assume that. There were many women in their fifties that did not look as young as she. It was not because life had been easy for her. No black person living in the American South during the country's midcentury civil rights conflicts escaped the emotional and often physical scarring from that frequently violent era. The scars Lula May wore on the inside were not noticeable in her outwardly appearance. Many white folks in Dixon marveled at her beauty, especially Lula May's complexion. One man even told her to her face, "girl you're the color of coffee with cream, why don't you let me have a taste?"

"There ain't no sugar in this coffee," she said with just the right squint in her eyes and lift of her eyebrows that the ole country boy knew he best not chase that cat.

Maybe it was being a black child raised in the American South that caused her senses to have such acuteness. Her hazel eyes needed no glasses to see. Her pierced ears, with their simple diamond studs, needed no hearing aids to hear, and her small European nose provided a sense of smell that was impeccable. Looking at Lula May at this given moment in time could not reflect her humble beginnings as the daughter of sharecroppers and the granddaughter of men and women born into slavery. Lula May was slave to no one. This was not to say that Lula May didn't work, she had held down more than one domestic job at the same time during her years of labor.

Ever since her very first job doing laundry for a prominent local family during the Second World War, Lula May spent money on her appearance, an act that being childless could only afford. Always slim, her body resembled that of a dancer and many of her era remarked that her beauty was equaled to that of Eartha Kitt's. On this special day she wore a royal-blue peplum dress with a ruffled shear gold mesh over-skirt adorned with bells and charms that she personally attached on every point. The flare of the over-skirt was not as broad and the length not as short as those worn by younger women, still its sensual nature was intact and caught the eye of both men and women alike who were all entranced by its elegance. Her gold broad-brimmed hat was the only hint that she was attending a Christmas wedding on this hot July day. That was because affixed to the blue silk hatband was a white poinsettia flower she had taken from an artificial Christmas decoration she kept in her attic 'til the proper season.

Slightly nervous, but not for what some would consider the obvious reasons, she removed her hat to fan herself and smiled from its stirring breeze and from the intake of freshly mowed grass and the roses that bordered the church's porch on either side. The roses' scent had left a taste of honey in the back of her throat which had given her the sensation of power she knew she would need by day's end. A power that gave her a Grinch like grin. "Loco," She called out as she put her hat back on covering her skunk-striped hair. Then from her gold sequined handbag she removed a compact and gazed into its mirror. "Oh, you devil, you behave yourself, you hear," Lula May said, as she snapped the compact shut, placing it safely away.

An angry hot dry breeze, seemingly from nowhere, blew through the pines and Lula May held on to her hat as the bells on her dress jangled along with the wind chimes that hung from the parishioner's porch, which presided proudly across the street. Startled, she suddenly withdrew a small gold cross from her bosom and kissed it before going indoors. As she opened the door, a second even stronger wind snatched the knob from her sweaty hand and slammed the door against the brick wall announcing her presence as she stepped inside. A third wind blew through the aisle before the bride's occupational partner, fellow paramedic Lloyd Parker, could close the door. Ushering with the rest of his unit, Parker was an easily bamboozled, slightly balding, extremely buff, and hairy blue-eyed blond constrained by his dress uniform due to his recent fitness routine. Mouth aghast, he watched the candles' flames as they danced and stretched high into the air before going out to his horror. The Yerby brothers, exotically handsome identical twin firemen, also in dress uniform, preceded Lula May relighting the candles as Parker, the name Lloyd's fellow firemen called him, escorted her to her seat.

A smart-ass boy of ten sang "Jingle Bells" before his horrified mother could put her hand over his mouth and whisper a warning in his ear. His eyes, while staring at the black woman, ballooned like a blowfish. Lula May did not have to hear the mother's forewarning to her son to know what she had told him. Teasing the boy, Lula May raised a single eyebrow and grinned before allowing Parker to continue ushering her to her seat. His mother, now frightened as the boy, cinched him to her side where he stayed 'til ceremony's end.

Generations perpetuated fear and hatred one right after the other, which stunted each succeeding generation's growth as human beings. God knows releasing prejudice is harder than changing religion for most folks, Lula May concluded in her mind, feeling slightly exhausted from the decades of hate she has beheld in Dixon. She tried to toss the thought aside by admiring the effort the bride's family had put into creating the holiday spirit. The church appeared as if Martha Stewart herself had come to Dixon and decorated it for Christmas. Poinsettias, magnolia, holly, ivy, ribbon and candles adorned the stained-glass building. Still, all faces continued to turn toward Lula May, which confirmed what she already knew as she proceeded down the aisle on Parker's arm, she was indeed the only African American in attendance.

She recognized many of her employer's bridge party, most of whom acknowledged her as she approached closer to the front of the sanctuary. Lula May was well respected by those in need of her distinctive manner of services. Distracted by the music, Lula May thought that the chiming created by her dress added to the wedding's ambiance as the pianist and a choir of children dressed as angels sang, "Christmas Time Is Here." She waved discreetly at those she knew and nodded as if accepting recognition for some fabled feat before facing forward. Placed directly behind the bride's family, she slid down the pew, patting the cushioned space by her before she sat down. "Sits right here," Lula May whispered.

In no time at all the church was packed to the gills with well-wishers and Dixon disbelievers alike who never thought they would ever see the day when Charity McRae would get married. "You'dz think this was a high school football game and we'z in the finals by the size of this here crowd," Lula May said to the couple behind her. "You know, I've known this family longer than anyone here, some four generations. I couldn't have been no more than seven or eight when Mrs. White, the bride's great grandmother, died during the last days of the Great Depression. Mrs. Marla-Belle was what most called her. She was a kind lady, yes, she was. It was the biggest funeral Dixon's ever seen. Still is I believe. Both blacks and whites, rich and poor, the good and the downright evil removed their hats as she moseyed on down Dixon's streets in a grand hearse one final time." She sighed with the memory then glanced at the compact. "Oh, look!" turning back, "Lordy, doesn't she look beautiful. You always knows the wedding is about to begin as soon as they seat the mother of the bride." Lula May smiled with pride at the adult woman she helped to raise. "Those girls are the closest thing I'dz gots to my owns," she continued babbling to the baffled couple, "As crazy as they is, I loves alls of 'em."

The lights flickered as the mother of the bride stepped from the church's foyer into the sanctuary. Thunder clapped and shook the old building, the overhead lights swayed during the downpour, it seemed to be a seasonal Southern afternoon storm as the rain began to pelt the stained-glass windows. "I don't remember any call for rain," a guest loudly whispered to be heard by her spouse. "There wasn't," another guest responded.

Lula May took her compact and while glancing into its mirror, she caught the reflection of the mother of the bride as she waited to be escorted up the aisle. Smiling and clacking her teeth together as if to examine them she whispered, "Satisfied? Nothin' more cleansing than a five o'clock rain, you'z can almost set your watch by it," she stated nonchalantly. With the rain's sudden end she finished, "Unfortunately, they last as 'bout as long as a good man." This caused a chuckle from some of the female company close enough to hear her quick wit.

With the compact opened on the arm of the pew, she sat the confine where every member of the bridal party could have a final rearview glance as they made their way straight toward the altar. With each step, they crossed the worn, unchanged course through the sanctuary, the same century's old, protracted procession taken by their countless ancestors prior. From their divine introduction into this transcendent tribe until their leaving it, as well as all the other spiritual sacraments expected of and by its congregate during their lives, these rituals commenced at path's holy end which proved that a straight line could also be a circle in Lula May's mind.

Walkin' down the aisle, each of my girls will stare back at where they's been and where they's at now and where they's going, and be proud, Lula May pondered while positioning the compact. *Yes sir, alls be promisin' for the future.* Following the veneer red path that could not hide the history that laid beneath, the whole family would reflect within this casing's mirror. Compressed, condensed, and concentrated, all could feel the spirits residing within, a spirit of ecstasy, a spirit of fervor, a spirit of grief.

Chapter Two

Bonnie White McRae Dickson was a Southern belle. She considered it her duty to be one, as well as the duty of her four daughters. All of her girls were from her first marriage to Major Thomas Newton McRae. He was killed during the Vietnam War while she was pregnant with her youngest. To her great embarrassment, her water broke during his funeral. Bonnie had hoped that the child would be a boy, instead she had another girl, Charity Thomasina, the bride.

Her second marriage was to Richard "Dickey" Dickson, which was just as tragic in Bonnie's eyes. Dickey, a descendant of the family from which the town was supposed to take its name (until a Postmaster changed the spelling on a form to reflect his father's Confederate service), was like Bonnie, a member of the old Southern aristocracy. Dickey had worked at his father's automobile dealership, and it was a fact that he had sold most of his cars to women. His slippery tongue had many women coming in for test-drives for he delivered the best ride in town, it had been said. Dickey disappeared on Christmas Eve 1986, close to twenty years ago. The inquiry into his disappearance brought to light his massive infidelities, as well as his father's, which caused many divorces to the embarrassment of Bonnie and also Dickey's mother, Betty. Though his body was never found, it's believed throughout Dixon that some jealous husband took Dickey for his final ride.

Bonnie had taken up smoking because all fashionable women had done so in the 50s and 60s. She seriously enjoyed smoking up until recently when statutes made it such a hassle. She saw her two-packs-a-day habit as her only vice, and considering all that she has been through in life, she believed she deserved at least this one flaw. Bonnie was a devout Southern Baptist and had been all of her sixty-two years on God's green earth. Her only other vice, though she did not consider it one, was her vanity. She had never been overweight, during her pregnancies she would not go out in public after the fifth or sixth month (when she began to show) and had lost the weight quickly after giving birth.

More than her cigarettes, Bonnie appeared to be addicted to all forms of make-up that were at a modern woman's disposal, liquid eyeliner, mascara, and a rainbow of eye shadows were just the beginning basics for the eyes. This resulted in her looking (especially after a couple of drinks chased with classic country music on the radio) as if she had attended a gay Tammy Faye Baker equal rights rally and lost. In her youth she had dark auburn hair but its current thinning, due to her blood pressure medication, had brought about her ten-year collection of Dolly Parton wigs. It was as a blonde that most now thought of her. Ethel, her younger sister and also her beautician, was the only person who had seen her without her wigs in many a year, which included her daughters. Excluding last year's tragedy, of course, when reality was revealed for all to see.

Bonnie waved at guests as her grandson, Oscar Job McCaskill, escorted her to her seat. Upon seeing members of her bridge club, Bonnie's penciled in eyebrows arose with glee for she knew that all of them had laughed behind her back at the thought of Charity ever marrying. What a great accomplishment I've achieved, she thought, as she continued down the aisle wearing her 1980s accessories, which she believed were in a revival. Besides, the accessories perfectly matched her sapphire-sequined dress cut tastefully below the knee.

Oscar, a fifteen-year-old with dirty-blond hair like his father's, was uncomfortable in his white suit and red tie, but liked the attention he received from the girls in attendance while he and his sister Sally stood by the guest book. When he was among strangers, Oscar embarrassed easily. His greatest fear that day was that he would get an erection sometime during the service. His fear was based on recent occurrences.

An incident toward the end of spring semester, when he was called to the blackboard to show an algebra equation, was the most embarrassing. The harrowing experience resulted in his new nickname at school, "Bulge," which his teasing friends aptly called him. After seating his grandmother, he returned to the back of the church as quickly as he could without giving the appearance of running due to his latest uncle-in-law's sister sitting in the pew two rows behind his grandmother. Iris was wearing a dress with a plunging neckline because it gave a false appearance of height, not to mention the dress exposed her most recent investment. She thought it also would give some of those in attendance a slight rise and laughed at her own internal double-entendre as earlier she dressed for the day's event while sliding on her stilettos. As Oscar hurried down the aisle after Iris lifted his eyes to her smile, she knew she was right.

"Another chip off the ole block," she thought turning her head to watch the boy return to the back of the church. Once Oscar reached the back, he took the arm of his Algebra teacher, Mrs. Coolie, who was always running late. Caught in the sudden burst of rain, Mrs. Coolie's dress clung to her form and showed the outline of her undergarments. Oscar turned and saw Iris looking back at him, she licked her lips to tease the boy before turning around to face the front. An instant protrusion announced itself and Oscar's face went flush with embarrassment. He couldn't believe it, if any of his friends in attendance noticed they would think he had the "hots" for his plain middle-aged math teacher. He quickly sat her, but not before she observed his predicament.

Twice now, she thought. *Maybe I should change my name to Mrs. Robinson.*

She smiled. "If you ever need some tutoring next year, Oscar," the dowdy woman said before she drew her mousey hair behind an ear, "let me know." Oscar wasn't sure but he thought one of his mother's best friends just hit on him. His predicament dissipated as fast as it arose.

"I'm getting it, Mrs. Coolie. Wait till you see my mom coming down the aisle, she looks like a movie star," Oscar whispered to his teacher before returning to his duties.

Lula May's thoughts were broken by the reflected gleam that hit her eyes from the Dr. Reverend's teeth as he mounted the pulpit. "Always smiling," Lula May grimaced.

"What a big name for such a small mans, you know he's a widower. And in a small town a single mans with a steady income is like honey to a bee. My business has reached new heights since the Dr. Rev. Three Names has come to town. Even Miss Ethel and Miss Bonnie came to me for one of my love potions." Dr. Reverend Paul Pruett-Peterson, the size of a horse jockey, took center stage. The five-foot-tall widower gazed over the crowd in amazement wishing he could have a congregation this size in attendance every Sunday.

The groom, Will Zemp, followed "The Good Dr. Reverend" (as his congregation referred to him) nervously up to the altar or pulpit as most Baptists express it. Will was a slender emaciated man in a white tuxedo with a matching red bow tie and cummerbund. The wide cummerbund helped to add weight to his lean svelte appearance. His straight fine hair, much longer than the bride's, elongated his face when he did not have it pulled back in a ponytail. He still bore the scars of homelessness in his demeanor. Though he was trying to overcome his humility, he was still in shock. *I, Will Zemp, will be marrying into one of the oldest families of influence in this small southern town*, he thought quietly. A Wal-Mart truck driver dropped him into Dixon not a year ago while he was hitch-hiking down Florida way. Honestly stupefied, Will tried to remember all the lies that were created by his future mother-in-law to cover up, as she put it, "your tawdry past."

Ethel White Fields, Bonnie's widowed single sister and the wedding's director, waved at the pianist to stop and play the chosen music for the bridal party's procession down the aisle, but the pianist was so immersed in the music he didn't notice Ethel's arms flouncing around. Frustrated, Ethel steamed up the aisle like a locomotive, stumbled over the flimsy red fabric used as a faux carpet, and crash-landed to the stifled snickering of the crowd. The Good Dr. Reverend, Will Zemp, and Noah Pruett-Peterson, The Good Dr. Reverend's fourteen-year-old son, helped the blush, red Ethel to her feet. As Ethel stood up, she smiled down at The Good Dr. Reverend with thanks. Never noticing the situation, the pianist continued his jazz solo from the "Charlie Brown Christmas" show. The carpet was now filled with even more wrinkles. Ethel worried that the same embarrassment could happen to the bridal party. Begrudgingly, she straightened the fabric with the help of Noah. *Noah sure has grown since the first time I met him*, Ethel thought noticing the boy's slacks were high waters.

Securing the compact, Lula May whispered to Ethel as she tugged the red cloth by Lula May's pew. "Leave good enough alone my sweet child, leave good enough alone. Lift your head, stand up and begin anew."

Ethel did as her mammy said without question. Upon standing from the straightened carpet, she was eye-to-eye with the Good Dr. Reverend. His standing on the pulpit, not to mention the rise in his shoes, made it possible. The swaying of the pianist caught the corner of her eye returning her immediately to her duties, but not before she used her muse-like stare on Paul Pruett-Peterson. "My dance card is open."

"So is mine," he replied.

"You're penciled in," as she two-stepped over and signaled to the pianist to begin.

"If poor Miss Ethel weren't so desperate for a man, we wouldn't be having this wedding on this fine Fourth of July weekend. We sure wouldn't." Returning her compact to the pew's arm Lula May continued, "It was a little over two years ago that The Good Dr. Reverend Three Names came to town. Ethel dressed up in her nicest winter coat and sacred crimson scarf and drove over to give the widower preacher a welcome with her homemade fruitcake." Looking out the window towards the parishioner's cottage, in Lula May's mind's eye, the summer's gorgeous green glory turned into that cold, dank, dark and dreary, deeply desolate December day.

Chapter Three

The street's trees, bare as their naked branches, danced and cackled in the cold wind. Beneath their winter laughter, opening her car door, was a desperate Miss Ethel. Like a lady should, with her legs together, she turned her body placing both her feet on the curb, gracefully lifting herself out of her late husband's pride and joy, a powder blue '67 Mustang. Standing with a package in her hands, she glanced up at the gyration of limbs above before placing her gift on the hood of the Ford classic. Out of nowhere a gust of wind slammed the car's door shut and lifted Ethel's scarf as it clung frenziedly to her long narrow neck. How it flapped like a flag wrapped around a pole, the blast even altered the beautician's sprayed-to-stone hairdo. The gift did not budge an inch during the icy gust, and thusly surprised even Ethel.

"Mercy," she exclaimed, as she watched a Scottish terrier, snapping at the wind, blown backward, and rolled uncontrollably with the race of autumn leaves across the holiday themed lawns. Facing the wind, she led with the brow of her head. Ethel heaved up to the modest cottage across from the church building and rang the doorbell while balancing her package. Noah, the Baptist preacher's son, opened the door. He was playing a video game and felt interrupted.

"Hi Noah, I'm Ethel Fields; I attend church where your daddy preaches. Do you remember me? Is your daddy in today?" Ethel uncontrollably chattered her teeth as she glanced over him, taking in as much of their home as she could. Noah knew the deal. Ethel was not the first church lady to "come-a-knocking." He thought she smelt of Aquanet mixed with some cheap Avon perfume. He knew the scent because his mother used to sell it to the old ladies of his father's past congregation. The inviting warmth from the opened door floated over the child and embraced Ethel.

"Yes 'um, he's sitting on the throne though. You'll have to wait." Noah slammed the door in Ethel's face. Her own self-generated heat rose into her head. Ethel huffed, steam escaped through her mouth and nostrils. She tapped her foot and re-rang the bell.

Noah re-opened the door, "he's still in the bathroom lady."

Ethel was caught off guard by the young man's curtness. Polite, but determined, Ethel's voice shivered, "but is there any way I can wait inside for your daddy? It's rather cold out here, young man."

Standing his ground, "dad said not to let anyone in the house unless…"

The Good Dr. Reverend interrupted as he walked up to the door, "I'm sorry Sister Fields, won't you come inside and warm yourself by the fire?" Ethel entered into the small foyer with her gift. Noah slammed the door and returned to his video game.

"Oh, please call me Ethel. I brought you something for your holiday sweet tooth."

Ethel smiled, extending the present forward, "I made it myself."

The Good Dr. Reverend smiled politely, "Why thank you and you must call me Paul." The weight of the gift caused Paul to exert himself. He tried desperately to place it on the table without a thud. He wondered what it could be. "Should I open it now?" Ethel did not notice his exertion as she removed her coat and scarf.

"Why of course."

"Let me take your coat first," Paul took her coat and scarf and hung them on the coat rack and quickly returned to the present. He took the gold bow off the red box and opened the lid. Pushing the tissue aside, he saw a dark brown brick with flowers on top made from bright red candied cherries, pineapple, and pecan halves. "Fruitcake," Paul said, trying to hide his disappointment. "Thank you." The phone rang. "Excuse me for just a moment," he said as he left the room. Hearing The Good Dr. Reverend in the other room, Ethel reached into her coat pocket and took out Lula May's potion and sprayed it on herself. As she returned it to her pocket, Noah entered the room. Ethel turned around disgruntled that it was the boy.

"Where's my dad?" the boy inquired, as he sniffed the aroma of Lula May's potion.

"He's on the phone, sugar," Ethel replied.

Like a baby tasting a lemon for the first time, Noah's face contorted. At first, he was repulsed, but with the second inhaling he smiled. He moved in closer to Ethel. "You sure do smell nice Mrs. Fields."

"You can call me Miss Ethel if you like, Noah," her voice sounded like heaven to the boy.

Nervous and eager to please, doe-eyed Noah reached into his pocket and pulled out a handful of Halloween candy and jutted it in her face just as Paul returned to the room. "Would you like some candy?"

"I'm sorry Sister Fields, I mean Ethel, a member of our flock is having a spiritual emergency and needs me right away. Sorry to have to cut our visit short. I'm sure we'll see you at church Sunday morning," Paul smiled and walked over to the coat rack and removed her coat.

Ethel squatted so Paul could help her put on her coat. The Good Dr. Reverend plunked on his winter attire. Ethel saw her scarf but did not mention it.

"Noah, watch over the place," Paul directed, "remember the rules. I'll be back shortly."

"Yes, sir," Noah replied. Paul and Ethel left shutting the door behind them. Noah noticed the scarf, took it off the rack and smelled it. Tiptoeing, the boy watched Ethel through the door window get in her car and drive away. "Miss Ethel," sighed Noah.

The very next day Ethel's car pulled up in front of the house. Noah peeked between the blinds. As Ethel got out of her car, Noah opened the door to his home. "Hi, Miss Ethel," Noah kindly greeted her. "Dad! Daddy! Miss Ethel is here," he shouted toward the kitchen.

"Hi Sister Fields, what brings you by again on such a cold windy day?"

"Just that," Ethel replied, "this cold windy day. I believe I left my scarf here the other day."

"Want you come in, Miss Ethel? You don't want to get sick," Noah said with concern. "Would you like some hot chocolate?"

While Ethel entered the house, Noah looked all starry-eyed at her. Ethel was caught aback by the penetrating gaze of the young man. *I wish your daddy looked at me that way*, she thought. "I think I have time for some hot chocolate," Ethel said, smiling at the boy. *Maybe the boy is the way to his father's heart.* She thought to herself as she moved her smile from the son to the father, never having to look up.

"Can I take your coat?" Paul asked.

"If you insist, but I can't stay long. It's just that scarf means a lot to me," Ethel said while she removed her coat. She then looked at the rack where she saw the scarf last.

Noah went into the kitchen.

"I'm sorry, I haven't seen it. Are you sure you left it here?" the Dr. Reverend inquired.

"I'm pretty sure." A microwave timer went off as the Good Dr. Reverend and Ethel came into the kitchen and took a seat at a 1980s beveled glass table.

The Good Dr. Reverend turned to his son, "Noah, have you've seen Sister Fields' scarf?" Noah dropped the hot cup and saucer with steaming hot chocolate, "No, sir."

"I'm sure I left it here," Ethel stressed. "Let me help." Ethel got up out of her seat to help Noah clean up the mess. Noah looked at her breasts, which didn't go unnoticed by Paul after he broke his own admiring gaze from the same monuments of womanhood.

"Miss Lula May, she took care of my sister and me. She made it for me when I was a girl. It means the world to me," she said lifting Noah's face with her finger under his chin, so he gazed into her eyes.

Noah broke his glance, "I'll go look for it." He sprang up and ran out of the room.

Ethel continued to clean up the mess as the Dr. Reverend handed her some paper towels and stood over her.

"So, how did you like my fruitcake?" Ethel rose to put the paper towels and broken cup in the trash.

"Let me help you with that." Paul hurried to take the shattered cup and wet towels from Ethel. He pressed the pedal that opens the trashcan's lid and dumped the debris inside, hiding the fruitcake at the bottom of the can. Paul turned around to face Ethel. "It was the prettiest fruitcake I'd ever seen. Noah and I sat down to it in one sitting."

"You ate the whole cake?" Noah runs into the kitchen with the scarf.

"And let it go to waste?" The Good Dr. Reverend said with a Mona Lisa smile.

"I found it. It was under my coat." Noah handed the scarf to Ethel.

"Why thank you Noah," Ethel said looking into the boy's eyes. "Thank you very much." Ethel took the scarf and gave Noah a hug. Noah was filled with happiness and hugged her back but was slow to let go. Ethel looked up and smiled at Paul, then glanced down at her watch.

"Oh, my! It's almost time for the ladies' auxiliary meeting. I must be going. I'll see you two at Church Sunday Morning," Ethel said wrapping the scarf around her neck.

"Don't forget your coat," Noah said.

Ethel rutted into her coat and left with a bounce in her step and her head held high. For the first time in her life, she could brag about her cooking. "The girls at the ladies' auxiliary will be eating their words," she said opening her car door.

"She made sure of it," Lula May chuckled, "Honey, Miss Ethel told anyone who would listen that the Dr. Rev. Three Names ate her fruitcake in one sittin'. Now honey, Ethel Fields has her faults, her cooking be the chief amongst them, but the one thing Miss Ethel don't do is lie, even when it is in her best interest to do so. So, when the single women of Dixon heard that the Good Dr. Rev. Three Names likes fruitcake, well, honey," she chuckled again. "What's they don't know is that I know the Good Dr. Rev. Three Names threw that fruitcake in the trash. The reason I know is my nephew, Hunter, works as a garbage man for the town and Ethel's fruitcake busted the bag and it fell out and broke my nephew's foot causing all sorts of trouble for him, but at his second job, well that's no concern of yourns."

Chapter Four

His parents sitting on the back row, a young Hispanic teenager whose face was slightly scarred, came forward and stood before the microphone. With the children's choir, he sang "Riu Chiu," a seventeenth century Spanish carol, as the bridal party in individual jewel-tone designer evening wear made its way down the aisle. The McRae sisters had auburn hair like their mother, just in different shades. Joy, Faith, and Grace, unlike their sister Charity, were striking beauties still with super model figures. It was not that Charity wasn't striking. No one who ever saw Charity could sat she wasn't. Yet, what most in Dixon said of Charity was that she was as big-hearted as she was big, and none of her sisters were as pretty as Charity was on the inside. Faith, of course, took offense at this, thinking herself as the only true Christian of the four. She dismissed the town's feelings and felt they were derived from Charity's job as a paramedic and volunteer firewoman.

The groomsmen, looking like diplomats, wore white tuxedos with sashes across their chests that matched the color of their respective bridesmaids' dress. Will Zemp had a big grin on his face as the procession made its way down the aisle. Most in the audience figured his grin was for his future bride or, with hair like a 70s hippy, he had gotten stoned beforehand. In reality, he thought the groomsmen looked funny because the only people he ever saw wearing sashes across their chests were beauty queen contestants.

The first down the aisle was Joy Beth McRae Hernandez Silverman Sakamoto, and though she was the oldest of Bonnie's daughters, she did not look her age. Some in town said it was because she was a stay-at-home mom, though seldom could one catch her there. Others used to say it was because she would not live with a man that stressed her out. But when she married the Sheriff, she became even more carefree and looked even younger. Others in town said that with all the money she received from each divorce she had a facelift. This, Joy denied adamantly. She claimed her key to youthfulness was finding something funny in even the darkest of events and help from Miss Clairol, of course.

Dressed in an emerald green gown, Joy strolled down the aisle with her current husband, Hector Sakamoto, the town's sheriff and in her mind, a profound key to her happiness. Hector was of Asian descent, but you would never have known it if you spoke to him on the phone. He sounded and acted like a Southern good old boy. Hector grew up in Dixon. His father was Japanese and was stationed in Korea during World War II where he met his mother. His parents were converted to Christianity and became Baptist missionaries at the end of World War II. Trying to spread the gospel in Korea, but not very successfully because of their mixed marriage, they fled with the onslaught at the end of the Korean War. With the help of the missionaries that converted them, they became household servants for the Dickson's and gave up the calling, though they stayed very devoutly Baptist. This, of course, was during the time of the Civil Rights movement when blacks refused to work for wages that could barely feed a family. And in this age of the New South, Hector's family had been treated just like white folk (except by a few veterans' families that lost their sons in the Pacific or Southeast Asian wars). Receiving better wages than their black predecessors, they participated in the same church and schools, to many a Yankee newcomer's surprise. Many in Dixon thought that the Sakamoto's treatment proved their lack of prejudice, but Hector knew better; one just had to drive through the "hood" on the east side of town for proof.

"How that hippie girl ended up married to the town sheriff is a mystery to even me. The question is can she keep him?" Lula May whispered.

Joy's three children, Mary Jane Hernandez, age fourteen, Herb Silverman, age nine, and Kind Sakamoto, age four, sat quietly with their aunt, Iris Sakamoto. Iris, the town madam, smiled at the many men in the church that were her customers, most of whom were receiving knife- cutting stares from their wives. Iris had her Doctorate in Business Administration and employed mainly college girls and graduates who had a hard time finding jobs that paid enough to pay back their student loans. In some cases, her girls made more than their husbands and boyfriends by dancing at her strip joints in the capitol city. But the real bread and butter of her business came from the Internet webcams she operated quietly out of the town's nicest trailer park. Iris kept everything low-key, to the point of living in the trailer park herself. No one, not even her brother or the IRS, had a clue as to her true worth. As for Joy's children, let it be said that the oldest was wise beyond her years, the middle child was a guilt machine, and the youngest, like most four-year-olds, was a joy to be around.

"I love her, but honey, sometimes I wonder if Joy ain't got a brain cell left in her head. What race she hadn't married, she's dated," Lula May worried. "That girl forgets she lives in a small Southern town. If youz ask me honey, I think that girl is trying to start her own U.N. right here in Dixon. Lord knows I do. I really do."

Faith Gail McRae McCaskill, Bonnie's second daughter, followed her sister Joy in the procession. She wore a gown of gold and reflected as she went down the aisle, "if I had wings, I'd appear angelic." After the rapture occurred, she imagined the gown to be the closest garment existing on earth to match what would be her rewarded robe in heaven.

Her husband Ellis, a striking attorney and known man-about-town, was pleased at his wife's appearance as well. With her newfound faith shortly after the birth of their second son, she had become dowdy and worked, in his opinion, at being a holy pain. They had four children, Matthew, age nineteen, Hope, age eighteen, Oscar, age fifteen, and Sally, the smartest of their children, age ten. Faith had agreed to dress up and wear make-up at her mother's pleading and on an oath that Bonnie would never ask her again to violate her beliefs. Her husband whispered lewd remarks to her that both enraged and excited her. Not since before Christmas last had they been intimate with each other. He planned to take advantage of her rare appearance and ravage her beauty at first chance. Her magnificent splendor reminded him why he'd gotten married to her in the first place. As they made their way down the aisle, he comprehended he had married a MIFL, just by how the Yerby twins watched her. Ellis knew the gaze. He'd been not just guilty but caught in the downright act of the ogle. A guy can't help but look, can he?

Faith felt uncomfortable all dressed up and looking pretty, and her husband's renewed interest only confirmed her belief that vanity inflamed the desires of the flesh. The only one of her sisters with non-pierced ears, she clutched her bouquet tightly in order to fight ripping off her earrings, mostly because they hurt from the clamps and also because she thought they might be offensive to the Lord. She said a prayer asking for forgiveness if she had led any man present to lust in his heart (she had and knew it) and ended her prayer with the aspiration that she might set an example that would lead her sisters back to the Lord.

Oh, my, look at Miss Faith, oooh honey, she ain't looked this good since her junior-senior prom, that's when she got knocked up with that oldest boy of herns. Lula May thought to herself. *Ever since she found the Lord she's been getting on her mother's last nerve. Can't stop singing hymns. It's not the traditional Baptist hymns that get on her mother's nerves, but them new-fangled one's she learns from them TV preachers. All them McRae girls has 'em a pretty voice. Oh, you should hears them when they sing together, they's like angels, except Grace of course, she's everything but an angel."*

Grace Anne McRae Weston was the most beautiful of Bonnie's daughters, many of the older town's folks in attendance were reminded of Rita Heyworth as she entered the sanctuary. She had a superb sultry singing voice, but she also had the most unusual speaking voice, almost childlike, but scratchy like a heavy smoker. Grace was neither a child nor a smoker. Most of the women in attendance were surprised at the modesty of her red evening gown. That was until she went past them down the aisle. It was then that men were pleased that her dress and reputation did not disappoint. Some women tried to cover their sons' eyes as they were exposed to the plunging cut that pointed to, but stopped just above, the crack of her buttocks, while yet others dug their nails deep into their husband's thighs.

Grace knew the effect she had on men. She had lost her husband because of it. It was not her fault that her brother-in-law was caught masturbating while he gazed upon her topless body as she slept. She did not even know he was in the room until the fight broke out between her husband and his brother. "What woman in her right mind would sleep with a bra on anyway?" she asked her then husband when he asked for a divorce.

Now she was in business with her sister-in-law, Iris, and knew that at least the Yerby twins were fans of the web-cam site. The paramedics, not much younger than herself (by that Grace meant that she hadn't graduated high school before they were in the first grade), had propositioned Grace as to what her interest in a three way might be as she came into the church. Grace made some catty remark, rubbed her fingers together indicating money, and made her way to the dressing room. She was glad that her mother was not around at the time to hear their remarks. Grace dreamed of Nashville and working with the country music stars as a songwriter. It would not be long 'til she had her Masters in Fine Arts and could put this town behind her, she thought.

Ted Zemp, the only member of Will's family in attendance, escorted Grace down the aisle. Unlike Will, Ted was a brawny man who obviously knew the inside of a gym. With a squared-off buzz cut of thick blond hair, he appeared to be every bit of a man until he opened his mouth and then the girl poured right out of him. Ted ran a hair salon in Knoxville, Tennessee and had begged his brother to let him cut and style his hair before the wedding.

"How will people know the bride from the groom?" Will asked his brother who was completely dumbfounded. To have the last word was a first for Will. Not being able to come up with a response was a first for Ted.

Ted contemplated the faux world his brother's future mother-in-law had created. It was so far from the abusive one he and his brother had gone through at the hands of their parents. He too decided to adopt the fantasy at that moment, and he made it his truth as well, at least while he was in Dixon. Both of their parents were now in jail for blowing up a rental home and the houses next to it while cooking up crystal-meth.

"Thank God it took place in West Virginia and not here in Tennessee," he told his teacher while he was in beauty school. "The explosion had killed both of their neighbors and they would have been sentenced to death and not just life in prison if the family they had killed had not been black that lived to the right of them and a registered sex offender to the left," he completed. He shook the memory from his mind.

Looking up, he and his brother locked eyes. Ted never thought he'd see his brother in a suit, much less a tuxedo. All his brother ever needed, Ted thought, were the right medications to make him stable. Ted was quite happy that this family had the money to make that so. He no longer had to worry about where his brother was or whether to wire him money for any of the sundry reasons his brother made up when he called him. He squeezed Grace's hand in a silent thank you, as they separated to either side of the aisle.

"She's an embarrassment to her mother," Lula May said, "I don't care if it is to pay her way through college. It ain't like Bonnie don't have any money to help her. She's got plenty. The bigger scandal, honey, is she works with that Jap hussy, the sheriff's sister. Ooh, if the sheriff knew half of what we black folks know about y'all white folk, ooh, child. We know more about youz white folks than you knows y'alls selves. Yes, honey. We do, we do, we do," Lula May said shaking her head back and forth.

Faith's oldest children, Hope and her brother Matthew, worked their way down the aisle. Hope tossed a mixture of magnolia and white rose petals onto the red fabric before them. Matthew held a white silk pillow with the family Bible on it. He had the same copper hair as their mother. Hope, on the other hand, had long, straight hair as black as coal. It was cut in such a way as to give her an adventurous mod look resembling that of a 1960s Emma Peel, which was accentuated even more by the sleek, silver, Bond-girl gown she wore.

Hope stood out when she was with her family, for Oscar and Sally were blond like their dad, Ellis. Because of this, Hope was thankful that her Aunt Joy had married ethnically. Otherwise, she would be the only brunette on either side of her family. Hope looked every bit the Irish lass with her pale skin and violet Liz Taylor eyes. It was the color of their eyes that linked these two as brother and sister. But it was the contrast of Matthew's hair that made his eyes appear more vibrant. Girls were drawn to Matthew's eyes and Bonnie loved him most of all because he looked the most like her father. At 5'11." Matthew's body was tight and lean. He was offered a wrestling scholarship by many colleges before he even graduated from high school, but Faith would not hear of it. At that time, she had other plans for secret reasons she kept to herself. Now that they were revealed, she continually worried if she could keep Matthew in the faith.

"Look at these two, appear so pure and innocent. They's ain't," Lula May paused ever so briefly, "ain't even twenty, and the things I know they do. Wild, just like you were, I bet," Lula May said, as the two siblings strolled down the aisle. Those around her thought the elderly black woman was delusional, for it seemed as if she was talking into thin air or talking to the open compact.

"Most likely she has Alzheimer's," whispered the husband to his wife who Lula May had spoken to earlier.

"She's too young to have Alzheimer's," the wife replied to her husband.

"Why thank you, honey," Lula May turned and said to the young woman who became beet-red realizing their conversation had been overheard. As the Spanish carol ended, the handsome Hispanic young man left the platform, but not before flashing his pearly-white, but slightly ragged smile at Hope. She smiled back at the boy and tossed some flower petals in his path as he strode quickly to his parents' pew as Handel's "Hallelujah Chorus" began.

With the motion of Ethel's arms, she lifted the well-wishers up from their pews and they all stood as Charity Thomasina McRae, the youngest and mightiest of Bonnie's daughters, proceeded down the aisle. Charity, not quite as tall as her sisters, was at the very least a good two hundred and fifty pounds. Her quadrangular physique was dressed in a white full-length bridal gown with lots of crinoline plus a veil that covered her face and shoulders. From every viewpoint, she appeared to be a huge white floating teepee. In dress uniform, Fire Chief Maxie Lee was indented into her gown as he escorted Charity down the aisle. He appeared to be emerging from the teepee's opening flap when he stumbled halfway down, only to be saved by Charity jack-lifting him back into position. Will Zemp's nervousness was obvious as Charity approached. Tall and skinny, he paled in comparison to her mass. The Good Dr. Reverend Three Names almost appeared to be in antipathy as the bride approached. If he had not been standing on an old concordance up on the pulpit, he would have disappeared in the white fluffiness that was Charity's wedding gown. Instead, the wedding party formed a fractured rainbow that was broken by a big puffy white cloud and the Good Dr. Reverend appeared to be floating like a cherub above it.

"You may be seated," The Good Dr. Reverend said to the crowd with the last 'Hallelujah' from the choir. As the congregation sat back down, Bonnie wiped away her tears. The Dr. Reverend cleared his throat and continued, "We are gathered here together to unite these two in holy matrimony. Who gives this woman to be wed to this man?"

The Chief replied, "Her mother, Mrs. Bonnie White McRae Dickson and the members of the Dixon Volunteer Fire Department." The members of the VFD whooped it up. Maxie motioned for them to take it down a notch as he took his seat beside Bonnie.

The Good Dr. Reverend began, "Genesis 2:18-25, And the Lord God said, 'It is not good that the man should be alone. I will make a helpmeet for him…'"

Lula May whispered under the ceremony, "Charity didn't believe me when I said this day would happen. She laughed in my face. The spirits told me that she would marry a boney man that knocked her outs cold and saved her soul. Charity said there wasn't a man in this town whose ass she couldn't whoop, and that she'd marry the man that was big enough to take her down without a fight. She said this in front of her momma, her sisters, and me. When you let the spirits out of the bottle, mmm, honey child, theys can make you eats your words, theys sure can."

Chapter Five

Everyone knew Lula May's connection to the family and rumors that she was also a root doctor. The congregation ignored her mumblings because of her age, though it did not go unnoticed by Ethel who watched her closely as if she were going to reveal an old family secret. There were twinkles in Lula May's eyes as she remembered, "It was two years ago on Pearl Harbor Day Miss Bonnie and me went to the Pig as we usually do to buy everything we need to makes her fruitcakes."

Bonnie's blue jeans were tight and the fuzzy sweater she wore caught the eyes of bag boys 'til they got close enough to realize Bonnie was the age of their grandmothers. Bonnie drew deep from her cigarette, remembering fondly the days one could smoke any place before putting it out in the ashtray provided at the grocery's doors. Lula May, rarely dressed in store-bought clothes, wore her homemade large floral print dress with matching turban. Bonnie grab her mama's fruitcake recipe out of her purse as each grabbed a cart and made their way inside the grocery store.

"Miss Lula May, I need a love potion," Bonnie said as bluntly as one could in a whisper. The two ladies made their way to the produce department. As they spoke, both gathered and placed great amounts of candied fruit and nuts in their buggies.

"I thought you said you'd sworn off of mens," Lula May said, staring at Bonnie in disapproval.

"It's not for me. It's for Charity," Bonnie said defensively while looking at the recipe.

"I's sure she has to," Lula May chuckled. "Now let me see it."

Bonnie handed the years old battered recipe over to her, "It's the best recipe when using one of your potions."

Mama's Fruitcake Recipe

Ingredients:

2 Cups Softened Butter

3 Cups Sugar

6 Large Eggs

3 Cups All Purpose Flour (set one cup aside)

1/8 Teaspoon Salt

2 Cups Raisins

1 ½ Cups coarsely chopped Candied Red

Cherries (set aside 4 cherries)

1 ½ Cups coarsely chopped Candied Green Cherries (set aside 4 cherries)

1 Cup coarsely chopped Candied Pineapple

1 Cup chopped Dates

4 Cups chopped Pecans

6 Cups White Grape Juice (set 2 ½ Cups aside)

½ Cup of favorite Dark Liquor

Directions:

Soak raisins in 3 ½ Cups of White Grape Juice for 8 hours, drain.

Mix 1/8 teaspoon of salt with 2 Cups of Flour, set aside.

Combine the candied fruit, dates, and pecans with 1 cup of plain flour, toss until coated.

Preheat oven to 275 degrees.

Cream together Butter and Sugar until light and fluffy.

Add one egg at a time to Creamed mixture until completely blended

Add mixed flour and salt to creamed mixture; beat until smooth.

Stir in flour coated fruit, raisin and nut mixture, blend well.

Grease 12 inch bunt cake pan, coat with flour.

Spoon cake batter into greased cake pan until ¾ full.

Alternate set aside green and red cherries on top of batter

(Make cookies if any batter is leftover.)

Bake in a 275 degree oven for two hours or until a long wooden pick inserted deep into the cake comes out clean.

Place wire rack over kitchen towels, place cake pan on rack to cool.

Heat 2 ½ Cups of White Grape Juice to a simmer, add ½ cup dark liquor.

Puncture cake several times with long wooden pick, while cake is still warm, pour 3 cups of hot juice liquor mixture slowly over cake so the cake can absorb it.

When the cake has completely cooled, remove from pan.

Serve with Milk, Coffee, or Tea.

Bonnie replied seriously, realizing the truth in the statement but not appreciating the insinuation, "the way she behaves sometimes I'd think so too, but who knows how long we'll be on this earth, and I don't want her to be alone. My baby needs a man to take care of her."

"And who is it you have in mind for her match?" Lula May said arching her eyebrow like Mr. Spock.

"Why, The Good Dr. Rev. Paul Pruett-Peterson," Bonnie gloated. "He has a steady and honest occupation. He's a widower. He's young enough to still have needs. Now that he is all alone, he needs a strong young woman to help him with that rambunctious son of his, too."

"Yeah, the Dr. Rev. Three P's has needs all right," Lula May said sarcastically under her breath remembering the story her niece Yvonne told her a few nights before. Yvonne worked at the local Texaco station on the outskirts of the black side of town. She was a light-skinned African American at the time in her mid-twenties, with green-tipped hair that's design gave the appearance of a potted Easter lily that had yet to bloom. Her nails, which she placed and still places great value and pride in (because they are real), were two inches long. As Yvonne was filing her nails, the Dr. Reverend Three Names walked into the gas station in blue jeans, a sports shirt, and dark sunglasses.

"I'd like some condoms please," the Good Dr. Reverend had asked.

"I need to see some ID," Yvonne demanded with attitude not believing some cracker ass, underage, teenage white boy, was going to try to buy condoms from her. She looked closely out the window into a parking lot on the other side of the street trying to tell if maybe the Reverend was part of some undercover sting.

"Since when do you need your ID to buy condoms?" Paul questioned, nervously fumbling for his identity.

"Ever since the churches made the city pass its teen abstinence law, and son, in my family, ten-year-olds is your height." Yvonne said, staring down at the short man.

Paul looked outside to his car where a young woman waited. He looked back at Yvonne and took out his ID. Yvonne looked at it and then laughed. "Take off them sunglasses," she said in disbelief. The Good Dr. Reverend did as she demanded and smiled at Yvonne as his eyes adjusted to the bright fluorescent lights. With the glasses removed he realized that her hair was green, resembling a potted plant and laughed uncontrollably. Both laughed without knowing each other's reason till Yvonne finally got out, "you're forty-five. I'm so sorry mister. What kind of condoms do you want? We have

Trojans regular and ribbed, with spermicide or without, and Lifestyles Sensitive, small, medium, and large."

"Lifestyles Sensitive, large please," The Dr. Reverend said, after collecting himself. With a nod of the head and a matter of fact smile he placed a ten-dollar bill on the counter.

"What God didn't give us in one area, He compensates in others," Yvonne said, as if she were testifying in church as she returned his change.

"Amen, Sister, Amen," he declared placing his sunglasses back on as he returned to his date with a spring in his step.

Lula May shook her head from the thought and continued shopping. Once the needed ingredients were gathered, Bonnie and Lula May waited in the checkout line as the grocery's cashier counted out change to the customer in front of them. "Miss Bonnie, did I ever tell you the story of when my daddy was a sharecropper for your ex-in-laws, the Dickson's, and the time a preacher came to visit while Daddy was working the fields?"

"No, I don't think you have," Bonnie replied.

"Well, I was helping Momma around the house, plucking a chicken as I remembers, when this preacher showed up right out of the blue, so Momma sent me out to fetch Daddy. Well, honey, it must have been at least a twenty-minute walk to the field Daddy was working in and I's tolds him a preacher had arrived, and Momma wanted him to come home rights away. Well, there were these storm clouds a'comin' and Daddy needed to finish his work. He said to me, 'Lula May, what kind of preacher is he?' I told him I didn't know. He then said to me, 'Go home and you'z finds out. If he's a Holy Roller, you put my shine away. If he's a Methodist, you make sure your momma puts aside a nice piece of chicken for me. And if he's Mormon, you sits on your momma's lap and don't you get up until I gets home."

Bonnie laughed out loud. Catching her breath she asked, "Well which one was he?"

Lula May responded in all seriousness, "He was a Baptist, so I did all three."

Bonnie, offended by the parable, went through the checkout without another word. While the young pimply bagboy loaded their groceries into the trunk, Bonnie broke her silence," the whole family is coming over Friday night to help me with the fruitcakes. I thought I'd pour a little of your love potion on the fruitcake I'm giving to the Good Dr. Rev. Pruett-Peterson."

Lula May sighed realizing that her story had not gotten through to Bonnie, "I need her hairbrush, her lipstick, her dirty panties, and whatever liquor you're using, and donts forgets to bring some sweet champagne. I'lls be calling on Erzulie tomorrow night. She starting to wears me out at my age. Oh, but whens I's young, Oh, honey child, let me tell you what! Ah ha, ooh, child, Erzulie make you hot. You'z got to have it. The Good Dr. Reverend Three Name's will come sniffing for Charity like a dog. All men's dogs. But I warns you, if anyone else gets a hold of that fruitcake with my love potion, anyone I's tells ya, they's going to fall madly in love with Charity whether she likes it or not."

"Ethel said he ate all of her fruitcake in one setting," Bonnie said still in disbelief, "You know I make the best fruitcake in the county." The words 'fruitcake in the county' echoed throughout the whole of Dixon as all the single women in town interested in the widower conversed with their friends over the phone. Bonnie, who was sometimes hard of hearing, heard the word 'county' ringing over and over and over in her head. Of course, this echo included the voice of Yvonne, who never forgot the name or face of a man who asks for large condoms. Yvonne, walked around her kitchen with a cordless phone glued to her ear, removed the wrappers from a bunch of Claxton fruitcakes, and placed them in a baking pan. She opened a cabinet, took down a quart of whisky and poured it slowly over the fruitcakes.

"Brenda girl, he's single, makes money and needed the large," she said. Then she sang a parody of "Son of a Preacher Man" changing the chorus to *A Big Dick Preacher Man*. And besides, you know I make the best fruitcake in the county," she said with a "hallelujah," shaking out the last drop of whisky.

Chapter Six

"This is as good as any," Bonnie said. She parked her car amongst a mass of vehicles and stepped out into a field, fairly filled with a menagerie of Lula May's followers. An early winter's wind's cold current choreographed a ballet of leaves across the hood of Bonnie's car. She watched the last of fallen autumn leaves as they blew high into the air, continuing their dance around and about the valley's voodoo sanctuary. In most eyes the old barn, in its state of disrepair, could hardly be called a sanctuary, but those there knew that to restore the old structure would reveal its sacred secrets.

All was silent Bonnie thought, ignoring the incessant wail from wind gust and the chattering chorus of fallen leaves. She looked up at the moon, not quite full, watching the whispering clouds speed across its surface. The smell of firewood and an up-coming snow blended and accentuated the air's chill with a sense of excitement. It had been the smell of snow that had become so rare with time. When she was a child, you could count on at least two major snows and several dustings a year. It had been three years since the last snow. *Maybe the environmentalists are right*, she contemplated while savoring her childhood memories of winters past.

Bonnie did not feel uncomfortable as one might expect of an older white woman amongst mostly people of color, the traditional African Americans and of recent years, a gathering of Hispanics. Besides, many of Lula May's family were in the crowd. Some had known Bonnie all her life, the younger members she had known all of theirs. Bonnie opened the back door of her car taking out a plastic Piggly-Wiggly bag. After she shut the door, a snap and crack infringed on her feeling of well-being until she noticed Hunter, Lula May's nephew, as he stepped out from a trail that led into the surrounding woods not too far from her car. "Hunter, is that you?" In relief Bonnie asked knowing the answer.

"Mrs. Bonnie, long time no see," Hunter walked up to the white woman and hugged her. Most would think it an odd sight to see a grown black man hug an older white woman, but to Hunter and his family, Bonnie and her sister were more like angels, secret messengers that proved there was still good in the world. He had not always felt this way about the woman. He thought his aunt, like most domestics, was underpaid and underappreciated. That was until he learned that Bonnie and Ethel gathered Lula May every Christmas when Hunter, his sisters, and their cousins, were children and went shopping for Santa. This annual bonus he found out about one summer when he was obviously overlooked for a job because of his color. He stomped into his mother's kitchen and cursed all white people as evil S.O.Bs in front of Lula May 'til the air turned blue with his words. His mom and Lula May just sat there as they continued to snap green beans.

"I wonts have dis," Lula May exclaimed slamming her bowl full of beans on the table. "I has seventeen nieces and nephews, not one of yous went without something special at Christmas whens yous kids, not one. The sixties and seventies were a tough time for our people. Most kids in this neighborhood were lucky just to get new shoes and clothes from Santa. You thinks that your momma and daddy could afford five brand new bikes, a G.I. Joe and Barbies for your sisters, or whatever yous told me you wanted from Santa Claus. Really Hunter, really, plus Sunday Church clothes right out of Sears' catalog, all the whilst theys worked as a domestic and a mill worker, strugglin' just to be puttin' food on the table and clothes on your backs? If it weren't for the White sisters, Christmas would have been nothing more than oranges an' nuts in your stockings and whatever handmade toys and clothes your momma, granny and I's made for you," Lula May looked over at her sister-in-law for conferment. She nodded her head and Lula May continued, "Theys goods and bads of every color of man's kind in this world. Believe me,

I's knows there is many evil white ass crackers out there. I's seen them and I's seen what they can do and have done. But yous tell me this, why's it today most of our people is kilt by our own people? Evil could care less about skin. All its wants is in the blood and once evil's in, it's hard to gets it out."

"Amen sister, amen," Hunter's mother said before the elder women returned to sipping iced tea and snapping beans in a kitchen cooled by box fans in the window and by the screened door.

"How's Charity doing Mrs. Bonnie?" Hunter said breaking his release and smiling down at the woman he towered above, "I haven't seen her at the Capitol Club in sometime. You tell her to get her rear-end over there next Saturday. I'll be performing."

"Performing?" Bonnie asked. "Lula May nor Charity ever told me you were in a band. Are you still playing your trumpet all these years out of high school? Good for you! I remember you and Charity side by side in marching band. Lula May and I never missed a Christmas parade while y'all were in band together. I just love a parade."

"I do too," Hunter said to the matriarch remembering marching in a pride parade earlier that summer. "I can't ever remember seeing you here on an Erzulie night, Mrs. Bonnie. Mrs. Ethel now, she's been a regular for the past few years, but I guess you know that since you'z two so tight and all."

"It's been a long time," Bonnie said wondering why her sister had not informed her of her recent visits to see Erzulie. "You're just too young to remember. The last time I was here to see Erzulie I ended up with that two-timing Dickey Dickson. Never use a love potion on a used-car salesman." Bonnie and Hunter laughed and turned their attention to the old barn as the music began. The sound of the band lured the crowd from the open field into the barn lined with glass voodoo candles for the protection against evil. The warm glow from the candles created sheer shadows stretched out on the walls. Sizzling incense sent swirls of smoke into the air creating a kaleidoscope for all the senses. Bonnie and Hunter entered the barn together scanning the vaulted room for those they knew.

While Hunter was assessing the boy to girl ratio, Bonnie quickly spotted Ethel gathered with two of her employees. Blake Chestnut, who always wore skintight pink t-shirts, was a flaming queen who was a master at coloring the years right off a woman. Also standing with

Ethel was Rachel DeCaro Bumgardener, a very young mother of twins who had recently lost her husband in Afghanistan to an IED. A Mid-Westerner, the striking girl with thick eyebrows and natural blue-black hair now lived with her in-laws on their farm. Her parents, both fourth generation Italian Americans were unemployed GM workers and were having difficulties supporting themselves and Rachel's younger two brothers still in high school. Supporting Rachel, the then unborn twins, plus all the expenses that come with proper prenatal care was a heavy weight on them, so Rachel moved South at her husband's request to live with his parents 'til he came home from Afghanistan. She never imagined his return home would be in a coffin. She never expected she would be in a barn with an overwhelming amount of people of color to that of whites. She wondered how she'd let her new boss talk her into seeking love advice from a seer possessed by some sort of Voodoo Venus in the first place. Ethel's new receptionist clutched her boss' arm in nervousness as men removed their shirts from the heat generated from the growing crowd. Bonnie, noticing the girl's fear, knew this was not a good time to approach her sister and smiled with a nod.

The followers hummed an ancient tune as the band played a driving low-bass rhythm. The crowd drifted around vis-à-vis in a tribal dance, tossing flowers into the center of the shrine, singing, "Come Erzulie, Erzulie come." With Hunter at her side, other than her big blonde Dolly Parton wig, Bonnie did not stick out in the performance of this circular ritual as the pace picked up like water going down a drain. Abruptly they stopped as Lula May, possessed by the spirit of Erzulie, the Voodoo Goddess of love, entered the sanctuary in nothing but a slip. Her shy shadow was the only announcement of her presence.

The menagerie of followers segregated into men and women whispering in a low chant, "Erzulie, Erzulie, Erzulie." Then the women, in the outer circle sang, "Ah! The beautiful woman," which was followed by a staccato chant by the men shoving for position in the inner circle, "Who is Erzulie? Who is Erzulie?"

Those who had business to do with Erzulie, which included Bonnie, sang, "Oh, I will give you a present before you, don't go away. Aabelo!" The female followers once again sang noticeably louder, "Ah! The Most Beautiful Woman."

"Who is Erzulie? Who is Erzulie?" the men chanted in a low deep guttural grunt. Yvonne, also in the crowd with Bonnie, as well as all men and women who wanted a blessing from Erzulie sang out, "Oh, I will give you a present before you, don't go away. Aabelo!" The music stopped as Lula May, possessed by Erzulie, broke through the circumference of the sacred circle. In a lovely sultry alto voice Erzulie acknowledged their praise. The crowd clapped their hands finding the rhythm set by her song. Dancing provocatively, her hands moved like serpents gently across the faces of her followers as she made her way to her makeshift shrine made of an upright harrow leaning against the hopper of an old, abandoned seed drill. Laid out before the shrine, atop the hopper were perfumes, make-up, and rings, from which she was to choose, while beautiful glamorous dresses, necklaces and bracelets hung on the spike-teeth of the harrow. The possessed woman, her hair now dyed black, made herself up from the gifts presented to Erzulie. Those whose gifts she chose to titivate reacted in great happiness.

Erzulie then walked into the center of her sanctuary, winked and with meaningless blown kisses, like those given by beauty contestants, flirted with her flock. With a glance from the Goddess, the band started playing. The male worshippers, fired up with a siring desire partially caused from basic hormonal drive and to a certain extent charged by a ceremonial brew prepared with herbs that have some of the same properties found in Viagra, danced around her showing their bodies during the first measure. They stood and faced the goddess as they thrust from their groin with each beat of the bass drum during the second measure, which ended with them grabbing their genitals through their pants in such a way as to show their manly excitement to Erzulie. As they circled her during the third measure, she moved counterclockwise running the tips of her fingers across their bodies. Erzulie chose her Adonis. The others turned their backs, forming a dancing wall around the goddess and her chosen, while continuing to show their sexual excitement to the women in the outer circle. As they licked their lips like hungry wolves, Erzulie kissed the chosen young man and rubbed her body across his before whispering in his ear. She turned him around and pushed him through the dancing wall. The Adonis looked among the circulating women and quickly chose a petite Hispanic girl, lifted her in his arms and ran out the barn with her hands wrapped around his neck. Bonnie noticed the bare-chested Hunter as he danced amongst the circle of men as the ritual continued.

"Champagne! Sweet Champagne!" Erzulie cried over the music gazing down at the men that surrounded her shrine. Bonnie did not hear Lula May in Erzulie's voice. The women, who wanted a blessing or a potion, had bottles of champagne for Erzulie as well as any required items, hairbrushes, lipsticks, the dirty panties of the woman or man who is to be desired, and alcohol, in Bonnie's case, a bottle of Jack Daniel's. The chain of dancing men encircled the Goddess, breaking only quickly enough for someone to pass into her presence. Bonnie budged her way next to Hunter and smiled. His abrupt stop allowed Bonnie to penetrate the circle. She popped a bottle of champagne to the crowd's cheers. Like sperm into a zygote, once penetrated, no other was admitted. Bonnie then produced a fluted glass from the Piggly-Wiggly bag and poured champagne for Erzulie. She sipped from the glass of bubbly and smiled at Bonnie. Bonnie reached deep into the bag and gave Erzulie Charity's hairbrush. Erzulie brushed her coarse hair with it. Bonnie then handed her Charity's Chap-Stick since she couldn't find any lipstick in her daughter's dresser. Erzulie drew it across her lips and tasted it. Erzulie sipped down her champagne and Bonnie quickly refilled her glass. Bonnie finally gave her the last of the required items, Charity's extra-large panties. Erzulie expanded the waistband, sniffed the crotch, and giggled. Erzulie looked into Bonnie's eyes, "Big Girl, but there was a man once, this girl needs love. I, Erzulie, will bless this woman. Let me taste your firewater."

Erzulie took the bottle of Jack from Bonnie and stole a swig. The Goddess rolled the liquor around her mouth and spit it back in the bottle. To Bonnie and the crowd's surprise the bottle glowed neon red. Erzulie smiled and returned the bottle to Bonnie. "You are pretty," Erzulie said running her fingers through the Dolly Parton wig, which slightly shifted. Bonnie straightened her wig and said, "Not as pretty as you are, Erzulie."

"No one is as beautiful as I am," The Goddess boasted. Provocatively, the men continued to dance around the pair. "Look at my dogs. Want one?" Erzulie asked Bonnie, indicating the throng of men surrounding her.

"Oh, my, they sure are handsome, but I'm afraid I must be going, got to get this love potion home. Maybe when I'm back for a personal visit, Erzulie, oh most beautiful Goddess. Thank you for the love potion, Erzulie," she said kissing the Goddess on the hand.

"I have a gift for you Erzulie," Bonnie said, placing a gold bracelet in her hand.

Erzulie, after biting it, smiled, slid the bracelet on her wrist to admire it, as Bonnie placed the glowing bottle of Jack back into the plastic bag. She made her way through the grinding shirtless men of muscle. She paused and glanced at one of the dancers, took a slug from what was left of the champagne and patted him on the face and moved her lips to say, "Good doggy." Bonnie exited the inner sanctuary as Yvonne waved her champagne bottle and moved into the inner circle. Ethel, with Rachel still latched onto her arm, made it to the cracked barn door in time to catch her sister.

"Bonnie, Bonnie!" Ethel hollered before clutching her sister's shoulder.

Turning around, "Hi darling, who's your friend?"

"Rachel Bumgardener, I'd like you to meet my sister, Bonnie. Bonnie, Rachel here was married to Ricky Bumgardener, Matthew's friend that was killed in Afghanistan. Rachel is worried about her babies, and I was wondering if you could give her a ride home so I could finish up business here."

"I don't see why not," Bonnie leaned into her sister and whispered, "See that real tall black man between the two shorter ones that are maybe five-eight? That's Hunter, Lula May's nephew, slide next to him. He'll let you pass." Ethel smiled at her sister before prying Rachel's hand from her arm, "Bonnie will get you home safely Rachel. Go with her dear."

Once outside, Bonnie took in a deep cold breath to clear her lungs, and still the aroma from the incense lingered in her nostrils. "Where are you parked?" Rachel asked. "By the woods darling, just follow me," Bonnie told the still frightened girl. Once inside the car Bonnie turned on her radio, tuning it to an oldies station and sang along to "Jingle Bell Rock" and "Blue Christmas" as she drove the girl home. Rachel sobbed during Bonnie's "Blue Christmas" rendition. "Everything will be alright," Bonnie promised the girl.

"How?" Rachel questioned. "I'm twenty, with twin boys not six months old, my husband is dead, and I live with his parents who cry more than I do. I don't know a soul in this backwoods town, hell, I don't even live in town. I live on a farm. I never saw a cow close up until I came here. If your sister hadn't giving me a job, I wouldn't have money for their first Christmas. I want to have the boys christened, but the closest Catholic church is some forty miles away and my in-laws don't approve," the girl ranted.

"There is an Episcopal church on the corner of Broad and Kershaw darling," Bonnie offered as a substitute. "It's not Roman Catholic, but it's damn near close and they do christen babies. I've been to a few of my bridge clubs' grand babies' christenings myself. The Bumgardeners are good people, they'll understand. Plus, those babies are all they have left to connect them to their son. They're going to want to do whatever it takes to keep you and your boys here. Now you live out on highway thirty-four, don't you?"

The girl nodded and was silent until Bonnie pulled into the Bumgardeners' drive.

"Thank you," Rachel said. "Ethel told me you lost your first husband during the Vietnam War. How do you ever get over it?"

"You don't. You move on for your children's sake, but you never get over it if you truly loved him."

"You said Kershaw and Broad?" Rachel asked as she stepped out of the car.

"That's right honey, just ask Ethel. She'll show you." Rachel shut the door, stood in the drive, and waved goodbye. Bonnie waved in return as she backed out onto the road. As she approached a stop sign at Jefferson Davis Highway, she thought of what Erzulie had said of her sweet Charity having been with only one man. She knew what man, and the spinning of her wheels and the scorching of pavement released her anger at the thought of him. But just being with her entire family tonight calmed her and she was soon at peace and slowed her vehicle down with the thought of her children. She wished the same for Rachel.

The moonlight had sifted through openings in a thin layer of fast-moving clouds.

The eerie light speckling the ground produced the energy of a discothèque along the dark drive that led to Bonnie's home. At the end of her driveway sat her Palladian home. A sense of pride filled her. Bonnie's mother had gone through piles of paperwork to have it placed on the national register. The entry porch had four two-story Tuscan columns, which had been wrapped with broad red ribbon creating an appearance of large candy canes. Wreathes of cedar, holly, and silver bells hung on the windows of the house's wings and across the windows on the second floor. A larger wreath had been placed on the paneled front door while a garland of pineapples, holly, and magnolia leaves hung over the door's elliptical fanlight. All that was left to do, Bonnie thought as she entered her home, was to decorate the Christmas tree. That would take place tonight. Decorating the tree on her beloved husband's birthday was a tradition she and her daughters had shared. That task had been passed to her son-in-law's and grandchildren while the women worked on her fruitcakes.

She had prepped the living room where the eight-foot-tall live blue spruce stood by a window. Years ago, she had grown out of room to plant the live trees her oldest daughter insisted upon in her own yard. A wall of trees now lined the old unpaved back road that leads to the old White family cemetery situated deep in the back woods off highway thirty-four near the long-forgotten lumber mill community of Lucknow. Boxes of decorations and colored lights were on the antique violet velvet Victorian sofa. She dropped a bag of icicles she had bought before her appointment with Lula May on top of the boxes. Bonnie looked up at the painting of her first husband, Tom McRae, which hung above the fireplace and lit a votive candle that she placed beneath it. "Happy birthday darling," Bonnie said aloud.

She remembered their first Christmas together, as she made her way to the kitchen. She laughed because it had been such a long time since she had remembered their annual lovemaking beneath the Christmas tree. Tom had joked that she had been the gift that kept on giving. She blamed the thoughts on Lula May's voodoo, which reminded her to hide the love potion before her family arrived. Wandering back to the kitchen, she took the bottle of Jack out of her purse and placed the potion, now returned to its normal coloring, under the blender cover and then went about the business of placing the fruitcake ingredients on the old oak table that had been in her family for generations. An apparition of Bonnie, Ethel, and her late brother Bobby as children sitting around that table watching Lula May cooking breakfast before they went off to school haunted her. She started to hum, "Mammy's Little Baby Love

Shortnin' Bread" along with the phantom of a youthful Lula May by the stove. Her heart was glad that Lula May was still alive and with her.

Chapter Seven

An unplanned convoy headed down a desolate country road lined with live oaks covered by Spanish moss. Headlights cut through the dark two-lane road that was only lit by the breaking of the moonlight through the clouds and a few sparse houses' porch lights off in the distance. The procession formed as they got farther away from town. At the head of the convoy was the McCaskill's SUV. The family inside, a poster ad for Land's End, sang "Over the River" with full vigor, of course with the exception of Hope, constantly looking over her shoulder at her boyfriend who followed behind the family in his beaten-up Ford pick-up truck with oversize wheels. Hope, without any warning, rolled down her window and stuck her head out giving a loud hoot. Her Hispanic boyfriend Raul weaved his truck back and forth while rolling down his window, took off his ball cap and stuck his head out with a holler in response to Hope.

"Hope McCaskill, roll that window up right this moment and sit in your seat like a lady!" Faith yelled. "I won't have you behaving like your Aunt Grace, throwing yourself at that boy. Shame on you!" Hope pretended not to hear her as she gave another hoot.

"Hope," Ellis snapped, "It's cold, roll up the window now!" Hope, after rolling up the window, threw herself into the seat with her arms folded.

"Why can't I have a little fun?" Hope hollered at her parents. "I put a curse on you. I hope whatever you've done to be so mean comes back to haunt you!"

"Someone's beat you to it," Faith snapped.

"You hang around Lula May too much," Oscar added to the fray.

"You lock yourself in the bathroom for way too long," Hope retorted.

"Cut it out both of you," Ellis steamed at his children.

"Why do we have to make fruitcakes every year?" Hope blurted out. "I hate it!"

Completely calm, but stern, Faith turned to face her oldest daughter, "It's what our family does for Christmas. We like it. It's a chance to draw names for gifts, let you kids decorate the tree. It reminds Mama of when we were girls and when Daddy was alive. It's when we learned how to sing together, when all our hearts were light and innocent. It's the time we put aside our differences for Mama's sake. And you're going to chop nuts, dates and candied fruit. And you and Raul will be in our presence at all times, and you will sing. And if you cause me any headaches, your license goes in my purse 'til school starts next January. No Christmas dance, no New Year's Eve dance. Nothing." Faith then turned to her husband, "I mean it too, Ellis. You hear me? I mean it."

Faith smiled, took a breath, and resumed singing, "Over the River" as if nothing had happened. Not hearing Hope singing, Faith leaned over to the rear-view mirror. Hope could see Faith's eyes upon her. Hope joined in with the rest of the family. But since she had to sing, she did so in a minor key. Sally, who had been quiet through the whole family dispute, took the octave above her sister to create a harmony. The sisters smiled at each other, both knowing their mother hated anything not done in a traditional way.

Running behind, Joy flew down the highway towards her mother's home. Stoned, as always for these occasions, she was putting eye-drops in her eyes when she noticed the swerving taillights of Raul's truck. "Amateur," she thought. Forced to slow down, Joy's VW van approached Raul's red pick-up. She could see her sister's SUV ahead and knew that Faith had insisted that her husband drive the speed limit. She assumed the truck in front of her wanted to pass the SUV, but for some reason would not, even though the road ahead was clear. With an erratically driven truck ahead Joy decided, since her children were aboard, not to pass and instead kept a safe distance. Joy had had the van since her days of following the Dead from city to city and had no plans of ever selling the 1980s vehicle though all her husbands had asked her to do so.

While Joy drove, she sung the Beatles' "Across the Universe" a cappella, while Herb and Mary Jane both harmonized effortlessly with their mother. But it was Kind, her youngest, whose laughs poetically chimed throughout the song and removed all the sentiment of melancholy that Joy usually felt on her father's birthday. Joy had just turned seven not a month before her father died. She remembered him more deeply than her sisters. She knew that she was her father's favorite. He would often take her with him and would make her lie down in the seat, so her sisters would not see them drive away together. This thought made her smile on the inside.

Joining the unplanned caravan to Bonnie's was Grace and Iris. Iris, who dressed like Janis Joplin or Macy Gray, depending on what generation you spoke to, drove with all ten gold-laden fingers on the wheel. Grace, dressed in a rhinestone cowboy ensemble, appeared as if she had just come off the set of a county music video shoot. The two, sporting a black Jaguar XJS, had come up on the three vehicles cruising at the legal speed limit. Iris pulled across the lane and hit the gas to pass the convoy. Joy waved at her sister as the 1988 sports car peeled past her VW van. Quickly, Iris had downshifted to check out the stranger in the red pick-up truck. At first Grace thought it might be Matthew, but it definitely was not, and with the burning of rubber, Iris flew past the pickup truck. The white SUV was next in line and Grace waved at her nieces and nephew blowing kisses as they passed. Oscar, sitting behind his mother had unbuckled his seatbelt and raised himself up in order to ogle at the car even more. Iris blew the horn as she passed the SUV and took the lead of the convoy.

"What nerve!" Faith spewed, before she noticed Oscar out of his seat. "Put your rear end back in your seat boy. You're not too old for me to take a switch to you, you hear?"

"Yes 'em."

The four vehicles pulled into Bonnie's yard, one right behind the other. Joy's kids jumped out first and ran up to their cousins in their SUV. Oscar and Sally were always interested in the music that Mary Jane and

Herb were listening to, since hip-hop and rap had been forbidden by Faith. Raul and Oscar both walked over to examine the Jaguar, as Hope trailed behind Raul like a new puppy. Hope was quick to introduce Raul to her Aunt Grace. Iris looked the boy in the eye to figure out what kind of man he might become. Iris considered this her greatest skill, for she had developed different categories for men and had only been wrong once, well, maybe twice, she thought. This boy was definitely a player, a deliverer of heartache. She knew that he was more than likely already a client on her web site, if not hers, somebody's. "He's a hotty," Grace said to Hope's delight.

Joy chimed in, "He reminds me of Salvador, the gorgeous son of a bitch! Not you honey, my ex-husband," she added at Raul's shocked response. Raul knew that Hope's immediate family was religious and had been shocked to hear any member of her family curse. The family worked its way inside. The interior had been designed with Victorian antiques along with newer family heirlooms from the Modern age. Upon first glance, nothing seemed unexpected for such an old house, Raul thought that was until closer inspection of the pictures on the walls. These were framed photographs of Bonnie and her daughters' families over time. The faces of ex-husbands including Bonnie's philandering husband, Dickey, had been cut out of them. Hope walked behind Raul and wrapped her arms around him as he stared at the collection. "Bonnie Gram doesn't like to be reminded of people she doesn't like," Hope told Raul, as he gazed at the beheaded men.

"Oh," he said with a strange accent that was somewhere between his parents' Cuban accent and the local southern drawl, "I thought she might be a radical feminist or a violent femme of some sort, not a grandma." Hope dragged Raul away from gawking at the foyer photos to a ball of mistletoe that hung in the door's archway. She looked up at the mistletoe and smiled at her new boyfriend. He bent down and kissed her, but not the deep kiss that she wanted. Raul was smarter than that. He saw Ellis out of the corner of his eye and had no intention of pissing off such a powerful man. Ellis had cleared his throat just as Raul broke off the kiss. Hope took Raul by the hand and pulled him into the living room away from her father's eye.

"So, Grace talked you into the annual Fruitcake gathering." Ellis said to Iris as they stood just inside the door.

"Yep," she replied, as a chain of children came running through the door dividing the two. The three sisters followed the children inside. Each woman placed her coat in Ellis' arms before walking into the living room. Iris took two of the coats so Ellis could hang up the first one. Bonnie, with cigarette in hand, made her way down the long hall to greet her family.

"Bonnie Gram!" her grandchildren hollered, encircling her like puppies hungry to nurse. She bent down and kissed them one by one giving a small peppermint candy cane to each grandchild.

"Hang your coats up," Bonnie demanded. The children ran into the foyer, loaded the coats into Iris' arms, and quickly returned back into the living room.

"Y'all hung your coats up that quickly?" Bonnie asked.

"Daddy's hanging them up for us," Sally replied.

"Well, that's nice of him." Bonnie knew what her grandchildren were waiting for. It had been her tradition since Matthew and Hope were toddlers.

"Mary Jane, keep an eye on Kind," Joy told her daughter. Joy, Faith, and Grace left their mother for the kitchen as Bonnie walked behind the couch where a red velvet bag with a gold braided drawstring was hidden. She opened the bag and drew out a handmade ornament she had created from her own perceptions of each grandchild on a plastic Legg pantyhose egg. On each egg she incorporated the grandchild's name in the design, as well as an animal she discerned to be the child's familiar. All of them personally hand painted. Designing the eggs came naturally to her, for years she designed greeting cards for Hallmark. The extra income came in handy for splurges on family and friends. Her father had instilled in her at an early age the importance of work, whether one needed the money or not. Having trained as a painter at Ringling Brothers in Sarasota, Florida, she worked for Hallmark 'til everything became computerized in the 90s. She did not care for modern technology, not even ATM cards. She enjoyed human interaction on all levels and blamed computers for the decline in the younger generations' manners. Now she painted on canvas mainly for pleasure, giving away most of her work as Christmas gifts every season.

"Herb," she called out. Herb came up and took his ornament from his Bonnie Gram, opened it, and withdrew the money she had placed inside.

After removing the money, he reassembled the handcrafted ornament and placed it on the tree. Bonnie, when she first started this tradition, had placed a dollar for every year that her grandchildren had lived, but with inflation she had increased the amount to five dollars for every year. Herb loved his ornament because his grandmother had placed a Star of David on it, since his father was Jewish. Bonnie fondly called him 'my little Jew' and loved to run her fingers through his dark curly hair. Pulling ornaments at random, Bonnie called out each grandchild's name. This was Kind's first year receiving an ornament and all the children were interested as to what special design their grandmother had created for him.

Iris got down on her knees and handed Ellis one of the two children's coats that had fallen on the floor, "So the ice queen's been keeping you on a leash? I haven't seen you for a couple of months."

"Not really, just saving money up for Christmas. I'm a cheating prick, I know, but not so big of one as to fuck my kids out of Christmas. Forgive the pun," he added. Her hand, hidden underneath the second coat, grabbed Ellis' crotch as he took it from her hand. "Yeah, you're a big prick, but I respect that."

Ellis had looked down into her eyes. "My prick or the fact that I love my family and I don't appreciate you putting that in jeopardy," he said under his breath, turning to hang up the coat, thus breaking her massaging grip.

"Both. Help me with my coat," she said as she stood turning her back to him, dropping her coat off her shoulders. Ellis took the coat and hung it in the closet. Iris winked at him as Bonnie came into the foyer.

"Where's Matthew?" she asked. She saw Iris' wink but was not sure if it was truly a wink or just a twitch in her eye.

"He said he was coming," Ellis said. "He said he has a big surprise."

"His ornament is on the mantle when he gets here," Bonnie said searching Ellis' eyes for some sign of guilt.

"What about Hector?" Bonnie added.

"He said he was coming but that he couldn't stay long," Iris said. "Joy probably can tell you the latest though. You know how quickly things change," she added.

"Ellis, the lights are on the couch. Iris, the women are in the kitchen, you're family now. I have a task just for you," Bonnie said leading Iris by the hand. "It's good for firming your breasts," she added as they approached the kitchen door.

When Bonnie and Iris entered the kitchen they saw Faith, Joy, and Grace sitting around a large round table for six. In front of each woman were stacks of candied fruit in small plastic containers. Red and green cherries, pineapple, dates, dried apricots and figs, boxes of raisins, as well as bags of pecans and black walnuts were piled on the counter by the sink. Sitting atop the island in the center of the kitchen sat a bag of lemons and oranges and a large stainless-steel bowl, the largest Iris had ever seen. "Iris, I need you to grate the zest of the lemons and oranges please," Bonnie said taking Iris to the island.

"I thought you said this was good for the breasts?" Iris questioned.

"It is," the girls rang out in unison.

"Did you see Hope, Mama?" Faith asked.

"She was stringing lights with that boyfriend of hers."

"She's growing up fast," Grace said, slicing candied cherries.

"I'm trying to slow her down. You in that get-up doesn't help you know," Faith said chopping nuts.

"Stop it," Joy said giving Grace, then Faith, the evil eye. "Where's Matthew?"

"He should be here shortly," Faith said.

"Does he have a girlfriend?" Iris asked across the room.

"He's dating some girl from Greenville," and with great pride she added, "He said he met her at church."

"That's nice," Bonnie added.

"Well of course he met her at church. What do you expect when you send the boy to a religious college?" Joy chuckled.

Grace said tauntingly to Faith, "I'm surprised he hasn't gotten thrown out. He has that wild twinkle in his eye just like..."

"Grace," Joy snapped.

"I'm sorry, she knows I'm just pulling her leg," Grace pleaded. "Let's change the subject. When's Hector coming?"

"I don't know. He said around seven, but you never know what's going to happen since they're calling for snow." Joy said.

"Where is Charity, Ms. Bonnie?" Iris asked.

"On duty," Bonnie said with a sigh, "same reason."

Grace looked up from the dried fruit, "I thought she had today off."

Bonnie lit up a cigarette and exhaled a stream of smoke, "She did. The Yerby Twins called in sick. Or was it their mother that was sick? I forgot. Anyway, she went in."

"That's funny, I saw them the other night and they seemed fine," Iris said, as she dragged the lemon across the grater. "Are you sure this will lift my tits?"

"You just wait 'til tomorrow, you'll feel it," Bonnie said as she poured the dry ingredients into the bowl.

"Do all of Dixon's firefighters live with their mothers?" Faith laughed, "The Yerby boys live with their mom, Lloyd Parker moved in with his mom after his divorce, and Charity still lives at home."

"Where's Lula May? I haven't seen her lately. I was hoping she would be here tonight," Joy muttered as she shoved a date in her mouth.

"It's a full moon tonight," Grace said, which answered the question in everyone's mind but Iris.

"So, it's a full moon tonight," Iris questioned, "what does that have to do with anything?"

"Let's just say Lula May conducts her special kind of church services when the moon is full." Iris, whose parents were missionaries, was even more confused by Bonnie's statement.

"Today's not Sunday or Wednesday, is it?" Iris asked hoping for some clarity.

There was a point of silence then Bonnie started to sing. "Ding, dingy, dong, that is the song, with joyful ring, all caroling, hark call the bells, sweet silver bells, all seem to say, throw cares away…" Each girl came in at her appropriate time, first Joy and Faith in the second soprano, Grace took the alto, when through the back door came Charity to sing the bass line. Iris had stopped the grinding caught up in pure amazement as the women sang. At the end of the song's "ding, dong, ding, dong," the last note held by Charity, they all broke into laughter and whatever hostility they held when they arrived was gone for the night. It was magic.

"Grab a seat and a knife, girl, and start chopping," Joy, now gleeful, called to her baby sister.

"I thought you were on duty," Bonnie stated lighting a cigarette.

"I'm on call," Charity lifted her walky-talky out of its holster. She placed it on the counter by the blender.

"What do you want to sing next?" asked Charity. "Any request Iris?"

"All I know is 'Jingle Bells," Iris admitted. The women started singing the classic as they chopped the dried fruit and nuts.

Chapter Eight

A pink sky silhouetted the tall pine that towered behind Matthew's grandmother's house. He could feel the nervousness radiating from his fiancée, Sweet Ride. Sweet's real name was Gertrude Geraldine Ride. She had hated the name since first grade when her classmates laughed at it. She immediately told the teacher to call her Sweet, her father's nickname for her, since he too hated the name, as well as his "hippy, tree hugging" mother-in-law, Gee Gee, for whom she was named. Her parents, though Protestant, did not believe in birth control. Thus, Sweet was one of nine children and very poor because of their belief. Though she was beautiful, her clothing was dated. The sight of such a grand house made her all the more self-conscious.

"Don't worry," Matthew told her as he cut off his Jeep, a high school graduation gift from his parents. "My folks are going to love you." He leaned over and kissed her gently on the lips.

"I didn't know your family was rich," Sweet said.

"We're not," Matthew assured her. "The house has been in the family for over a century, that's all. We're regular folks, nothing special, you'll see."

"Look, it's snowing," Sweet said with an excitement in her voice that is only heard from Southerners who marvel at its rarity. Sweet hopped out of the Jeep to play in the falling snow, her tongue stuck out to catch the flakes. Matthew ran up behind the beauty and wrapped his arms around her, spinning, laughing, teasing. Dizzy to the point of falling, Matthew landed on the earth's newly moist wetness with his girl on top of him. Lifting her securely to her feet, he stepped around to face her and took her tongue into his mouth. The moistness of her lips jolted through Matthew. He pulled her closer to hide his obtrusive shame. She broke free. Both were embarrassed. He put his arm around her, and they stared quietly at the house together, the cold flakes removed the flushness from their faces.

"I love you," he said, "and my family will love you, too."

"Your family are not regular folk. One look at this house and anyone would tell you the folks that live here are special."

"What do you mean?" Matthew asked slightly surprised.

"It's like a Christmas present, all wrapped up with ribbon and bows, hiding some big secret gift that no matter how hard you shook it, you'd never guess what it was."

"Well, when you open this present, you'll see that it's a homemade knitted sweater that you'll wear once on Christmas day, and that it is so run-of-the-mill that you can't even return it. You'll be stuck with it, just like me," he said smiling.

She shook her head, "You really don't know who you are, do you?"

"Yes, I do." Sweet gave him a leery smile, looked into his violet-blue eyes, and kissed him on the cheek. Matthew smiled and pulled her tightly into his side, "Let's go meet the family."

Ellis and Oscar had just strung the lights around the eight-foot blue spruce as the children opened the boxes filled with ornaments. Raul sat on the couch, flapping his legs together, while he watched the family in action. Hope teased Raul all evening long as she bent over hanging ornaments on the lower branches of the tree. With her fine behind facing him, it became impossible for the teenager to get up from the couch without saluting Hope's father from the hip. Hope walked over to Raul and sat on his lap, instantly recognizing the results of her teasing. She draped her arms around his neck and kissed him.

"Hope. Do you want to be grounded?" Ellis said.

"No sir," she said sliding off Raul's lap to sit next to him.

Matthew stood in the living room doorway, "Hi everybody."

Sally ran up to her big brother and gave him a hug. She noticed the stranger still standing at the entry door. "Who's she?" Sally asked.

Matthew motioned for Sweet to come closer, "Everyone, I'd like you to meet Sweet."

"Hi, Sweet?" Ellis said, not sure that he had heard the name right. "I'm Matthew's father."

"Hi," Sweet said extending her hand.

"This is my brother Oscar, my cousins Mary Jane, Herb, and Kind, my sisters.

Sally and Hope. And that's Raul Gomez. What are you doing here?"

Hope stood up taking Raul's hand and pulled him off the couch. He nonchalantly adjusted himself shaking his leg 'til his excitement fell into place. "I'm dating your sister," Raul replied with a grin while rocking back and forth on his feet with his hands in his pockets.

"Since when?" Matthew spewed, knowing that Raul was a player.

"We've been dating since homecoming weekend," Hope squared off to her brother. "Why do you care?"

"Matthew, is that you?" Bonnie cried out from the kitchen.

Matthew tore his gaze from his sister. "Yes mam, Bonnie Gram, it's me," he yelled toward the kitchen.

Bonnie was cleaning her hands on her apron as she backed out of the swinging kitchen door. Turning, she noticed the stranger clinging to her grandson's arm and gave Sweet a genuine smile. "Who is your guest?" Bonnie smiled.

"Is mama here?" Matthew asked.

"Of course," Bonnie looked toward the kitchen, "everyone's here."

"Mama, Aunt Joy, Aunt Grace, Aunt Charity," Matthew yelled, "come in here, I want y'all to meet somebody." All four women came through the swinging kitchen door with Iris trailing behind. Matthew walked into the living room and over to the fireplace with Sweet on his arm. They stood under his grandfather's portrait. "Everybody, I'd like to y'all to meet Sweet Ride, my fiancée."

The family was in complete silence with the exception of Hope, who tried to withhold her laughter. "Did you say her last name was Ride?" Hope said as her laughter ripped.

Iris could not contain herself either, "Honey, did I hear him correctly? Did he say your name was Sweet Ride?"

"Yes, mam," Sweet responded without shame.

"Is that your given name, Sugar?" Faith asked the girl, mortified by the overall situation. Internally Faith said, "Strike one, Hope. How rude of you." Quickly followed by, "Damn! Damn! Damn! Forgive me Jesus, but he's done knocked up another girl."

"No, my given name is Gertrude Geraldine. Sweet's my dad's nickname for me,"she explained.

"If my name was Gertrude, I'd change it too," Herb said and was quickly smacked in the back of the head by Mary Jane. "What?!" he said in response to his sister's reaction.

"Are you kin to Sally Ride, the astronaut?" Sally asked Sweet, trying to distract the girl from Hope's snickering. Hope ignored the piercing stares of both of her brothers.

"I don't think so," Sweet told the little girl.

"Sweet, this is my mother, Faith, my Aunt Joy, her sister-n-law Iris, my Aunt Grace, my Aunt Charity, and Bonnie Gram, my grandmother."

Bonnie overcame the initial shock, "Let me be the first to welcome you to the family." She hugged the two then said, "You have to be a very special girl to catch our Matthew. Come on back to the kitchen with us, we're making fruitcakes." Bonnie took Sweet by the hand and led her through the crowd, "Now where are you from?"

"Greenville," the girl replied nervously as the women followed behind the others.

After the women had cleared, Ellis glared at Matthew with great intensity. Matthew felt confusion at his father's silent response. He thought the family would be happy. Ellis took a deep breath and then sighed, "Son, let's take a step outside for some fresh air." The two put on their coats and stepped onto the porch. The snow had continued to fall but had not begun to stick to the ground. "Let's go sit in the car," Ellis said to his son walking toward his SUV. Matthew trailed behind his father 'til they reached the vehicle. Ellis unlocked the doors with his remote and the two jumped inside. "So, is she pregnant?" Ellis said to his son.

Matthew felt the anger in his voice and responded defensively, "No! I can't believe you're asking me that."

"Son, don't lie to me. I'm tired of paying for abortions for you."

"You've paid for one abortion, not abortions."

"Oh, that's right, I forgot, the James girl miscarried two days before the appointment. Lucky me. It's my pocket the money was going to come from, not yours. You're so damn addicted to pussy I'm surprised you haven't come to me for money to get rid of the clap. Damn, boy, you're too young to get married. You're not even old enough to drink, not that that's stopped you from stealing my liquor either. Don't deny it. So how in the hell do you plan on taking care of this family? You haven't finished your first year of college. Can't you wrap that dick, boy? Do I have to go buy a banana and show you how to put on a rubber, son? Damn it! Fuck! I'm tired of your shittin' irresponsibility," Ellis finally stopped to catch his breath. His rant had steamed up the windows of the SUV.

Hope had watched her brother and father from the living room window. Noticing the fogged-up windows, she took advantage of the fact by sneaking out with Raul, unnoticed by adults.

"Are you done? Good," Matthew said not giving his father a chance to respond, "she is a virgin Dad and so am I."

"You're a what?" Ellis said dumbfounded.

"I'm a born-again virgin, Dad," Matthew said in complete sincerity.

Ellis' laughter could not be contained. He had heard of such ridiculousness and thought of it as a phony form of Alcoholics Anonymous used as a control mechanism by religious extremists. If you can successfully grab hold of a man's balls psychologically and twist them, you have great power. Regaining his composure, Ellis said, "So is she a born-again virgin, too?"

"She's a true virgin," Matthew said.

"Oh, I'm sorry son, you have such a track record, I just thought…"

"That's okay, Dad."

"So, how long have you been a virgin?"

"This Sunday makes two weeks."

"It's gotta' be hard... abstaining like that." Ellis looked over at his son with a smirk. The two chuckled.

"You have no idea how hard it gets," the two laughed some more. "Dad, how far can a guy go and still maintain his virginity? Is there a law that says what that is? I mean," Matthew paused feeling awkward, "can a guy, uh-mm, can a guy jerk off and still be a virgin? Reverend Lewis said to always ask yourself, 'What would Jesus do?' But I just can't ask Jesus that, I mean he's the Son of God. God didn't even do it with Mary, he sent an Angel to do it for him."

The eighteen-year-old was almost in tears, "I'm so horny I can't stand it. But I don't want to break my word to Jesus." Ellis' range of emotions were hard to contain. He had been angry, not with his son, but at his wife for insisting that Matthew attend Bob Jones University. Matthew had good grades. He was a fine athlete too, pursued by many state universities. The pressure placed on his son by his mother to attend the religious university had been overwhelming. He blamed himself for caving in to his wife's constant nagging. The boy should be enjoying his youth and not be forced into becoming a religious zombie like his mother. But Ellis also found humor in the situation as well. The idea of being a born-again virgin was silly enough, but his son's sincerity could only be compared to the heroes in Gilbert and Sullivan operettas. Ellis was also disheartened by his son's bewilderment and felt that this was what led to his son asking the girl to marry him. Absolute denial of one's animal instinct, Ellis had always thought, led to an imbalance in the psyche, which led to bad decisions.

"First son, as to the law, there is no law on the books in this state that defines what male virginity is. And Clinton didn't even know what "is" is, as far as the definition of sex is concerned. That's something that every man has to answer for himself. Matthew, unless you have amnesia, there is no way you can reclaim your virginity, no matter how much you pray. You have carnal knowledge, it cannot be erased any more than knowing what watermelon tastes like, or the pain of a sunburn, the sound of an owl's hoot, or even the sight and smell of the sea. Your knowledge of these things can't be erased any more than your knowledge of sex. All that your so-called born-again virginity is doing is giving you the knowledge of what it feels like to deny yourself sexual pleasure. That said, I do know that to lose one's virginity, it takes two. I also know that Oscar has a Playboy hidden in your grandmother's spare bathroom. Look under the sink behind the jumbo pack of toilet paper. As to Sweet, I need to think son. As far as you marrying this girl, I think you are too young but you're an adult and I can't stop you. When we get home, we'll talk a little more. You need to get back to that girl before your mother and grandmother pick her apart." As the two got out of the vehicle, they saw Charity coming from around the back of the house. "You got yourself a real beauty," Charity said to her nephew.

"Did you get called in?" Ellis asked.

"Yeah, a domestic dispute," Charity replied in a hurry. "The Kelso's are at it again. Lisa was beaten up pretty bad the last time." Charity jumped into the emergency vehicle, turned on the lights and siren, and sped down the long drive out onto the highway. The children came out onto the porch and watched the gem- colored lights speed through the trunks of the deciduous trees. Soon the sirens were a faint whisper that blended with the wind-whipped willows that adorned the front yard. Still the fallen snow had yet to stick to anything but Matthew's hair. Ellis had thought the snow looked as if it was trying to douse the flame of his son's hair in much the same way Bob Jones University had doused his son's sexual nature. Faith may not like it, but this will be their son's only year there, especially if he had to pay the bill.

"Come on kids, let's go back inside," Ellis said to the crowd of cousins who had come out to play in the falling snow. "I think it's time to turn on the tree lights." He placed his arms around his sons, rubbed the top of their full heads of hair dusted with the falling snow, and patted them on their behinds, sending them back inside before him. "Born-again virgins," he chuckled to himself. "Indeed."

Chapter Nine

Close to the woods that bordered the property, in the back of the house stood an old evergreen tree. Hope could not ever remember it not being there. Its broad evergreen branches, like an expanded southern belle's fan, hid the young couple's embrace. The lip balm Hope had placed on Raul smelled of cherries. It was at her insistence he let her put the lip balm on him. He felt that any lip care was gay and was very apprehensive at being caught wearing it, especially by Matthew. "Are you sure this is not lipstick?" Raul whispered, not putting it past his new girlfriend to do so.

Mary Jane watched the couple from the upstairs bathroom. "Kiss me," Hope told the young man after applying the balm to her lips. Mary Jane pressed her own lips on the window and mimicked their kiss when there was a knock on the door. Mary Jane told Matthew she would be right out. No hurry Matthew had said, he'd find another one.

"Matthew, have you seen Hope?" Faith yelled up the stairwell, "We're about to light the Christmas tree."

"Mary Jane tapped on the window trying to get Hope's attention. It was Raul who noticed her.

"Isn't that your cousin? Up there," Raul pointed. Hope gave Mary Jane the finger. Luckily for Hope, Mary Jane didn't see Hope's gesture because she had fogged up the window with her breath. With the window fogged up, Mary Jane wrote backwards so Hope could read it, *Your Mom's coming*. "Oh shit," Hope said. She grabbed Raul by the hand and dragged him through the woods that belonged to the property.

"Come on, let's go around front and onto the porch. If anyone asks, we were on the porch watching it snow, okay?"

Nodding, Raul was amazed at how quickly Hope thought on her feet. He followed her closely as they meandered through the woods.

"Why through the woods?" Raul asked.

"So, my mother can't find our trail. She's just looking for an excuse to break us up."

"But if we cut across the yard at any point, won't she figure it out?

"We'll come out by the cars where our footprints will mingle with all the rest. Quiet."

"Hope, Raul, Are you two back here?" Hope could hear her mother calling for them from the back porch.

"Hope! Raul!" Faith screamed loudly in anger before stepping into the yard. "Where are you young lady!?" Faith called out again, scanning the back yard like a hunting dog.

Faith walked up to the tree and felt the cold breeze on her face. She looked up at the falling snow, "Merry Christmas you bastard, thanks for the mess." She brushed the snow off her face, "Jesus forgive me."

Faith contemplated the anger she felt. If she could forgive the wrongs she felt were done to her, maybe love and not hate could fill her heart. She bowed her head in prayer, "Dear Jesus," she said aloud, "I pray that you'll forgive all those that have wronged me and set free from burden all those I have wronged. Help me to be a stronger leader for Thy cause and set a true Christian example for my family so that we may all celebrate Thy glory in Heaven together, in Jesus' name I pray, Amen."

With the end of the prayer, she turned to go back inside when a chill went up her spine followed by a warm sensation, which felt much the same as a shot of whisky resting in your gullet. A hot dry breeze seemed to be rising up from the earth. The snow that had gathered on the evergreen's branches melted. Faith's skirt flew up like Marilyn Monroe's as if she was standing over the same New York street vent in *Seven Year Itch*. She moved as quickly as she could, running up the back porch steps. Faith slipped on the steps, but her grip on the banister kept her from falling to her knees. She looked over her shoulder at the tree as its branches swayed and slapped together as if they were trying to snatch her and pull her into its snare, before they fell into place, calm, unmoving. "Just the south wind," Faith whispered. "Damn Lula May, you've made me so superstitious."

Once Faith felt secure on the screened-in porch she turned around and looked back at the tree. Faith jumped as another gust of wind rattled the back windows. It seemed as if something was begging to go within. As the wind came, icicles formed on the tree from the melted snow. Shaken by the miraculous sight, she shivered from head to toe, unsure if she saw what she saw. Taking a deep breath, she turned to go inside. With a new draft of wind she looked down between her legs for she swore she felt something crawl between them as she opened the door. Nothing.

"You look like you've seen a ghost," Grace said to Faith.

Faith thought to tell her sisters what she just witnessed but didn't want to be the brunt of Grace's jokes and chose to ignore it.

"Mama, has anyone found Hope and that boy yet?" Faith asked as her mother opened the oven door to place the first of the fruitcakes in to bake. Bonnie too looked down at the floor thinking something had brushed her legs.

With cigarette in her mouth, Bonnie shut the door to the gas oven. "Have you looked out front, Hun?" The flames in the oven shot up at the sound of Bonnie's voice and danced around the fruitcake like stars circling the head of a cartoon character after it's been whacked on the head.

"I saw a bottle of Jack Daniel's in the cabinet just the other day Mama, where did you put it?" Grace said in frustration looking through the cabinet.

"I don't want any drinking in this house, the Jack is for the fruitcakes," Bonnie said in her yearly scolding manner. "Dickey Dickson was the last to drink in my house, Damnation! Damnation! Damnation! The spirit goes in the fruitcake; it goes in the fruitcake, the fruitcake understand?!"

No one saw as the flames in the oven ceased their dance, nor all of the candied cherries that sat on top of the bunt cake began to illuminate with each blood-flushing rush of what only could be described as a heartbeat. Its creator, unlike Dr. Frankenstein, did not rejoice at the restoration of consciousness to this being, or that he was once again on this celestial plane. No, she was completely unaware that her repeated words had given life to a fruitcake possession, a birth of sorts.

No one drank inside, it was always outside, so if they got caught, they could respond, "Mama, I'm not drinking inside the house." Usually, drinking outside was not such an issue, there were many a time during the first week in December temperatures were in the upper sixties or lower seventies even after sunset. This year was obviously an exception.

"Mama, I know the rules, I just can't find the booze. Your fruitcakes are not the same without the Jack, they are dry just like everybody else's," Grace snorted at her mother, but in all reality Grace really needed a drink, especially when she was around her family.

"Oh, damn, I forgot, I gave it to Lula May. Her grandniece needed a toddy for the cold," Bonnie lied, with her face turned away from her children. She wasn't as lousy at telling lies as her sister Ethel, but her children could always tell.

"I'll send Ellis after a bottle before the liquor stores closes," Faith said.

"There's no need to do that," Iris said, "I got a C.B. radio as an early Christmas gift for myself. I'll just go outside and radio Hector, he can run by a Red Dot."

"Could you do that, Hun?" Bonnie asked happily, "tell him I'll pay him back."

"Joy, Faith, you want to join us?" Grace added as she and Iris were heading for the door. Before anyone could respond the kitchen door squeaked and all heads turned toward it. Hope dragged Raul into the kitchen. Tensions were tight and the stress was still fully mounting on Faith's face.

"Momma, were you looking for me?" Hope asked.

Grace and Iris slid past Hope and Raul. Joy originally had not planned to join her sister-n-law and Grace, but she didn't want to be around the incoming fireworks that she knew would be coming her niece's way.

"Wait for me," Joy said while getting out of her chair.

"Where have you been?" Faith took aim.

"We were out on the front porch watching the snow," Hope responded. Faith's sixth sense had told her Hope was lying.

"Why don't y'all have a seat," Faith ordered. The three women sneaked by the children as they watched the animated version of "How the Grinch Stole Christmas." Ellis noticed the three and thought they were sliding outside for a drink. He took Sally off his lap giving the excuse of having to go to the bathroom. Knowing that Sally would have noticed if he went right instead of left, Ellis decided to cut through the kitchen. As he got to the kitchen door, he could hear his wife drilling his daughter. He was caught in limbo.

"Panda Bear," Iris called on the CB, "This is Little Red ride your hood, you read 10-4?"

"Coming in loud and clear, Red, heading your way," Hector responded as Grace and Joy stood at the open car door and listened. Joy was reminded of the mid-seventies fad and laughed.

"Got Grace and Joy here by me, Mrs. Bonnie forgot the booze. Can you stop by a Red Dot, copy?"

"Already have," Hector responded. "I'll be there in 10 minutes, copy."

"Ask him if he's got Jack," Grace said.

"Is that a bottle of Jack, Panda Bear, copy?" Iris asked.

"That's a 10-4 plus a whole lot more, tell Mama Panda I confiscated her favorite.

Panda Bear signing out," Hector said to an elated Joy dancing around the Jaguar.

"Whatever her favorite is it must be good," Iris said looking up at Grace.

"What's your favorite?" Grace asked her sister.

"You'll see, let's just say it's seasonal for right now," Joy said giddily. Joy also knew that whenever Hector brought her favorite, he must be horny, because upon its consumption he just had to lay back and she was more than glad to do all the work.

Ellis stood still by the kitchen door as the women came back inside. Grace noticed her brother-n-law and pointed him out to the other two. After they hung their coats, they tiptoed up to the kitchen door and joined together in the eavesdropping. Faith was in full swing with her interrogation of Raul. "So, do you go to Church, Raul?" Faith asked.

"Sometimes," Raul responded.

"Only sometimes?" Faith questioned the teen. "Why not all the time? Do your parents not believe in God?"

"We have to drive to just outside the capitol to attend mass," he said defensively. "Sometimes they're just wiped out from working twelve-hour days, six days a week."

"So, you're Catholic?"

"Yes, mam."

"So, Raul, how long have you been in the states?" Bonnie asked in curiosity.

"I was born here," he replied coughing at the cigarette smoke that Bonnie exhaled.

"And your parents?" Bonnie asked politely.

"Good cop, bad cop," Iris whispered on the other side of the door.

"They came over on the Cuban boatlift in the 80s," Raul explained.

"Really, so your parents are communist?" Faith said, as she circled the table like a buzzard waiting for its prey to fall.

"No mam, trust me when I say they're real capitalists. They own the One Day Dry Cleaners on the south side of town," Raul added. "If you come in while I'm working, I'll give you a discount."

"Were you born in Florida?" Bonnie asked as she drew in another smoked filled breath.

"Yes, mam. In Ft. Lauderdale," Raul responded in his peculiar accent.

"Is the US flag still flying in Florida? Are they still a part of the United States?" Faith asked, embarrassing her husband deeply on the other side of the door.

"Of course, Mama, remember the 2000 election, Bush v. Gore," Hope said sarcastically, doing her best to defend her boyfriend.

"Oh, that's right. Florida's still a state just not part of the South," Faith smirked.

"Faith, shame on you. How can you say that Florida's more southern than we are? They kill abortion doctors, execute murderers cruelly and without mercy, and they keep blacks from the polls. How much more southern can they get?" Bonnie chastised her daughter putting out her cigarette, "Leave the poor boy alone."

"Thanks Bonnie Gram," Hope whispered in her grandmother's ear before kissing her cheek.

"We're going to turn on the Christmas lights, everyone to the living room," Bonnie instructed the young couple as she wrapped her arm around her daughter's waist and pulled her tightly to her side. "He's just a boy, Hun, a horny red-blooded, born in America, boy," Bonny whispered making her way to the door, "Put your girl on the pill." Faith sent darts toward her mother through her eyes but said nothing.

Having heard the chairs being pushed away from the table, the four adults hightailed it to the other end of the hall. Grace had opened the foyer closet door and closed it as soon as she saw the kitchen door open. As they reached the living room where they had all gathered, Bonnie looked over her family, "Who wants to turn on the Christmas lights this year?"

"I do," Sally said.

"You did it last year," Herb said to his cousin.

"You did it the year before that," Sally shot back, "And you're not even a Christian."

"Now, Sally, let's not forget that Jesus was Jewish," Bonnie said to her granddaughter.

Joy held Kind, his head resting on her shoulder. She was saddened by Faith's influence on Sally, but she knew that the pre-teen was too smart to continue in her mother's religious misgivings. Kind noticed his father's police car immediately and lifted his head off his mother's shoulder in excitement. "Daddy," the toddler said, pointing out the window as the police car parked.

"Hectors never had the privilege, has he Joy?" Bonnie asked.

"I don't think so," Joy replied.

"Mary Jane, go tell your Papa Hector to step on it. He's turning on the lights." Mary Jane left the room, and everyone looked out the window as Mary Jane made her way to her stepfather. Mary Jane pulled the town sheriff into the house.

"Hector," Bonnie called, "It's your year."

"No, let one of the kids do it," Hector resisted.

"All those in favor of Hector turning on the lights raise your hand," Bonnie instructed her family, "it's unanimous," Bonnie added, though Sally didn't raise hers.

"Kind, do you want to help your daddy?" Hector held out his arms and the two-year-old was handed off to his father as he made his way to the switch.

"Watch," Matthew said to Sweet. "Look out the windows." With Hector holding Kind's little hand, they flipped the switch and watched the lights as they lit-up, coming on around the family Christmas tree like an elaborate chain of dominos. From the bottom up, the round bulbs shined bright red, blue, green, yellow, pink, with a few clear replacements 'til they reached the animated angel atop the tree. The angel held a bell in her hand which chimed carols as it rang. Simultaneously, with the ringing of the bell, the bare skeletons of deciduous trees that stood guard like a squadron of soldiers in Bonnie's front yard started to light up, each a different color, first a blue, then a yellow, followed by a pink, white, green, clear, and finally a red. They all watched in glee as the lights reflected in the dusting of snow like an oil slick on the road after a rainy day. Mouths agape, both Sweet and Raul were amazed by the theatrical display of lights.

"Wow," Sweet said to Matthew as they all bundled up in their coats to go out and see the army of trees aglow in color.

"How did they do that?" Raul asked Hope.

"Mary Jane's dad did it the year she was born," Hope responded.

"He designs light shows for rock concerts," Mary Jane said with much pride.

"Who have you seen in concert?" Raul asked his fellow Hispanic teenager.

"He keeps telling me he won't take me to one 'til I'm married," Mary Jane said. "Mom says it's his new wife that doesn't want me around."

"That's because you look like mom with black hair, that's all," said Herb. "Anyway, his new wife doesn't want any reminders of how much child support your dad pays that doesn't go into her pocket."

"My stepmom doesn't call me names," Mary Jane paused for a second knowing that she most likely did. "Well at least not in front of everyone."

"Who calls who names and what do they call you?" Matthew asked his young cousins.

"My stepmom, I don't know what, something in Yiddish I think, Granny Levine backslapped her though," Herb said also with pride, "Sophie hasn't been back since."

"Lula May put a curse on her as well," Hope added.

"Where is Lula May anyway?" Matthew asked Hope and then turned to Sweet before Hope could answer, "You'll never meet a more loving, straight-forward, tell you how it is human being."

Grace started singing "Let It Snow" and her mom and two sisters joined her in harmonies reminiscent of The Mamas and the Papas. "Being around your family is like being thrown into the middle of *The Sound of Music*," Sweet whispered to Matthew. "And you think they're ordinary, run-of-the-mill?"

After a couple more songs were sung, Hector went to his patrol car and took out a bottle of Jack from the trunk. "Mrs. Bonnie," Hector said with respect, "here is that liquor you asked for."

"Thanks Hector, I better go inside and check on my cake," Bonnie said leaving her family to play in the snow. She took out the fruitcake, which was not as firm as she liked. In fact, it bubbled like lava all around the center, which she had never experienced with her cakes. As she waited for the cake to cool, she decided to make herself a Jack and Coke. After all, she knew her children were probably at that very moment doing the same out of Hector's trunk. She finished the drink before she felt the cake was cool enough, so she decided to have another drink with a cigarette. After her second drink, the cake seemed cool enough as to not evaporate the liquor. She took the love potion from under the blender cover and began to pour the elixir over the cake when the phone rang.

"Damn," Bonnie said as she re-covered the potion and then made her way to the phone on the foyer table. It was times like these that she wished she had bought a portable cell phone, but some things you cling to, and if it has worked for you like this phone has all your life, why change mid-stream she thought.

This was a trick that Matthew and Hope had been doing for years. Using her cellphone, Hope would call Bonnie and Matthew would run inside and make a couple of drinks for them as their grandmother made her way down the hall. From the back porch Matthew went in and made drinks for Hope, Raul, and himself as Sweet stood as watchman out back. Hope was great at accents and would call as the same charity each year. Hope wanted to be an actress and considered it a great success that her grandmother didn't recognize her voice. Matthew made the drinks successfully and got outside where the four hid behind the evergreen where Hope and Raul were earlier in the evening.

"Here, have a taste," Matthew offered his fiancée. Sweet thought, what the heck, a taste won't hurt. She was surprised at how good it tasted. Matthew made his drink weaker than usual, not wanting to use so much Jack that his grandmother would notice some missing.

"I wish I had had you make me one," Sweet said.

"Your wish is my command," Matthew said double clicking the heels of his boots.

In the meantime, Bonnie had come back to the kitchen, taken the potion out once more and had started to pour it slowly over the fruitcake. It pleased her that the cake seemed to be soaking up the concoction quite well. When once again the phone rang, this time it was Raul on the line readied to imitate his father's voice. When Matthew went inside, he saw both bottles sitting on the stove. He got a glass, then some ice and reached for the bottle that had the greatest amount of liquor in it. He quickly poured it over the ice, added the Coke, and made his way outside with great stealth. He gave Sweet the drink, and they went back behind the tree and listened to Raul conduct a survey on the widows of Vietnam Vets.

"Hope, Matthew, where are you?" Faith called from the front yard. Raul quickly hung up the phone, trusting Hope's grandmother did not hear Hope's mother calling for them. The four quickly downed their drinks and set the glasses down by the tree and made their way toward the front. Sweet started to feel funny. Truthfully, she had never felt this way before. She passed it off on the drink as she held Matthew's hand. Soon, Sweet started feeling pretty good. There was a hint of something in the air that stirred her. No wonder people become alcoholics she thought, one drink and you feel like you're in love. She looked at Matthew and put her head on his shoulder, soon after she sniffed, and then she sniffed again. It was the same smell that just earlier today sent waves through her, but now she was repulsed by his smell and thought he should go take a shower.

"Where were y'all?" Faith inquired.

"Just showing Sweet and Raul around, that's all," Matthew told his mother.

"Why don't y'all take the kids inside and watch another movie, it's getting too cold for them to stay outside," Ellis said to his oldest two.

Bonnie finally finished pouring the love potion into the cake. She pulled out a holiday tin and placed the cake inside it, sealed it and placed it on top of the refrigerator.

"You two go on ahead, I'll be there shortly," Hope said to Matthew and Sweet.

"What's up?" Matthew asked his sister.

"We're just gonna' grab the glasses and slide them inside before anyone notices," Hope said deceivingly to her brother. Raul and Hope went back behind the tree and immediately started making out. Raul slid his tongue into her ear and down the side of her neck. His hands slipped inside her coat and fumbled over the thick white fabric, not the silky bras that most girls wear. Faith did not allow her children to buy their own clothes. Faith reminded her daughter constantly she was just sixteen and had no need for that kind of underwear. Lucky for Raul, the bra unfastened in the front, and in no time his cold hands had cupped her breasts, and his thumbs rubbed her nipples which quickly became erect. Hope's hands found their way to his crotch, she had been teasing him all night and right now she wanted to be bad. She unzipped his jeans, he was wearing no underwear. She thought this was real sexy as she slid her hand between the brass teeth and secured his nuts in her hand. "These belong to me," lightly slapping his balls underneath. Raul pulled his hips back but Hope had hold and pulled him forward as she stood for a kiss. She bent over and took his penis out. She examined it closely noticing that unlike her other beaus, Raul was not circumcised. This fascinated her, she wondered if it would taste different.

Bonnie was about to throw the empty bottle in the kitchen's trash can, but noticed a dribble resting in the bottom and thought better of it. The power of the potion that once filled the bottle could not be chanced, especially around teenagers. Bonnie felt the need to be rid of it and scanned the kitchen in search of where. Oscar, at the same instance, had gone up stairs to pee. While standing at the toilet he looked out the window and saw his sister in action. He could not believe what she was doing to the Latino. Hope was squatted in front of the young man and with one clean swoop his jeans were down, and his bare ass was in the wind. Oscar missed the bowl.

"Damn it," he said taking aim once more. Hitting his mark, he looked back out the window when all of a sudden, they froze. What were they doing Oscar wondered. Did he cum? Raul wanted to pull his pants up, but Hope would not let him. She nodded no and lifted her finger to her mouth. Oscar wished he could see the expression on Raul's face, but he was at such an angle that this was not possible. Then he saw the reason; Bonnie Gram was out in the yard.

Without her coat, Bonnie thought it too cold to take the bottle all the way back to the trash cans in the back of the yard. Pulling back her arm like a baseball pitcher, she let the bottle rip. Oscar could not believe his eyes; his grandmother could not have planned this if she tried. Up and over the bottle went and clocked Raul on the side of the head. He went down cold. He was unable to stumble because his pants were down around his knees. He fell like a tree. Hope clasped her mouth to keep from screaming. Bonnie heard not a thing. Hope was in a complete panic. She tried to wake Raul up, she slapped his face and scooped up a handful of snow rubbing it in his face to no avail. Oscar knew of only one relative that would handle this discreetly, Aunt Grace.

He opened the bathroom door then turned around to flush and put the lid back down. Without washing his hands, he ran down the stairs into the living room. "Where's Aunt Grace?" Oscar asked his brother.

"Outside with the other adults," Matthew responded.

Oscar stepped out on the porch and saw his aunt sipping on a drink. "Aunt Grace, Aunt Grace," he yelled until he got her attention. "Come here, I want to show you something."

"What is it, Oscar?" Grace hollered from behind the trunk.

"It's a surprise, just for you," Oscar called back so that no one else would bother.

Grace made her way to her nephew, being number three out of four made them tight in both of their minds. "What is it, Oscar?" Grace said when she was closer.

"Follow me," Oscar replied taking Grace around to the back. When they got to the couple, Raul was still out cold, his pants were still down, and Hope was in tears shaking the young man by the shoulders.

"What happened?" Grace said in shock.

"Bonnie Gram threw something and clocked him on the side of the head while Sis here was blowing him," Oscar told his aunt.

"How do you know?" Hope asked her brother.

"I watched it all happen from up there," pointing to the bathroom window.

"I can't get him up," Hope said to her aunt.

"You…," Grace put her hand over her nephew's mouth. "There is a time and place for jokes," she whispered in his ear. "She'll rip our privates off if you say the wrong thing right now. First of all, we need to get his pants up before someone else comes back here," Grace said. "Hope, you and Oscar grab a leg each and lift his legs up while I pull his pants back up." They did as she instructed, and all went as plan. "Oscar, on the back porch is a folding lounge chair. Bring it here," Grace told her nephew. Oscar got the chair and set it up. "Help me lift him up and set him in the chair."

Raul's head fell back, his body still limp.

"Is he dead?" Wide-eyed, Oscar asked.

"No Doll, he's still breathing," Grace said looking into his eyes. "Now Hope, we got to bend him over, so his head falls between his knees."

The two women tilted Raul forward and immediately the chair folded on the guy like a bug in a Venus flytrap. After freeing the young man from the chair Grace set the chair up again and said with a smile, "Oscar, hold the back of the chair for us dear." Never once did she lose her cool. This time they bent the teenager over with his head below his knees. Grace rubbed his back and shortly he woke.

With his head still lowered Raul asked, "What happened?" Oscar, seeing the Jack Daniels bottle, picked it up and showed it to Raul.

"This is what happened, you got whacked upside the head with it," Oscar said. "I'm not sure if Bonnie Gram saw you two, but if I were you, I wouldn't ask."

"You need to get into some dry clothes," Grace said. "You look about Matthew's size, Oscar, go ask him if he has any clothes here. Tell him that Raul and your sister were playing rough and she knocked him into some wet mud and that he's soaked through. And Oscar, not a word of this to anyone, do you understand me?" Grace told the boy before patting him on the back and sending him on his mission.

"Who could I tell but you," the fourteen-year-old said with a smile before running into the house.

"Okay you two, the same story goes for you," Grace said in all seriousness. "I didn't see a condom on him, and I don't see a wrapper lying around. This is not good, that goes for both of you. Your braces could have scratched him. If he has anything you could have it, and vice-versa young man. Play safe. Now, get inside. Raul go upstairs into the guest bathroom. Take a shower, a cold one," she said as they stepped from behind the tree. She saw four glasses lying on the ground by the empty bottle of Jack. She picked up the bottle and threw it deep into the woods then grabbed the glasses and went inside.

Raul was obviously taller than Matthew by three inches. Raul's classic red high-top Converse tennis shoes were below the hem of the khakis Matthew had loaned him. Raul stood by the fire and warmed himself, still a little light-headed from earlier. He wore a pullover long sleeve shirt that was also too small. Hope sat across the room admiring the exposed stream of black hair that ran from just below Raul's bellybutton into his waistband. He did taste different, she thought as she smiled at him. Trying to read if Bonnie saw anything, Raul did not respond to her smiles. He was too busy watching the old woman as she set the dining room table. The dining room was directly across the foyer from the living room. He could not help but notice once again all the photos with the heads of men cut off of them, especially the large family portrait of Bonnie, her daughters as teenagers and a headless man in a suit. It made him all the more nervous.

Charity had stopped at the KFC and brought back three buckets of chicken with all the fixings.

"With all these guests we need to add leaves to the table, Charity," Bonnie told her daughter. "Would you do that for me?"

"Sure Mom," Charity replied knowing no one else would do so.

Standing under the mistletoe, Sweet watched the large family interact in the living room and wondered about the future. Charity saw the young beauty and passed by her on her way to the dining room. Sweet, catching a whiff of the paramedic, absorbed the amiable alluring essences of Charity. Her nose locked onto the scent like that of a bloodhound to a fox. Sweet did not know what had come over her, but she followed the woman in uniform into the dining room. In her mind's eye a halo appeared around Charity's head.

Sweet was drawn to the square block of a woman. "I'll help you," Sweet volunteered. She felt some great energy just being around Charity, some wild sensation filled her. Sweet thought she must be filled with the Holy Ghost or was she a witness to some great saint, the long-haired girl pondered as the two women tugged the table apart.

Charity was tired after pulling two shifts. She did not even noticed Sweet's attention. After all, though the girl was beautiful and her voice pleasant and calm, Sweet was barely legal and was also her nephew's girlfriend.

"So how was work?" Sweet asked, as she helped Charity lay the first leaf in alignment to the male spokes.

"The same as always," Charity said. "Sweet, right?" verifying her name.

"Yeah," Sweet let loose of the word almost in a sigh from hearing her name spoken by this beautiful woman.

"Why women stay with men that beat them, cut them down, and treat them like slaves is beyond me," Charity shook her head. "Take tonight's case, this is the third time this year I've taken her to the emergency room. This time he knocked her braces through her mouth. But will she leave him, No." Charity mimics the abused woman as they place the second leaf on the table, 'The Bible says I can only leave him if he commits adultery, we're bound for life, it's a sin to leave him.'" Returning to her natural voice, "She didn't even finish high school, her parents married her off at fifteen to a man whose wife died. She's not twenty-five, yet she looks forty. The thing is, without an education you don't have to be black to have a Color Purple life."

"Quoting Lula May, are we?" Joy said, coming in with plates at the end of Charity's rant.

"Sorry Darling, I didn't mean to soliloquize," Charity said to the young woman as they shoved the table together, "it's just been one of those days."

Bonnie placed the KFC buckets and all the side dishes on top of the buffet and the family helped themselves, sitting down around the table after they made their plates.

"Who wants to say grace?" Bonnie asked, followed by, "We hold each other's hands Sweet, Raul." Sweet was situated between Matthew and Charity.

"I do," Matthew spoke up. "Dear Lord, make us truly thankful for Thy many blessings and Thy generosity. Guide us in Thy heavenly manner to do the right thing always so that we may share a home with you in Heaven. And Dear Lord, I want to give you my personal thanks for my family and especially to the woman who led me to salvation and the truth," Faith beamed with pride that her son loved her so much, "Sweet Ride, my future bride," Faith's eyes sent bullets across the table, "in the name of Jesus Christ, Our Lord and Savior, Amen."

Sweet was slightly embarrassed by the prayer and became flushed. She was unprepared for the strong squeezes she received from both Matthew and Charity. Faith smiled so sweetly at Sweet she felt like sugar was crystallizing in her mouth. Faith was thinking about how she was going to rid herself of this poor white trash. As far as Matthew was concerned, Sweet was thinking of how to rid herself of the shallow materialistic bourgeoisie.

Raul was sitting across the table from Charity. "How did you get that knot on the side of your head?" she asked.

"Who, me?" Raul said looking apprehensively at Bonnie. "Hope and I were playing, and I slipped and fell in the mud."

"Something must have smacked your head when you landed," Charity observed.

"It was too dark to see what it was," Hope fostered.

"Well, with all this snow, we need to figure out sleeping arrangements," Bonnie said.

"Raul," Raul snapped his head toward Bonnie, "do you want to call your parents and let them know that you're spending the night? With that bump on your head, and that jacked up truck of yours, I don't think you should be driving in falling snow, do you Hector?"

"I don't think they'll go for that. I'm sure my dad will come and pick me up," Raul said first to Bonnie, quickly turning to the sheriff.

"Young man, if you want, I'll give you a lift home, where about do you live?"

"In Springdale," Raul said.

"Springdale, really, I didn't know there were any Hispanics living in our neighborhood," said Faith in disbelief turning to Ellis.

"You don't have to do that, Sweet and I will drop him off," Matthew volunteered.

"No sir, you and Sweet will not be sleeping under my roof until you're married, it's unchristian like and I won't have it," Faith said to her son.

"But Mom," was all Matthew was able to get out of his mouth.

"I don't care if it is the twenty-first century, it sets a bad example and I'm not going to make Sweet sleep on the couch." Changing personalities like Sybil, Faith said congenially, "Momma, you don't mind if Sweet spends the night here, do you?"

"Why of course not, Grace and Iris can sleep in yours and Joy's old room and Sweet can bunk with Charity," Bonnie said, pleased that she was not going to have people up to the gills.

"Momma, Mary Jane wanted to spend the night, is that okay?" Joy asked.

"Why of course, she can bunk with me," one more won't hurt she thought.

"I'll be by tomorrow to get my van if the roads are good," Joy added.

"Hey, Matt, do you still think I could get a lift?" Raul asked. Matthew hated being called Matt.

"Sure," Matthew said, disappointed at the sleeping arrangements. Everyone that was leaving said his or her goodbyes. Matthew brought Sweet's luggage in and tried to kiss her goodnight under the mistletoe. Faith and Charity were watching the young couple. Sweet turned slightly and Matthew's kiss landed on her cheek. His mother's watching was the reasoning he placed behind Sweet's behavior. He gave his mother the evil eye as he went out the door.

Grace hugged her nieces and nephews goodnight. When she came to Oscar she whispered in his ear, "Remember sugar, The French and Latino's don't hold anything over us Southerners when it comes to sex. We just don't talk about it, especially in mixed company."

Raul hopped into the Jeep. Hope climbed onto the sideboard and kissed him properly on the mouth. "That's enough of that," Matthew said, cranking up the jeep.

"Hope, get your fanny in this car," her mother yelled.

"Better luck next time," Hope said, both young men thinking the statement was for them.

"What street do you live on?" Matthew asked.

"Chestnut," Raul replied, "the corner of Chestnut and Fair Street."

It wasn't long after they left that Charity was called to duty once again, and Matthew pulled off the side of the road to let his aunt pass by him with sirens blaring. "My Aunt Charity was the first woman to become a part of the Dixon Fire Department," Matthew said with pride.

"I guess somebody has to put out all the fires that your other aunts start," especially your Aunt Grace, what a MILF!" Raul said with much enthusiasm.

"Don't talk about my family like that. And if I as much as see you squeezing my sister's ass, I'll be the first in line to kick yours."

"You should talk to your sister. She can't keep her hands off mine. And as far as you kicking my ass, I'm benching close to twice your weight," Raul pulled his arm out of his coat and flexed it to show off his muscles. Nothing more was said between the two until they got to Raul's home. "Thanks for the lift," Raul said before Matthew drove off. "Asshole."

Raul walked up the steps to his house. His parents were asleep, only the porch light was on. He looked back at the sidewalk and saw his footprints in the snow, stuck his tongue out to catch some snowflakes. It was something he would never do if anyone were around. It was childish he thought, but if no one is there to see and judge, is it anything at all but a secret memory?

Matthew and Oscar lay in their twin beds with the blind up so they could watch the snow. The light from the streetlamp allowed them to view the frozen puffs of white. It also cast a stripe of angular light across their faces and along the wall. Both slept in nothing but their underwear, Oscar in briefs and Matthew in boxers. Matthew had recently switched to boxers because he thought that boxers were what men wore. Both propped their pillows up and reclined in their beds with their hands behind their heads and the covers pulled up below their armpits. The sound of the wind howling and an occasional vehicle passing by were the only noises they heard. They laid there waiting for the all's clear, the sound that was their parent's snoring, and in no more than ten minutes, like clockwork, it started and they could talk. Oscar missed their conversations and was full of questions he could not have asked at their grandmothers.

"So, are you fucking Sweet?" Oscar asked his big brother.

"No," he said to his brother, "I've found the Lord."

Oscar turned his head from the window and looked over at his brother in disbelief.

"We're not going to have sex 'til we're married," Matthew added.

"Not even a hand job?" Oscar inquired.

"No, all we've done is kissed," Matthew tried to change the subject, "God sure has blessed us with this beautiful snow. Have you thought about being saved Oscar?"

"You're sounding like Mama," Oscar paused, "Have you played with her tits?" Like most fourteen-year-olds, his inquiring mind wanted to know. He knew of his older brother's exploits in the past. His brother often talked dirty to his girlfriends on the phone thinking he was asleep. Who could sleep with the bed squeaking? Oscar hadn't reached puberty then, but now that he had he was eager to learn the things his parents thought he was too young to know about.

"I told ya' all we've done is kiss," Matthew said. "But when we get married, I'm going to make love to my wife night and day, day and night. We're gonna' have three kids of our own. I hope two boys and a girl. And I'm gonna study pharmaceutical research and Sweet is gonna' become a nurse. And when we get our degrees, we're gonna' become missionaries and minister to the poor communist Chinese that aren't allowed to know about Jesus and adopt little Chinese girls and raised them in the Lord. Couples over there are only allowed to have one child and so there are a lot of girls up for adoption. And I hope the Lord uses me as his vessel to stamp out the great social diseases. Can you imagine popping a pill or getting a shot that will stop diseases like alcoholism and homosexuality?"

"I sure hope not," Oscar said in a loud whisper just in case Sally might be able to hear them, I've got a porn with lesbians rubbin' each other with oil, sucking on each other's boobies and eating pussy. I've got a boner just thinking about it. One of the girls has a black dildo and…"

"Man stop, I told you I've found the Lord," Matthew demanded. "I don't want to hear about that stuff anymore. Let's pray together that Jesus will lead us away from the temptations of the flesh."

"You go ahead, I don't need it," Oscar said. "The only thing I'm praying for is to get laid and I don't care when, where, how or who."

The two were quiet and returned to looking out the window.

"Matthew, you awake?"

"Yeah," Matthew said, his eyes closed.

"Has a girl ever stuck her finger up your ass?"

"No," Matthew snapped at Oscar with an angry whisper, "but if you don't shut-up and go to sleep I'm gonna stick my fist up yours."

"Just asking," Oscar whined quietly. "No need to get mean about it."

"Good night," Matthew said finally.

"And wet dreams," Oscar said before turning on his side and pulling the covers over his shoulders. Matthew couldn't help but snicker before doing the same.

Chapter Ten

Charity was tired when she got home from work. It was quiet and still because all had gone to bed. She figured her sister Grace and Iris had a bit too much and were spending the night from Iris' car still parked out front. She really didn't mind. Last time Iris spent the night she had flashed her tits at Charity. Iris teased Charity quite often in private and Charity was delighted to see a set of relatively firm breasts considering that most often the only real breasts she saw were those of old women who have had heart attacks and need defibrillators to revive them. Seldom did she make it to the capitol city to visit the state's only exclusively lesbian bar, a smoke-filled room of drunken women in plaid drooling over the handful of lipsticks was not worth the headache brought on by the competition. Charity felt poor, unattractive, and incomplete every time she attended, and usually ended up going to see Lula May's nephew Hunter, AKA Virginia Headhunter perform at the Capitol Drag. The last time she went out, Virginia performed Whitney Houston's "Saving All My Love." During the last chorus, the tranny slung condoms filled with Ivory Liquid into the audience to the applause and laughter of all in attendance. The constant craving for finding love was building and Charity knew that once again she would put herself on the market in hopes of finding love. The question was what she would do with it once she found it. She was still closeted with her mother, and though she knew her sisters knew, she never mentioned her exploits. Charity felt that her mother's generation was lost to the reality that gay people do exist and can be healthy, happy, and even heroic, though Charity deemed none of those qualities to herself. Who would want to love a fat depressed dyke who doesn't have the nerve to reveal her sexuality to her own mother and the world?

"Gloom, despair, and agony on me, deep, dark, depression, excessive misery, if it weren't for bad luck, I'd have no luck at all, gloom, despair, and agony on me," she sang to herself. The old *Hee-Haw* tune always put her in better spirits. As she went into the kitchen, fruitcakes filled the counters. A large bottle of Jack Daniels sat beside the cakes with a note on it.

Charity, please add a quarter cup to each cake before you go to bed. Love, Mom. PS, Sweet, Matthew's new girl, is spending the night. You'll have to share your bed since you took down the twin beds. Sorry about that.

Charity tossed the note in the trash, opened up the refrigerator, took out the two-liter bottle of Coke, filled a glass with ice and made a drink. As she sipped on the nightcap, she measured out a quarter cup and poured it over each cake. After finishing the task, she sat down at the table to finish off her drink when she saw the round tin atop the fridge. The tin was green with red Ho! Ho! Ho!'s circling the base. She got back up, took the tin down, and struggled to take the lid off the tin, which had Santa drinking a Coke illustrated on top of it. She finally got the tin open and was overcome by the smell. "It's him," she said loudly as shivers visibly shook her whole body.

She ran out on the porch and looked out at the snow-covered tree that's branches drooped not only from snow but icicles. Charity breathed deeply. She returned back into the kitchen that was completely filled with the smell of Brut. It took everything for her to maintain her composure, but she could not, she ran to the sink and vomited. Gazing at the cake she grabbed the bottle of Jack and poured the remaining half bottle onto the cake and quickly closed it. As the smell dissipated, she stared at the tin. "Lula May," Charity said, "Who is this cake for?" Charity looked for a tag and could not find one. *I wonder who Mom is after this time*, she thought.

Charity rinsed her mouth out with water, poured the rest of her cocktail into the sink and went upstairs. As she opened the door, she remembered the note once seeing the beautiful young woman lying in her bed. Sweet's blonde hair cascaded across the pillow and Charity was reminded of Sleeping Beauty.

"I'll be your fairy godmother anytime you want. Where is the magic fairy dust?" She'd be happy if only she had a girl like this to come home to every night, she thought to herself. She plopped down in the chair by the vanity. It had been a long time since she looked into the cracked mirror. Charity broke the mirror when her mother forced her to participate in Joy's second wedding. She had gained weight between the fitting and the wedding date. As she glanced into the mirror, pulling the slip down over her boxers, she felt she looked like an over-stuffed kielbasa. Who knew kosher food could be so fattening. With one clean punch, the beveled lead glass mirror cracked in two. God, how her mother raked her over the coals, saying words she had never heard come out of her mouth. She broke the mirror over seven years ago, "…isn't it time for my bad luck to be over?"

She sat in the chair and played with her hair, "Maybe a new cut," she whispered.

Sweet's nostrils flared open like dilated pupils vacuuming Charity's scent into her olfactory system. The chemical reaction in her brain was spontaneous and her mouth began to water. She took in another breath, her eyes opened, and with the third intake of Charity's scent, Sweet smiled. She saw the most beautiful woman in the world. How could anyone be more perfect? Charity's androgyny was not confusing, or repulsive, or any of the other evils she had been taught. The androgyny was more like a rare, beautiful gem that should be coveted, not tossed to the swine. Oh, the smell of her, Sweet got out of bed and walked over to Charity still gazing at herself in the mirror. "I didn't mean to wake you," Charity said to the young beauty that wore nothing but a t-shirt that she had taken from her father before going to college.

"You're beautiful, you know?" Sweet cooed.

"Darling, you need to get your eyes checked."

"No, you really are beautiful," Sweet said picking up the hair brush off the vanity. Sweet began to brush Charity's hair. No one had brushed Charity's hair besides herself since before Dickey Dickson went away.

"Look at me for a moment," Sweet asked. Charity looked at Sweet who took her fingers to brush Charity's bangs to the right. "Now look," she said. Charity gazed into the mirror. She did look better she believed. Smiling, she looked up in thanks to the near stranger. Their eyes locked. Charity then broke the stare remembering that this girl was her nephew's fiancée.

"What's wrong?" Sweet questioned.

"Nothing."

"Then why did you turn away like that?"

"Because you're my nephew's fiancée and I want to kiss you. I'll go sleep on the couch."

"No, don't. I wanted to kiss you, too. I was just a little nervous," Sweet confessed. "I never kissed a girl before."

"So, have you and Matthew had sex?"

"Oh, no, not 'til we're married," Sweet paused, "I'm not gonna marry Matthew. It's not that I don't love him; I do, but not that way. I'm too young to get married. Matthew's the only guy I've ever dated. I was just doing what my parents wanted me to do. I've always done what my parents wanted. I'm gonna' do what I want to do. I'm gonna' kiss you Charity." As those words escaped her lips, her mouth led her to Charity's mouth, and sweet Sweet would soon be innocent no more.

"Iris, did you hear that?" Grace asked.

"It's just somebody having sex. Go back to sleep." Iris replied.

"We're not at your place, we're at my mom's," Grace whispered.

"So, Charity's gettin' laid. Go back to sleep."

"Did you hear what you just said?"

"So Sweet is getting laid."

"Oh, thank God. Matthew's back to his old self. I was afraid he was going Jerry Falwell on us."

"Now he's gone Jim Baker on us. Go to sleep." Grace rolled over on her side and faced the wall. She could never go to sleep while she knew people were engaging in sex, so she pretended to sleep for Iris' sake. She looked at the light through the window projected on the wall. The eyelet pattern from the curtains was like a stencil in their stillness. All was quiet.

"Oh, yes," Charity followed with a moan of satisfaction. Grace turned back over to see Iris sitting up in her bed. The two women looked at each other and smiled.

"Are you alright?" Sweet could be heard barely through the wall.

"I am now darlin', I am now," Charity's muffled voice came through the wall,"It's my turn now."

"All hell is going to break lose," Grace whispered to Iris. "I can feel it."

"No shit," Iris responded. "I hope the roads are clear tomorrow. I don't want to stick around for the fireworks."

"I do. I'm curious as how the perfect Mrs. Faith is going to handle this one."

"It's not Faith that I'm worried about, it's your mother."

Grace and Iris were already downstairs sipping coffee when they heard Charity make her way down singing a Cole Porter classic, "Tell me why should it be, you have the heart to hypnotize me. Let me live beneath your spell, do do that voodoo that you do so well, for you do something to me that nobody else can do."

"Somebody is in a good mood," Grace said to her sister.

"It's Christmas time I guess," Charity responded while pulling out the egg basket from the refrigerator.

"Santa bring an early present last night?" Iris said before sipping her coffee. Charity dropped an egg and blushed.

"Good morning girls," Bonnie said coming into the kitchen, "Did y'all sleep okay?"

"Slept fine momma," Grace said.

"Did the snow stick?" Bonnie said while poring herself a cup of coffee, "What would you girls like for breakfast?"

"I think Charity wants her eggs scrambled," Iris chucked.

"Is that Ride girl up?" Bonnie asked Charity.

"No Ma'am," Charity replied. "I don't think she slept so well."

"Well, I didn't either with Mary Jane in my bed. Can you take her over to Faith's? I told Matthew last night that you would."

Charity could not find words to say in response. Grace stepped in, "Momma don't wake the girl, she would have to get ready and that would make Charity late for work. Besides, Matthew has a Jeep, he can come get her."

"Charity, are you gonna clean up that egg?"

"Sorry momma," Charity said grabbing a paper towel.

"Well, if you're not gonna take Sweet to Matthew, why don't you drop this fruitcake off at the Good Dr. Rev. Pruitt-Peterson's. Charity was obviously lost in a dream. Bonnie snapped her fingers in front of Charity's face, "Charity, Pruitt-Peterson's fruitcake, can you drop it off?"

"What?" Charity said dazed. "Sorry momma, sure I'll drop it off for you."

"What's got into you this morning?"

"Sweet," Iris said after sipping her coffee. Grace was taking a sip and sprayed coffee across the table.

"What was that?" Bonnie asked.

"Hot," Grace said.

"Sweet, I put too much sugar in my coffee," Iris covered.

The phone rang. "That must be Matthew," Bonnie said leaving the room.

"I'll get you two later," Charity said.

"Like a virgin, touched for the very first time, like a virgin with your heartbeat close to mine," Grace sang mockingly. Charity grabbed an egg and threw it at Grace who reached up and grabbed it in front of her face. Broken, egg ran down her arm. "Damn it, Charity! I was just joking."

"No, it's more like," Iris, barely able to hold a tune, sang the chorus of the Guns N' Roses' classic, "Sweet Child of Mine."

There was a knock on the back door and Lula May let herself in. She walked over to Charity and slid her bangs over, "You's needs to shows your pretty face girl. How's my Gracie?" Lula May saw the egg running down her arm. "What's you do to Charity?"

"Why do you think I did anything to Charity?" Grace said.

"Do's you regularly squeeze raw egg in the morning or does that ho you work for have you doing some new ball breakin' exercise?"

"Why good morning, Lula May," Iris said to the woman who insulted her.

"Mornin' Ho," Lula May said flippantly, "Streets too cold for you this mornin'?" Bonnie came back into the kitchen.

"Good morning, Lula May. That was Matthew, I told him Sweet wasn't up yet."

"Sweet?" Lula May asked.

"Matthew's fiancée," Grace said, "Her name is Sweet Ride."

Lula May started laughing, "You's jokin' me."

Sweet came down in Charity's flannel shirt rubbing her eyes, "Good mornin' everybody. Do I smell coffee?"

"Good morning Sweet," Charity said. "Let me get you a cup. How do you like it?"

"Do y'all have any of that flavored creamer?" Sweet responded.

"Just milk, honey," Bonnie said.

"Milk and three teaspoons of sugar please," Sweet said as she sat at the table with Grace and Iris.

"Girl after my own heart," Charity said smiling at the dismantled girl.

"You sure do live up to your name. Sweet, I'd like you to meet Lula May Dixon, the oldest and nicest member of our family. Sweet is about to become the newest member of our family. She's Matthew's fiancée," Bonnie said.

"Is that so?" Lula May said sitting down next to Sweet, "Let me see your palm." Lula May took the girl's palm into her hand. As she examined it, she noticed that there was a scar in the shape of a crescent moon securely within the palm, but ever so close to the wrist casting its shadow on the rest of the lines.

"Where did you get this scar?" Lula May asked the girl.

"My daddy was spanking me and when I broke loose, I fell off the porch onto a broken Coke bottle."

"Yo's daddy thoughts musta' been unclean, 'cause everything yo's Daddy wants out of you will not take place. You'lls have a great love in yo life, but not that yo's daddy will like. You will feel loved and happy, but yo daddy will be ashamed and condemnin'. Your life will be shadowed by this scar, what cause yo daddy great sadness wills bring you's great happiness, but great danger as well."

"Will Matthew and Sweet get married?" Bonnie asked staring down at the girl's hand.

"No," both Sweet and Lula May said at the same time.

"I like Matthew a lot, but do you think it's wise to marry the first person you date? I'm giving him back the ring today. Is there any way that I can get y'all to call Greyhound for me? I need to get a bus back to Greenville," Sweet said to the stunned relief of Bonnie and Charity.

"There is no need for that. I'll drive you home," Charity said, "If you can wait 'til I get off my shift."

"Thanks, that would be nice," Sweet said. "I'll pay for the gas."

"Don't worry about it," Charity said with a smile.

"Let me fix y'all breakfast. Y'alls sits down a visits for a while," Lula May said to the women. Nothing much was said after Sweet's announcement. Sweet and Charity sat across from each other. Their smiles were contagious.

"Charity, you're gonna' be late if you're gonna' drop the fruitcake off by the good Dr. Reverend's," Bonnie said oblivious to the nonverbal conversation between Sweet and Charity. Lula May was not.

"I'll see you after I get off work," Charity smiled at Sweet while sliding on her paramedic jacket. "I get home around six."

"Don't forget the fruitcake," Bonnie said as she handed the tin to Charity as she stepped out the door.

Chapter Eleven

"Come on in," the Good Dr. Reverend said to the big-boned gal standing at his door. "I was just fixing breakfast for Noah and myself. Can I offer you some coffee?"

"No thank you. Momma just wanted me to drop this off to you," Charity said putting the fruitcake in his hands.

"Another cake, what kind is this one?" The Good Dr. Reverend said with sarcastic smile. Charity told him it was Fruitcake. "Really, why thank you. By the looks of you I thought it might be pound cake. Won't you come in for just a moment, I got something for you."

Charity looked down at her watch, "Well, I guess I've got a couple of minutes."

"Before my wife got ill and died, she was a big woman. Never lost the weight after Noah was born. Anyway, she had some nice clothes that she only wore a few times before she got sick with the cancer. I'm sure they are about your size." The Good Dr. Reverend said as he started pulling dresses out of a box he had tucked away in a closet. He held them up and placed them under his neck to show them off. "Real nice and feminine, don't you think? Better than wearing slacks to church," he said with a smile.

"Those are pretty, but…"

"And there's diet books, Lord knows she tried to lose the weight. See, here is Suzanne Summers' Eat Great Lose Weight, and the South Beach Diet, Adkins, oh there are so many, I'm sure you can use them." Charity was dumbfounded as the good Dr. Reverend place the heavy box in her hands, "Will we see you and your sisters at choir practice tonight?"

"Not me anyway, I'm taking a friend home to Greenville," Charity said, pleased to have a legitimate excuse not to be there.

"Too bad, well I don't want to keep you from work," he said before hustling Charity out the door. "See you at church, bye now."

"Great, nothing better than being told you look like a big fat dyke first thing in the morning," Charity said tossing the box on to the passenger's seat. "If I hadn't just been with a beautiful eighteen-year-old virgin, I'd of flattened that self-righteous asshole," Charity said aloud to herself as she cranked up the vehicle. "Good Dr. Reverend indeed, well they got the G–D–right."

The resonance created from the engine of Matthew's jeep was loud enough for the women sitting around the table to hear as he pulled into the drive. Iris and Grace looked at each other. Grace quickly took a last sip of her coffee.

"It was nice meeting you, Sweet," Iris said pushing away from the table.

"Matthew is a strong, resilient young man, don't worry about him. You do what's right for you," Grace said before she kissed her mother and Lula May goodbye. The two women made their way to the back door, Grace waving goodbye as she shut the door.

Matthew groomed himself in the rearview mirror as he noticed his aunt and her friend coming out to their car. "Is Sweet up?" he asked as he hopped down from the jeep.

"Yep, she's in the kitchen with Momma and Lula May. We've got to get to work, talk to you soon," Grace said before Iris was able to crank up the car. "Love you, Matthew."

Iris gave the sports car a rev before she pulled out on to the highway. Matthew looked on thinking that he would like to give that car a spin around the block sometime as they drove out of site. Matthew went around to the back door noticing the evergreen tree and how it had grown over the years. He had wondered why this tree had never been decorated at Christmas as he made his way onto the screened in back porch. Before he opened up the door, he took a slight moment gazing at the three women gathered around the table. As his Bonnie Gram drew from her morning cigarette, he wished she would stop smoking before it killed her.

"Good morning and Merry Christmas," he exclaimed cheerfully as he entered the kitchen. He went immediately to Sweet and tried to kiss her on the lips, she turned her head and offered her cheek as a blurry-eyed Mary Jane made her way into the kitchen.

"Why lets me take a look at you, Rooster," Lula May said, holding Matthew by the shoulders. "You's ain't no boy no mo. No sir-re, you's a full fledge college man, dressing sharp in the mornin', hair combed."

"Rooster?" Sweet asked.

"That's whats I's called him since that first red curl popped on top of his head like a rooster's comb. I's right by calling him that too, always struttin' around town the way he do," Lula May said as they exchanged hugs.

"Lula May has been taking care of Hope and me since we were born. Said she was the only one who could keep us right and make sure we were good. I swear she killed that holly bush on the edge of the woods from taking too many switches off of it," Matthew laughed.

"I's taken care of three generations of this family froms the times they were born," Lula May boasted to Sweet. "They is my family since I's no chillen of my own."

"You are family," Bonnie said in all sincerity. "Lula May I don't know what we do without you."

"Matthew, has you had breakfast?" Lula May asked.

"No, Ma'am," he stated before sitting down next to Sweet and reaching under the table for her hand. Sweet took her hand away and used both hands to drink her coffee.

"Scrambled eggs with ham and onions sound good?" Lula May asked. "How about you Mary Jane?"

"If you don't tell Mom," Mary Jane stated knowing her mom had been against eating pork ever since she was married to Herb's father.

"Sweet, you want to go shopping with me, Lula May and Mary Jane?" Bonnie said as Lula May placed butter and the onions into the cast iron skillet. "I was thinking about driving over to Capitol Mall and taking a look around."

"Lula May did anyone tell you that Sweet and I are engaged to get married?" Matthew asked as she added the ham. Only the sound of the frying ham and onions in the butter could be heard. Bonnie raised her eyebrows at Sweet.

"What?" Matthew said looking around the room as if there were some surprise lying about of which he had been unaware.

"We need to talk," Sweet paused, "alone."

"Why don't y'all go into the living room. No one is here but us girls. Y'all can talk in there," Bonnie informed the young couple as Lula May cracked the eggs. Matthew got up pulling Sweet's chair out from the table. They walked out of the kitchen.

"He ain't never been dumped before has he?" Lula May said, cracking the last egg.

"No, I don't think so. He's always been the one doing the dumping," Bonnie said refilling her coffee cup.

"Sweet's dumping Matthew?" Mary Jane asked before getting up and turning on a baby speaker Joy left at her mom's for when she babysat Kind, "I got to hear this."

"I guess we're the ones going to be eating these eggs then," Lula May said pulling the wooden spatula across the frying eggs.

"What's up?" Matthew asked as they reached the living room.

"I can't marry you," she said looking down at the floor.

"Why not?" he asked lifting her chin to look her in the eyes.

"I don't love you that way. The fact is I really don't know what love is. You're the first guy I ever dated," she stated before turning her back and walking away from him. "I have nothing to compare this to," she lied, thinking of her night with Charity. "I know my parents sent me to college to find a husband and live a good Christian life, but I want a real degree, not just a M-R-S degree."

Matthew was shocked by her words and walked over to her, "I love you Sweet, I really do. You have no idea how much I love you." He turned her around to face him. "Kneel with me," he said sliding onto his knees. "Let's pray about this before we make any rash decisions."

"I already have Matthew," she said looking down at him.

"But I love you," he said wrapping his arms around her legs. "Don't leave me, please."

"I'm sorry Matthew, but it's over."

"No, it's not, just think about it over the holidays. I know you'll change your mind. Just let me know when we get back to Bob Jones," Matthew pleaded.

"I'm not going back there. I'm transferring to State," Sweet said. "Go back there if you like, but I think they are out of touch with reality... and the Bible."

"What's gotten into you?!" Matthew declared rising from his knees and taking a step back.

"I don't know, but I'm glad it did," she said, seeing a photo of Charity in her uniform, "you're a good guy Matthew, let's just be friends."

"It's my family, isn't it?"

"No, you have a wonderful family. I hope to stay in touch with you all, but I want to live my life as I want to live it. Not the way my parents, or Bob Jones, or the church thinks I should live it. God has a plan for us all if we listen. My ears were just opened last night, and he told me that marrying you was not part of it. I'm sorry Matthew."

"Do you want me to take you home? Give me a chance, please Sweet," he begged.

"Your Aunt Charity has already volunteered to do that after she gets off work," she said noticing the tears building up in Matthew's eyes. "I gave your grandmother her ring back this morning, please don't cry," she said trying to smile at him.

"But I love you. I became a virgin for you," he shouted at her in anger.

Lula May and Bonnie looked at each other as they listened through Kind's crib speaker. Lula May looked up at Bonnie, "how can you do that?"

"I'll explain it to you later," Bonnie said.

"I want to know too, Bonnie Gram," Mary Jane requested.

"I'm sorry Matthew," Sweet said. Matthew stormed out of the living room and went out the front door slamming it behind him. Sweet looked back to the photo of Charity in her uniform, took it off the wall and kissed it before she returned it as Mary Jane, Bonnie and Lula May entered.

"Are you alright darling?" Bonnie asked.

"Yes mam, I'm fine," she stated. "Not so sure about Matthew though."

Lula May examined the girl from head to toe, "I was just straightening Charity's photo. It went crooked as Matthew slammed the door," she lied.

"Well, we're going to Capitol Mall shortly to do a little Christmas shopping. The offer still stands. It will be a few hours before Charity gets off work," Bonnie said.

"That sounds like a plan. Just give me a minute to get ready," Sweet left the room and passed Mary Jane who had watched her cousin tear out the drive. She smiled at the girl before she went upstairs and into Charity's bedroom. Sweet fell on the bed, rolled over on her tummy and inhaled Charity's pillow. "It's you I love," she said before burying her head deep into the purple covered pillow. She came up like a cat that had gotten into the catnip.

Matthew was frustrated beyond recall. He wiped his bleary eyes as he sped down the old county road and back into town. His jeep beeped at him telling him his gas was low. "Damn it to hell, I need gas and I got to pee," he shouted turning on the music desperately looking for a gas station. He whipped his jeep into the Shell on the black side of town. He quickly slid the debit card into the gas pump, stuck the nozzle into the tank, and left it pumping as he jogged into the store. Desperately, he looked for the bathroom. Yvonne watched the redhead boy walk across the store like a duck in a target gallery. "Can I help you find something?" Yvonne shouted across the store.

Stopping in his tracks, Matthew turned to her, "You got a bathroom?"

Yvonne held up a key attached to a paddle that once had a rubber ball attached to it. "It's around back," she said.

"Thank you," Matthew said as Yvonne handed it over to him. He did his best not to run out the door as he hurried around back. Yvonne chuckled once the door shut. The paddle had much graffiti written on it, the kind of stuff that would cause his mother to piss herself whether she needed to or not. As he opened the bathroom door an aroma he had not smelled since camp, where the only facilities were outhouses, hit him in the face. "Damn," he said before he went inside.

Next to the toilet was a condom machine. Everywhere he turned filth of some sort offended his newly sanctified mind, bikini-clad girls on the dispenser and sordid messages written on the wall. It had been months now that he had gone without touching himself other than to urinate or shower. Matthew had loads bottled up inside him, rumpus frustration, phenomenal anger, speculating doubt. A lurid horniness he couldn't deny overcame him as held his penis in his hand.

"What would Jesus do? What would Jesus do? What would Jesus do?" He repeated over and over to himself before giving himself a shake, zipping, and fleeing the foul, vulgar toilet.

Chapter Twelve

No town is free of vice, no matter how big or small. Dixon was no different. An old, vacated bait and tackle gas station on the lakeside of town was where one ventured in order to find a cheap 'date.' Once the prostitute knew what her 'john' was looking to buy, she'd encourage a trip to the Motel Johnson, a relic from the 1950s that was designed in the period's modern style. The motel in its heyday housed fisherman, salesmen, and families passing through Dixon. This was of course in the years before the interstate highway system was built two and a half decades later, which made the motel out of the way.

After Charity left, the Good Dr. Reverend wasn't feeling so 'Good' anymore, as a matter of fact he wanted to be 'Bad' and couldn't wait to get his little bugger Noah off to school. As soon as his son's bus pulled away, he ran to his car and made a beeline to the old bait and tackle. The Good Dr. Reverend shot down the highway until about half a mile or so and stopped his car. Confused and baffled, Paul pulled off the road, placed his car into park and rolled down his window in hopes that the cold air would shock him into reality. The urge, which overwhelmed him earlier, had come and gone as quickly as it had arrived. He knew what he was thinking about, but he took none of the precautions that were his practice prior to setting out on such an exploit. Uncomfortable on the roadside, he drove up to the Motel Johnson, turned into its parking lot and parked. He was here the last weekend before Thanksgiving when he let Noah spend the night with a new friend he had made from school. Eyes shut, his head pushed against the headrest, his arms locked on the wheel, Paul took in deep breaths, memories of the night flowed through his mind.

Dark-eyed Darla wore tight denim blue jeans and a tattered jacket she had owned since she was a teenager. Because of the cold, the denim jacket covered most of her silver sequined tube top. She ringed the contours of her small, puckered mouth with lipstick in what the Reverend could only describe to be as 'chicken-ass red' in color. Deliberately dropping her leather-fringed bag, Darla slithered up to his window and watched the little man, his eyes squeezed closed, breathing nervously. Aware that the man was alone, she unbuttoned her jacket. Her sequined tube-top burst open to the elements and changed colors as the Motel Johnson's Road sign flashed each neon word of its name before the silhouette of an arrow, pointed upward toward the establishment, followed suit. The red neon phallic shaped arrow flashed three times before the sign repeated the sequence.

Paul thought he was watching a David Lynch movie as he followed the arrow to the motel. Before a door near the end of the corridor of rooms, he witnessed two whores dancing. Not in a typical modern writhing lascivious manner, as would be expected, but in a haunting-like tempo last practiced in the years the structure was built. The Good Dr. Reverend watched as Marsha, a formally trained dancer now hooked on meth, sang the melody of the Blue Danube as she taught Brenda, a formally trained pole-dancer, the waltz. Both high on different cocktail drugs coupled with alcohol danced dizzily, spinning to the pulse of the flashing lights. Brenda stopped suddenly and vomited over the curb; Marsha laughed and then continued the dance without her partner. The girls that worked the Motel Johnson said their use of the motor inn's flashing sign set a pace that promoted heightened pleasure. Other than Marsha, they were ignorant that they serviced their clients with a mouth waltz. Either way, all took pride in their street slogan, "The best B Js are found at M Js."

Darla could tell by Paul's quirkiness that he wasn't a cop. She had not seen his car under the flashing neon banner before that night. His silver hair danced with neon red as he turned his eyes away from the motel to her. Startled, she stood up from her kneeling position due to another car pulling into the parking lot. The Reverend was eyeball to eyeball with Darla's jumbo ruby-eyed navel piercing that stared back at him. "Demon eye," Paul thought out loud, pulling his head away from the window.

Dropping back down, dipping her glittering squeezed breast into the car's window secured Paul's gaze, this was ever so brief as her face entered his view with those electric blues piercing out of her crack-sunken raccoon eyes. Not phased, his hardcore horniness was in control. Her red gooey lips parted, "I'm Darla."

"Hey Mister," a blond headed cooze said to Paul, snapping him out of his daydream. Startled, he followed the blonde's gaze down to the protrusion in his pants. Paul quickly reached into his glove compartment, grabbed out Bible tracts and threw them at her before rolling up his window and backing out of the lot. Praying there were no witnesses to his presence there during daylight hours, he burned rubber pulling out of the motor inn's entrance and out onto the highway.

He sang his favorite gospel tunes trying to erase his horniness and shame. But no sooner had the small man returned to his drive than he found himself throbbing as if he were twenty, he backed out the drive once more. Possessed, this time he found himself pulling into some stranger's yard just around the block from fast-food alley. He knocked on the door, "Jessica, it's Dickey. Open up."

Jessica, an unclean meth addict missing her front teeth, opened the marred door as the vaporous Paul shoved some bills into her cleavage. Paul, overcome by the demon possessing his mind, entered the room and Jessica shut the door. The woman Dickey knew as a young vibrant woman was twenty-five years older and looking much older than her forty plus years. Jessica smelled like one of hell's offerings. The demon remembered the smells of hell, which he associated with the cooking of meth that lingered in the room. He would not even tap this decrepit creature with the Reverend's dick. Her scent sent his demon self back to the torturous realms he had just escaped. "Standards son, standards," Dickey heard his father Joe saying, which Paul also heard resonating in his head. He fled Paul's body as the junky kneeled before him. Paul regained control of himself as he heard the unzipping of his pants. Looking down at the wretched toothless woman who had her hand in his pants he gasped in horror, "No!" He shouted as he broke through the possession zone, slapping the woman's hand away. The preacher zipped up his pants and fled the shanty looking over his shoulder as the monster created by Dr. Meth-n-stein stood dumbfounded in her doorway.

"Thank God for standards," Paul said, driving home in fear. *Do I have Alzheimer's?* He wondered pulling into his drive, running inside and slamming the door. He went to the living room and removed the photo of his late wife, kneeling down on his knees, he tried to pray, but his overwhelming horniness would not allow him to concentrate on the subjects divine. He fondly remembered fondling her enormous breast smothered in baby oil. He removed his engorged member from his pants, unaware that another member of the ladies auxiliary had arrived with yet another fruitcake. Gazing through a wreath that acted as a porthole view into the living room, the primly dressed woman stood on the sidewalk in a state of disbelief as to what she was witnessing. Dickey, on the other hand, felt he was witnessing what he heard other souls in hell describe as everyday occurrences at the Roman forum. He applauded the vigor and stamina displayed in the Reverend's memory. As his relief spewed forth before the flames and onto the hearth, the natural release of chemicals connecting with the synapses in the minister's brain felt like a junkie's sweet rush of heroin to Dickey. "What else was an incubus other than an orgasm addict," Dickey thought as both spirits steeped in the afterglow.

The doorbell rang breaking the spell. Paul glanced down at the mess he made, grabbed a pillow off the couch and wiped his bodily fluids up, throwing the pillow in a hall closet before he answered the door. When he opened the door no one was there. He heard the sound of a car door closing, when he saw another fruitcake tin at sidewalk's end. As the car pulled away, Paul saw his neighbors, an older man and wife, out walking their dog and waved at them. As Paul retrieved what he knew to be another fruitcake, the old man popped his wife on the bottom before kissing her.

Paul would not understand why, but over the following days he would notice many of the couples in the neighborhood walking around with smiles on their faces. He blamed it on the holiday season, but he knew through his therapy training that the season was usually stressful and led to much marital strife. He had witnessed one man with a black eye and a couple of men grabbing their lower backs. These men must be sleeping on the couch he originally thought, but each man wore a smile on his face and had a swagger in their stride. Paul did not know what to think and smiled.

Chapter Thirteen

Over the next few days, the Good Dr. Reverend received over two dozen fruitcakes. Because he was relatively new to the congregation, he figured that this was a tradition started by the previous pastor. He could not recall telling anyone that he liked the holiday staple. One cake, well he could serve it to guests, but what to do with twenty-seven fruitcakes plagued the Good Dr. Reverend. It was while watching a re-run of *Seinfeld* with his son that it came to him. He would re-gift the cakes to the church choir. Charity McRae was the only member of the choir that gave him a fruitcake, and as of late, if she wasn't working during rehearsals, she was visiting some new friend in Greenville. He checked the rehearsal schedule and found that Charity would be working on the twenty-second. That would be fruitcake day he thought to himself and chuckled.

"Noah, Hey Noah, where are you?" the Good Dr. Reverend called out for his son.

Not getting a response, the Good Dr. Reverend went upstairs looking for the thirteen-year-old. He knocked on Noah's bedroom door and opened it, but Noah wasn't there.

"Strange," he said. "Noah if you're up here you better answer me."

It was out of character for Noah not to answer him. Paul started back down the hall when he heard sounds coming out of the bathroom.

It was a slurping rhythmic pounding that was unmistakably the sound of masturbation. Since his wife had died it had become a more common sound in his life than he liked. His son was coming of age, he thought to himself and continued down the hall, but he stopped in his tracks when he heard an unfamiliar voice coming out of the bathroom.

"Oh, yeah, I'm gonna fuck you," a deep man's voice echoed, "again and again and again."

The Good Dr. Reverend went back to the bathroom and tried to open the door, but it was locked. Paul pounded on the door, "Noah, are you in there? Noah if you're in there you better open this door!"

"Ah yeah, oh, yeah, I'm cumming, yeah, ah, ah, ah, yes," the erratic noise churned in a continual climb, which blended with a rhythmic pounding. That was not the voice of his son. The good Dr. Reverend just knew that his son was being molested in his own house. He hurried to his bedroom and pulled the forty-five off the top shelf in the closet and ran back out into the hall.

"I don't know who's in there, but if you've hurt my son, I'm going to kill you, you son of a bitch!" the Good Dr. Reverend shouted at the door. Once again Paul tried to open the door. He was a small man and knew that neither his brute force nor his weight thrown against it would open the door. He cocked the gun and pointed it at the doorknob and fired. He slung open the door and there sat Noah on the toilet, his pants down to his ankles, computer printouts of Grace, nude from Iris' porn site, were on the floor with cum showered all over them.

Noah's head turned to his father and the voice of Dickey Dickson came out of Noah's mouth, "Can't a man have some privacy?" This was followed by a deep dark chuckle that sent chills down Paul's spine.

"Who are you?" Paul asked.

"Tricky Dickey," Dickey Dickson said through Noah. Has the spirit of Richard Nixon possessed my son the Good Dr. Reverend thought for a split second. Noah's head tilted back, and his eyes rolled back in his head. This was followed by a loud crash down in the kitchen. Noah looked back at his dad, looked down at the nude pictures of Grace, felt the gooey semen on his hand, and blushed. Noah quickly covered his genitals. "Dad, please shut the door," Noah demanded in his regular thirteen years old voice.

"We need to talk, son," Paul said quietly pulling the door shut as best he could. His gun still in his hand, he turned and started running down the stairs. When the Good Dr. Reverend got down to the kitchen the fruitcakes were all on the floor. Before they were stacked neatly on the counter. He picked them up and placed them back where they were, but the cake Charity had given him was ice cold. The sweat that developed on his hand earlier caused his hand to stick to the tin. "Ouch," he shouted as his hand pulled free. Paul's phone rang and he answered, "Hello, yes, everything's alright. Thanks for your concern," he heard the sound of sirens as Sheriff Sakamoto pulled into the Reverend's drive. "The police are here, got to go."

Hector knocked on Paul's door, "Good evening, Reverend, we have reports of a gunshot coming from your home. Is everything alright?"

"Yes, Sheriff, won't you and your deputy please come inside. It's embarrassing."

Hector's deputy stood by the car with his gun drawn. He waved for him to put his gun down and with a nod of his head for him to come inside. The Deputy and Sheriff slowly walked into the kitchen. Hector noticed the gun lying on the table, "is this your gun Reverend? Is it registered?"

"Yes, to both questions Sheriff. Please have a seat. Coffee, fruitcake?" the Reverend asked pointing to the stacked tins on the counter.

"I'll have a cup of coffee," Hector replied.

"You deputy?"

"Why not, but no fruitcake," the Deputy said trying to hide his smirk.

Before turning a chair around and sitting in it backwards. Sipping from his cup the Reverend addressed the officers, "This is a bit embarrassing, and I hope what I say will stay at this table. Earlier, I called for my son and did not hear a response. I went upstairs to his bedroom to see what he was up to, but he wasn't there. As I was returning downstairs, I heard what I thought was a strange voice coming out of the bathroom. I asked Noah if that was he, but got no response. I knocked on the door and heard once again a strange voice, the words he was saying made me think that my son was being molested in my own home. I ran to my room, got my gun, and shot the doorknob. To my horror, but mainly my son's, I caught him in the last stages of masturbation. Apparently, my son's voice is changing," Paul ended laughing out loud. The two policemen joined in the laughter.

"Do you mind if I check on your son? It's just regulation."

"Not at all." The three gentlemen went up the stairs together to find Noah picking up the porn off the floor.

Hector asked, "Noah, you mind if I have a word with you, son?" Noah walked into the hall, his head hanging low in shame. The Deputy walked into the bathroom. He noticed the pornographic images of the Sheriff's sister-in-law on the floor. "Son, I understand that your father caught you in a private moment."

"Yes, sir."

"Do you realize that looking at pornographic images at your age is against the law? What site did you get these images?" Noah doesn't answer.

The Reverend scolded, "Answer the Sheriff."

The Deputy holding the printout with a latex glove on his hand brings the photo of his sister-in-law to the Sheriff. The Sheriff notices that it is from his sister's site. "Never mind, son. I'm going to look the other way this time to save your father public embarrassment, but the next time your father asks you to answer, answer him no matter what you're doing. We're all men here. We've all done the same thing you were doing. No need to be ashamed. We'll let your father talk to you more about it."

"Yes, sir."

The Sheriff folded the photo and put it in his pocket. "I'll write this down as an accidental discharge, Reverend," the Sheriff said before realizing his accidental double entendre with a smirk.

"Thank you, Sheriff," Paul said trying not to laugh.

"We'll see ourselves out."

"Goodnight, Sheriff."

"Goodnight, Reverend, Noah," Hector said as he and the Deputy descend down the stairs and out the front door.

"Not a word about this to anyone and I mean any of this to anyone," Hector said to his Deputy.

"If your wife looks anything like your sister-in-law," the Deputy said opening the patrol car door.

"Hamp, I said not a word to anyone, and that includes me."

After a talk about the birds and the bees with his son, Reverend Paul sent Noah to bed. The last thing the boy remembered was finding porn on the Internet. Noah's next memory was of Paul standing in the bathroom door and his own right hand covered with bodily fluids. He did not remember his father pounding on the door or the gunshot. Paul had never witnessed anything like what had happened. He worried that his own sins had brought some evil spirit into his house. He was quite sure that his son must have been possessed. He returned to the bathroom and saw the cum-covered printouts that the Sheriff didn't take balled up in the trashcan. He took one out with the tips of his fingers, unraveling the paper. He thought he recognized the nude woman in the photos. "I wonder if her mother is aware of this. Shameful, just shameful."

Returning the photo to the trash, he carried the waste basket downstairs to the living room and with his fingertips tossed each ball of porn into the fire. "Well, at least my boy is straight," he thought as the last ball of fire disintegrated in the fireplace's flames. Paul reassured himself that he must be doing the Lord's work or Satan would not have bothered with him. He prayed mightily all night long before the fireplace for forgiveness of his own carnal sins and protection against evil for his son.

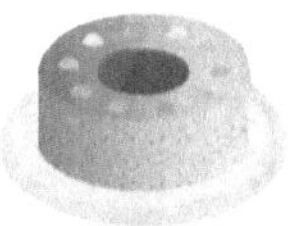

Chapter Fourteen

Raul arrived at five pm to pick up Hope for their date. Like all young men, Raul had become immune to the discerning eyes of most parents, but the McCaskill's were another story. He still was not sure if the Jack Daniels bottle that knocked him out cold was an accident or deliberate. With that thought in mind, he approached the traditional Craftsman home with clear Christmas lights draped over the azaleas with caution and reverence. Hope watched his approach from her bedroom that had been converted from an old sleeping porch. She tapped on the window to garner his attention. Raul looked up and motioned for her to meet him. The chilling wind caught the seasonal Snoopy flag and the icicle lights, which swayed as Raul climbed the porch steps holding Matthew's dry-cleaned clothes. Hope opened the door.

"Are you ready?" Raul asked.

"Yep," Hope replied, closing the door quietly behind her. "Just leave those hanging on the door," she said, taking the hangers from him and hooking them on the door knocker.

When they got down to the bottom of the steps, the door reopened. "Hope, I want you home by eleven o'clock," Faith yelled to her daughter while stirring the contents of a bowl. "Raul, do you have a watch?"

Raul turned to answer Faith, "Yes, Ma'am, Mrs. McCaskill."

"Eleven O'clock, not a minute after," Faith said in all sincerity.

"Eleven O'clock. Will do Mrs. McCaskill," Raul yelled from his truck adding, "That's Matthew's clothes hanging on the door. My mom and dad said to tell y'all thank you."

Raul locked his fingers together. Hope slid her right foot between them and, with a clean lift, landed gracefully in the passenger's seat of the elevated four-wheeled vehicle. The couple pulled into the drive-thru of a locally owned hamburger joint. After eating, Raul reached into his glove compartment and pulled out a pre-rolled joint. He pressed in the cigarette lighter and torched the joint up as soon as its lighter popped out. He passed the joint to Hope, who took a toke with glee.

"What you wanna' do?" Hope asked.

"I've got something special planned, but first let's get stoned and look at the Christmas lights," Raul said.

After the choir finished "Joy to the World," the good Dr. Reverend said, "Beautiful, just beautiful." Then Paul said to the choir director, "I have a gift for all the members of the choir." By the doors to the church was a large cardboard box. As each person left, the good Dr. Reverend handed out tin after tin of fruitcakes.

Betsy Gaddis, the secretary of Mayor James "J-Bird" Weldon, was eager to leave. Rehearsal had run over, and she was late. She took the Ho! Ho! Ho! tin that Bonnie had placed the Good Dr. Reverend's cake in. Betsy felt that the tin was appropriate for she deemed her affair with the Mayor would appear in many eyes to make her a "ho." Betsy was single and attractive, she knew that it was her extra-large breast and not her skills as a secretary that got her the job with the Mayor. Though she was just twenty-five, she wore her hair in a braided bun. Many thought it was because she was conservative. The real reason was two-fold. The chief motivation was to keep the wayward Mayor's jealous wife from being suspicious. It was also the reason she wore little make-up to work. The other motive was to keep the Mayor from pulling her hair during their lovemaking.

She drove through town as fast as she could to meet J-Bird. Putting on her lipstick, Betsy looked down at the speedometer and looked back up to see blue lights in her rearview mirror. "Damn," she said placing her lipstick back in her purse only to pull out her license.

Hector walked up to Betsy's Accord. "Hi Betsy, what's the hurry?" Hector said. "You know you were doing fifty-five in a thirty-five? You got your license and registration?"

"Hi Sheriff, I'm sorry, choir practice ran long, and I was running late for a date," Betsy said after blotting her mouth.

"Who are you dating on this side of town?"

"I'm dating Guy Kress in Bone Town," she said knowing that Guy Kress, her second cousin, was a closeted divorced gay man. They had a mutual agreement between themselves, she used him to hide her affair with the Mayor, he used her to hide his homosexuality from his straight friends. Hector let his flashlight investigate the interior of Betsy's car. He spotted the tin in the passenger's seat. He wasn't sure, but he thought the tin was breathing. Betsy noticed that the light rested on the tin. "The Good Dr. Reverend gave the choir fruitcakes for Christmas," Betsy explained, "I don't like fruitcake, do you?"

"My mother-in-law makes enough fruitcake every year to feed the whole town," Hector said returning the light to Betty's face, which slid down to her breast. There was something about Betsy that reminded Hector of Joy. The shape of her face and the color of her eyes were the main shared characteristics. If fact, Betsy looked like youthful pictures of Joy with a boob job. He smiled at Betsy and wondered what Joy was up to tonight. "Merry Christmas Betsy, take this as a warning. Watch your speed, okay?"

"Thanks Sheriff," Betsy said slowly pulling off the shoulder. The Motel Johnson's main form of business came from one-night stands and those who were conducting extramarital affairs. The Mayor's high school football pal, Keith Fudge, owned the motel and kept room eight reserved for him. The Mayor never had to sign in at the desk. Mayor Weldon had parked his car so no one could read his license tag. He was pacing in nothing but his boxer-briefs and navy dress socks while staring at his watch and looking out of the window from time to time. Betsy pulled out her cell phone, "Hi J-Bird what you doing?"

"Waiting on you, darlin. How soon before you're here?"

"Choir ran long, I'll be there in less than five minutes."

"I'll be waiting," he said. "The door is unlocked." The Mayor, unlike many of his friends, had maintained his fitness. With sixty-eight percent of Dixon's women voting for him, he attributed his fitness and good looks to his winning the last election. Marrying a descendant of a founding town father didn't hurt either, considering he grew up one step above white trash. Weldon checked himself out in the mirror. He turned around to check out his butt while flexing his ass muscles. This had become a strange habit since a college girlfriend complemented him on his derrière. Women like men's butts the same way men like women's boobs she explained. His mother having died of breast cancer made him wonder if there was such a thing as ass cancer. The forty-year-old lay back on the bed and started to massage himself through his shorts. Time was waning, when Betsy arrived, he knew the sex was going to have to be quick if he were to make it home to his wife on time. As he heard the car pull up, Weldon pulled off his underwear and turned over and posed himself on his side. He propped his head up with one hand and in the other hand twirled his shorts on his index finger. When the door opened, he let the underwear fly.

Betsy, with fruitcake in hand, caught the shorts in her mouth as they slapped her across the face. Shutting the door behind her with her hip, she kicked off her shoes and ran toward the smiling naked man sprawled across the bed. Tossing the fruitcake on the end of the bed she wrestled with the Mayor trying to shove his underwear in his mouth. J-Bird's eyes rolled back. Betsy thought he did this to let her win. "Hush," Betsy said. Her tongue flicked across his nipples while she worked herself out of her hose. She stopped to pick the hair out of her mouth, mounted him with her blouse still on, and removed the underwear from his mouth so she could kiss him. The fruitcake bounced on the bed in rhythm with Betsy's rise and fall. If they had noticed it, the tin would have appeared as if it were expanding. A strange, possessed moan escaped J-Bird's mouth. Betsy looked at him peculiarly, she had not ever seen Weldon respond so fervently as he moaned over and over again with the voice of Dickey Dickson. The voice and look in Weldon's eyes stopped Betsy on the down stroke, "Are you okay?"

Weldon's body flexed upwards for a movement. He sat up, tossed Betsy on her back and took control of the sex. With each thrust the fruitcake surged closer to the bed's edge.

"Oh," Dickey Dickson's voice bellowed as Weldon's taut body quaked with his orgasm, the whole double bed quivered as if it were a vibrating bed. The tin fell off the bed and Weldon's eyes rolled back into his head once more. As he shook his head, Weldon's eyes returned to normal. He smiled. "I've got to go," the Mayor said after he looked at his watch. He quickly got dressed as Betsy sat on the bed flabbergasted by what just took place.

As Mayor Weldon was heading out the door, Betsy said, "Oh, where's that fruitcake. I'm allergic to nuts, take it home to your wife." She picked the cake off the floor and handed it to him with a kiss, "Merry Christmas."

"Thanks," Weldon said sarcastically as he quickly slid out the door. Trying to conceive of another reason for being late, Weldon sped down the dark road with all haste. Alice, his wife, bordered on a level of mental illness that was so severe he often considered having her committed. The only thing that stopped him was the political power her family buoyed and the certainty that they would turn on him if he did. Her obsessive-compulsive behavior was repulsive to him. The fact that she had to wear white gloves in public to cover her constant house cleaning and the washing of her hands 'til they bled, he thought, impeded his ability to run for Governor. The Mayor felt cowardly and thus placed part of the blame on his shoulders, but the majority mainly on her family. Thinking to himself, *I just need to wait 'til Betty and Joe are gone, put Alice away and...* "Damn it!" he shouted as the blue lights appeared in his mirror. Hector got out of his car slowly and walked up to the car.

"Hi Hector," Weldon said through his cracked window.

"Got a new car J-bird?"

"When you're married to a Dickson, you're a member of the car of the month club," the Mayor chuckled.

"Something must be in the coffee down at city hall. I just stopped your secretary not thirty minutes ago. What's the hurry?"

"Just getting home to Alice before she goes off the deep end. You know how she gets when I'm late. How are Joy and the kids?"

"Great. Hey, slow it down a little. I'll let you get home to the wife, Merry Christmas J-bird," Hector said returning to his car.

Weldon rolled back up his window when his excuse struck him. He rolled his window down again and yelled back to the Sheriff's. "Hey Hector, can you give me that ticket?"

Hector started to laugh, "Now that's a first. Why the hell do you want a ticket?"

"Why the hell do you think, an excuse for being late," J-Bird said.

"Are you trying to tell me that you would rather pay a fine than face your wife without an excuse? Damn, J-Bird, she's got you pussy whipped," Sakamoto chuckled.

"Well shit if that's what you want. Do you want me to make it out for the four-pointer you were driving or just a two-pointer?"

"Two will be fine, I don't want to lose my driving privileges," he laughed jokingly, but knew Alice had enough sway with her father, owner of Dickson Motors and the real power in town, to change his ride to a beat-up 70s Gremlin if she wanted. Hector handed the mayor the ticket and the Mayor tried to hand the Sheriff the fruitcake.

"Take this fruitcake home to the wife," the Mayor said.

Hector could not help notice that it was the same fruitcake that Betsy offered him. "No, thanks Mayor, the wifes already made one for us, thanks anyway," the Sheriff replied as Betsy slowly drove by, honking her horn and waving.

"Guy Kress must not have been at home," Hector smiled.

"Why do you say that?"

"I just stopped Betsy not thirty minutes ago. She said she was heading out to see Guy Kress. She sure as hell didn't pay any attention to that warning I gave her. Can't drive all the way out to Bone Town and turn around like that in that short of time. You know, she tried to give me a fruitcake that looked just like that one, too. Merry Christmas J-Bird, make sure to say hello to that paranoid wife of yours. I haven't got a clue as to why Alice should have any concern about you," Hector said with a wink and headed back to his unmarked patrol car.

Weldon rolled up his window, "Damn it! Damn it! Damn it!" The Sheriff knew Alice. His parents worked for hers. All J-Bird could count on was that secret unspoken bond between men not to say anything. "Fucking fruitcake," he shouted.

"We all are if we are married," said Dickey. Weldon looked over at the seat. Nothing was there. He dismissed the voice as something in his head. "Hurry up, time to tap the wife," Dickey said.

"Why do I want to go home to that terminally dried up cunt," Weldon said, thinking he was talking to himself.

"Grudge fuck! Grudge fuck!" Dickey chanted. Weldon quickly joined in the chant, "Grudge Fuck! Grudge Fuck! Grudge Fuck!" Weldon pulled into his drive and started to think about how he was going to ravage his wife. These thoughts opened the portal for his repossession by Dickey and with the rolling of Weldon's eyes Dickey Dickson was once again a man. Dickey had always had the hots for his sister, used to whack-off sniffing her panties when he was but a teenager, and now he had the chance to do in death what he only fantasized about in life.

Dickey grabbed Weldon's briefcase and the fruitcake and went into the house.

Alice was at the sink washing her hands, "James, is that you?"

"Yeah, sorry I'm late, got a speeding ticket," Dickey said through Weldon.

"What's wrong with your voice," Alice asked.

"Nothing, just scratchy from talking all day," Dickey said remembering Weldon's thoughts earlier. "I got something for ya," Dickey said, putting the fruitcake on the table.

Alice looked over her shoulder as she heard the thud of the cake on the table. She did not notice the erection sticking out of her husband's pants. Alice returned to doing dishes, scrubbing each one with intensity before placing it in the dishwasher, "who'd that come from, is it cake or cookies?"

"I'm not talking about the cake, Alice," Dickey said, walking up to his sister, lifting her dress, and rubbing his penis against her panties. Dickey grabbed Alice's breasts and rotated them pulling her tightly against his body.

"Are you drunk?" Alice said in disapproval.

"Just fucking horny," Dickey grunted thrusting up against her.

"I started my period today," Alice said with a frigidity that would stop most men cold.

"More lotion for the motion," Dickey said tearing Alice's dress open and quickly turning her around for a kiss. The kiss was the big mistake. Weldon, unlike Dickey, always showered first thing when getting home. Betsy's lipstick was coated all over Weldon's mouth. Every woman knows the taste of her own lipstick, and this was not only a brand, but also a color that she would never use.

With all her force she pushed the possessed man off her and looked him in the eye, "Who are you fucking you lowdown son of a bitch?"

"You," Dickey said making a move for her.

Alice turned around and grabbed a glass out of the dishwasher and threw it at him. "Don't lie to me, I can still taste her nasty sticky cheap lipstick," Alice screamed, drawing her arm across her mouth.

"You psycho bitch, somebody should have put your ass in the crazy farm the time you killed Jug Head," Dickey screamed at his sister through Weldon.

"Did my mother tell you about that?"

"Jug Head died because mom and dad tried to stop you from giving him enemas. But nothing and no one would stop you. So, you stuck a hose up the poor dog's ass when mom took your Massengill's Floral Fresh douche away. It always has and still is your brand, but the only thing floral fresh about you are the flowers on your victims' graves. Why'd you kill Jug Head you crazy bitch? He loved you. You turned that water on and blew the poor dog up like a Macy's Thanksgiving Day balloon. You just couldn't stop, and he was Dad's best hunting dog, too."

"How dare you!"

"What was it you said? I remember, 'well at least he won't be stinking up the place with his stinky farts,' ain't that right you dog killer?"

Alice went over the edge to say the least. Her eyes bulged out of her red face and her ears turned purple. Everything she could place her hands on became airborne as she hurled the objects with all her might at her possessed husband. He ducked to his left and jumped to his right to avoid pots and pans, knives, and glasses, and even the electric can opener that came his way. Alice screamed, "So you're calling my parents Mom and Dad now! You're in cahoots with them to put me away, aren't you?"

"How about the time you put superglue in Jason Riddle's Vaseline because you found out he was not just fucking Veronica Harris, you found out he was fucking her up the ass. You gave yourself chlorine poisoning from putting bleach up your pussy. Lucky for Veronica, Jason needed to rub one out and found out what you did the hard way. The only way Dad stopped that one from going to court was because Veronica was just fifteen. You were never fifteen! You've been an old fart all your fucking life!"

Alice continued to hurl anything she could get her hands on. The blender followed quickly by the toaster, "Stop it! You son of a Bitch, stop it!"

"How about the time you…" Before Dickey said the word you, Alice had spied the fruitcake on the table along with a set of poultry shears she had thrown earlier, which had landed on the table. She grabbed the fruitcake and hurled it at him full force. Dickey jumped out of the way before he realized what it was she had thrown. The fruitcake had burst through the window and landed on top of the car. J-Bird's eyes rolled to the back of his head and by the time the Mayor had control of his mind, Alice was stabbing him repeatedly with the shears, "Die, you son of a bitch, die!"

"Alice," Weldon said in shock to his wife, quickly realizing that he was done.

"You're making a mess," Alice said stepping out of her torn dress that was barely clinging to her. In shock, J-Bird watched as she scrubbed the floor with her dress. His jaw dropped open as he died. She tried to close it, "You look surprised."

Alice was furious that her mother and father would tell, of all people, James, her husband of only six years, her sacred childhood secrets. Such weaponry in the hands of non-relatives was dangerous if not handled carefully, and that included husbands. If her brother Dickey were around, she wouldn't be so sure that it was her parents that broke the oath of silence. "I'm sensitive, very sensitive. You should have known that by now!" Alice shouted at the body, his eyes still open and mouth still agape. She threw her blood-soaked dress at him, "stop looking at me!" She screamed before striking the body. She obsessed on how to get revenge. Alice knew she was going to kill them, but how? She thought pacing back and forth in her blood-stained slippers. She left the hardwood floor and went to her bedroom while tracking her husband's drained blood over the champagne-colored carpet. Alice removed her stained slip, turned on the shower in the master bath, placed a shower cap on her head to protect the perm she just received that morning and scrubbed her skin free of blood, turning it into a rosy pink. After drying with a plush Ralph Lauren towel, she removed from the closet the dress she had intended to wear to church on Christmas and draped it across their immaculately made bed.

"Lovely," she commented before she opened her dresser to take out her undergarments. She glanced at a framed photograph of her and her five siblings at the base of a big tree in their yard, all of them dead now.

She wondered why she never noticed the black woman in the slight distance hanging clothes on the line, she was too beautiful by today's standards to have such a job. Alice was barely five when the photo was taken, with six years between she and Dickey, who stood next to her, she knew she had been an unplanned mistake. In another photo, her mother held her as an infant in a wing-backed chair as her father towered above them. Alice was born when her parents were in their mid-forties, now in their late seventies and early eighties, taking the two out would be easy enough, but … "How? How do I get rid of them?"

As she had just finished dressing, the buzzer on the stove blared, startling Alice.

Giving herself one final look in the mirror she returned to the kitchen, she looked over at the body, "Dinner is ready, Shake and Bake pork chops." Alice walked over to the stove, opened the oven door, and took out the pork chops. It was then that the idea came to her while her head was close to the oven. She placed the food on the counter, cut off the oven and washed her hands. Grabbing her coat and keys she looked once more at her dead husband. Noticing the poinsettia on the table, she snapped stems from the plant and tossed them on her husband's corpse. "Floral fresh," she cackled.

Alice didn't notice the fruitcake sitting on the roof of her car as she backed down the drive. The Mayor's home, a wedding gift from Alice's parents, was on top of a hill that overlooked the town. As she threw the car into drive and hit the gas, the fruitcake slid off the roof, hit the trunk, caught the bumper, landed on its side, and rolled downhill. The fruitcake smacked a small branch in the road and bounced onto the sidewalk gaining more and more speed as if it were trying to catch Alice as her taillights blended with the holiday light gawkers trolling the neighborhood.

Chapter Fifteen

Tired of the limited music selection on the radio, Hope placed a mix of music into the player as Raul turned into one of the most affluent developments in Dixon. As they drove up a hill, they looked down into a yard that had a large red numeral three amongst a life size manger scene. Hope started to laugh. "What's so funny?" Raul asked.

"Momma thought the large number three was for the Trinity. Dad had to explain to her that it stood for Dale Earnhardt. Momma could hardly contain her laughter at her own ignorance. After Momma gathered herself, she said, 'Well, that's special, maybe they think he's Jesus' chauffer.' Even Dad had to laugh."

As they continued up the hill, they looked in amazement at all the extravagant displays. Some had a sense of style while others were extremely tacky. Several had their entire house outlined in lights with bonus animated reindeer, elves, and or snowmen. Hope pointed out Herb's father's home, which had a large menorah made of large plastic candles that had five lit. The giant air-blown snow globes were the latest trend, they ran a wide gamut of scenes. Every Christmas theme created, from Disney to the classical Currier & Ives, was represented. Raul and Hope drove around slowly in awe of the elaborate unofficial neighborhood competition. At the bottom of the hill Raul stopped and looked into Hope's eyes, "Will you be my Maid Marian?"

"What does that mean?"

"Every year Christmas comes and goes for most of the immigrants that keep this town going. They don't have enough money to buy their kids gifts, much less decorate. So, I go around neighborhoods like this and take decorations from the rich and give them to the poor."

"How long have you been doing this?"

"This is my second year stealing Christmas decorations," Raul said. "If my parents knew they would kill me. Poppa, ever since I was a little kid, would buy and drop off Christmas presents on migrants' porches, he started bringing me along when I was thirteen. We would hide and watch as the kids went crazy. I noticed that most families didn't even have a Christmas tree, so with your help I want to give some poor family a fully decorated tree."

"Don't you think someone will notice that we're digging up their tree?" Hope asked.

"Not soon enough," he nodded. "I brought a chain saw. What I need you to do is to unplug the lights and help me toss it in the back. Then we're gonna haul ass."

"So, whom are we stealing from?"

"These folks right here," Raul pointed at a small evergreen tree standing around seven feet tall. The tree was completely decorated with lights and plastic ornaments of silver and gold. An animated angel sat on top flapping its wings back and forth. Hope thought it was one of the ugliest angels she ever saw. The angel's face looked as if she was constipated or that the top of the tree had been shoved up her ass. Raul took the chainsaw from the tool chest that sat on the back of his truck. As soon as it was cranked and Raul was in place, Hope disconnected the lights and the tree fell in no time flat. "Grab the chainsaw and throw it in back," Raul yelled at Hope. She did as she was ordered as Raul dragged the tree to the curb. Raul lowered the tailgate placing the trunk of the tree on it, lifted Hope up into the back and the two quickly pulled the tree onto the truck bed. They jumped out on opposite sides. Raul shut the tailgate as Hope climbed into the cab floorboard first before rising into her seat. Like Tigger, Raul bounced inside, and they were off climbing up the hill and descending it just as fast. The lights that they had observed earlier were a blur. More citizens were gawking at the lights and Raul made a sharp turn down a not so decorated street. Their hearts pounded as if they were tympani drums.

"We did it, we did it!" Hope yelled bouncing in her seat filled with excitement. Raul reached over and kissed her on the mouth not noticing the black cat that crossed slightly up the road under the streetlamp.

Olivia was an old scraggly black cat always in heat. Her meows and moans for a mate could be heard for blocks. Pacing the sidewalk like a street whore, she called out in cat speak, "Hot pussy, I'm a hot pussy for you! Get your free hot pussy here!" Olivia heard a rushing sound and looked up the hill. The old cat's night vision was not what it used to be, and the speeding fruitcake was a blur to her eyes. *I still got it,* the bony old cat thought to herself. She quickly bent over with a lick to clean herself, turned her back to the approaching fruitcake, and lifted up her tail for what she believed was a looming tomcat. The fruitcake slammed into the old cat lifting them both off the ground. Olivia gave a long drawn out meooooow of satisfaction. The fruitcake took flight in an arcing elevation and descended crashing through the windshield of Raul's oncoming truck.

Hope's screaming commenced where Olivia's meow left off. Raul lost control of his truck and swerved off the road into the decorated yards of the affluent neighborhood. It all seemed to be moving in slow motion to Raul and Hope. The red truck first struck Santa and his reindeer. The carolers, three doors down, watched as the reindeer flew through the air, pulling Santa and his sleigh to a crash-landing on the neighbor's roof. With their jaws wide open, they stood like deer caught in headlights as Raul drove through a nativity scene. Mary, Joseph, and the three kings fell over like bowling pins. Raul crossed himself as the baby Jesus was shot out from beneath his truck like a punted football only to crash into the back passenger window of a car stopped at an intersection. The car's driver screamed, Jesus! Only to turn around and see the baby Jesus safely landed into an empty child seat. This caused the man driving to piss himself and he repeated the Lord's name once again.

With the stolen tree in the truck's bed Raul didn't want to stop. The carolers ran into his path as he tried to veer away. Some jumped high, some low, and the high school high-jump champion jumped over the truck and crash-landed onto the tree in back. Hope grabbed the wheel pulling the truck in the other direction. The truck plowed into a house while pinning a plastic Frosty the Snowman between the bumper and the porch, its severed head rested on the truck's hood. The abrupt stop caused Raul's head to slam into the windshield. Hope's arm snapped against the dashboard. Bloodied, Raul fell back into his seat before he lifted himself upright and asked Hope, "Are you okay?" Just then the airbag opened up and pounded his head against the back window, knocking Raul out cold.

"Raul, Raul!" Hope opened the door, "Call 9-1-1 somebody, call 9-1-1!" Forgetting she was in a jacked-up truck she fell out with a thud compounding her fracture. She stood back up with the help of one of the carolers. She looked back at the path of destruction. *Mom is going to kill me*, she said to herself. Looking down at her bleeding arm, she fainted.

With the door still open, Olivia, the cat, jumped inside the truck purring very loudly. She butted her head and brushed her whiskers against the tin and then circled the cake, finally resting her body against it. She licked her paw feeling very satisfied. "Meow," she said to the crowd that hovered over the passed-out girl. The crowd looked up and stepped back, partly out of nervousness from Olivia's blue-black razorback fur, partly because the fruitcake tin appeared to be breathing.

Zack and Jack Yerby were the first to arrive on the scene. The twin paramedics went quickly to work. Hector was not far behind. Once he saw Hope on the ground, he quickly called Joy and informed her of the accident. Joy called Faith and her mom and, before you knew it, Joy and Faith were on site. Bonnie and Lula May were on their way to the hospital. Joy went directly to her husband. Faith went looking for Hope who was sedated on a stretcher and on her way into the back of the ambulance.

"Where's Charity?" Faith asked Zack walking along.

"Don't know, ask Jack," Zack said to Faith.

"Jack, do you know where Charity is?"

Jack, who was loading Raul onto a stretcher, was too busy stabilizing the young man to pay close attention to Faith. "Damn it woman, call her! She has a cell," Jack snapped.

Faith went back to Zack who was currently working on the high jumper sitting on the opened tailgate. "Zack, do you know Charity's cell phone number?"

"Are you telling me you don't know your own sister's number?" Zack sneered.

"It's on caller ID at home," Faith stomped getting frustrated.

Quickly glancing at his cell phone Zack said, "2-5-7-9-2-8-6, I think she's in Greenville."

"What is she doing in Greenville?"

Hector pulled Faith aside, "Look Faith, Hope has a compound fracture, her arm is broken in two places. She has minor abrasions to her face and arms and suffers from a concussion. The boy who was driving is in much worse shape. We didn't find a license on him, and I can't remember his last name. Do you know his parents?"

"Raul, Raul, damn it, I can't think of the wetback's last name," Hector said. "I told Hope that they were nothing but trouble. They're hell bound Catholics for God's sake. She went out with him just to spite me."

Joy took the keys out of the ignition and opened the locked glove compartment of the wrecked truck, a bag of pot fell out. She quickly placed it in her bra and grabbed the insurance information and took it to her husband, "Where did you get this?"

"The glove compartment."

"It was locked."

"I know, there was nothing in there but this, I don't think it's going to be a problem."

"Good, there was nothing in the ashtray either," Hector said to his wife with a smile.

"Did you see what was on the seat?" Hector asked.

"One of our fruitcakes," Joy said. "I guess Hope gave it to Raul to give to his family."

"Maybe," Hector nodded. "But I think I've seen this Fruitcake twice today already."

Chapter Sixteen

Like a hyena finding a dead carcass, Frank Payne was the first tow truck to arrive on the scene. He went through the motions of securing his prey, giving the evil eye to all those hungry, salivating tow truck drivers who drove by the crash site. Frank was all man. Wearing form-fitting overalls with work boots, his six-two frame, broad shoulders, blue eyes, and unkempt ash-blond hair was nothing less than Hitler's wet dream. Frank had one flaw, he was accident prone.

With all the emergency vehicles gone, Frank backed his tow truck up to the crash, connected the hook and cable to the truck's axle, and lifted up its tail end. He opened up the driver's door to place the truck in neutral and spotted the fruitcake sitting on the seat and bet Penelope liked fruitcake, if not, her momma did. "Damn it!" He screamed cutting himself on a shard of glass. Olivia, seeing Frank with the fruitcake, arched her back, spit and hissed at him.

He went to kick the cat, but she was quicker and jumped, claws extended, onto the man's leg. In a jig, Frank tried to shake the cat lose. Olivia ascended his leg driving her claws deep into his flesh. "Ahhh!" God damn it you crazy cat!" Frank Payne screamed in pain. He picked up the black cat by the back of the neck and tossed her as far as he could throw her, quickly jumped inside his tow truck and drove off. As if her kittens were being taken from her prematurely, Olivia let out the most sorrowful of meows. *The good ones never stick around,* the cat thought as she watched Raul's truck fishtail down the road.

After dropping off Raul's truck, Frank Payne headed home to freshen up for his date. He never thought he would be so lucky as to date Penelope Price. Of course, she didn't look so good when they were in high school together. Tall and lanky, Penelope in those days was quite mousy and to be quite honest, very strange, and not in a good way either. Frank was on the wrestling team with her brother Peter. Peter, also a member of the ROTC, had gone into the army right out of high school. Peter, unlike his sister, was well-liked and sociable. Peter and Frank hung out together during the summer of Frank's parents' divorce. Frank's father had moved into the same trailer park as the Prices. Peter and he walked around the woods that surrounded the trailer park talking about girls, football, and dreams now long forgotten. While in the woods they came across the ruins of an old farm. The house had burned down leaving nothing but chimneys that stood as tall as the pines. Pines replaced tobacco in the region, which replaced cotton and now dominated the county's agricultural lands. A tobacco barn was still standing amidst the pines as a reminder of the economic institution that dominated 'til the current century. Once Frank and Peter shared watered down gin, they poured into a soda bottle Frank had taken from his mom's car when she dropped him off. They got drunk, not as drunk as they both claimed after their walk amongst the pine needles but drunk enough that they never walked alone together in the woods again, drunk or sober. The last Frank had heard was that Peter was in Bosnia, but that was years ago.

It was fate, Frank thought, as to how he ran into Penelope in the first place. Penelope was at Frank's brother's mobile home outlet. Frank brought biscuits from Hardee's and the two shared breakfast together just like they promised their mother on her deathbed. This time it was in Earnest's office when Leroy, one of the salesmen, came running in to announce that Penelope Price was on the premises. Everyone was shocked to see the wrestling superstar was at Earnest Payne's Mobile Home Outlet. Penelope was a true knockout, long luscious hair, huge breasts, and Cher-esque waist and legs. Frank knew from the first time he saw her on TV that she had a lot of plastic surgery, but who cared when this was the result.

"I tried to buy Momma a house, but my momma said to me, 'I was raised in a trailer, went through three husbands in a trailer, raised you in a trailer, and by damn I'm going to retire and die in a trailer too!'" Penelope told the crowd that gathered around her.

Frank couldn't believe he had the nerve to ask her out and was even more surprised when she said yes. Penelope had requested that Frank meet her at the trailer she had bought that day as a Christmas gift for her mom. So Frank was off to Heritage Mobile Home Park, without a doubt the nicest trailer park in the county. Penelope had explained that she chose the park because of the pool, gym, and clubhouse. Frank knew the park well for two reasons. First, many a divorced man lived there since that was all a working-class man could afford after paying child support, but not that many complained. That was because of the second reason. Iris owned over twenty trailers with two to three beautiful girls in each. For a few, being caught at the Heritage was the cause of their divorce in the first place. Mrs. Price will be truly proud, probably as proud as she was when Peter graduated from boot camp.

Penelope arrived at the trailer park as the massive truck was pulling away from the newly placed mobile home. She had to buy an older trailer that same day and have it removed in order to place her mother's new home in the upscale Heritage "MHP" as its younger residents referred to the mobile home park. Back on standard time, darkness came early, and the workers were unable to tie the trailer down, but they did hook up the electricity and promised to return first thing in the morning to finish the job. Penelope thanked the men and admired the fitness of a handsome young man that had to be the baby brother or nephew of one of the Joseph brothers she went to school with all those years ago. The concrete steps she had ordered did not arrive with the delivery. The doorknob was at eye level. She opened the door and prepared to crawl inside.

Peter Price was honorably discharged from the army a year prior to the second Iraqi War. It all came about from a physical. He had been in the Army for nearly ten years when they discovered knots in the region of his intestines. Blood tests showed that it was not cancerous, but they decided to do surgery to be on the safe side. The results led to a psychological review and eventually to his discharge. What they had discovered and removed were his ovaries. Peter was born a hermaphrodite, but because he had a fully functioning penis and testicles, no one suspected.

After he and his wife tried to have another child, he discovered he was sterile. Keeping his sterility to himself, he had a DNA test performed and the results confirmed his suspicions. Maybe she wasn't sure who the father was and just guessed, heaven knows he was hitting whatever came his way when she announced her pregnancy. So, he kept the knowledge to himself until she announced she was pregnant again with their second child. His sterility revealed, he discovered his commanding officer was the father of both children. It was the cleanest divorce, no arguments, no alimony. She got nothing but walking papers. Which she did, right over to his commanding officer's wife. Of course, this was before the unwanted discovery.

Peter had always struggled with his feminine side. He had a few homosexual encounters in high school, a few dates with red bugs from wrestling in pine straw. Of course, he was drunk at the time and had used that as part of his denial later in life. But now that he discovered that he was part woman he decided to explore that half of himself more thoroughly. So, he went out and bought himself a wig, make-up, and what he thought was a hot sexy dress.

All dolled up, Peter looked into his mirror and sang in his deep bass voice the Helen Reddy classic, "I am woman, hear me roar, in numbers too big to ignore, And I know too much to go back and pretend." He could not stop himself from laughing, but the laughter soon turned to tears. He couldn't go out, what would he call himself? How do you wipe your eyes without smearing your mascara? How do you hide that bulge where no bulge should be on a woman? Then the call came.

"Am I speaking to Peter Price," said a voice he did not know, "Mr. Price, this is Dr. Walkup at the Faber Home. I've got some bad news Mr. Price. Penelope was killed today. She broke away from a group during an outing to the movie theater and ran out in front of a bus. I'm truly sorry."

Peter and his mother had placed Penelope in Faber after her last suicide attempt, "Have you called my mother?"

"Yes, but there was no answer, so we didn't leave a message."

"Don't worry, I'll call her. It's best if it comes from me. Where's the body?"

"The city morgue here in Atlanta. I just want you to know that Faber is conducting a full investigation."

"Deal with me and not my mother please. She didn't handle our father's death very well and they had been divorced for over twenty years when he died. I'll be by to get my sister's things tomorrow along with the body," Peter said and hung up the phone. He looked out the window at a twinkling star, "Thanks Penelope, wherever you are." Peter never made an announcement in the local papers of her death. He had her buried in Savannah, he loved the town, even honeymooned there. He bought a tombstone that had both his and his sister's name on it along with their dates of birth. But Penelope was buried under Peter's name with her date of death chiseled under his date of birth. So, the dates were a little crisscrossed, they were too. Penelope, though dead, didn't need a death date because Penelope was only beginning to live. Peter was now Penelope. He had his sex change surgery with the money he received from her life insurance.

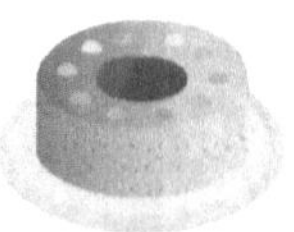

Chapter Seventeen

Frank, with fruitcake in hand, knocked on the door of the brand-new trailer. There were no steps installed yet, so his chest came up to floor level. When Penelope, in tight black stretch jeans and a low V-neck red fuzzy sweater, came to open the door the trailer tilted so that the floor was now at his knees, "I'm sorry about this, but it got dark before they were able to tie the trailer down," Penelope explained to her guest.

"Don't worry about it. Merry Christmas," Frank said lifting his leg up to the trailer's floor.

"Let me help," Penelope said offering Frank her hand and pulling him up into the trailer with a "Welcome aboard." They both laughed.

"I hope you like fruitcake," Frank said. "Maybe your momma will like it," Frank placed it on the counter.

"If it's loaded with booze, I'm sure she will. Speaking of which, can I make you a drink? Do you still drink gin and tonics?"

"Yep, I can't believe you remembered that. Peter, Ernie, and I use to keep it premixed in a Sprite bottle and passed it around at the pool."

"I know," Penelope remembered. "I used to watch out for momma while Peter mixed it up. I don't know what y'all were thinking. To think that momma wouldn't notice her booze watered down. God how many times she beat Pete over that."

"I remember putting lotion on the welts on his back," he said sadly. "How is Pete doing these days? Is he still in the army?"

"He's doing great. He fell in love with some Bosnian girl and got married shortly after his divorce. Works for some corporation over there I can't pronounce. We hear from him at Christmas and our birthdays, that's about it."

"I guess war really changes people," Frank offered. "I never took Peter to be a European."

"Enough about Peter, how are you doing these days? I'm surprised you haven't got married yet. Didn't Susie Klein have you wrapped around her fingers?"

"Damn, it's been a while since you were in town," he shook his head. "Susie and I broke-up years ago. Dated Beverly Steel for a while, but that ended when she got promoted and moved to Chicago. I thought about moving up there. Even went to visit her once, but my southern blood is too thin for Lake Michigan winters. Just dating around these days. So how about you? How did you become a professional wrestler?"

"I dated one," Penelope said, handing Frank his cocktail.

"Really?" Frank said sipping from his drink.

"Yep, I was in this car accident, won a lot of money and had these done," she said cupping her breast. "You like 'em?"

Those were the words that opened the door in Frank's mind for forward possession. Frank fell back in the couch and closed his eyes. "Yeah," Dickey said, now possessing Frank's body, reaching out for her breast.

Penelope slapped his hands down, "If you want to see them you're gonna' have to pin me, do you think you can pin me Frank?"

"I'm sure gonna' try," Dickey graveled.

"You must have developed a slight allergy to quinine, your voice has changed. Here's the deal, we're gonna play strip wrestling. You pin me down and I will remove a piece of clothing, I pin you down and you remove a piece of clothing, deal?"

"Deal." Penelope kicked off her high heels and assumed the standard Greco-Roman wrestling position. Frank saddled up next to her.

"At the count of three," Penelope said, "One, two, three." The two moved around the trailer. Peneope's Hip Toss tilted the trailer to one side. The fruitcake slid across the counter ever closer to the edge with each move of the match. Crossfade to body slam were the moves that pinned Frank, the fruitcake fell off the counter.

"Damn, you're strong woman."

"Off with the sweater," she demanded. He took off his sweater and dropped down to the floor on all fours. Penelope saddled him this time. The trailer again started to sway from one side to the other with her fireman's carry. She flipped the possessed Frank onto his back. She almost had him pinned when he bucked his lower body. This caused the trailer to tilt, and the fruitcake slid across the floor smacking Frank in the head.

"Ouch, Mother fucking fruitcake," Dickey screamed, pushing the fruitcake away. Distracted, Penelope pinned the one-time jock again. "All right," Dickey said frustrated, "I'm getting serious here, this ain't right! No woman has ever whooped my ass like this before."

"Do you want to take off your pants or your shirt?" Dickey took off Frank's shirt so that the man was in his t-shirt and jeans. Having lost the last round, Dickey put Frank on all fours once again. Penelope took her time working Frank's body over, tossing him one way then the other, groping him freely. The groping was the only reason Dickey even continued with the sport. As the trailer moved so did the fruitcake, placed on its side by Dickey's recent anger the fruitcake smacked Frank against the head several times. If the fruitcake didn't hit some part of Frank's body as it moved across the floor, it banged against the walls. When Penelope pinned Frank once more, Dickey went ballistic.

"How can a woman be that God damn mother fucking strong?! Let's return to our neutral corners," Dickey demanded. "I need a drink."

"Take off the t-shirt or the jeans," she smiled deviously.

Dickey decided to remove Frank's jeans. Frank wore his jeans tighter than he liked anyway and he felt this would give him a little more agility. Now in nothing but boxers and a t-shirt, Dickey picked the plastic gin and tonic bottles off the floor and made himself a drink. Having downed his first drink, he started to make a second. He started humming at first, and then remembering the words he started to sing, "You made life fun for me, Oh, what it's done for me, having you around, Sweet Charity." Dickey changed the words to the Broadway classic, "A warm place my dick's never been, makes it pop out my shorts for head again, It's incredible."

"Put that away," Penelope said. "I never took you as a musical kind of guy, Frank."

"Suddenly I'm the guy I never dared to be, watch me touch those tits quite easily," Dickey sang stealing a pinch only to be slapped down. He started down the hall to the bathroom, "I've got to go and pee, my Sweet Charity, please belong to me, Sweet, Sweet Charity."

"It's on the right," Penelope yelled down the hall.

"You know, you remind me of somebody who use to wrestle hard against me," Dickey yelled back over the sound of his urinating.

"Did they whoop your ass the way I'm mopping the floor with yours?"

"Nope, but it's not that she didn't try. God, she brought out the monster in me."

"From what Peter told me, it doesn't take much gin to do that."

At this same moment, Ellis had Matthew tag along as he took his Boy Scout troop out to sing Christmas carols. He decided to take the mostly privileged troop to sing to the not so privileged. That said, he sent the Boy Scout troop on its merry way to sing trailer to trailer as he took Matthew in to visit with Iris. .Iris was not surprised to see Ellis, but she was surprised to see Ellis with Matthew at her place. "What a nice surprise! Come in, come in," Iris said to the father-son pair. "Take your coats off and have a seat. I was in the middle of something on the computer, give me one moment and I'll be right back."

"Where's Grace?"

"This late, I'll bet she's at Wal-Mart shopping, it's the only place around here open twenty-four hours a day," she said finishing a porn conversation and having one of the girls at another site take over. Iris turned off her computer and attended to her guests, "So what do I owe this visit to?"

"Just in the area," Ellis said. "My scout troop is singing carols tonight and I thought I'd have them sing in a place that doesn't often experience the custom."

"Can I offer you something to drink?"

"Scotch and soda for me, what would you like son?"

"Nothing," Matthew said still depressed from his breakup with Sweet.

"Are you sure honey?" Iris said disappointed. "He's old enough to have a beer. Can I get you a beer?"

"No thanks, still not legal," Matthew pouted. "Just nineteen. Don't think Jesus would anyway."

"Jesus, right," Iris smiled. "Well, I think I'll join your dad with a screwdriver."

"Let me help," Ellis volunteered walking with Iris into the kitchen.

"You mind if I turn it to the game?" Matthew asked his hostess.

"Go for it honey. Why'd you bring him here?" she said, under her breath to Ellis.

"To get him laid, he has been down ever since that girl dumped him. He hasn't gone out of the house since. I think some other distraction will break this spell."

"Ah ha, I see, and whom did you have in mind?"

"Someone a little older, but not too old," Ellis pondered, "under twenty-five. Sexy, not slutty. Not an obvious whore."

"Well, I guess I could call over a few girls to watch the game with him," Iris offered. "It's Christmas time and it's for the boy not you, three girls, five hundred. And if he likes one and wants to date her, no extra charge until he goes back to school."

"Damn woman that's a little high."

"Getting high costs extra," Iris teased. "All my girls are clean and tested. None of these girls are virgins, but they haven't been rode hard and left out to dry either. He's family."

"Here's the deal," Ellis played hard ball. "Three hundred, and if he gets laid, I'll throw in the extra two."

"You drive a hard bargain," Iris held out her hand. "Deal. By the way I have a new toy. Maybe Mrs. Claus will show it to you later. Let me get on the phone and get the girls over."

Oscar and the other members of his troop were a little pissed at his father for bringing them to carol at a trailer park. But as trailer after trailer, they came across beautiful sexy women, their spirits rose high. And boy how they were racking up contributions for UNICEF. "I don't think we would be doing any better if we were caroling at Knight's Ridge," a scout said. "Who would have thought that people who live in trailer parks made this kind of money." another scout said as they walked to the next trailer. Between the trailers the Boy Scouts sung parodies of Christmas songs. Juvenile as their renditions were the scouts enjoyed them immensely. They sang them with the same bravado of drunken sailors, though the only thing they were drunk on was their youth. "Feliz Navidad" became "Please suck my knob, please suck my knob, please suck my knob or I will have to get a hand job." And "Silver Bells" became "Pull my Balls, pull my balls, or I will cum upon your titties, my ding-a-ling, is about to cream, soon I will cum upon your face." As crude and tawdry as their songs may had been, the jaded men of the park who had long lost their youth to bad marriages, the responsibilities of fatherhood, and the daily rigors of life, saw a beautiful lightheartedness in the scouts that caused more longing than any woman, car, or possession. The longing was for the reversal of time, a time when most only had the burden of homework and little in the way of their actions for which to answer. Those lonely men, though many with new young brides and or girlfriends, gave money to the scouts. These boys were genuinely happy, not pretending as so many in the populous do during holidays. Though things were tight, most gave heartily.

The teens wandered the hundred-trailer Heritage Trailer Park brighter than Rudolph's nose, knocking on door after door. At a trailer on Stonewall Circle, two women, one a brunette with pale white skin and the other a bleached-blonde Hispanic, opened their door and the boys began to sing, "O Come, O Come, Emmanuel."

"That was beautiful boys, now let's hear your version," said the bleached blonde buzzed on something.

"What do you mean?" asked Oscar.

"We like your other carols better. What was the one y'all were singing between homes on General Lee Boulevard? 'I sucked your tits on Christmas day on Christmas day, on Christmas day, I sucked your tits on Christmas day on Christmas day in the morning.' Y'all know that one, don't you?" The brunette girl laughed at the blushing young men. "Y'all sing that one while we find you some money."

Oscar led the scouts in the parody watching the women bending over in their tight jeans retrieving money from their purses. Each took out a twenty. Handing the tallest scout in the troop who was holding the money bucket a twenty, the Hispanic woman said, "Feliz Navidad, boys," deliberately bending over enough to reveal she wore no bra.

The brunette woman stuck her twenty in her cleavage and said, "Who wants to retrieve this twenty to help out all those starving children in Africa?"

"I do, I do," the scouts yelled out raising their hands like first graders that know the answer to a question.

"You," Angelina, a Southern girl from North Alabama, pointed to Oscar, "you come right here and stand up for your troop." Oscar made his way up the stairs to the small porch attached to the trailer. Like most from Florence, Alabama, Angelina's 'R's were drawn out long, "I know you want it. How hard can it be for a young… strong… strappin' young man like yourself to put his hand on it and rub it between your fingers, make sure it's real, now take your hard rough fingers and wrap them around it and jerk it, come on, come jerk it out of there? Come now, you can do it. Do it for Angelina."

As the thirty-something bent over, showing the fullness of her breast to all, Oscar let his fingers go down between the woman's v-neck sweater. He made sure that his fingers felt the softness of her bosoms before he pinched the twenty, snug tight between her breasts. He retrieved the twenty to the cheers of his troop members, waving the money in the air. The brunette, taking his head in her hands, kissed Oscar on the mouth as her blonde roommate held mistletoe over their heads. The scouts whooped it up. "Merry Christmas," she said and then whispered, "What's your name?"

"Oscar."

"Merry Christmas, Oscar," she said loud and clear, "You're one good kisser." She turned the boy around by his shoulders and slapped him on his butt as he descended the stairs to rejoin his troop.

"Y'all come back next year," said the brunette as she winked at the boys.

The scouts heard, "they're so cute," by one of the girls as she shut the door.

"I've got your cute for you right here," said Oscar as he strutted like a peacock, grabbing his crotch. "I think they were strippers. Who else would have a metal pole in the middle of their living room?"

"I guess it's something for Santa to slide down on Christmas Eve," joked a scout.

"Santa's gonna be doing some sliding alright, but with his own pole," Oscar replied.

The boys walked over to the next trailer and knocked. Again, two women opened the door, but these girls were why the word flamboyant was invented. One woman looked like Grace Jones in leather, while the Asian girl looked like Lucy Liu dressed up as May West in a corset. The boys sang, "Have a Holly, Jolly Christmas" for the women and they too gave the boys twenty dollars each. "Did you see the tits on that Asian girl," one boy said. "Do you think they were real?" the tall lanky scout asked.

"Who cares if they were real, I just want her to smother me with them," Oscar said shaking his head and making an 'mmm good' sound from the old Campbell soups ads. "How about that Nubian princess wearing leather? Mommy, I've been a very bad boy," Oscar imitated a child's voice to everyone's laughter, "I need a spanking." Oscar bent over putting his hands against the hood of a car, "Spank me, Mommy." A scout took his caroling book and whacked Oscar across the ass. "Harder Mommy, Harder." This time when the scout whacked Oscar, it was so hard that it set off the car's alarm. The troop quickly took off running 'til they came to a trailer that was rocking from side to side.

"Damn, I wonder what is going on in there?"

"There's one way to find out," Oscar said leading the troop all dressed in their uniforms up to the rocking mobile home. The tall scout in the troop knocked on the door.

"Who the fuck could that be?" Dickey said, caught in a headlock. Penelope, not releasing Frank, who was now in nothing but his boxers, dragged the man to the door. By doing so the trailer tilted, the fruitcake rolled and smacked the wall and the scouts standing outside the door in unplanned unison took one step back. Penelope asked how she might help the fellows.

Before she could finish her question, a scout screamed out, "Oh my God, It's Penelope the Punisher, the world's greatest female wrestler!" The scouts went wild with abandonment. It was as if Santa Claus himself had opened the door. These guys were beyond themselves with excitement. They jumped and gave each other a high fives. It was like a scene from when the Beatles played the Ed Sullivan Show, but instead of girls screaming, it was boys. Penelope Price aka the Punisher was a star. "Okay guys, what should we sing for Penelope?"

"Can't you see we're busy here guys," Dickey said.

"Hush, Frank," Penelope said with a squeeze. "Do you boys know the Little Drummer Boy?" The boys sang the carol like no other they had sung that night. After the song was done the scouts volunteered to sing another. "I'm sorry boys," Penelope stopped them. "I do have company as you can see."

"Will you show us one of your moves?" a scout shouted.

"I don't see why not, what do you say Frank?" He nodded, anything to send them away. "Okay boys, watch this," Penelope picked Frank up and put him across the back of her shoulders. She started to spin Frank around and let him loose. He smacked into the wall and slid to the floor, knocking his head on the fruitcake, which fell flat and into view of the scouts. "How was that?" The scouts applauded and Penelope grabbed some money out of her pocketbook and handed it to Oscar. "Do any of you boys like fruitcake?" The guys all raised their hands straight up. "Well, I'll treat this like a bridal bouquet," she said turning her back to the scouts. She slung the cake out the door shutting it behind her.

Dickey could be heard saying, "Nooooo..." The cake hit the street and Frank's eyes rolled to the back of his head. Released from Dickey, Frank was not quite sure why he was in his boxers, what caused the bump on his head, nor did he care as he watched Penelope take her clothes off.

"Do you give Frank?"

"I give."

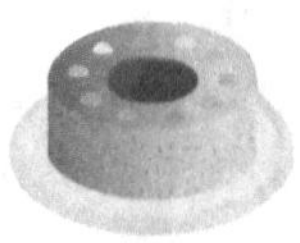

Chapter Eighteen

"This is Emily Fisher, Anne King, and Charlotte Butcher," Iris said to the three girls, offering them a seat on the couch. "I would like y'all to meet my brother's brother-in-law and our company attorney Ellis McCaskill and this is his son Matthew. We were watching college football. Do you want to join us?"

"Sounds great, Peach Bowl, right?" Charlotte said. "Do you like the Vols?"

"The coach is an ass," Ellis said, "I liked them when, ah, you're too young to remember."

"Who do you like, Matthew, right?" Anne asked.

"Good memory, I pull for Clemson in the ACC and LSU in the SEC. How about you, was it Charlotte?"

"No, I'm Anne," she said. "And I'm a huge Cocks fan."

"How about you Emily?" Matthew smiled.

"I'm from Oregon, went to State, so I'm a big Beavers fan. But living with these two, all I hear is Cocks and Vols, Cocks and Vols. It makes a Beaver want to shake those nuts. So, you're a Tiger either way you pull."

"Oh Ellis," Iris interrupted, "I was going to show you my gifts for Grace and Hector." Iris led Ellis back to her bedroom. Iris took out a black glove with silver beads attached to it. She slid the glove on her hand and flipped a switch that caused a humming sound. "Have you ever seen one of these?"

"I can't say that I have," Ellis said. Iris let her gloved hand fall onto Ellis' crotch, "Oh, oh, that feels good."

"Iris! Ellis!" Grace screamed, "Hope's been in an accident."

Ellis ran out and down the hall yelling, "What happened?"

"I don't know the details. I just know that she and her boyfriend are in the hospital. Faith, Joy, Mom and Lula May are there right now."

"Matthew, go find the troop, round them up," Ellis called out. "You're going to have to take them home. Can you get me to the hospital, Grace?"

"Sure," Grace rushed to say. Ellis tossed Mathew his keys, and he and Grace were out the door.

"It was nice to meet y'all," Matthew said to the girls on the couch.

"Same here. Is there any way we can help?" asked Anne.

"Do y'all hang out with Iris and Grace very much?" Matthew asked.

"All the time," said Charlotte.

"We're having a party," Charlotte said. "We'll call you."

"Do that," Matthew said from the door. "I got to go, Bye."

"Drive carefully," Iris shouted out to Matthew as he left.

Harold Leadbetter ended up with the cake by the time Matthew arrived. Not one scout's uniform was clean. Many had holes in their knees, or the elbow was torn out. The fruitcake squabble that took place between the scouts in the trailer park streets was more akin to a rugby match than wrestling. Harold, the shortest in the troop used his height, or lack thereof, to his advantage. Being more centered, it was Harold that elbowed, kneed, and punched his way to victory.

"What the hell?" Matthew yelled at the scouts.

"Matthew, you're not going to believe this. Penelope the Punisher is in that trailer," Oscar said pointing. "Where's Dad?"

"Hope's been in an accident," Matthew told them. "I've got to take everyone home. They had to take her to the hospital." Matthew dropped Harold off first. The Leadbetter's home was decorated in the latest of modern country. No old antiques here, all new furniture deliberately distressed to give the look of antiques without any of the value. Stenciled hand-painted ducks waddled one after the other across the chair rail in the kitchen. Harold came in and tossed the fruitcake on the counter.

"Is that you Harold?" his mother called from the living room. She was watching some decorating show on HGTV. Besides HGTV, QVC, Fox News, and weekend sports on all the ESPN channels, Harold could not think of any scripted television program that his parents watched. A commercial came on and his mother came into the kitchen, "What happened to you? Vince, get in here." Harold shook his head and said nothing had happened. "Your uniform is torn to shreds and you say nothing? Vince, come look at your son."

Vince made his way into the kitchen and asked Harold where he'd been, and what had he been up to. "And what is that?" his mother added, pointing at the battered fruitcake tin.

"I got it from Penelope the Punisher, the World Wrestling Federation's greatest female wrestler and her half-naked boyfriend while caroling at the Heritage Mobile Home Park with my Boy Scout troop tonight. After we sang a carol, she gave us her fruitcake and we wrestled for it and I won," he said with great pride. Not noticing any appreciation for his victory, "Is there any other questions?" the teenager added sarcastically.

"Don't talk to your mother like that," Harold's father scolded.

"I make the fruitcakes around here," Tina Leadbetter said.

"You can say that again," Harold threw at his mom.

"March your ass upstairs young man, just for that I'm taking that cake to the homeless shelter along with the other can goods I've collected," Tina shouted.

Ellis and Grace ran into the emergency waiting room. Faith stood up and wrapped her arms around her husband. "Is she alright?"

"She broke her arm in two places, that's all I know."

Raul Gomez's parents were completely and utterly distraught when they came into the emergency room. The Cuban couple had long lost the broken English that was often associated with immigrants. As they stood by the desk, Nacha clutched the arm of Roberto and they waited patiently until the nurse gave them papers to fill out. After Roberto presented their insurance card, the staff that sat by idly went to work. Doctors were called down, x-rays were ordered. Raul moved from third world to first world medical treatment in the flash of a card.

"Can you's believe that," Lula May commented as she watched the medical staff in hyper drive. "The type of service you's get has nothing to do with the color of your skin. That's whats I used to think. That's how it use to be, but the first thing they asked for, even you's white McCaskill's, was your insurance card. The only color a doctor sees now days is green, and that piece of plastic screams green, just look ats em go. Either you's got a layer of plastic green skin ors you's don't and the thicker your green hide is the better. Doctors must have the Christmas spirit year-round with as much green and red they see. Un hunh, you knows that be'z right."

"I'm going outside for a cigarette, anyone want to join me?" Bonnie asked.

Nacha Gomez walked over to the McCaskills, "How is Hope?"

"We're waiting on the doctor," Faith said coldly.

"Do you know what happened?"

"Other than Raul driving through three yards and destroying a block of Christmas decorations, almost running over and killing the high school chorus, and landing both himself and my daughter in the hospital, no, I do not," Faith snapped.

The curtness of Faith caught Nacha completely off guard, "Hope is a good girl. I pray that nothing serious has happened to her. Raul does nothing but talk about her, I know he didn't deliberately hurt her."

"Why in Jesus' sweet name did you buy your son a vehicle like that?"

"He's all we have, it's hard to say no," Nacha told her. "Surely you know how hard it is to say no to a child when you have so much. All you want is for them to be happy."

Doctors came out into the lobby, and both sets of parents gathered around. "Mr. and Mrs. Gomez, we need your permission to operate. Raul's brain is swelling, and we need to release the pressure." Nacha howled and fell to her knees in tears.

Lula May immediately went to the woman and comforted her, "Don't worry chile, the spirits aren't here for his soul, he's gonna to be fine, just fine. He's gonna give you many grandchillen'. You wait and see. Lula May knows." She lifted Nacha up and moved her to a chair.

"Do it," Roberto said. "Where's the paperwork?" A nurse took Roberto aside with a clipboard full of documents.

"Hope has two compound fractures in her right arm, but she will live. We're going to keep her overnight for observation if you don't mind."

Faith wrapped her arms around husband, "Praise Jesus."

"Can I stay with her?" Bonnie said, in from her cigarette.

"I don't think that will be a problem, Bonnie," the Doctor replied. "But only one person can spend the night."

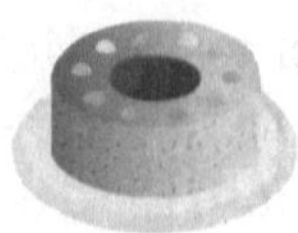

Chapter Nineteen

"It's the last full day of shopping and we're staying open for twenty-four hours today, come on down to Dickson Motors, we've got a deal for you. Y'all hurry on now, you only have three hours and eleven minutes left to come and register for a new car, there will be a live drawing at the stroke of twelve and somebody is going away with the vehicle of their choice tonight," the car salesman said over the radio.

Alice would have her revenge. Arriving at her childhood home, her parents, Joe, and Betty, were sitting in front of the television in their respective chairs. A bowl game was on, but her father was sleeping, her mother, busy knitting, looked up at the game from time to time knowing her husband would ask about it when he woke. Alice stood there in silence watching them for the longest time. Tears streamed down her face.

Her memories raced down her cheeks, many not her own, but those of her siblings, parents, aunts, and uncles, who in days long gone filled her head with stories of their family's glory days. What she now realized were these tales of the "Old South" were tales of its metamorphosing into the "New." Her parents had placed much hope that she and James would have children, for though her parents had six children, all her older siblings had died without a legitimate heir to carry on with the family fortune and this was worrisome to her father.

"Is that you Alice?" her mother asked.

"My therapist asked me to bring some things from my childhood to our next session," Alice said, before she trotted up the stairs of her parents' old antebellum residence. Her father had been born here, she remembered.

"I hope it's not that repressed memory therapy. You know that's been proven not to work," Betty said before she continued to knit. "Can't it wait?"

"James and I have many engagements over the rest of the holidays. Now's the only time I have open."

"Come say bye before you leave."

"I will, Mom," Alice said from the top of the stairs. *It's a promise*, she said to herself as she made a left toward her childhood bedroom. She could not help herself. She opened the door to her oldest brother, Laurence's room, whom she barely remembered. The room was frozen in time and was still a shrine to him all these decades later. Her last memory of him was when they posed for the photo she now cherished. Wearing his Navy uniform, he was fifteen years her senior. She was but five when he died shortly after he came home from basic training. The room had an old early 50s radio on the dresser covered in dust. Next to it was the same photograph she had with the same beautiful black maid hanging clothes out on the line. She tried to gather who her brother was. She was never allowed into the room and had only seen the inside of it once since his death and that was when she saw her father exit the room, his eyes reddened from tears. She opened the door to his closet and witnessed a series of garments neatly hung inside; recognizing the next to last article of clothing, Alice stepped back in shock. On the shelf, above each garment, was a framed photograph, many she had never seen. Laurence's first day in school, a cub scouts' uniform, his first Sunday suit, the tuxedo he wore to the Prom. Between that and his dress Navy uniform was the shocker. She had known that her dad had once belonged to the Klan, but not her brother. Maybe the garment belonged to her farther, but above it on the closet shelf was a framed photo of her father and her two older brothers, all in Klan regalia holding their hoods in their hands. With the Confederate battle flag draped over what she believed to be her brother's Bible, Alice realized that the closet was her father's private shine to her brother Laurence. She shut the door in shame and went out into the hall.

Curiosity had hold of her. She opened the door to her second oldest brother's room, directly across from Laurence's. Kevin's room, too, was also a shrine, very similar to his brother's room but with antiques of a slightly later age. Model cars lined the shelves and the dusty remains of one not completely assembled sat on his desk just as he left it all those years ago. Ironically, Kevin died in a car crash, killing himself and his best friend Sam. Alice remembered how her sister Cathy had a crush on Sam and how her mother often made Cathy leave her brother's room. Laurence hadn't been dead but two years when Kevin died the night of his high school graduation. He and Sam had been drinking, so the story goes, and crashed. When Alice opened Kevin's closet there, too, was the same kind of shrine created for Laurence. Between his tux and his cap and gown hung the Klan regalia that appeared in the same photo of father and sons that sat on the closet shelf in Laurence's closet. Alice quietly closed the closet door, and was about to leave, but not before noticing another framed photograph of Kevin and Sam posing by the same car in which they died. Though she was slightly older, the same maid was hanging out what were clearly white sheets on the same clothesline.

Who was that woman? Alice thought. With the new discoveries, she was now curious about her sisters, whose rooms were next to her parents. She first went to her oldest sister's room. Cathy was selfish and self-centered her mother had said. She had fallen victim to the sinful wicked ways of the 1960s as many Republican ladies of today would say. It was this shame that caused her to commit suicide, Betty, her mother, had told her during her sister's funeral. Cathy was just two years younger than Kevin and soon after graduation she left Dixon for California on the back of Clive Jackson's Harley. She knew her parents had planned a coming-out ball for her, but Cathy would have none of it. Cathy sent home pictures of herself from all over California. Alice's favorite was of Cathy in San Francisco as a flower child. She got pregnant once but thought it best to abort considering all of the acid she was doing when she conceived. Mother was just mortified, not so much about the abortion because she later admitted she thought it was the right thing to do, by no means was Cathy fit to be a mother. What got to Betty was that she sent the information on the back of a postcard, a postcard of David Bowie's *Diamond Dogs* album cover, uncensored no less. Shortly after the postcard, Betty started driving out of town to get her hair done so she wouldn't be asked about her wayward daughter's latest shenanigans.

Alice quietly opened the door to her sister's room. It had not been turned into a shrine like her brothers. Often family guests that visited would be given Cathy's old room. At the end of the bed was the hope chest that Betty had given to Cathy when she turned twelve, a tradition Betty had with each of her daughters. Out of curiosity, brought on by the discoveries in her brothers' rooms, she opened the trunk. Inside the trunk, sitting on top of a quilt, sat a box. The box was wrapped in ribbon and had small stains splattered on its burgundy cardboard cover. Alice thought they could have been made from tears. Inside the box sat envelopes of letters and postcards that Cathy had sent over the years. She opened the top envelope that included a photo of a mulatto baby that had been torn and taped back together with scotch tape. On the back was written, "Joey–2 months." As Alice continued looking in the box, she found another photograph of Cathy, at most she was sixteen, in a crinoline dress readying for a party or dance. also in it was the same maid as in the other photographs, brushing Cathy's hair. Alice felt very confused. She was away at college when Cathy came home and committed suicide. Why would you drive across a continent just to kill yourself? She opened the window and tossed the box into the yard before going to Georgia's room.

Georgia was thirteen months older than Dickey, and more man than he'd ever be. Betty worked hard at making Georgia a young lady, Georgia, on the other hand, (often with both hands) punched anyone but her mom for calling her by her given name, she preferred George. As a young girl she clung to her father Joe and mimicked his every move. As a teenager George toiled at becoming a young baseball playing, shit-kicking, truck driving, gambling, skirt-chaser, just like her father.

"Like father, like... well you know," town's folk would say when seeing them together. Betty tolerated George's deeds because she thought her daughter's behavior helped console her husband's grief after the death of Laurence and Kevin. There was nothing more fun to George than fishing, hunting, smoking, and drinking with her dad and brother Dickey, she forgot she was a girl when they were at play. As a matter of fact, Dickey often boasted about how it was George that got him drunk and took him down to Madam Zelda's when he turned sixteen for his first piece of ass. It was at Madam Zelda's that the two were known as the Dickson Brothers, and where their father would sometimes join them. As long as what they did didn't take place in Dixon, Betty turned a blind eye.

George met her downfall when she took a fancy to a gal in "Cow Town" as the two siblings called Lee County's County seat. Dickey preferred Madam Zelda's because it was always a sure nut, but George's gal had a pretty friend who wanted to double date. He thought it smart to date a "real girl," as in, not a whore. He didn't mind being sociable at first, especially when they went carousing in the next county over.

In "Cow Town" no one knew George was actually a girl, well at least not 'til George got a girl alone. What Dickey didn't know was that George had the hots for one of Lee County's elite daughters. With the full moon rising over the lake, the Dickson 'brothers' as they were called in those parts, took the girls to the dam. Dickey and his date took a walk along the shore and after some coercion via Jack Daniels, Dickey persuaded his date to go skinny-dipping, while George and her date made out in the back seat of the car. Dickey saw another car coming and his date wanted to leave the summer waters and return to shore. Persistent, his date broke away and quickly got out of the water, but Dickey just thought it was another couple coming to the county's favorite make-out spot and floated on his back saluting his date by flexing his erection.

"That's a new shirt," Dickey said as she dried herself. She was fully dressed and skipped a stone across the water toward Dickey's penis periscope as the car arrived. Using the moonlight, the car cut off its lights and quietly pulled into the dark parking lot lit by one light post at the end of the docking ramp. "See, just another couple coming to do the same thing we're doing."

The car's door opened, and it was then, as the interior lights came on that Dickey could see the silhouette of the Sheriff's patrol hat. Sheriff Riperton most often ignored his own citizenships' hanky-panky, but the Sheriff knew every car in his small rural county and the Chevy, which he admired (and was looking for some reason to confiscate), wasn't one of them. Dickey quietly moved toward the shore unnoticed, but he knew the same was not going to happen for his sister. As the Sheriff pointed his flashlight toward the Chevy, its light tore a hole in the darkness and exposed George's date with her patent leather shoes in the air and her panties around her ankles, while George was face down in her wetness.

Sheriff Riperton threw open the backdoor, "Young man, you need to stop what you're doing and slowly get out of the car." As George stood the Sheriff let his beam of light move to the girl's face. Without a word or hint the Sheriff leveled George with a left hook and drew out his pistol.

"Daddy! Don't Daddy!" George's date screamed, "That's George Dickson, Joe Dickson's son." With her knees now pulled to her chest, she continued, "Dickson Motors, Dickson Tool Company, Dickson Pharmacy. They own everything in Dixon."

"Pull your panties up, Patty," the Sheriff demanded. "Where's Irene?"

"Over here, Sheriff Riperton," as Dickey's date made her way to the boat landing.

The Sheriff pointed his flashlight in her direction and caught Dickey zipping his jeans. "Get your ass over here boy!" pausing for just a second, "Now boy! Move it!" Dickey grabbed his shoes and wet shirt off the ground and made his way to the landing lifting his legs like a Tennessee walking horse due to the coarse shore. Shining the light into his face he asked, "What's your name, son?"

"Richard Dickson, sir."

"And yours?" pointing his light down at George who had lifted herself onto her elbows.

"George Dickson, sir."

"So y'alls daddy is Joe Dickson," he addressed Dickey and finished his sentence looking at George, "my DAUGHTER tells me."

"Yes, sir," The siblings said in unison.

"Are you married George Dickson?"

"No, sir."

"Good, we're going to go talk to your daddy. Richard Dickson, you get your ass in that there Chevy and lead the way to your daddy's house. I'm going to be right behind you all the way with your brother in the back seat of my car. You don't mind riding in the back seat, do you George?" The sheriff said sarcastically.

Nodding toward his date, "Can she ride with me?" Dickey asked forgetting Irene's name.

"I don't mind if she don't mind." Irene hopped in the front seat of the Chevy and Dickey lead the way to his parents' home. When they arrived, the Sheriff turned on his lights and pulsed the siren. Joe Dickson came out into his yard in nothing but his boxers and a housecoat while Betty, also in her housecoat stood in the doorway.

"How can I help you, Sheriff?" Joe asked. Sheriff Riperton told Joe that he caught George having sex with his daughter in the back seat of the Chevy, as the Sheriff pointed toward the car, he saw Dickey and Irene mouth-locked in the front seat.

"And exactly what did you catch them doing?"

"Your son had my daughter's feet in the air and her panties around her ankles," said the Sheriff.

"Is this true George?"

"Yes, sir," George said.

"I expect George to do the right thing and marry my daughter, Mr. Dickson." Joe at first snorted, then started to chuckle and finally fell on the ground and belly rolled. "What's so damn funny?" the Sheriff demanded.

Catching his breath Joe yelled, "George, show the Sheriff what you're working with." The Sheriff quickly covered his daughter's eyes with his hand as George walked up to the pair unbuckling her belt. George dropped her trousers revealing her womanhood to them both. Sheriff Riperton's jaw dropped along with his hand from his daughter's eyes. Patty clung to her father's arm as she started vomiting.

"I should arrest you boy, I mean girl… that's illegal in this state," the Sheriff declared still not believing what he was seeing.

Once again, Joe rolled on the ground in pure laughter, "And let all of Lee County know your daughter's a lezzy?"

"I ain't no lezzy," the young girl screamed wiping her mouth with the back of her hand.

"You are now," George announced to her licking her lips.

"Get in the car," the sheriff screamed at his daughter. The girl climbed into the patrol car. Dickey and his date were still making out when Irene heard the slammed doors. They started to peel down the long drive and stopped short as Dickey's date chased after them screaming, "Don't leave me, don't leave me here."

"Georgia, you should be ashamed of yourself," Betty screamed at her daughter. "Get up to your room right now. Things are gonna' change. You're gonna' start behaving like the young woman the Lord made you!" Betty would have none of "George" anymore. She refused to let Georgia go out of the house dressed like a boy again and took all the clothes George had confiscated from her late brothers and replaced them all with newly bought dresses. When George threw all her dresses in her hope chest and set fire to it, the fire department had to be called to douse the flames. Betty had thought she'd seen it all. Of course, she hadn't, because as the fire department arrived to douse the flames, George walked out of the house naked.

"I told ya' mother, I'd rather go naked than wear another dress," George screamed as she walked out the house toward her family making Dickey take off his shirt to cover her. Joe no longer considered George's behavior cute when he got the repair bill. As a matter of fact, he was a bit frightened by George because she was more like him than any of his other children, living or dead. Betty had Georgia committed to the state mental institution where she suffered years of electric shock therapy to help change her sexual orientation. During one of the treatments George had irreparable brain damage and was sent home comatose. She lay in her room for years, turned by the help to prevent bedsores from developing.

Alice referred to her sister as George only once after her parents committed her. "I gave birth to Georgia, not George. Don't ever refer to her as George again!" Betty demanded, first to Alice, but with a longer stare at her husband.

Alice didn't like Georgia much, not since she shot up her favorite doll with a shotgun while playing soldiers with Dickey. She was shocked when she walked into her sister's room. The old double bed was still dismantled and resting against a wall. In its place was the hospital bed that had been purchased to make the nurse's life that tended to her sister easier. Still situated by the bed were the medical devices that helped deliver vital nutrition to Georgia through a feeding tube. As she looked around for signs of the fire her sister had set, she saw a doll. It was not a Barbie doll, or a porcelain doll, but an antique blacked face rag doll that was male in gender. On the nightstand was another photo, once again of the beautiful African American woman in an old rocking chair holding a six-year-old Georgia, the child was topless and wearing boy's underwear, holding that same doll that Alice now held in her hand. In the mirror behind them, the photographer could be seen in the photograph. It was an older black woman with a darker complexion than the woman Alice had seen in the earlier photographs. *Who are these people? Why don't I remember them?* She wondered.

Alice looked in the closet filled with dresses, tons of them. On the top shelf laid a Confederate battle flag folded in a triangle and a photo of Joe standing behind George holding a big fish. They both had on ball caps that displayed patches of the "Bars and Stars" front and center. She shut the door. Alice couldn't remember witnessing Georgia in a dress 'til the day of her funeral. *Did mother buy all these dresses just to figure out which dress she was going to bury Georgia in?* She thought to herself. "You always get the last word, don't you mother," Alice said audibly. Alice placed the doll on the bed, stepped into the hall and took one more look into the room. "They'll never put me in an asylum," Alice said closing the door to Georgia's room. She made the journey down the hall to Dickey's bedroom and walked with as much fortitude as she could muster. Alice was actually afraid to admit herself into Dickey's room. He tortured her from time to time after she entered first grade. "It's for your own good," Dickey said. She had to develop a meanness of her own if she were to reach the level of survival standards needed to withstand life with her devious brother and sister and prove to all she was a true Dickson.

Dickey and George ruled Dixon. They considered the town theirs by right of birth and all who were in their sphere were their subjects and allocated to their scrutiny. Unlike the nonchalant customs of the three older Dickson's, George and Dickey from an early age had endeavors in business and ventures of intimidations on both the social and economic side that gave their father hope for the future of the Dickson family. Neither child minded getting their hands dirty, no matter what the job entailed, and actually took joy in it.

Alice kept this in mind as she opened the door, not knowing if one of Dickey's teenaged booby traps might still be in place. Dickey, being the only son left, avoided the draft and upon graduation moved to the capitol city to attend university. During the spring semester of his junior year, he was expelled for cheating and returned home in shame, locking himself in his room 'til the semester was over. That was when Joe started

Dickey's career as a salesman at Dickson Motors. Alice had not been in this room since Betty found Dickey wrestling with her on his bed when she was in eighth grade and Dickey a senior in high school. For Alice, it had all been innocent, but Betty's attention had been brought to a pair of Alice's panties found amongst Dickey's bed linen by the maid at the time, Sheriff Sakamoto's mother.

Dickey hated Mrs. Sakamoto who left no object unturned during her cleaning. Many of his vices had been revealed to his mother with the hiring of the Sakamoto's, and he laid it at the housekeeper's feet for the renewed piousness of his mother and/or the appearance thereof, which was why he felt George was sent to the state asylum in the first place.

Betty had hired the Sakamoto's shortly after Kevin's death to manage the house affairs. This gave Betty more time to follow her 'social responsibilities,' which mainly included her bridge parties accompanied by gin martinis at the Pecan Grove Country Club for which Joe's father had donated the land prior to World War II. Also, Betty thought it more prestigious to have Asians running the house than the typical blacks, which she and generations prior had so much depended upon. At the time, Betty felt she had to keep a close eye on the 'coloreds' due to the likes of Martin Luther King, Jr., and other civil rights leaders in the region.

Unlike her oldest brothers, Dickey's room was not a dust-covered shrine. It had obviously been kept clean awaiting his return that never came. Dickey had been married twice before marrying Bonnie White McRae. On his chest-of-drawers sat framed photos from doomed marriages that in Alice's mind had made him meaner and more ornery than when he was as a child. His first marriage came shortly after his expulsion from the university. Belinda was the youngest daughter of Dixon's most beloved family, the Tilson's. Dickey and she had two boys, Adam and Kendall, the three died a fiery death when rear-ended in an automobile accident. Alice picked up the photo of the three during a Christmas party her parents had given the year prior. In the photo was the same maid, significantly older, but still as beautiful, placing a cake on the banquet table.

Next to it was a photograph of Dickey and his second wife, Carol Bratlie, lounging by the pool where she would accidentally drown. Carol died on her nineteenth birthday. According to the autopsy, the combination of alcohol and barbiturates ended the newlyweds' marriage before they could celebrate their first anniversary. It was another scandal as the police searched for the source of the prescribed medications. Alice perused the photo for the African American beauty almost giving up until she noticed the slight gape of a curtain in the French door that led to the patio by the pool. "There you are," Alice said, "I see you."

Alice sat the photo back down and turned to the closet. She had to know if her father had created a shrine to Dickey as well. When she opened the door, she was disappointed not to see the white garments her other brothers had hanging in their closets, but as she looked up onto the closet shelf, she saw for the first time a photo she had never seen before. She took the photo down and examined it. The photo had been taken before she was born and had every member of her family in it but her. There were others in the photo, some she had recognized, some she had not, but in the background of this photo, standing in a field all alone was an obviously poor African American girl in a ragged shirtdress with her fist clinched. The girl was too distant to tell if she were the woman that appeared in the other photographs, but in her gut, she believed it was so. Alice wondered if the light-colored black man dangling from the tree was the black girl's father or some other relative.

As Alice examined the face of the executed black man, she noticed a birthmark above his left temple, it was the same birthmark on the portrait of her grandfather that hung over the fireplace in the den where her parents now sat. It was the same birthmark that both her father and all her brothers bore as well. The man hanging was not much older than her father. *Look at them, standing so proud*, Alice thought to herself before returning the photo. *Where's Dickey's journal? I know he kept one.*

Standing in the hall as a girl she remembered George screaming at the teenaged Dickey, "Write whatever you want about yourself, but leave me out of it." She heard the ripping of paper and the struggle between the two. "I'll crush your head with my thighs, Richard Donald Dickson, this is the kind of stuff that could land the whole fucking family in prison you asshole!"

"Give it back!" Dickey yelled.

"Dad would whoop your ass if he knew you wrote this shit down!"

"No one is ever going to see it!" he pleaded.

"I saw it," George stared at her brother sternly.

"You wouldn't have if you hadn't of broken into my chest!"

"Hide the key better," George said before she heard Dickey howl in pain. She slung the door open and came stomping out of the room with the torn pages in one hand and what Alice assumed to be a bottle of 'shine in the other. Dickey had obviously taken a blow to the nuts and was rolling in pain on the floor.

"Bitch, I'm going to get you back!" Dickey screamed before noticing Alice standing in the hall. "What are you looking at? Shut the door!" Dickey demanded, which she did, but not before noticing a black leather journal lying on the floor and Laurence's navy chest opened on top of the bed. *Where is that chest?* Alice searched over the room. It was not in plain sight.

Alice looked under the bed, *Why do men try to hide things under the bed? Don't they know that's the first place women look?* She said dragging the chest out from under the bed with some effort. She was not surprised when she noticed the padlock on the old vintage foot chest. She simply walked over to Dickey's desk, pulled out the drawer, and to her surprise it wasn't there. *Where did you hide the key Dickey?*

Alice walked back over to the bed, lifted the covers exposing the mattress and box springs, and stuck her arm in between them in a sweeping motion. She smiled and pulled her arm out holding the key in her hand. Alice was not prepared for what she saw upon opening the chest. Under a now dated 35mm Cannon and a bottle of single malt Scotch were tons of nude photos of young adolescent girls. Alice could tell by the girls' hairdos' what decade the photo's had been taken. Dickey had photographed his crimes of molestation and Alice noticed the splattered cum stains on some images where her brother obviously took pleasure from his violent memories. Alice was sickened by what she saw, but the search for the journal kept her lifting the photographs up by her fingertips, placing them in categorical stacks as her own OCD mandated. *God, what I wouldn't do for a pair of gloves.*

As the photos went from decade to decade, she supposed someone else was involved at the scene with the varying angles contained within the images of Dickey in the act. After stacking hundreds of Polaroids, she saw who Dickey's accomplice was. Her heart fell into her gut. It was bad enough to witness pornographic images of your brother, but to see images of her father receiving a blowjob by a girl no older than fourteen,

Alice stopped and cried. When she heard the old grandfather clock begin the chime, she wiped her eyes dry. Now numb to what she witnessed captured in the photography, she did not stop again until she came upon pictures of her brother and sister, nude and obviously dancing, drinking, and participating in a full-fledged orgy. Upon lifting the photo up and out of the chest, she saw the edge of the black leather journal she had seen as a girl. She nervously opened the book. On the first page was a reference to the photo sitting on the shelf in her brother's closet. "My first clear memory is of my father…"

After reading as much as she could endure, Alice stood up, walked over to her brother's desk, took out a pen from the still opened drawer, and she simply wrote, "This is why - Alice Faye Dickson-Weldon" next to "This is the journal of Richard 'Dickey' Donald Dickson." She then thought, *Should I add 'and I killed my husband due to his infidelity?' I'm sure they'll wonder why.* She thought better of it. It would be best to leave some mystery about this night.

She opened her brother's window, and a cold blast of wind stung her. As the gust subsided, she slung the journal deep into the yard and watched it land in a clearing by the pump house next to the pool. She shut the window, and was about to leave the room when she saw all of the work she had done stacking the photos blown into a montage across her brother's bed. On top of them all rested the image of her naked brother and sister at an orgy, both holding a bottle of booze with their arms around each other's shoulders, posing for who Alice assumed was their father. They looked so happy she thought. Alice took the bottle of Scotch still lying on the floor and poured it over the photos lying on the bed. She went back to the desk for the box of matches she had noticed next to an old cigarette case earlier. By the case she saw Dickey's old switchblade. She opened it, drew it across a piece of paper. It was still sharp. Taking a match out of the box, she lit it and tossed it on the bed.

"Here's to you George," she said as she lifted the Scotch bottle and swallowed what was left. She shut the door quickly behind her taking one quick glance at the blaze she had set. Switchblade in hand, Alice walked across the hall to her room. She knew she didn't have long, turning on the light she noticed her favorite doll and picked it up. By her bed she saw the framed photo of her and her parents and like all the other photos, unnoticed until this day, the same maid held her ten-year-old birthday cake as she blew out the candles. She took the doll and descended the stairs in fervor. She calmly placed her doll on the couch by her mother. With her back to Betty, she reopened the switchblade, walked behind the chair of her sleeping father and slit his throat.

"Alice!" her mother screamed, "Why?"

Alice ran at her mother with the knife, but her mother wasn't going to give up without a fight. Alice went to stab her mother, but her mother crossed her knitting needles and stopped Alice's downward thrust of the bloody knife. As Alice withdrew the knife her mother quickly stabbed her in the gut with a knitting needle. "You bitch!" Alice screamed at her mother as she pushed Betty away.

The two women circled the chair. Betty, taking a fencing stance, kept her knitting needle pointed at her daughter. "I was a member of the fencing team at my alma mater," Betty announced while flailing her needle back and forth.

"Well, la, de, da, da," Alice snarled back at her mom. "I'm from a long line of lying, thieving, backstabbing, nigger lynching, good ole' fashion shit kickers and I'm putting an end to us all!"

"Not without a fight!" Betty said trusting her needle at Alice.

"You're no match for me old lady!" Alice screamed running at her mother.

Betty maneuvered out of her way sticking her leg out tripping Alice. As the football game blared in the background, the sports announcer seemed to be watching the women as they fight, "The Bull Dogs inflict an injury to the running back…" Alice fell on her hands and knees by the hearth and Betty stabbed her with both needles in the back. "What a fake," the announcer screams, "it's a two-point conversion for the Bull Dogs. Can the Tigers recover? The kick was good and what a return!" Alice reared up on her knees and knocked her mother back. Betty landed on her shoulder by the old Chippendale desk, and one could hear her bones as they cracked. Betty howled in agony. "What a game we have here, looks like no one is giving up," said one sports announcer. The other anchor responds, "Yep, there is blood in the water, no doubt." Alice stood up and reached behind her pulling the knitting needles out of her back with a shriek. After tossing the needles into the fireplace, she felt her wounds and examined the blood on her hands. Betty pulled herself up using the desk with her good arm. "The snap is clean, Johnson took a loss on the play. A flag is on the field, a player down." The fans moan. "There's an injury on the field. It looks like Coach Smith is calling a time out. I guess this is a good time to go to our sponsors," a body soap commercial appears on the tube with young athletes in the shower.

Hearing the jingle and knowing her daughter has OCD Betty suggested, "Alice, were your hands clean? You better go wash them. You don't want those cuts to get infected." She spied the phone on the desk.

Alice looked at her bloody hands and dropped them by her side, "I don't think it's going to matter mother." With a rush to her head, Alice picks up the knife off the floor. Slowly standing she balanced herself on the mantle. "Why didn't you tell me?" Alice asked. Betty picked up the phone as a Vonage commercial aired. "I cut the lines mother. If you weren't so stingy and had spent money on a cell phone, I wouldn't have even considered this."

Betty snatched up the crystal port decanter with her good arm and broke it across the desk. "Who told you?" Betty asked as Alice let go of the mantle and moved toward her.

"My dead husband, mother," Alice screamed.

"It was a quick affair before the two of you were ever married. Your dad had been out gallivanting around with your brother like a twenty-year-old fool," Betty said in shame. "I saw J-Bird on the lot. He was young and handsome, and I wanted revenge after being publicly humiliated by the investigation into your brother's disappearance. Afterwards, I pointed him in your direction. I thought a good lay would cure your OCD. It obviously did not. But why did you kill your father?" Betty squealed, inching her back against the wall that hung their family photos.

"We're back, Major is out of the game and Peterson is now on the field," The announcer embarks to the TV fans over the "Tiger Rag" being played in the background.

"At first it was because he told him about Jug Head. It was a sworn secret between the four of us never to tell anyone," Alice stated.

"You killed your father over some old hunting dog you killed!" Betty was beyond furious. "I should have had you institutionalized then and there, right next to your sister, but your father stopped me, and this is what he gets in return!" Betty, with the broken decanter in hand, points at the bled-out man in his easy chair. "You have been nothing but a curse!" Betty in her rage charged her daughter, knocked the knife out of her hand

and with a slash of the decanter cut Alice across her chest. Falling back on the desk, Alice pushed Betty away with the force of her legs. Betty crashed into the TV and hollered in pain before sliding down to the floor.

Alice picked up the desk lamp, "But after I read Dickey's journal, and how you helped to cover-up the molestation of all those girls committed by both of them, and how you forced Dad to kill his own brother to gain his small puny share of an inheritance, I feel possessed to put an end to us all." Alice stepped over to her mother and brought the lamp down on her head. Alice fell on her knees and took the cord from the lamp into her bleeding hand, wrapping it around her mother's neck, she strangled her. Betty went limp.

The smoke from upstairs descended the steps and set off the fire alarm. Bleeding, Alice didn't waste any time. She went into the kitchen and turned on the gas stove and oven. She then went back outside and sat in her vehicle. She turned on the radio, found a contemporary Christian radio station, and pulled a nail file out and methodically filed the nails she had broken in the fight. After she listened to the end of a sermon on Salome, the preacher on the radio asked, "Is there any Evil in your life? Is the only joy in your life perched on your kitchen sink? Are your hands ragged with worry? Is the only good, ("good" pronounced in two syllables) you see coming into your life-ah, coming to you in the form of your magazine subscription (the radio-evangelist takes a breathable pause) to Good Housekeeping? Find faith in Jesus. Let God's grace come into your life. He will keep coming if you let Him in. Let Him light up your life. Don't hide that light under a bushel. Let the world know you believe and that you're going to stomp out Evil with a Zionist fire burning in your soul. We're here to help. And the Lord needs your charity to make it happen, you can send your donations to Holy Liberty's Burning Light Ministries, P.O. Box number three, just remember the Trinity, here in Lynchburg, VA, two, four, double 0 seven, let's all go to Heaven. Hallelujah! Praise Jesus! Or just go to our secure donation's web site at WWW Liberty's Burning Light Ministries, dot COM. Help us to stomp out the evil in the world."

Alice took out her checkbook, looked at the balance and wrote out a check to Liberty's Burning Light Ministries for that amount. She opened up the cable bill she had yet to mail, crossed out their address and wrote that of the ministry's. She got out of her SUV and stumbled down the drive clutching her wounds and put the now bloody envelope in the mailbox and lifted the flag. When she returned to her vehicle, "I Don't Need Nobody Else" from Mercy Seat was playing. She cranked up the SUV and drove it directly into the kitchen with a "I'm coming, Jesus! I'm coming!"

Three angels shook their heads, their winged silhouettes framed by the flames.

Without fear they entered the broiling flames and retrieved the souls from the collapse of the antebellum structure. The three souls, unaware of their deaths, were engaged in a brawl when their angels found them. Secured within the angels' grasps, it appeared the angels were acting more as bar bouncers removing the unwanted from a drinking establishment than the feared creatures of death that they were.

Boom! Buildings all through Dixon shook. Anyone that could run outside did. Up on the hill a fire doused the darkness of night. "That's the Dickson's mansion," Bonnie said. The huge white old Greek antebellum home could be seen clearly in the wintertime. Shortly, the sounds of the fire engines were heard wailing throughout the town.

Lula May, with her arms still around Nacha, walked out into the hospital parking lot, "See, the angels of death are not here for your boy." Lula May tried to comfort her, "These angels of death here in Dixon today are heres to deliver souls directly to the mouth of hell. They's not here for your boy."

Nacha noticed the seriousness within Lula May's face and separated herself from the old woman while making the sign of the cross. "You are a sentinel," she said. "My mother told me your kind existed, but I did not believe her."

"Believe," Lula May said, staring into the Cuban born's fearful eyes, "believe."

Bonnie noticed the fear in Nacha's eyes. She walked over to the women to subdue what her intuition told her dealt with Lula May's calling. Jolted by a secondary explosion, all three women turned and stared at the iconic building as a pillar of flames reached higher into the night sky.

"Evil's loose in this town," Lula May said as she watched the fire engines with their swelling sirens surge toward the engulfed mansion on the hill.

"It does seem like something's loose," Bonnie replied, "I feel it in my bones."

Nacha crossed herself once more, "God have mercy," she said before joining her husband who had come outside to find his wife.

Chapter Twenty

The Leadbetter's lived out of town on a state highway a mile from the next living soul. Dickey first had attempted to possess Harold, but after being speared up his ass for a rotisserie pit BBQ during his days in hell, as well as being the prom date of various demons with deep penetrating sadistic temperaments, Dickey was not in tune with Harold's homoerotic nature and exited the young man as quickly as he entered. So, this Christmas Eve morning, Vince received a gift from heaven (well maybe not heaven), this morning Vince Leadbetter woke up with a raging boner, something that had not happened to the five-foot ten-inch, two hundred-eighty-pound man without the help of erectile dysfunction drugs since he was diagnosed as a diabetic. Dickey's spirit loomed over the house waiting for the scent of eroticism to announce its presence. The moment Vince had an erotic dream it was the welcome mat placed before the door, and Dickey entered… into the contemporary mind of Vince at work sneaking glances at his secretary's tits, a QVC shopper in her late thirties. She was not Dickey's type. As Vince placed his hand on her shoulder, Dickey came off the office elevators and introduced himself to Vince as his boss' nephew and new co-worker, "My uncle said we were hitting the town. Take me to your favorite places, all your lucky ones."

Dickey worked Vince through his entire sexual history, even the college ones Vince was too drunk to remember. Back and back and back in time until Vince was once again living his teenage years with the very first girls he ever had sex with along with his favorite memories from quality time spent with his fifteen-year-old girlfriend at her parent's lake house. It was a weekend when their parents were both away and Vince learned how to truly make love to a woman. Dickey experienced Vince's memories like an addict savors morphine. It was more than just the sight of the beautiful young lovers as they made out. By way of Vince, Dickey could taste her lips, feel her erect nipples on the palm of his hands, quiver as her hot breath is released onto his ear, and savor the sound as they rutted and slogged in their denim. Dickey, who wanted, needed, to feel uncontrollable teenage lust, quickly found control of Vince's motor skills and possessed the giant in whole. He threw the covers off the petite Mrs. Leadbetter, lifted her onto her knees, threw her nightgown over her head, yanked her panties down and with a spit and a shove, no Viagra needed. Dickey turned Tina every which way but loose that Christmas Eve morning. Dickey's and Vince's minds entwined, Dickey experienced all the pleasure Vince had experienced with the fifteen-year-old girl and Vince experienced his wife through Dickey's mind. It became very animal, grunting, huffing, slapping flesh. It was rapturous pounding pleasure. The Leadbetters rattled the dining room chandelier. This was the first time Harold ever heard a groan out of his father much less, "I'm going to fuck that tight little ass of yours." This was the first time he heard his mother's voice go on for minutes without saying the first intelligible word. The last time Harold could remember his mother mildly exulting some kind of pleasure was the time he came home early from school and caught his mom with a Mexican from the lawn service. Not only did Pedro get an extra tip (Harold called all Mexicans Pedro) but Harold also got a hundred bucks for his silence. He didn't care, his father was a beer-guzzling ass.

Harold was sitting down in the kitchen eating a bowl of cereal when his mother came downstairs all smiles, "Did you hear what happened? It was all over the news this morning. The Mayor was found murdered." Mrs. Leadbetter dropped her head whispering, poor Alice.

"Poor Alice my ass," Harold said. "She's the one that did it, killed her parents too. Murder-suicide with major issues, she blew her whole family up."

"What is this world coming to? I've got errands to run. You're going to be spending time with your dad today. He said something about joining a gym. You two should have a good time. It's like a new person's got a hold of him." Tina took the fruitcake and put it in a box, "Son, put this box in the trunk."

"Mom, can't I keep the fruitcake?"

"Do you want to go to the dance, or do you want the fruitcake?" It took Harold a moment to think about it. Bill would be at the dance with Sheila, of course. Bill drank too much. Harold remembered the last time Bill drank too much. He decided on the dance.

Sally and her church group had chosen to volunteer for the Mission Homeless Shelter as their act of benevolence this season of giving and she wasn't going to let her sister's accident stand in her way. She and her friends had walked around the entire neighborhood collecting can goods all season. Sally intended on delivering them even if it meant placing the collected can goods in the back of her brother's old red wagon and pulling it down to the Mission herself. "Dad, can you take me down to the homeless shelter?" Sally asked. "I've got to deliver the can goods we collected from our church group. They are depending on me."

"I don't see why not. We can do it before we get your sister out of the hospital," Ellis said to his daughter. "How does that sound?"

"Great, thanks Dad."

Tina was heading out of the Mission when she saw Faith, Ellis, and Sally as they carried a box each into the shelter. She ran up to Faith. Ellis and Sally continued inside. "Is it true? I'm so sorry, I can't believe she's dead."

Faith dropped her box. The canned goods went all over the sidewalk, "Dead? Ellis! Ellis!" Faith began sobbing. Tina was doing her best to comfort her church friend. Homeless people started gathering around the sobbing woman. Ellis ran back outside thinking that some homeless man had attacked his wife.

"I'm sorry Ellis. I didn't know she was so close to Alice."

"Alice?" Faith said. "I thought you were talking about my Hope, not Alice. What happened to Alice?"

The two started gossiping as Sally and Ellis picked up the cans strewn all over the sidewalk. "What happened to Hope?" asked Tina.

"She was in a car accident last night."

"Faith, sweetie, I'm so sorry, I thought you and Alice were cousins. I had no idea about Hope's accident. It wasn't too serious, I pray Jesus."

"Hope will be fine. Broke her arm in two places. As for Alice, she was my step-aunt. She was a senior when Joy entered high school. I really didn't know her that well. How did she die?"

"I was hoping you knew more. She killed J-Bird and then blew herself and her parents up."

"That was Alice?"

"She rocked this town, literally, I've been told," Tina laughed. "The national media is already in town. They're going to be all over the church tomorrow, you can count on it. Got to run sweetie, see you during church, Merry Christmas."

As she ran to her car she passed Will Zemp, standing across the street holding a sign that said, Will Work for Food. Ellis and Sally came outside and joined Faith. They could not help but notice Will. He was scraggly, unshaven, and quite smelly even from a distance. Sally pulled on her father's arm, looked up at him with her big round eyes and said in all sincerity, "Daddy, what would Jesus do?"

What would Jesus do? Ellis thought to himself. Faith had bought Sally a charm with WWJD on it. *What an annoying hypocritical phrase, used by most as a political weapon, not to mention a brainwashing symbol no different from a silver watch or a black and white pinwheel waved by moneychangers pretending to be men of God. What would Jesus do? Jesus wouldn't crawl in a diaper in front of an abortion clinic pretending to be an aborted baby as their neighbor had done one week and the very next week demanding that a man be executed. Either life is precious, or it isn't. What Jesus wouldn't do is give money to someone to do his work in exchange for a charm and in turn wear that charm to relieve his own conscience for not doing the job himself.* Ellis let go of Faith's hand and went across the street to Will Zemp.

"What are you doing?" Faith shouted at Ellis.

"What Jesus would do," Ellis shouted back to his wife over the blare of a car's horn.

"Hi," Ellis said to smelly Will, "I don't have any work for you, but I would like to invite you to our family dinner." Ellis took out his business card and wrote the address of his mother-in-laws on it along with his cell phone number. "Do come, I mean it. My mother-in-law is a great cook."

Will took the card from Ellis, "Thanks, I doubt I'll make it, but appreciate your offer.. Merry Christmas," Will looked at the card. "Mr. McCaskill, and God bless you and yours."

Ellis returned across the street to his wife and daughter. "What did you just do?" Faith demanded.

"What Jesus would do, Faith," Ellis said. "What Jesus would do." There are those who are filled with the Lord, and then there are those who say they are filled with the Lord, but in all actuality, most are just filled with themselves.

Harradine and Owen O'Brian were newlywed missionaries that were filled with such a piety that they prayed over every action they did no matter when, where, or what they might be up to. They didn't just pray at meals, or religious gatherings, as was expected of religious leaders, they prayed about the everyday things, including having a good bowel movement, though they were way too young to have such concerns. They even gave credit to the Lord when they no longer suffered from gas. All glory goes to God. These missionaries forced the homeless to sit through their sermons if they were to eat. Every evening of the week, if they were not sitting in the pews by seven o'clock, the doors were shut and locked. So there, Will sat most nights. The exceptions came when he could afford to feed himself from doing yard work or some other type of manual labor and still have enough to buy a case of Milwaukee's Best. This Christmas Eve night, Will had become aware of a truism. In his thirty some-odd years of dealing with so called men of faith, he noticed that all preachers that had hair, had the most perfect part in it, not even one strand out of place. Owen was no exception. He also believed that without evangelists, Vitalis would no longer exist on the market. Will knew this tight-assed preacher used it because he could smell it. It was a smell he associated with his grandfather and early childhood, but seldom did he see or come by men of that age anymore.

While Harradine, a pretty, long-haired girl fresh out of some Bible college, played the organ, Owen preached to the homeless as if they were depraved and deserving of their poor wretched conditions. These missionaries based their beliefs not just on the concept of original sin but like most televangelists, on the compounding of their original sin by not following the word of God and living Godless lives. This was the reason for their poverty, Owen O' Brian taught. If ungodly living was the reason for poverty, how come Hugh Hefner lives in a mansion?

The real reason that most of these men are here is because Reagan cut funding to mental institutions. Todd, an old Vietnam vet Will watched after, was fine on his meds, but without them, there was no telling what he would do. "What have we done to deserve this other than having no security blanket to fall on," Will thought out loud as the preacher rambled on and on and on about Hell being a living eternity.

After a traditional Protestant televangelist-inspired Christmas sermon, sister O'Brian got up from her organ and stood before the forced gathering of the homeless, and said, "A gift for a Bible verse, or should I say a Bible verse gives you a gift," she chuckled. Now, Will Zemp knew the Bible very well, while his grandmother was alive she took him to church every time the doors were open. This was going to be Will's Christmas present to himself he thought. Sitting in the back row, he whispered Bible verses to the men in the row in front of him. "Come, let us make our father drink wine," he whispered into the ear of an old black man that got up and repeated the verse to the young white twenty-year-old, "and we will lie with him, that we may preserve the seed of our father, Genesis 19:32." Then Will yelled, "Hallelujah!"

Harradine gave the man a coat, "Is there anyone else that has a Bible verse they would like to share?"

Will could not help himself. He had to check if he could teach 'Little Sam' his brother's favorite verse, "The soul of Jonathan was knit with the soul of David, and Jonathan loved him as his own soul. And Jonathan stripped himself of his garments and gave his sword to David. First Samuel, 18." Will repeatedly whispered in the ear of an emaciated drug addict who got up and quoted it word for word to the shock of Will and to the bewilderment of the missionary. "It's a miracle!" Will shouted.

Harradine reached into a box and gave the man a canteen, "You there, you in the back, you seem to know the Bible, why don't you come up and testify with a verse?" Harradine said with raised hands in the air. Will looked from side to side, hoping someone else would volunteer though he knew she was talking to him. Feeling he had no choice, Will got up and went forward.

"So, brother," Harradine challenged. "What verse are you going to testify with?"

Will turned around and looked at the room filled with homeless men and said, "Jesus wept." The crowd of men broke out into laughter. The short verse was an unexpected Christmas gift, one you really wanted, but couldn't bring yourself to ask. Harradine reached into the box and pulled out the fruitcake Tina Leadbetter had brought by earlier that day. She handed Will the fruitcake and that caused an even greater roar amongst the homeless, the men taking her deadpan behavior as part of a joke. The O'Brian's were not amused.

Will placed the fruitcake under his bunk bed before he pulled down the covers and crawled onto the lumpy mattress. He looked around the hall lined on either side with bunk beds that originated from a closed military base. Todd, who usually slept in the bed across from Will was missing. "Where's Todd?" Will asked.

'Grover,' so called due to his voice's similarity to the Muppet on Sesame Street, said, "Todd's dead, man." Only Grover could deliver something so serious that sounded so silly.

"How?" a voice from across the room asked.

"A seventeen and fourteen-year-old trying to take his drugs is what the news said," Grover explained. "Did you know Todd was a decorated Iraqi vet? Captain Todd Bowie, homeless no more," Grover continued.

"How could anyone kill someone in a wheelchair?" a sleepy, confused man asked. "What kind of kids are we making today?" asked another.

"Desperate," said Grover, "They're plainly desperate, just like the rest of us."

"Lights out," Owen O'Brian shouted.

In the darkness, Will said, "Goodnight Todd," turned over and went to sleep. It did not take long for Dickey to do his work. The moonlight revealed a series of pup tents along both rows of bunk beds, above and below, from mountains to molehills, the covers revealed dreams of happier Christmases past. With the mission on lockdown 'til morning and only one woman in the entire building, plus only one man that had access to her, Dickey would wait 'til sunrise to play with the mind of Owen O'Brian. Now his spirit felt like Marley's, only instead of his pal Scrooge getting richer and meaner, his buddy lost a fortune and became a homeless drunk.

Devin Whittaker became Dickey's sideman shortly after the parents put George away in an institution. Whittaker, as Dickey called him, greeted him after work with a six-pack, some blow, and a list of skirts to chase 'til morning light. Whittaker was a reporter on the local NBC affiliate when Dickey died and went to hell, a drunken pass at the new female anchor apparently was the beginning of Whittaker's living descent. Whittaker's uncle, who owned the station, was facing a harassment suit from the new feminist anchor if he didn't let his nephew go. "She'll move on soon and you can come on back," his uncle said to him. His uncle is long gone, and she is still the evening news anchor twenty-five years later. For Whittaker, coke led to crack, which led to divorce and alimony, which led to meth-sex, which led to herpes, which led to another lawsuit and public humiliation, which led to bankruptcy and an inability to get a job, which led shortly thereafter to living on the street. If it were not for Whittaker's scent, Dickey would not have even recognized him. Tonight, Dickey was going to direct Whittaker's dreams to the good times they shared when they first met at Zelda's all those years ago, as base and degenerate as they were, shots of tequila, lines of coke, a little weed, and dancing with topless girls to James Brown. "I got mine, don't worry about his," Whittaker sang in his sleep.

Chapter Twenty-One

Christmas morning Charity got up and went through her regular routine, but before she could get a cup of coffee down, her cell phone rang with an emergency at the homeless shelter. When she and Parker arrived on the scene, she gauged the situation and quickly loaded the O'Brian's, still feuding, into the ambulance and rushed them to the hospital. Most of the homeless were asleep until awakened by the siren. They were in no hurry to go outside this cold Christmas morn. Opening the door at County Hospital, Charity found the chill refreshing which made her nose red. Charity's rosy nose made Harradine remember her childhood and all the stop-motion animation her mother and brothers watched together on VHS. "We are Santa's elves," Harradine sang, her voice slightly slurred from the pain medication administered at the scene.

One by one, members of the family arrived at Bonnie's, and as usual, some brought unexpected guests. There was always more to eat than there were people, and Bonnie realized that non-wed-bound strangers kept the infighting down. Matthew invited Emily, Charlotte, and Anne to both Ellis and Iris' happiness. Bonnie gave out presents to her family members, each and every one of them. Hope demanded to go by the hospital to visit Raul who was in an induced coma and promised the Gomez's that they would return with a home-cooked meal. Faith had objected on the drive to grandma's house. Ellis reminded her that it was

Jesus' birthday and enjoyed using one of Faith's self-righteous weapons on her, WWJD.

The battle between Hope and Faith continued. The presence of strangers had done nothing to cool her anger at her mom. Any chance Hope saw to fire, she made no qualms about taking the shot. Her father deserted any notion of protecting his wife against the rebellion. He too had reached the limit to all of Faith's haughtiness and condescension he could stand, though he would not enter into the fray amongst friend or foe, "Why do you treat those poor people the way you do? Their son is lying there in a coma, you would think you would have a little sympathy."

Faith sneered in a whisper yell, "Their son almost cost me my daughter. Don't you realize that could easily be you lying in that hospital bed, or worse, in your final bed of rest?"

"Faith, darling, will you and Hope help me set the table?"

"Sure Bonnie Gram," Hope said, and the feuding pair went to the dining room where Grace and Joy were adding leaves to the table.

"Where's Hector?" Grace asked her oldest sister.

"He's still dealing with the press over the Dickson's fiasco," Joy replied.

"Alice," Faith said looking upward with raised eyebrows.

Will went into the dining hall and got in line with all the other homeless men for their Christmas dinner. There were all sorts of rumors as to what happened to the O' Brian's this morning, but in truth, no one knew. Volunteers were there anyway. They were different year to year, seldom did they see the same volunteers twice, unless of course they were doing some sort of court-ordered community service. This year it was some church's singles group. One man was very annoying to watch as he hit on the female volunteers. He would bring the aluminum wrapped dish to the steam table, singing the George Michael classic, "Faith." It would be something else if his voice didn't sound like some possessed hollow soul, or the way he shook his ass and then looked over his shoulder with a wink at his intended target. Man by man, tray by tray, the volunteers slopped the food onto their plates.

It was then that the idea struck Will, "I've been invited to a real family Christmas, and I have dessert." Will went up to the lodging and found clean clothes that had been donated to the shelter. He took a shower, brushed his teeth, and with fruitcake in hand he headed out the shelter for the trek to Bonnie's home.

Charity arrived home with a massive headache and went directly to the kitchen. She knew the cause was due to a lack of caffeine. But she had been so busy with the O'Brian's she had not had the chance to even stop by a drive-thru. Lula May, Ethel, and Bonnie sat around the table sipping coffee while the desserts finished cooking.

"Hi Charity," Ethel said, "I'm glad to see you're home. How was work?"

"I'll tell you all about it but let me pop some aspirin first."

"Has you's found yourself a husband in Greenville, girl?" Lula May asked, "Your momma tells me you's been going there a lots."

"I'll marry the man who can knock me out cold first or save my life better than I can in a dangerous situation, Lula May," Charity said. "That means I ain't ever getting married." After popping the pills, Charity made herself a cup of coffee and sat down with the women, "I'm swearing y'all to silence, okay?" The women agreed. "It took a while to get the truth out of them."

"Who's them?" Lula May asked.

"Owen and Harradine O' Brian, the new missionaries down at the shelter," Charity took a sip of her coffee before continuing. "Anyway, between Dr. Walkup and me we finally got the truth out of them. It seems that the newlyweds decided to give each other a special treat. As part of his Christmas gift Owen was going to make breakfast for his new bride. Well, it seems Owen asked Harradine if she would like an appetizer of sausage while he fixed her breakfast. Anyway, while she was eating his sausage, he stiffened up at the wrong moment and spilt hot grease on her back."

"Poor girl," Ethel said.

"Not as poor as Owen," Charity explained. "When the grease hit her back, she still had his sausage in her mouth and she clenched down on it."

"No, she didn't," Lula May said clasping her mouth trying not to laugh.

"She didn't sever it in two, but she sure as hell mangled it."

"And they are the missionaries at the shelter?" Ethel asked.

"Yep," Charity said.

"You're pulling our legs," Bonnie said.

"Nope," she shook her head. "Anyway, he beat her directly afterward. She has a broken jaw, two black eyes, and second-degree burns down her back. He on the other hand is going through reconstructive surgery as we speak and will never be able to stand straight again. Oh, Hector said he might be running behind, has to file the report after dealing with the press."

"Poor Alice," Ethel said.

"Poor Alice my ass, "Lula May said. "That girl was Dickson through and through. Why, the only Dickson meaner was he whose name can't be spoken."

"You know, I don't think there are any Dicksons left," Ethel said.

"You's knows, you's right," Lula May agreed. "Alice and her daddy was the last two blood Dickson's left. Mrs. Bonnie, Merry Christmas, I believe you'z the sole heir to the Dickson fortune."

Bonnie got up and ran out of the kitchen, "Ellis! Ellis! Where are you?" Ellis was sitting in the living room watching a game when Bonnie came running into the room. "Ellis, as the widow of the man who will not be named, am I entitled to the Dickson fortune?"

"I don't know, depends on the will. If old man Dickson left everything to Alice, and since she's dead with no heir, it could be."

"But Bonnie Gram, she blew up everything," Mary Jane said.

"Fire is cleansing," Bonnie said, "besides they own much more than that house. They own that Ford dealership, they own God knows how much stock, and they own half the property downtown."

"What's the ruckus? Why are you so happy Momma?" Grace asked.

"We're rich, Honey," Bonnie squealed. "We're rich. When Alice killed her husband and then blew herself and her parents up, she left no heir. As the widow of that bastard whose name I will not mention, I'm the only Dickson left in this town. I'm the sole heir."

Faith thought for a moment, *what would Jesus do? There is no telling how this fortune will be spent. The Lord would want it to be spent on heavenly things,* and with that last thought she knew what she had to do. "You are not the last Dickson, Momma, you know that."

"Well what other Dickson's are there?" Bonnie replied.

"Why Hope of course." Faith threw out into the room.

Hope had not a clue, "What do you mean Momma?"

"I don't think this is a conversation to be had in front of strangers," Joy said nodding toward Matthew's girlfriends. "Hope, will you and Matthew join us in the kitchen. Ethel, will you and Mary Jane entertain our guests while we have this family conversation."

"Why does Matthew need to be in on this?" Ellis asked.

"He's an adult," Joy said. She could tell by the look on Faith's face that she did not anticipate her asking Matthew to the table. Lula May, Bonnie, Joy, Faith and Ellis, Grace, Charity, Hope and Matthew, in that order made their way to the kitchen. "Well momma, do you want to be the one or do you want me to do it?"

"I think you should do it. I think your momma feels stabbed in the back right now," Lula May said.

"Very well then," Joy took a deep breath, "there is a reason why we don't say Dickey Dickson's name. He raped us one by one. Hope, Charity is your mother, she gave birth to you. Dickey Dickson is your father. Lucky me, I did not get pregnant, but both Faith and Grace did. Grace had an abortion, Faith do you want to tell the rest?" Faith was in tears, she said nothing.

"Matthew, Dickey Dickson is your father too," Joy blurted out.

"What do you mean Matthew is..."

"When Faith knew she was pregnant, she chose you, Ellis. Faith was the first to get pregnant, but Dickey threatened to throw us all out in the street. She was just sixteen, she didn't know what to do. Dickey was very powerful, and his family carried a great deal of influence, so she chose you. And two weeks after you slept together, she came to you and told you she was pregnant. He weighed over seven pounds. Did you really think he was born two months premature? Momma didn't have a clue, not about Faith anyway. But Charity, she was just twelve years old. She had always been on the heavy side, so no one noticed. Faith persuaded her not to abort you, that she and Ellis would adopt you and raise you as their own. But momma did find out about Charity and what Dickey had done to all of us."

"So that's where I's comes in," Lula May began, "Me and Mrs. Bonnie here plotted ons how to kill that bastard so no's one would ever find out. I made a poisonous potion and Mrs. Bonnie here puts it on his fruitcake, 'cause Dickey Dickson loved him some fruitcake. And after eating a big chunk of it, he's died a painful death, and we just stood around and watched him squirm until he died. We also decided on how's to gets rid of the body. Joy, being the hippy chick that she was, had plenty excuse to buy a Christmas tree with a root on it. We buried that Bastard right out there, under that tree. We's drove his car to the next town and left it there and I's drove Mrs. Bonnie back. Nows y'alls knows the truth."

"So, Faith, do you want to bring this all out? Do you want to claim the Dickson fortune? Do you want us all to spend the rest of our lives in jail?" Joy asked.

"No," Faith said sobbing. "Ellis will you forgive me?" Ellis stood there dumbfounded.

Herb ran into the kitchen, "Mommy, Hector is here, and he's got someone with him."

"Excuse me everyone, but I've got a splitting headache. Do you mind, I'm going to my room to lie down," Charity said.

"Before you leave, we will never speak of this again," Bonnie said to her family, "Is that understood?" No one said anything. "Good." Bonnie said, and the family left the kitchen and went out to mingle with their guests.

"What was that all about?" Iris asked Grace.

"Nothing to speak of," Grace said.

"Liar. What about Hope?"

"Another time Iris, it's all settled."

Ellis hardly recognized the man, but he remembered the card when Hector showed it to him, "You're the guy by the mission."

"Yes, sir," he said.

"Call me Ellis, and your name is?"

"Will Zemp," he nodded.

"Glad you could make it, Will," Ellis smiled.

"I didn't come empty handed," Will said. "Who do I give this to?"

"That would be me of course," Bonnie said taking the cake from Will. "That tin looks familiar, I wonder if it's one of ours. Set it there on the buffet and open it up for me." Will did as he was ordered. He had great difficulty getting the lid off the scratched battered-up tin. Finally getting it opened, Bonnie looked down at the cake just as she was lighting her cigarette. With one big puff, a flame shot up and caught Bonnie's Dolly Parton wig on fire. Lula May noticed the spirit of Dickey

Dickson pulling on the wig as the flames got higher. Will quickly closed the lid back on the cake and tried to put the fire out, but Bonnie would not stand still. Bonnie ran around the dining room knocking everything on the floor. The fruitcake fell off the buffet onto the floor and rolled next to the hall stairwell. Bonnie was screaming, "Get it off, get it off!"

The haunting voice of Dickey could be heard throughout, "Die you bitch! Die! You're gonna' burn in hell with me, you mother fucking whore. Die!" Pulling as she may, she was catching the curtains on fire. The room ablaze, she ran into the living room, finally getting the wig off her head. As it flew through the air you could see Dickey's flaming spirit as he crawled across the ceiling to get back to Bonnie. The wig in its descent landed on the Christmas tree. The ornaments went off like firecrackers, popping one by one and shooting flames onto everything in the room. "Grab the children, everyone get out," Hector ordered. Everyone filed out onto the yard with light-filled trees.

Lula May did a count, "Charity, Oh my Lord! Charity is still inside."

"Where would she be?" Will asked the old lady.

"She said she was going to her bedroom," Lula May told him. "It's the first room at the top of the stairs," Will immediately ran back into the house. He tripped and fell on the fruitcake. He grabbed it and took it with him because he knew the metal doorknobs would be hot. "Charity!" Will yelled running up the smoke-filled staircase, "Charity! I'm coming to save you!

Charity woke up from the smell of smoke. She always put earplugs in her ears when the children were over or she couldn't sleep. When Will got to the top of the stairs he took the fruitcake tin and knocked the doorknob off. He opened the door and BAM! The door caught Charity right in the head, knocking her out cold. Will found her on the floor and believed she had passed out from smoke inhalation. He tried to carry the big woman, but he could not lift her. He then grabbed her feet and started to pull with all his might. He dragged her out into the hallway and pulled her down the stairs. Her head hit each step with a bang. *Maybe I should have pulled her down holding her shoulders*, he thought, but it was too late for that. Bang, bang, bang, her head caught every step. Her body landed on a Persian carpet, which made it easier to pull her since her shirt was now above her head exposing her sports bra. Will pulled her through the front door and out onto the porch where

Hector and Ellis helped to get Charity out into the yard. The family watched as their beloved home went up in flames.

Lula May noticed how the tall old evergreen tree that served as Dickey's marker was burning, sending fire high into the sky. The smoke from the burning tree billowed upward forming a cloud chamber that attached itself to the low-lying clouds of winter. A newly formed vestibule behaved like a placenta that holds a child within the womb. Lula May noticed the impression of an embryo growing inside his mother. As the cloud mutated with the billowing smoke, Lula May perceived the form of a growing man inside. Hope noticed Lula May and followed her eye to the new cloud formation. She too saw the dark shape and felt as if she were watching the sonogram of a child in the womb. Hope turned her attention back to Matthew, who was surrounded by his invited guests. The two locked eyes and Hope guided his attention to the elderly black woman looking upward. Matthew followed her gaze into the sky. The face of Dickey turned and looked down on the gathering and smiled with an evilness that made Lula May shiver. Matthew and Hope both watched in amazement, not noticing Lula May's discernment. Hector had called emergency services and once they realized it was the McRae's home that was ablaze, the Yerby twins, who were supposed to have the holiday off, were the first to arrive not living far away. The Yerby twins argued over who would perform what task of CPR on their beloved friend until Ellis brought the pair into reality.

"I'll take both your asses to court if one of you doesn't do something now!" The elder twin did mouth-to-mouth as the younger worked Charity's chest. Lloyd Parker followed in the ambulance just as Charity was revived. The fire engine behind Lloyd quickly went to work to extinguish the flames. All the family clamored around the heavy woman now wrapped in a blanket and planted kisses on her cheek. Realizing she would be fine, the Yerby twins joined in the fight to save the home from total destruction. The youngest grandchildren complained of hunger, but not a single adult had an appetite as they watched the historic home burn.

"Hand me that newfangled phone of yourns Ho!" Lula May said to Iris.

"Who're you calling?" Iris snapped back.

"That be none of your business," Lula May retorted.

"Then no phone," Iris raised her eyebrows.

"I use to work with your momma and daddy. I knows where they live, twenty-seven Precipice Road. They still has a good old-fashion phone like me and is listed in the phone book. Now hand me your phone, HO!" Iris handed the old woman her phone. "Show me hows to use it."

"What's the number?" Iris said softly.

"7-4-3-7-6-2-7."

"It's ringing," said Iris handing Lula May the phone. Lula May walked over to her car to make her call private.

When Lula May was finished, she returned the phone to Iris. "Here, Ho!"

"You could at least say thank you and stop calling me Ho!"

"You're the one who will be saying thank you and I'lls stop calling you Ho when you stop Ho-in'."

Hours passed before the firemen got the flames under control. "It's like hellfire itself was released," the Chief said to his fellow fire fighters. The chimney on the East side of the structure was left standing alone as the house's wing collapsed on it. After the edifice's flames were extinguished, the evergreen continued to burn. The Yerby twins had to double team what appeared to them to be the world's largest matchstick as it continued to burn until it reached the earth. The two were assured the flames were out. Having not been able to urinate for hours, the twins pulled their penises out and pissed on the stump for good measure. A final gush of steam leaped forward, and the umbilical cord was cut with a couple of shakes of their cocks. Holding a handheld fire extinguisher, the Chief walked around the house surveying the damage done. Not a morsel was left in one wing of the house, no photos, no furniture, no clothes. On second floor, in the other wing, there was no roof, just open sky.

"What a strange looking cloud," he thought as his foot kicked something in the ashes. The Chief looked down and, to his surprise, what was obviously a fruitcake tin was at his feet. Picking it up with his gloved hand, he brushed the ashes off the container. "How in hell," he said in disbelief as he gazed at the uncharred vessel for the seasonal staple. "Ho, Ho, Ho indeed," he laughed. He continued his search through the rubble.

"Bonnie Gram, are we going to have Christmas dinner?" Herb asked. "I'm really hungry," he added.

The matriarch took her grandson in her arms, "Real soon, my love, real soon."

"Why Bonnie Gram, why did this happen?" Sally asked, "You're the nicest person in town."

"God just wanted to make me grateful and show me what's most important in life."

"What's that?" Herb questioned.

"Why my family, darling, you and Sally, and Charity and all the rest made it out alive. See, look around you, I really didn't lose anything that couldn't be replaced. Everything that is precious to me is all around me. God will take care of us, you just watch and see."

Chief Maxie Lee made his way from the rubble with his hands behind his back.

"I'm sorry folks," the Chief said, "all we were able to save was this." The Chief pulled the fruitcake out from behind his back and placed the smoke charred fruitcake tin before them.

Bonnie opened the cake tin and Lula May nodded her head no. "Mr. Zemp, since you saved my daughter's life, I would like you to have the first piece."

"I can't," Will said.

"I insist," Bonnie said breaking off a piece of the cake. Will took the cake and ate it. "Well, how is it?" Bonnie asked.

Will looked at Bonnie and the rest of the family finally resting his eyes on Charity, "It's the best I've ever had."

"See children, like I told you, the Lord will provide."

They all broke into laughter. Instantly, Charity liked the man, more than any other man she had ever met, not sexually of course, but she knew they would be friends, "thanks for saving my life, Mr. Zemp."

Will raised the fruitcake up as if it were a toast, "The pleasure is mine."

Unbeknownst to the family, their tragedy had spread through town like wildfire, "Look at the vultures gawk," Faith snorted as cars began to line the road.

"Well, what's open on Christmas Day?" Mary Jane asked.

"In this small town on Christmas Day, nothing," Iris remarked.

"You'd think Fort Knox had opened its gates," Ellis remarked.

In full drag, Lula May's nephew Hunter was the first to arrive in his old beat-up pick-up truck. Riding with him in the front seat was

Sunshine, a tall southern man of German descent who lived in a trailer park with his wife and three kids and worked as a mechanic by day. He told Hunter that his real name was Trey Jones, but Hunter found no record of a Trey Jones ever living in these parts. *He'll let me know when he wants to. Some guys never feel safe, not when they're into this*, Hunter thought as he cut the truck off, "How do I look?"

"Like Whitney Houston on crack," Hunter's companion snapped.

"Thanks Sunshine," Hunter was indeed dressed like Whitney Houston, and he was stoned from some really good weed. With one more glance in the mirror, he opened the door and sashayed his way over to the family. His companion got out of the truck and waited by the tailgate smoking a cigarette in a tight white rabbit mini dress and a long florescent blue bobbed wig and a pair of platforms. She had been practicing, "White Rabbit" at Hunter's when Hunter got the call to come help. Because of his angular German features, the drag queen appeared like a mod 60s spokesmodel promoting a new cigarette. "Where should we set up Auntie?" Hunter asked Lula May.

"Did you bring the generator like I told ya'?"

"Yes 'um," he said. "In the front yard amongst the trees." As people got out of their vehicles, most of them were African American, some Hispanics and a sprinkle of White folks became a part of the mix. Ethel recognized one of Lula May's 'dogs' she had taken a liken' to from the blue moon ceremony earlier in the season. In fact, all these folks were followers of Lula May. As they unloaded their vehicles it became apparent that they were setting up for a feast. As the electric line that fed the bare trees was found, Sunshine removed her elbow-length gloves and revealed the hard rough hands of a mechanic.

Sunshine was a church-going Southern Baptist. Yep, a seven days and six nights a week father and husband, an all-around man's man, who became a female impersonator extraordinaire every Friday night and on Christmas Day while his wife and kids went across state lines to visit her parents. Sunshine gleamed as she attached the magical lights to the generator, and they all came on. Tables were set amongst the trees and a feast of untold proportions appeared almost by magic as if it had been planned this way. "It's a true Christmas miracle," Bonnie said in tears as she wrapped her arms around Lula May.

"As many miracles as you and Ethel have performed for the folks that would have had nuttin' in this town on Christmas Day, you'z my girls as if I gave birth to you'n myself. I love none better."

The celebration continued, feasting, dancing, singing, even a tawdry drag performance by Hunter as Virginia Headhunter, of course, and Sunshine cheered what would have otherwise been a day of sorrow. All clapped as Sunshine tapped her heart out to "Dueling Banjos" wearing a green and white gingham square dance costume. Her auburn pigtails flapped in the wind as Hunter, in braided blond ponytails, wore a red and white gingham square dancing costume and stepped onto the makeshift stage and challenged the 'mountain lass.' Faith, originally offended and as uptight as she could muster, could not contain her laughter, which sparked her sister Charity to reach hold of her sister and give her a big hug. Hope played fiddle as Grace played guitar and sang, "Silver Bells."

"You've made her a lady, that's more than I could have ever done," Charity leaned over and said to Faith as they watched Hope and their sister perform. It was the only gift she had to give to her sister that meant anything.

Oscar sang his version of Silver Bells in his father's ear to his delight, who demonstrated his appreciation with a big grin and a manly slap across his son's back. He then sent the dirty blond boy on his way to hang with his cousins as he discussed their in-law's current legal issues with Hector. Ethel ran back to her shop and secured a wig she had set aside to give Bonny to wear on New Year's Eve. Knowing her sister's vanity, Ethel took her sister aside, cleaned her face and attached the new wig. It was just the gift Bonnie needed to face everyone. Bonnie in her new wig, and with a survivor's attitude, strutted from table to table thanking everyone for their generosity and promised to have them back when the house was rebuilt.

But as the sun began to set, the dark cloud that hung above the crowd as a reminder of the tragic day released its tears. Very slowly at first, a few huge drops fell indiscriminately upon the heads that had gathered by the newly formed ruins. A large drop landed on Matthew's head and as he looked up at the gray cloud above, he noticed the dark figure of a nude male body that appeared to be pissing on the gathering. Another drop descended onto his head and this time rolled down over a birthmark on his temple, which drew the raindrop into his head. The birthmark dried out and with a rush of air began to crumble off Matthew's face leaving no sign of blemish. A great thunderclap followed, and rain doused the crowd into a wild frenzy. No one noticed Matthew as he stood in the rain with a wicked grin, no one but Hope. Hope looked to the sky, but the figure of the man in the cloud was gone. She felt a sense of relief. She worried about her brother, something didn't seem right. Considering the fire, the breakup with Sweet, and his new religious conversion, she figured he was awash with confusion.

Emily, Anne, and Charlotte ran up to Matthew, "Iris said we have to go. Are you coming to your Aunt's New Year's Eve party?" Anne asked.

Coughing, his voice sounded ragged, "If y'all are going to be there you better believe it." The girls all kissed Matthew on the cheek and ran to the pick-up, wringing the rain out of their hair before sliding in on the bench seat, Anne blew the horn at him and drove off, all girls waving. Unmoved, unstirred, the rain continued to fall. Matthew didn't blink until his mother ran up to him, put her arm around him and lead him to the SUV asking if he was alright. Coughing once more, he told her, "Not sure, I think I've caught something."

As quickly as the party arrived, they disappeared. Charity went home with Lloyd Parker, his momma had three spare bedrooms after her children left the nest, that left two for Charity to choose from since Parker moved back home.

"Momma, come stay with Hector and me."

"Thank you honey, but Ethel already asked me to stay with her. I just want to have a moment alone if you don't mind."

"Of course, Momma," she said.

Will stood in the rain. If he ran, he might get back to the shelter by curfew. Hunter, still dressed as Virginia Headhunter, and Sunshine pulled up to the sprinting homeless man. "Need a lift?" Sunshine asked. If it weren't not for the cold rain Will would had said no, but with a thunderclap he jumped into the truck like a scared rabbit. "Where to, hero?"

"Corner of Gay and Jackson."

When they arrived at the destination and the drag queens saw that it was a homeless shelter, Hunter turned to Will, "Are you homeless? Oh, no, you ain't staying here, not tonight anyway. My aunt would have my hide if I didn't offer you a place to stay. You're staying with me, my friend."

"I'm not gay."

"Did I say you were? No, I didn't. I got a spare couch that sleeps good. Anyways, I prefers my men with a little meat on 'em. We'll figure you out some future sleeping arrangements tomorrow. You smoke, of course you do. I gots some green that smells just like a Christmas tree waiting in my stockin'. Christmas ain't over 'til the clock strikes twelve and yes, I am Virginia, and I am your Santa Claus." Sunshine enjoyed Virginia's candor and laughed. Before Will could say no, "We made it here before seven," Virginia Headhunter pushed the pedal to the floor and throttled the old truck down the road. "Say goodbye to Lonely Street Will. When you saved Charity McRae, you just got yourself a whole new bunch of family and friends."

Lula May slid into Bonnie's car and took the woman's hand, which allowed her to release the tears that she had buried the whole day. "Thank you, Lula May. I don't know what I'd do without you, I love you so much," Bonnie tried to say through the uncontrollable sobbing.

"I loves you, too. You go on and cry now. You've been strong all day long, you deserves a cry."

"I have everything that matters."

"And like Job, you'll have more."

Chapter Twenty-Two

Matthew examined his home as if he'd never been there. Hope, Oscar, and Sally thought there was something strange going on with Matthew. Everything seemed new and exciting to the usually subdued redhead; as he meandered around the house, he allowed his hands to touch everything, with every new idem his face expanded into a big stupid grin, then he coughed or cleared his throat before he laughed. "Did one of those girls give you some Extasy?" Hope asked.

A look of confusion came across his face, "Ecstasy? Not yet."

"Is that a, 'I'm coming down with something' cough', a 'I've been smoking cigarettes or weed maybe kind of cough' or is it simply a burning wig inhalation cough?" Sally asked Oscar. Oscar looked at his youngest sister and smirked.

"Time for bed everyone, it's been a long day," Faith demanded, wanting time with her husband.

It was not 'til Dickey saw Matthew's high school graduation photo that he remembered he shared the same abode with his brother. Oscar stood behind him wondering why his brother was gazing inside their room. "Are you sure you're okay?" Oscar asked his brother nudging him inside and shutting the door. Matthew sat and bounced on Oscar's bed checking it out for comfort. Matthew nodded yes. "Then what are you doing on my bed?"

"Just looking out the window," he said before getting up. Oscar started to disrobe and felt a little creeped out when he noticed his brother watching him undress.

"What?" Oscar said. Dickey ignored him and became fascinated with Matthew's personification in the full body mirror attached to the closet door. Garment by garment Dickey did a silent striptease examining the tone and tightness of Matthew that Dickey never possessed.

Oscar sat on the edge of his bed in his briefs and watched his brother flex each muscle, "I don't know what's gotten into you, but you're behaving so gay tonight."

Matthew allowed the heaviness of his belt to pull the lower garment around his ankles, as he stood before the mirror, his Jo-Boxers still on, he checked for a tan line, his thumbs went beneath the waist band and he slid them to his knees and let the underwear fall. Standing, he reached down into his groin and loosened what had been cramped up in his hip-hugging cords all day.

"Well, I see you inherited the family jewels," he said as he twisted his hips back and forth. Oscar burst out laughing as he heard the slapping sounds. "Yep, you're a Dickson," Matthew looked over his shoulder then grinned at the fourteen-year-old on the bed and began to laugh too.

"Man, your voice is getting deeper. How many times do men go through voice changes? Sleeping commando, I see." A quick look of, oh, I get it, came over Matthew's face as he walked over to his bed, pulled down the covers and jumped in. "Goodnight bro."

Coughing, "Goodnight," Matthew reached over and cut off the lamp and smiled.

"What do you mean you're a Dickson?"

Dickey dreamed of how the body he now possessed came into being. Madam Zelda's went out of business with the coming of AIDS. Dickey's refuge for the consumption of innocent youth no longer existed and the relative conservative turn, even by Southern standards, of the nation as a whole forced Dickey to visit the dregs of 'City View,' one of the poorer regions of the state's capitol. 'City View' was once a thriving mill village filled with poor working class rough Scotch-Irish with absolutely no political clout. The region was still unpaved until the late 80s, just in time for the ending of the US textile industry. Poverty had sent many a teenager, both male and female, out onto the street to make party money their parents no longer had to give, especially if they were both out of work, or alcoholics, and in most cases, both.

Dickey road through 'City View' with his father's old college chum, 'The Judge' who sat on the federal bench and who had just as much a liking for the 'innocent' boys as Dickey had for the girls. Occasionally the pair would pick up siblings and take them to some retreat off the beaten path and party with enough booze and cocaine to kill a horse. Well, the coke didn't kill a horse, but it took the obese jolly judge out during what sounded like the deflowering of the sixteen-year-old he picked up off the street.

"Help me, God help me! Help please, somebody please. I'm in pain, please, get this man off of me, please!" It was not 'til Dickey finished using the girl that he allowed her to check on the continuous cries of her brother. Her blood-curdling scream caused Dickey to come running out of his room flapping in the wind. Nude, standing in the door, he saw what had happened. 'The Judge' had collapsed dead on the boy and tore the inner ligaments of the boy's thighs. Weighing over three hundred pounds, the six-foot-two man was too heavy for the boy to escape. Not even Dickey with the girl's help could roll the giant off the boy who was obviously in anguishing pain. Dickey had no other option than to call his father.

When Dickey opened the door for his father, Joe witnessed the fourteen-year-old girl wearing just a robe, who sat cross-legged on the bed sharing a cigarette with her brother. "The man has a wife, five kids, and eight grand kids. I had no idea we had a fucking homo in the Klan," Joe said upon viewing the scene.

Joe had brought with him two black men who pulled the dead man off the naked boy, being unable to hold him, the robust judge slid out of their grip and hit the floor with a thud. "Roy," Joe said to one man, "throw a blanket over The Judge. Howard, get that little faggot dressed. Then bring him in here." Joe grabbed the girl off the bed by the arm and pulled the now- frightened girl, an obvious member of her high school's 'Future Drug Addicts of the World' Club, out into the main room of the cabin.

"Who's your family, girl?"

"I'm Liz Johnson, Bruce Johnson's daughter," the girl said.

"And your momma's family?"

"My momma was a Kelley."

"And what do they do for a living?"

"Mom still works at Spring Hill. My daddy was laid off from there two years ago."

The black men, holding the hustler under his armpits, brought him into the room, "What's your name boy?"

"Steve."

"Do y'all have a record?" The siblings were obviously scared stiff. "Have y'all ever been arrested?"

"No, sir. Our daddy was for drunk and disorderly," the girl said.

"But that was a couple of years ago," the boy added.

"Now you two listen here and listen to me good. The Judge brought y'all to help him on his hunting trip. You girl, to keep the cabin clean, and you boy to help if he bagged a deer. Y'all met him at a gas station close to where y'all live and asked him for a job over a month ago. Yesterday, he picked you up and brought y'all out here. These men found you and the judge out in the woods, Steve. The Judge was ahead of you on a hill, turned around clutching his chest and fell on you. These men were out hunting and found y'all. Now repeat the story." Steve repeated the story first, then Liz.

"Harold here works for me, called me worried because they were black men and didn't know how the authorities would look at the situation. That's when me and my son arrived, understand that girl?" She nodded yes. "Repeat it!" She did.

They got the Judge dressed and placed the body on the bed. They removed all the illegal substances from the premises, but not before Dickey got in another bump. Joe called the police. After Joe hung up the phone he said to the streetwalkers, "I'm giving you both one thousand dollars. If I see or hear of either of you on my property or in Dickson County ever again, I will have Roy and Harold here kill your asses."

Prior to the police's arrival, Dickey looked down on his father's disgraced friend. After a moment of contemplation, he went into the den, stepped onto the hearth of the fireplace, and took a rifle from above the mantle. He cocked the gun and examined it for ammunition. Seeing none, he walked over to the desk and took a box of buckshot from a drawer. This caught the attention of everyone in the room. He loaded the rifle and cocked it once more. Looking down the length of the barrel he pointed the gun toward the boy, who wet himself. Dickey discerned with a smirk, dropped the gun's barrel down and laughed. Dickey turned the barrel upward. Joe took notice and for a quick second thought his boy was going to kill himself until he noticed that he was moving his hands down the hard hollow rod hand over hand.

A decision made, Dickey returned to where the judge laid at rest. Dickey placed 'The Judge's' one hand with the finger on the trigger and the other about the cock, pointing the barrel down between his legs. He covered him with a sheet. Dickey noticed The Judge had died with a smile on his face and roared in laughter. He went to his room. "Details," he took his Instamatic from his bag and captured the image, "I'll call this one 'Happily at Rest.' After taking the picture he returned the rifle to the fireplace and waited with the rest for the police's arrival. Once all was done at the cabin, being questioned by the police, the body removed, the children returned home, and the black men handsomely paid, Joe addressed his son with a seriousness that he had never seen.

"Boy, you'll be forty before you know it and fifty will come fast after, it's time to get your act together. I expect you married by year's end or I'm cutting you off." Joe walked up to his son, pointed his finger rhythmically into Dickey's chest in the same manner as when he was a boy and said, "I'm dead serious son, you're my last boy and you got to fly right. I'll have an accounting of every penny you spend 'til you're married son, every dime, nickel, and penny, you understand boy?" Dickey hated being called 'boy.'

"I would never have met your mom, if that damn Judge hadn't died causing Dad to demand I find a wife," Dickey uttered to himself, which sounded like scrambled eggs to Oscar.

"Matthew," pausing for a response, "Matthew, you're talking in your sleep." Dickey grumbled for show and turned his back to him. Facing the wall, Dickey thought of the first time he laid eyes on the four girls and their mother. It was a hot summer day when they arrived at the dealership, all five in designer jogging suits and matching headbands. His mind went roaming to when he first had sex with Bonnie, followed by the year and month with each of the McRae girls. He looked over at the snoring Oscar, "Your mom was my favorite. She was the passionate one."

A fox crossed Lula May's path and she stopped her car. The red animal smiled at her before disappearing into the woods. Lula May drove herself home in the same car she had driven since 1969, that was how long it took Lula May to save for a Cadillac working as a domestic and a little root-doctoring on the side. "When you buy the best and takes care of it, you'z can gets a lots of mileage offs it." She turned on a dime and returned to the cottage that had been her father's instead of her own home, a small post-war brick bungalow she had bought in town. She pulled her car under the old oak that stood between the screened porch cottage and an old wooden garage that was bigger than the old house with its apartment roosted on top. Lula May rented the apartment to Hunter to keep an eye on the old place. It was hard for a big sissy like Hunter to find a place to rest his heels, especially amongst his Black church-going community. Lula May noticed a pick-up truck that wasn't Hunter's pulled under the other side of the old oak. She knew it must belong to Hunter's friend that he played dress-up with, just like he and Grace use to do she thought. "Both of them wanna' be stars," she said shaking her head.

The old wooden steps creaked, and the screened porch door squeaked as Lula May stepped onto the old chestnut planks where her mother had given birth to her. Mattie was unable to make it into the house after working in her garden on that hot September day. There was not a soul around that morning but her toddlers playing in the yard. Mattie brought Lula May, her third child of nine, into this world on her own. Lula May thought of her mother briefly before placing the key in the house door and letting herself inside. She reached over on the old plaster wall and pushed the top button of the old light switch, this turned on the bare pendant light that hung in the center of the room above an old faded green Formica table wrapped with a scratched band of chrome. The kitchen's light revealed a post-World War II kitchen that had never been updated. She closed the door and turned on the porch light so Hunter would know she was there.

Lula May opened the pantry doors where Mason jar after Mason jar was organized and labeled. She chose a few and set them on top of the Formica table's tinged swirls of green before she sat in one of its matching plastic-covered chairs, clean of course, no crud found between the seat and piping, but showing their age. She hummed to herself as she opened the cabinet above the sink and took out a cup and saucer, setting the porcelain on the countertop closest to the stove.

She saw the lights of Hunter's truck before she heard the humpty, thump, thump of the music rattling the vehicle as it arrived at the backwoods home deep in the county. She heard the men as they climbed the steps of the garage apartment. She pulled a kettle off the old wood-burning stove and placed water from the tap inside it before she set it back on the range top and went outside for the chopped wood that was piled by the garage. As she placed the elongated pie- shaped wood across her forearm, she heard the descent of the tall blonde man down the stairs that flanked the other side of the garage. He stepped into the old woman's view due to the glow generated by a mounted light above the old carriage house doors. In jeans, a flannel shirt, and ragged ball cap, she watched in amazement at what once appeared to be a woman stride across the grassless yard under the old tree. Trey cranked up his truck and drove off blaring the distorted discord of some old 80s rock hair band song that Lula May never liked. She shook her head as it disturbed the spirit songs sung by the winter sirens in the backwoods' night.

Trey's taillights in the distance, an old barn owl rested in the oak before it hooted. It swooped down and captured its prey as the elderly woman watched. The barn rat writhed trying to twist itself free of the grip of death. The owl landed on a fence post, raised a talon, snapped the ruddy-haired rodent's neck with its beak, and ripped into the belly of the creature.

"Lord, I hope's not," she said whilst she watched nature's revelation revealed before her.

"Aunt Lula May, do you need my help?" Hunter inquired from a window.

"Nots with the firewood."

"Cans I bring Will Zemp with me? He's the man who saved Charity's life."

"I knows whose he is. Best bring him withs ya'," Lula May sat at the old table with a pestle and mortar before her as the men entered the time capsule that Mattie had left behind. Before Lula May said a word, she took the left hand of Will and examined it closely. She motioned for Hunter to come observe, "See this line, how it holds a wish bone dangling above the lifeline."

"Yes, Auntie."

"Remember's whats I tolds you about wishbones?" She asked. "Watch this man, he can break it into and think he wins because he holds both sides."

"Hibbery-gibberish, it ain't nothing," Will said.

"Do you's believes in nothin'?" Lula May looked at him. "I believes in nothin'. Nothin' is for sure Mr. Will, nothin' is for sure. I don't force people to believe in the old ways, they hears and sees its for themselves, then theys believes on their own free will or they denies what they saw or heard. Maybe they say what they saw was a hallucination. But who is to say that this life is not just that?" Lula May chuckled at her own musings, "It only matters just to me," as she prepared the mortar to grind.

"Mr. Will, now that's you are family, tells us a little about yourself," she grunted as she turned the lids off the Mason jars.

"Well, I was born in Oklahoma, my mother was half Cherokee, her mother was full blooded Cherokee, but Granny Thelma never lived on the reservation. Mom's daddy died in Korea. Granny married a bullhead Marine sergeant when I was little and moved to Paris Island, South Carolina. Dad was, is crazy, I think, always looking to make a quick buck with the least bit of effort required. Dad said his mama was Polish, his dad saw her when he went into Pittsburg for a picture show after a week in the mining camps. I asked him about our last name, he didn't know. Didn't really care what kind of name Zemp was, it means nothing, my father told me."

"Your grandfather ran off with another woman when your father was young," my mother told me. "The last time your father saw his father was when he was leaving them as his mother kneeled, pleaded, and begged, trying to block the front door while praying to God for him to stay. Your father held his sobbing mom after his father pushed her aside and walked out the door leaving her with three kids to rear alone. He never saw him again."

"We, my brother and I, lived with my Granny and her husband, who made us call him Pappy. I must have been eight when we first went down there. I had never seen the ocean before. Whenever mom and dad got arrested, which was often, and had to go to jail, which is where they are now…" Will paused, changed his mind about what he was about to say. "Believe me when I tell ya, Bonnie and Clyde was their favorite movie. They almost went out in a blaze of glory. My fourteenth birthday was the last time I saw them out of jail. Of course, they were on the run, very paranoid as I remember. Beaufort's where I graduated high school. So, I call South Carolina home. It wasn't long after I graduated high school that the episodes began. I'm schizophrenic they say. Granny Thelma said it was caused from all the drugs my momma was doing when she was pregnant with me. Said she popped acid like Pez."

"You just has sight of whats things could have been, they seem real 'cause they could have been," Lula May said opening another jar. "Sometimes you'lls be forced to see whethers you wants to or not," she sniffed the contents. "No modern medications wills ever stop that. But Lula May cans help you know what world you's inside of," she said before tasting a dried mushroom. Only after she pinched what she thought was enough of the mushrooms did she grind the ingredients into a paste with the pestle and mortar. The kettle blew as it had thousands of times before on the old stove. She walked in the old path of worn linoleum created by the generations that had visited the matriarchs that held court here spanning over three centuries and retrieved the whistling water. Will did not recognize the old grain pattern of wormy chestnut, but he took note of it. By the house's ancient nature, it was a holy place to her family.

Hunter took a small Florida souvenir spoon and scooped a small heap of the paste and with his finger pushed it into the teacup that sat before him. He did the same for Will and Lula May. His aunt made her way around the table filling their cups. Hunter stirred the concoction he knew would not taste good just by the smell. He passed the spoon to Will who looked at his hosts twice as the steam rose into his nose. Lula May poured the water into her cup and set the kettle on a trivet, shaped like an iron, resting in the center of the table. Lula May took the spoon out of Will's cup and swirled the paste and water together in her own cup. Eyes watering, she sipped her tea. The two men followed suit.

The old Felix clock ticked, keeping rhythm for the few animals left in the winter's woods making song. "It won't take long," Lula May warned.

With a rush of wind, the door opened, and a fox entered. He joined the table, jumping into the fourth chair and snickered at Lula May. He got up on the table and groomed his long tail when a barn owl flew in and perched on top of the refrigerator. The owl hooted over and over drawing Lula May's attention away from the fox. A rush of red rats ran through the door. The owl's eyes closed like a camera lens and the sound of advancing film echoed, as fast as the shutter closed, the owl snapped their necks and stacked the dead creatures into a perfect pyramid on the stove before they caught flame. The owl flew and rested on the windowsill and pecked on the pane. Lula May stood up and walked to the window. Opening the window, the owl flew out and rested on a chicken coop. A beautiful rooster strutted around a roost of chickens and mounted each in a wild frenzy, as one rooster left another took his place. It amounted to a mad chicken orgy. Each consecutive rooster crowed louder and louder with each and every chicken he bred. Lula May placed her hands over her ears.

The walls of the old house melted away and Will was once again at the day's fire. He watched the smoke rising from the burning house. He stood horrified as he observed the formation of an embryo within the cloud that rose from the burning house. The embryo grew quickly into a grown man. Thunder clapped, the rain began to fall, draining the human cloud above them. As the rain hit the cold ground, steam turned to fog and hugged the ground around them all. Will saw Matthew freeze in mid-step for no apparent reason, a doorframe appeared around him. Matthew looked directly at Lula May and Bonnie and grinned. The redheaded young man turned within the door and stared at Will sitting at the table with Hunter and Lula May. Will watched as everyone else got drenched but Matthew. His skin sucked in the rain like a sponge. As Will surveyed all around him he noticed that Bonnie took Matthew's hand and lead him out of the downpour. With Matthew's back now to his view, Will observed another face on the back of Matthew's head. Will felt as if he were witnessing the Roman God Janus manifest in human form before him. Will's face shone with amazement. He was dumbfounded.

Hunter dreamed he was a white girl, a girl who had nothing to lose. A girl who would do anything for the right amount of cash. Hunter sensed she was a super model extraordinaire and posed for her photographer, apparently a very rich photographer. Cash was surrounding Hunter. It fell like rain around her as the photographer moved close to the girl for her close-ups. The photographer then grabbed Hunter and kissed her, and swiftly a hand took hold of her breast, this she expected and made sensuous moans as she had been instructed to do by her agent.

The photographer brushed the hair away from her eyes while taking it in his hand. He snapped Hunter's head back and like a starving vampire, he fed on her fear, beads of panic-sweat crystallized like cocaine lines, and he snorted and licked the powder off of her skin before stuffing her mouth with money at every scream. Hunter felt the fear from every morphed mounting as he watched himself change from one squirming terrified girl to the next in the mirror above the bed. Then Hunter saw the photographer's head watching her from the mirror, but it was a different face than that of the photographer, it was the face of a Mrs. Bonnie's grandson, Matthew, and Hunter screamed as the sadist's head spun slowly around. Matthew's beautiful angelic face turned to face Hunter's in eye-to-eye contact before he kissed Hunter's lips, gently at first, before he rose to look into Hunter's eyes. Quickly, the redheaded youth's countenance turned mean and demonic. His lips came down and sucked the breath from her and his mouth rooted in each girls' soul before placing Hunter on all fours. The redheaded monster, with his frog-like tongue, fed on each smoke-ring cry uttered by every girl. He pounded their sex whilst he pulled their hair like the reins of a horse. Slapping them, he demanded more anguish with each crack of his riding crop.

After he had his way, each girl, though still alive, laid motionless, blooded, and psychologically flayed as the nude photographer stood over her and took one last photo. Matthew held a pillow over Hunter, his eyes inside a white girl widened with fear. Hunter, again the black man, gasped for breath. His dilated eyes shot open and the fear he felt faded slowly away. The racing of his heart mellowed and tears, now capable of being released, ran down the cheeks of his face.

Thunder clapped and wind and rain blew into the cottage through an open window. Revealing the landscape with each bolt that broke the darkness, Lula May shut the window as the storm still brewed. While she was returning to the table, she saw a snake curled up by the stove watching her as it was obviously warming itself. She took her broom and held the snake down before grabbing it behind its head and slinging it outside into the darkness. When the snake hit the ground, many heads sprung forth from it. Both men were stunned by what they witnessed and were not sure as to what reality they were residing. Lula May pointed at the fox and it cowered out the door tucking its tail as small birds cascaded down from Heaven, pecking on his head. Prepared to strike, the multiple-headed serpent rose up against the fox, which fled into the tall grass of a kept-back, untended field of tall brown pasture fluttering like flames in the hearth. The mutant serpent gave pursuit. Slamming the door shut, Lula May seemed to float to her chair. Three of the small birds perched in the window watched. She hastily grabbed hold of each man's hand, "Now tell me what you saw. Don't leave anything out."

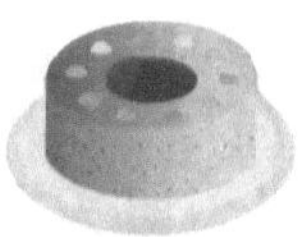

Chapter Twenty-Three

Ellis arrived early with Matthew and Oscar in tow. On the 28th of December, Iris threw her annual lingerie party for adults. Because of this, Iris was not happy about Oscar being present. It was shortly afterwards that Joy arrived with Mary Jane, both forms. The weed she was glad to see, the living girl, not so much. It was not that she didn't like her step-niece, she was worried that one of her clients might mistake her for one of her employees. Also, she did not want to get the reputation as a madam that supplied minors.

"Joy, what are you thinking?" Iris scolded. "I'm a madam, I have clients who may mistake her as one of my employees."

"They're not going to touch the Sheriff's daughter," Joy said.

"They have no clue who my brother is, or who you are," Iris countered. "It's bad enough that Ellis brought Oscar."

"Ellis brought Oscar?" Joy searched the room. I don't see him. A boy should lose his virginity with a normal girl his own age, don't you think?"

Iris scanned the room. She looked in the bedrooms where her girls were getting prepared for the show. In her most demanding dominatrix voice, "Oscar McCaskill, are you in here?" No response, she continued her search. Not finding the adolescent, she followed the barreling chuckle of Ellis as he politely laughed at a bad joke told by one of her regulars.

"Ellis, where are your boys?" Ellis looked around and raised his shoulders. Iris grabbed Ellis by his coat sleeve and hauled him over to Joy. "All guests under the age of twenty-one must be accompanied by a responsible adult at all times. Find them."

"They haven't gone far, Matthew is not going to miss your girls on the catwalk," Ellis snorted. "Especially Anne. They most likely stepped outside to drink from the pint they stole out of my desk that they think I didn't notice,"

Now that Matthew was back to his old self, Oscar wanted to party with his brother before he went back to college. Oscar figured if he played his cards right, he just might lose his virginity tonight. Most of the women he had caroled to not a week or so ago were engaged, or so they said. Oscar dragged his brother from trailer to trailer. "I'm serious man, these are women, not girls."

"I like girls, you can train them. Women have minds and needs of their own that must be satisfied first. I like it to be all about me bro," Dickey told Oscar. "Let's go back to the party."

Handing Matthew the pint they stole from their father's desk, Oscar said, "Let me show you one more place before we go back." Dickey was uneasy at first, he thought he knew the place, but neither he nor his host could recollect the trailer. How could one forget all of the concrete lawn decorations? He took the last swallow from the pint and tossed the empty onto the neighbor's lawn. Unable to conceal his excitement by his ridiculous grin, Oscar knocked. The dirty blond teen looked at the door, then his brother, then back to the door. For Oscar it was as if he were waiting for Santa Claus to come down the chimney. With the opening of the door, promptly Dickey remembered why he felt so nerved from the place.

"Shit no," Dickey exclaimed as his body drained to white in fear of Penelope.

Wiping her mouth with the back of her hand, "Can I help you?" Penelope asked the star-struck Oscar.

"My Aunt Grace and Aunt Iris are having a party and I came to invite you."

"Iris Sakamoto?" a voice articulated from inside, followed by the head and bare shoulders of Frank Payne jutting in the doorframe parallel to the floor.

"One and the same," Oscar replied tilting his head.

"You remember Iris, she was the Asian girl that rode on your brother's bus," Frank said looking up, trying to make eye contact with Penelope. "You have to remember her. She and her brother were the first Asians to attend Dixon High."

"Of course, I remember, I thought she got her MBA at State. She lives here?"

"She owns here," Oscar said with pride.

"Well, I guess we must attend if the owner of this fine establishment has invited us. Give us a minute will you, please?" Penelope requested placing her large hand on Frank's head, shoving him out of the way as she shut the door.

"She was giving him head when you knocked, you know," Dickey uttered through Matthew to Oscar.

"How do you know?"

"The way she wiped her mouth when she opened the door and the fact that her friend was butt naked or he would have stood in the door to ask about Aunt Iris. You'll learn," Dickey chuckled as the couple came outside.

"Lead the way boys," Penelope, in her faux rabbit fur coat Frank gave her for Christmas, said, locking hands with her beau.

When the brothers and their guests arrived, Iris' fashion show was about to begin. While Joy to Mary Jane debated as to where to sit, Grace and Iris teased and delighted dozens of guests, mostly men, as they mingled in what no one would guess was the interior of a modular home. Oscar was extremely proud of his guest, "Aunt Grace, I'd like you to meet Penelope the Punisher."

At the utterance of her name, men in the know, those with teenage sons, turned toward the boy and the Amazon, some even gasped, "It is her."

"How do you do, thank you so much for the invite, Grace, I'm sure you remember my boyfriend, Frank Payne."

Grace shook their hands and made small talk. Dickey immediately went and stood by Mary Jane, "Hi, Mary Jane."

"Hey, Matthew."

"There you are. I was wondering where you and your brother got off to. Y'all didn't get into any trouble, did you?" Iris asked.

"No mam', not unless you consider lying and telling a professional female wrestler and her tow-truck-driving boyfriend that your aunts invited them to their party is trouble, nothing happened," Matthew answered.

"Damn, she's tall. Guess I'd better go introduce myself. Both of you stay in clear view," Iris said as she meandered over to her first celebrity guest.

"You're pretty, you know," Dickey flirted with the twelve-year-old.

"Thanks Matthew. No one but my mom has ever told me that."

"She's right. Do you have a boyfriend yet?"

"Kelly Gardner asked me to the movies Thanksgiving weekend, he tried to kiss me, but it didn't work out."

"Why not?"

"When he leaned over to kiss me, he farted and I started laughing. I couldn't help myself. He tried again, but his brothers, who sat behind us, made farting sounds every time he leaned my way and I'd start laughing again."

"It's rough being the youngest brother," Dickey remembered. Realizing Matthew was the oldest he added, "a couple of my friends were the youngest brother and got hell."

Before Dickey could get out another word, Grace announced, "Folks, take your seats, the show is about to begin." Joy found Mary Jane and sat next to her. Oscar sat next to Penelope across the room from Matthew. Ellis, who was sitting next to Oscar, motioned for Matthew to come sit next to him. But before Matthew could move, the music started, which was the cue for the show to begin.

Anne, Charlotte, and Emily, each in different colors of red, white, and black leatherette bustiers with matching stilettos, stepped into the living room in perfect sequence to Peaches' erotically provocative grooves. They reached their position, snapped their whips, and chrome poles rose from the floor to the ceiling. Each girl gave a swing around the pole before moving to the clientele. Anne and Emily first made their way to Matthew. Anne wrapped her whip around his neck and plunged his face into her breast and Emily placed the tip of her stiletto under Matthew's crotch drawing the handle of her whip from his belt buckle to his chin, lifting his face to a kiss on the nose. As Emily left to tease another guest, Mary Jane noticed her cousin's undeniable erection.

Joy turned and became aware of what her daughter was staring at, bent over and whispered in her ear, "Don't stare darling. See Oscar across the room, look at how funny he's sitting? Boys around your age just can't help it. Watch the models."

Charlotte was the last of the girls to show her wares to Matthew. She noticed the effect the others had on him and jiggled her whip's tip, tickling his trousers bulging mass before turning to her left. Bent over at just the right level so as to expose her cleavage, she extended her right leg and ran her fingers over the roman styled straps of her stilettos and with the extended nail of her index finger, his gaze, in almost a metaphysical jealousy, distinguished each of her buckles as they ran up high along her long leg. Dickey was salivating, it was more than Dickey could bear. He turned her so her bumper was in his face, stood tall against her and grounded rhythmically into her, running his hands to her breast. The redhead lifted her straight against his body to her surprise and everyone else in the room, especially Mary Jane's. Charlotte searched the room for Iris to read how to respond. Before she could find her madam, Dickey took his hand and turned the girl's face to his for a kiss. The next set of models came into the room followed by Iris.

Iris, noticing the dirty dancing that was taking place, made her way to the pair when she heard a pounding at the door. "Matthew, this is a fashion show. Charlotte needs to change into her next outfit. Y'all can dance later." Dickey ignored her. Iris made her way to the door.

"Iris, Grace, open this door and open it now!" Faith screamed.

"Oh shit, it's Faith." Iris pointed at Ellis and with her finger she dragged him to her. "Your wife is at the door."

Ellis opened the door and Faith bulldozed into the room and the music stopped. Faith noticed Matthew with his hands firmly on the dominatrix breast. "What in God's name is going on here?" Faith said to her husband.

"I am having a lingerie party," Iris said. "You're late, so have a seat or take your concerns with your husband outside."

"Well, I never," Faith gasped. "You have children here."

"With their parents. Your sister and husband chose to bring them. They know what kind of party I am throwing."

"Matthew, what are you doing to that girl?" Faith screamed at her son.

"I'm hiding my boner in her butt cheeks and playing with her tits!" Dickey said to every one's surprise.

"Don't talk to your mother that way," Ellis said to Matthew.

"Anything else would be an obvious lie, and we shouldn't lie, should we mother?"

Faith stormed over to Oscar, grabbed the boy by his ear and dragged him toward the door. "It was nice meeting you, Penelope," Oscar shouted, waving goodbye to the professional wrestler.

"Ellis, we'll talk more when you get home," Faith said over her tears. She dragged her youngest son through the door leaving it open. Ellis walked over to his other son, pulling him apart from the model, he said, "Son, the model needs to go change into another outfit." Ellis noticed that they were the center of attention, "Forgive my wife, she's having difficulties with her baby boy becoming a man." Placing his arm around Matthew, they walked over to the wrestler and her boyfriend and took their seats. There was another knock at the door.

"I've got this," Grace said. When she opened the door, there stood her other sister, Charity, with Will Zemp beside her. "Come on in. Glad you could make it. You just missed a scene made by our sister Faith. Joy is here with Mary Jane. Why don't y'all have a seat next to them?"

After the fashion show, the guests mingled with the 'models.' Ellis opened his wallet and counted out seven Franklins, five for Matthew and two for the new Slavic girl for himself. Iris and Ellis stood in the kitchen and watched as Charlotte, Anne, and Emily danced provocatively with Matthew. Matthew called them his angels. Ellis was stunned at his son's lascivious style of dancing. His lack of shame was startling. He wasn't sure if this behavior was generational or peculiar to Matthew. "I love these angels, they're sent from heaven just for me!" Matthew belted above the music. Charity henceforth referred to the evening as "Matthew's Angel Party."

This was that night that Charity grew a beard. She had not originally planned to proposition Will, but there was a clarity that cascaded into an obvious solution, and as she and Will stood outside catching the clear clean air, Charity said, "My mother has always wanted me to be with a man. It's only happened once, which led to Hope, and it will never happen again. I'm a proud lesbian and I have no plans of even trying to change. But if you marry me and set my mother's mind at ease, you'll have an allowance and will never be homeless again."

"How about seeing other women?" Will asked.

"I don't plan on giving them up, "Charity snickered. "I don't see why you should either. Just be discreet for Momma's sake. If you fall in love by chance, I'll give you a divorce. But please try to wait 'til mother has passed, or she'll try to find another man for me."

"Are there any other conditions?"

"It will all be spelled out in the prenuptial. Will you marry me, Mr. Zemp?"

"I will," Will said. The two shook hands, looked at each other, then kissed ever so briefly on the lips as Grace snapped a photo of the two.

"Let's go tell my mom. And remember, you were the one to ask me." Grace took photos of most of the guests. Matthew, Anne, Emily, and Charlotte posed for Grace, at first in the Charlie's Angels' pose, followed by various romantic Vanity Fair style compositions. She printed the artistic images she thought her mom might enjoy and sent them home with Charity as she and Will left.

When Charity and Will returned to Ethel's, they found Lula May and Hunter sitting with the White sisters around the kitchen table. As they sipped on coffee, slices of Ethel's fruitcake sat barely touched on the plates before them. "So, how was the party?" Hunter asked.

"Well, apparently, we missed the main action. Faith showed up not too happy that Matthew and Oscar were there, much less Ellis. Matthew refused to leave, but she dragged poor Oscar out by his ear."

"So, did you enjoy the party Will?"

"What was there not to like? Women in lingerie, Matthew's Angels, meeting a professional female wrestler, and asking the woman I love to marry me and her saying yes."

"Who's that?" Hunter teased, "Are you talkin' 'bout Miss Charity?" Will grinned. Bonnie stood up; "Thank you, Jesus," she shouted running around the table to embrace her 'baby girl.'

"I's told you," Lula May said. "Now, didn't I?"

"Well congratulations," Ethel said and then squealed. "We're going to have a wedding."

"Oh," Charity said, hearing the paper crunch in her coat as her mother hugged her, "Grace took some pictures tonight. She printed out some copies for you."

Bonnie glanced at the pictures and set them on the table. Hunter picked them up and started looking at them. The look on his face caught Lula May's attention. "What's wrong?" Lula May asked.

"That's me as a white girl," Hunter pointed at the image of Anne.

"Lord no, I feared it so," Lula May said.

Bonnie was too involved with Charity and Will, but Ethel heard her second mother's words. "Feared what so?" Ethel asked.

"Dickey Dickson's soul is free from hell. What's worse is he's possessed ours' little Rooster."

"But how? We sealed Dickey with evergreen," Ethel questioned.

"Somehow, he was released from hell before the fire, the sly fox told me so. But when the house burned down and caught the seal on fire, it destroyed the passage to send him back. Only Damballah can return him to where he belongs. I have never called on him because he can take the living as well as the dead. He has many mouths to feed."

"Chillen'," Lula May stood, "we have a freed demon to capture."

"What demon?" Bonnie said, "We have a wedding to plan."

"Dickey Dickson is free."

"It can't be," Bonnie said.

"I knew it!" Charity said, "It was the night we made the fruitcakes. I opened the tin you had set aside for the Preacher. His smell filled the room."

"All seven who sealed him in hell were present that night," Lula May said realizing that was the night, "it was the only way for the seal to be broken."

"But who would do such a thing?" Hunter asked.

"Faith," Bonnie said shaking her head, "She prays as she breathes."

"She didn't do it intentionally. I know the heart of the girl, she wouldn't do it after all that he did to her," Ethel said.

"I'm sure you'z right, cause she'd never knowingly bring a demon to reside under her roof."

"What do you mean?" Bonnie inquired.

"Will," Lula May startled the lanky man, "Will drank the tea of the Mother with me and Hunter Christmas night. His vision is pure. Come sit next to Lula May, tell my chillen' what you saw." They all sat around the table as Will told them his vision.

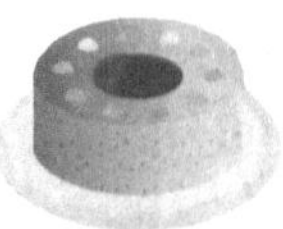

Chapter Twenty-Four

Dickey Dickson now possessed the body and stamina of a nineteen-year-old, almost twenty years in hell only to be reprieved into the fine specimen that is his own flesh and blood. The male form in his first life was not of much importance to his generation. Although never fat, Dickey never worked out or developed any definition to his outer shell. It was as if his son had created a new, more perfect, body for him. Because of this and knowing Matthew had been fantasizing about this moment for days, he didn't mind sharing these women with his son. It would be like the old days with George, Dickey thought, but with the advantage of being inside her head and doubling his pleasure. He brought forth Matthew's consciousness to enjoy and share in the delight that these three beauties were supplying. Indeed, Dickey was giving training to Matthew that most men, married or not, were ill equipped to give from simple lack of experience in the art of multiple lovers in the same bed.

The commands Dickey was giving the girls penetrated the bedroom walls of the mobile home Iris had supplied for Ellis and his son. Ellis, now aware of the ruse Faith had pulled almost twenty years ago, felt no guilt receiving head while propped up in the king-sized bed, cigar in one hand and a single malt Scotch in the other. This was indeed an act of revenge against his wife. He wondered if she had not shown up if he would have paid for Oscar to lose his virginity. He knew in his heart that he brought Oscar as a way out, but single malt has a way of making a man want to find a means into that warm, soft and moist spot on a woman. The spot on his wife had long been cold, dry, and frigid for him anyways. He laid back and enjoyed the Gypsy woman, admiring her hourglass form which sprawled before him.

Matthew went muff diving with Dickey as his guide. It was not the first time Matthew had the taste of a woman in his mouth, but it was the first time he had made a girl squirm. Emily was surprised by the skill of the youth, only other women and older men had been able to manipulate her in such a glorious fashion, but their sex and/or their age was always a reminder that she was at work. With Matthew she was able to let go of herself and indulge in the pleasure. "Eat Me!" she screamed wrapping her hands around the post of the old brass bed. "Oh, God, don't stop!"

Matthew came up for air, his sex buried deep in Anne's mouth, her warm nasal exhale overwrought his pubic region to a breaking point. "Slap my balls somebody!" Dickey said, realizing Matthew was about to release. He knew the results Matthew wouldn't anticipate. Enjoying Anne's sex, Charlotte lifted up and did as commanded. Popping them firmly from underneath, she watched as the furry red globes descended from their perched position as Matthew let out a yelp of joyous pain and shivered. She gently stroked them as he continued to quake, pulling them further down 'til they sank to the periphery of his scrotum and rested tenderly on Anne's chin. "Slap my ass, Charlotte!" Dickey demanded before he once again dove into Emily. "Sorry, but we want this to last, son. The night's just begun," Dickey said to Matthew inside their shared head.

Ellis could not believe the groans vibrating from his son and those three girls.

"What kind of porn has this boy been watching?" Ellis wondered, after he heard Matthew demand that Charlotte eat his ass. It was something Ellis had never experienced. He, for some unknown reason, thought it very gay to play with your anus other than to wipe it. Even when he went in for a physical, he never considered the act anything but medical.

Anne, who was being ground into a royal jelly by Matthew, watched the young man's face as Charlotte tunneled into his nether regions. the original surprise expressed was followed by a succession of matchless faces. Emily, who lacked interest in women sexually, ran her nails lightly up his back into the cusp of Matthew's auburn hair before trailing them down deep into his firm broad back leaving vertical ribbons of red. This caused a monstrous moan to be bellowed out of Matthew's mouth.

"Doesn't it hurt so good?" Dickey groaned to his son.

Emily, no longer the object of Matthew's attention, said, "I'm gonna light this joint." Charlotte looked at the clock, it was a quarter 'til two. Charlotte's nipples followed the red tracks Emily's nails had made. She placed her tongue in his ear and then quietly whispered to Matthew, "You've been a very bad boy. Should mama get daddy's belt?"

Anne took note at the fear that was on Matthew's face as his mouth uttered something different than what it seemed he wanted to say, "Yes, mam."

As Charlotte rose off Matthew she said, "I'll be right back boy." Emily held the joint to Matthew and Anne's lips with the shut of the door. Charlotte knocked gently and entered into Ellis' room. Nina was spooned against Ellis as he stoked his cigar. Ever the businesswoman, Charlotte, a little disheveled, sat on the edge of the bare bed in a robe she retrieved from the bathroom.

"I hate to interrupt Mr. McCaskill, but since you are paying for our services, I need to know if you would like us to continue with your son. Another hour will be three hundred more for all three of us." Ellis asked how much longer before those rates kicked in. "Fifteen minutes," Charlotte said after looking up at the clock. There was one ticking in every room.

"Do what you have to do to get the boy off," Ellis said. "Christmas has already shot my bonus load. Charlotte, right?"

"Yes, sir."

"Thanks for asking."

"Yes, sir, I need to borrow your belt," Charlotte drew the belt from Ellis pants and left the room. As Charlotte walked in, she caught the other girls' eyes and looked up to the clock. "So, you've been a bad boy," Charlotte said, not giving Matthew time to respond before bringing the belt down across his white buttocks. Matthew drove deep into Anne, she moaned louder than she ever had earlier.

"God Damn it woman!" Dickey screamed turning back to look at Charlotte.

"Cursing like that in front of ladies," Charlotte brought the belt quickly down once again. "Answer me, Boy!" Charlotte demanded as a red warm glow radiated from her strikes across Matthew's mounds of whiteness.

"Yes, mam," Dickey growled. "Please stop," Matthew begged. The voices seemed to be made by two different people, Emily thought. "You can take it boy," Dickey told Matthew, "Dickson's can take anything… I deserve another," Dickey told Charlotte who obliged by striking at a different angle. "Oh, God," Matthew cried out arching his back finding himself as deep as he'd ever been inside a woman. The pain and pleasure rattled all that was in him. "Feel that boy, don't it hurt so good?" Dickey said in terseness to Matthew.

"Fuck me hard, Matthew, Fuck Me!" Anne squealed.

Dickey directed Matthew in a rotating grinding with fast short strokes that placed a true face of pleasure to Anne's demands. Just as the heat on his butt was dissipating, Matthew lifted his buttocks upward. Charlotte greeted the flesh with the leather strap sending Matthew plowing his hardness deep again into Anne. His pulsing rod of nerves reached into Anne, and she shuddered beneath him. "Again," Dickey cried aloud, "You can hold on boy, take another," he said in the young man's head. "Please, I don't want another," Matthew cried out, but it was too late, the belt struck flesh causing Matthew to wail. Matthew was to the point of tears, never had he had such a conflict of sensations pouring through his body.

Charlotte looked at the clock, stuck her finger in her mouth, and said to Anne, "I need to drive the point home."

"Fuck me, Matthew!" Anne demanded again.

As Matthew lifted his rear-end up, Charlotte drove her wet finger deep into Matthew's anus. He screamed, "Lord Jesus!" as he fell into Anne's warm softness. He released himself into Anne, jerking in convulsions. Charlotte thought, *This is the kind of night that would have even made Anais Nin proud,* as she continued to massage his prostate milking all his seed into the condom deeply planted within Anne. Matthew started to cry.

"Don't cry boy, damn it, don't cry," Dickey demanded. It was too late, the tears descended onto Anne. Matthew was released, not just from his own angst, but from Dickey as well.

A quick rap on the door, Matthew looked over his shoulder as Ellis entered the room. He witnessed Charlotte removing her finger from Matthew's anus. "All done here," she said to the man wearing just his boxer shorts. Breathing heavily, Matthew turned back and looked deep into Anne's eyes.

"Damn, I'm a woman," Dickey said huskily. Only Matthew was aware it came from Anne's mouth. He jolted off of her, condom still attached and filled with his bodily fluids. Matthew wondered if he had just fucked a transvestite. He looked at his father, and then back at Anne, now propped up on her elbows.

"Son, we've got to go, it's 2 AM and I'm sure your mother is still up waiting for us. Get dressed and say goodbye to your angels," Ellis said to a still quivering Matthew. Emily walked over to Matthew and offered him the joint. He declined to Emily's surprise. She rolled the condom off his still-throbbing penis.

"Damn," she said holding the condom up for all to see. "How long have you been holding on to that load?" Ellis, seeing more than he wanted to see, returned to his room to finish dressing. Before he finished buttoning his shirt, Matthew was standing inside, staring at the woman who lay naked on the bed, snoring. His pants now on, Ellis took out a twenty-dollar tip and placed it on the dresser.

Anne knocked on the door before opening it. Ellis with his wallet still opened pulled out sixty more and gave it to Matthew. All in their underclothes, Emily and Charlotte stood behind Anne. An embarrassed Matthew stuttered, "I thought y'all were just college girls, I had no idea that y'all were…"

"Whores?" Charlotte stated, handing Ellis his belt.

Emily took the twenty from him. "Let me give you a tip, Matthew. We are college girls, women that will have degrees with no debt," Emily said assuredly.

Charlotte, dismayed at the change in Matthew's attitude began to rant, "Please tell me why it is guys can fuck as many girls as they like, wallow like pigs in mud and come up clean, smelling like roses, no taint for the deeds done? But if a girl does the same, she's a slut. Give this some thought, if you take a girl out on a date to McDonald's, do you think you're gonna get laid? But if you take a girl fine dining, you count on it. Did she like you, maybe, maybe not? But you just laid out some major bucks on dinner, so she fucks you. It just makes you both feel better that it was paid with by food and not cash. It doesn't change the fact that she is still a whore. We all just had a really good time for less than it cost for a really good dinner for four at Capital Grill. Ask your dad if you don't believe me," she added.

Matthew dropped his head staring at the money in his hand.

"I'll say this about you, I've never seen a guy behave so differently after sex. It's as if you are scared of us. We're the ones who should be scared of you after all the rough play you demanded," Charlotte said to Matthew with a "Thank you" when handed the twenty, "my ass is going to be sore for days."

"You're really good at sex Matthew, you should consider going to work for your aunts," Emily said in all bluntness. "Trust me, no one 'til you has ever given me a true orgasm from oral sex. You're a true champ."

"Can't I get a kiss?" Anne asked. "Forgive my voice, it's just a little raw."

Realizing all that he had done with and to the girls, Matthew turned beet-red in shame and shook his head no, "God, please forgive me," he said. He hung his head and left the trailer completely distraught.

Anne started to cry, not from anything Matthew had said, nor the fact that he didn't kiss her, though her business associates thought so. During Charlotte and Emily's rants, Dickey had gone deep into the girl's psyche to find her weaknesses. Dickey used these against her, taking her into memories of childhood abuse, not physical or sexual, but the constant emotional debasement she suffered from her parents' words, which caused a feeling of worthlessness.

Ellis sighed loudly before yammering, "It's that damn Bob Jones University that has fucked him up girls, be glad you're going to a real university. I thought I had Matthew back to normal, but this born-again virgin shit is just too much."

"Hope he finds a Mary Magdalene, because whoever he ends up with, they sure have a freak show on their hands," Emily added.

"He's anything but normal," Dickey grinned in Anne's scratchy voice. "But that's a good thing." Ellis wiped the tears from Anne's face, "Thank you, Mr. McCaskill." Anne reached up on her toes, her wet damp cheeks touching his as she kissed him. Ellis, like Anne before him, absorbed the demon's tears. Dickey was once again in a man's body. Dickey wrapped his arms around the girl, and then slapped Anne on the ass as he departed with a swagger in his stride. Nina snored and the girls jumped having forgotten she was there.

"I guess we know what side the freak falls on," Emily noted.

"That goes down as the strangest fuck ever," Anne said feeling a bit dizzy from Dickey's release, "I'm still reeling from it."

"Iris owes us a bonus," Charlotte added.

"Good point, Lord Jesus," Emily mocked with enthusiasm as they all laughed together.

As they drove home, Dickey wasn't sure what to say to Matthew. He searched Ellis' memory to try to understand his son. The more he searched through Ellis' memories, the more the demon side of him broiled. The oddest thing about being a demon, Dickey thought, was knowing the universal truth, Heaven and Hell, everything in between and all the creatures of the universe that reside in its abodes. The 'saintly' he toyed with regularly in Hell. He would not return to damnation if he could help it, but if he had to return to the realms of eternal torment, he would take a thousand gashes upon his soul to have the honor of torturing Faith. He may have placed her on the path to her own vain holiness, but she plowed her own grave by denouncing her humanity long before her last breath.

"Son, are you alright?"

"You don't have to call me son anymore, I know who my real father was."

With the combined fury of Ellis and Dickey an unnatural roar bellowed, "I am your father, you are my son!" The voice waves penetrated through Matthew, rattling the windows. Matthew was frightened because within the voice of Ellis, which he had known all his life, was also the voice of Dickey, which he recently found speaking to him inside his head.

"Son, talk to me, I am your father," the combined voices demanded.

"I broke my vow to God to stay pure. I am ashamed of what I have done. I feel you think less of me as a man because you found me with a woman's finger up my ass. I'm confused because of the pleasure it caused. I'm angry that I know what that feels like and even angrier that I want to feel it again. I'm angry that there is a God. I'm angry that there is a Heaven and Hell. I'm angry at the voices in my head. I'm angry with you and Anne and Charlotte and Emily. I'm angry that my entire family lied to me about who I am. I don't know who I am. I'm confused."

"It's okay, son," the combined voices said.

"It's not okay. I'm not okay. I've got to figure this out on my own," Matthew said nothing more. When they arrived home both men went to their bedrooms without saying another word.

Faith was sitting up in bed when Ellis walked into the room. Dickey allowed Ellis to come forth to the front. He knew a woman scorned when he saw one and he had no interest in tangling with her. His mind was on his boy, he realized for the first time how his own father must have felt.

"I want a divorce," Faith barked at Ellis as he undressed.

"On what grounds?"

"Adultery."

"I'm the one with adultery and fraud charges, missy!"

"You've cheated on me. I know you have."

"Prove it," Ellis demanded as he made his way into the bathroom turning on the shower.

Faith in her flannel nightgown stared at him looking for tell-tale signs of his behavior, hickeys, bite marks, the leftover remains of bodily fluids. *Nothing,* she said to herself as she watched Ellis step into the shower. "I saw you at a whorehouse with those women dressed in you know what."

"You saw me at a lingerie party with your sister Joy, the sheriff's wife, her daughter Mary Jane, Iris, the Sheriff's sister and your other two sisters were there as well. I'd call that a family reunion myself. By the way, if your mother hasn't already told you, Charity is engaged to that homeless man with the fruitcake from the shelter. The one who went back into the fire and saved her life, what's his name," Ellis paused to think. "Will Zemp," Dickey told him. "Will Zemp, that's right"

"Charity is getting married?"

"Yep."

"To a man?"

"It's the only kind of marriage this state allows."

"God be praised," Faith said.

"I paid for Matthew to get laid. He's angry at himself for, what did he say, oh yeah, breaking his vow to God to stay pure."

Faith's face turned red, "You ungodly man, you are bound for Hell!" she screamed at him. "I need to go pray with my baby."

"The hell you are!" Soap still in his hair, he stepped out of the shower and grabbed her before she reached the bedroom door. "You have fucked that boy's mind up enough. It's going to take years of psychiatric treatment to get the boy straight." Faith turned and slapped Ellis. This turned Dickey on and for Faith, not in a good way. Like a teenage boy, Dickey was immediately to the point in his desires. Lifting Faith up, he tossed her onto the bed, after one bounce of her body, Dickey had lifted her gown with one hand and removed her panties with the other. Faith, after looking into her husband eyes, knew his intentions. Propping up on her elbows like a crab, she tried to retreat from his physically expressed intentions. Grabbing the lanky woman by the ankles, he dragged Faith toward him, her auburn hair created a fan that framed the white features of her face and flamed the desires of Dickey.

"All these years and you have maintained your figure for me," Dickey growled.

"You're drunk!"

"With lust!" Dickey said, "By God, you are going to serve your husband and perform your wifely duties!" With ease, Dickey reached down and removed Faith's bra. Placing his other hand under the small of her back, he lifted her up against him taking her breast in his mouth.

"Dear Jesus, please don't," Faith cried.

"No prayers are going to save you. You are mine under God and I'm going to have you," Dickey said staring into Faith's watering eyes. Dickey brushed back her hair before drawing his tongue along her long neck. Feeling her tears fall, he licked the wetness from her cheeks and smiled. Pulling the flannel gown off of her, he placed her on the bed like a plate on a table, examining the dish he was about to devour, the demon salivated. *What to eat first?* he thought.

When Matthew came into his room, he turned on the lamp by the bed. Oscar had been waiting up all night to find out if he had gotten laid. He turned over on his elbow to ask his brother about the night, but his eyes popped and his jaw dropped. Oscar was speechless. The removal of his brother's shirt revealed the scratches Emily made down his back. When Matthew dropped his pants, Oscar saw the bright red bruising stripes across his brother's buttocks. Matthew was in such a hurry to leave the scene he did not bother to retrieve his underwear.

"Holy shit, bro, looks like you got real kinky tonight."

Turning to see his brother awake, Matthew replied, "I guess you can say that." Wincing as he sat down, Matthew started to sob.

"What happen bro, you can tell me," Oscar said sincerely.

"I'm going to Hell, Oscar," Matthew cried. "I'm going to Hell."

"What'd you do?"

"What didn't I do would be a quicker answer."

"Who with?"

"All three of 'em, Anne, Emily, and Charlotte." Matthew said, "I did everything the voice in my head told me to do."

"What do you mean the voice in your head?"

"Satan had hold of me Oscar. He showed me the ways of sin and I enjoyed every minute of it. Satan has a hold of me. He spoke to me and through me. I did things to those girls and he had them do things to me, things I'd never thought of doing or ever wanted done."

"Did you enjoy it?"

"Too much, way too much," Matthew sobbed uncontrollably. "God has left me Oscar. I'm going to hell."

Oscar wanted to ask if he could smell his fingers but thought better of it. Oscar got out of bed and retrieved a pair of sweats and handed them to his brother, "Do you still love Jesus?" Pulling on a pair of sweatpants, Matthew nodded yes. "Then I wouldn't worry too much about it, Matthew. Jesus forgives everything if you are truly repentant, and it doesn't take an elder or a preacher to tell that you are truly remorseful. Jesus will forgive you, hell, he already has," Oscar said before returning to his bed.

"What happen to your frigid ways, bitch?" Dickey demanded. Oscar and Matthew heard what they thought was bound to be one hell of a fight coming from their parents' bedroom. "You're wanting it, tell me you want it!" Dickey continued.

Oscar chuckled, "I've never heard them in the act before." Matthew, recognizing Dickey's voice, shivered with fear, and said, "Satan." With that statement, Oscar became very worried about his brother. Matthew pulled up his covers to his neck. Whispering in prayer, the red head started quoting the twenty-third Psalm.

Turning over, staring into the night, Oscar thought to himself, "I'll call Aunt Grace, she'll know what to do."

Chapter Twenty-Five

Dickey woke up to Faith singing in the shower, her voice was heaven compared to the shrill screams of torture he had endured without end for nearly two decades. She sang the chorus to "I'll Fly Away" over and over, which Dickey noticed was like shrieking to Ellis' mind. With a shower cap still on her head and a towel around her body, she came into the bedroom and went directly to her closet.

"Morning," Dickey said.

"Good, you're up. Tracey called from the office first thing this morning. She said to remind you that you have to be at the county courthouse at 10:00 am for the Todd case and that you forgot the file. I have to go pick up Sally, she has a dental appointment at 10:30. It's nine, you better get a rollin'," Faith said coming out of the closet fully dressed. She returned the towel and shower cap to the bathroom. Looking in the mirror as she combed her hair she thought, *the beauty of being a Christian is the time it saves not dealing with make-up.* Satisfied with her hair, she sauntered out the bathroom straight to the bedroom door, leaving with a "Ciao."

Dickey was astonished, she had conducted herself as if he hadn't breached every cavity in her body last night. He had turned her into a depraved wanton woman. He searched Ellis' memory for moments spent in marital sport only to find missionary boredom. Dickey was intrigued. He heard from the bottom of the stairs, "Court, 10:00 AM!" and the shutting of the door. There was no need to bring attention to Ellis, the attorney had slept most of the night. It was time to let him out. "File at office, court at ten, it's a little after nine," Dickey told Ellis before retreating to the back of his mind.

Ellis made his way down to the kitchen. Oscar was downstairs eating cereal and playing video games on his PlayStation, "You and mom were sure loud last night."

"Sorry about that," Ellis said throwing a frozen sausage biscuit into the microwave. "Couples fight."

"That's the kind of fightin' I'm looking forward to," Oscar smirked.

"What?" The microwave dinged. "I'm running late son, got to run by the office and be at court in," looking at his watch, "twenty minutes." Briefcase and sausage biscuit in one hand, Ellis poured some coffee in his thermos and ran out the door as the home phone began to ring. "Answer that Oscar," Ellis requested, "if it's the office tell them I'm on my way."

"Hello, McCaskill residence," Oscar answered.

"Oscar, it's your Aunt Ethel calling, is your mother around?"

"No mam', she took Sally to the dentist."

"How about your sister Hope?"

"I'm not sure," she answered.

"Will you check for me, I need to talk to her, please."

Oscar knocked on his sisters' door, "Hey Hope, Aunt Ethel is on the house phone. She wants to talk to you."

Groggily Hope answered, "What's she want? Tell her I'll be there in a minute."

Oscar returned to the kitchen, "Hi Aunt Ethel, she'll be right down."

"Oscar, how's Matthew doing?"

"Weirdly, that college has gotten hold of him, that's for sure," he said.

"What you mean sugar?"

"I'd rather not say, it's kind of embarrassing. Let's just say I ain't ever known him to be this religious." Oscar heard the trampling of Hope down the stairs. "Here's Hope, Aunt Ethel, say hi to Bonnie Gram for me."

"Hello," Hope answered.

"Hope darling, it's your Aunt Ethel. I was going over to Lula May's old house to visit and have lunch and I was wondering if you'd like to tag along for the ride? She always makes extra you know."

"Sure, that sounds like fun," Hope smiled.

"Pick you up shortly after eleven then, goodbye."

"Goodbye."

"What was that all about?" Oscar asked.

"Aunt Ethel and I are going to have lunch with Miss Lula May," Hope said sticking out her tongue at her younger brother, who quickly returned the gesture with his middle finger.

"Lula May likes me best you know!" Oscar shouted at his sister.

Ellis had called ahead to Tracey, his secretary, who walked out of his office and handed him the file. "Call the courthouse, tell them I may be a few minutes behind. Then call Rick Todd and tell him the same." Ellis looked at his watch as he sat at the stoplight waiting for it to turn green. He thought about what Oscar had said and then pondered on Matthew's behavior at Iris' party. He took a sip of coffee as he pulled into the intersection when the light turned green.

Jackie Williams was running late as well when the light turned yellow, "I can make it, I can make it," he hit the accelerator. The old Mercury plowed into the Jeep Cherokee's driver's door, turning the vehicle on its side as it glided down Broad Street, smearing a pedestrian into the road before mangling a Grand AM and trapping its driver inside. Before turning over, Ellis smacked his head on the door knocking him out cold. He dangled from his seatbelt as coffee poured over the airbags onto the passenger window. Jackie Williams would be late for work no more. Not wearing his seatbelt because it no longer worked, he hit the steering wheel, and it crushed his chest. When thrown back against a seat with no headrest, his neck snapped. Jackie Williams, a man always hustling for a dime at everyone else's expense, was dead.

When Charity and Lloyd Parker arrived on the scene, Charity immediately noticed her brother-in-law's vehicle. Lloyd, on the other hand, straight away recognized his best childhood bud's classic. Charity evaluated the state of affairs and called for backup. She calmly made her way to Ellis' Jeep, looked inside, and could tell he was breathing. She tried to open the door. That wasn't happening. She then saw a set of legs in a pair of red Converse poking out from beneath the rear of Ellis'

SUV. She rolled up the pants leg and felt for a pulse. She shook her head, seeing Charity, the man in the Grand AM honked his horn. Charity rushed to the passenger's side and opened the car's unlocked door, "It's alright, we'll get you out. Are you hurt anywhere?"

"I heard my leg snap and I think my nose is broken," the man said, his hand over his face. "I'm a hemophiliac."

"I know it hurts, but you've got to keep pressure on your nose. I'll be right back with the 'jaws of life' to get you out of there."

When Charity turned the corner, she saw Parker performing CPR on his friend. He stopped to check for a pulse, nothing. He returned to CPR, "Come on Jackie, you've got a wife and kids!"

The Yerby Twins were on the scene as Charity reached Lloyd, "We have a hemophiliac trapped in the Grand AM that needs the 'jaws of life,' a casualty under the SUV, my brother-in-law's unconscious inside the SUV," she felt for a pulse then looked into the eyes of the man lying on the street, "another casualty from the Mercury."

"Parker, he's gone," Charity said. "You've got to go work on Ellis. He's part of my family, I can't. You know regulations. I have a hemophiliac that is bleeding and is trapped. The Yerby twins are going to have to pry him out while I work to keep him stabilized. Please, go help Ellis."

When Ellis regained consciousness, Dickey saw two Principalities and a Guardian amongst the pile-up. The one Principality he could not identify had locks of white hair that whirled like the hands of a belly dancer. His wings of black had the blue sheen of a raven's and his eyes were a hard piercing sapphire blue, like the Principality Dickey recognized, his nude body was perfection. The angel Dickey knew was called Omeguel, his wings of brown were marked like those of a Carolina wren, his black hair was as chaotic as the other Principality in its constant churning, his amber eyes were a color rarely seen other than in the crystallized sap of pines. Omeguel brought Dickey to judgment. He trembled. Though the angels were benevolent, they never budged from their duties. The Principality unknown to Dickey walked toward the SUV. Dickey felt like an escaped convict and retreated deep into Ellis trying not to be noticed.

Dickey heard the angel say as he passed from view, "I am Zebruel, Brandon John Howard. I have been sent by the creator to prepare you for judgment. We have three days 'til the heavenly winds will retrieve you."

The guardian angel addressed Zebruel, his superior, "I will meet thee at the appointed gathering." The guardian angel kissed the boy and disappeared before the child-spirit's eyes.

"Am I dead?" Brandon asked.

"Your animal form no longer functions, Brandon John Howard," Zebruel said. "But you, like all created in the heavenly realm, will live forever. Whether you are given some new task to fulfill or adjudicated to bliss or torment is for the Creator to decide."

"I want my mommy," Brandon said.

"I will take you to her, take my hand," the angel assured. Brandon took Zebruel's hand as they passed in front of the toppled Jeep, Dickey saw the angel holding the hand of the twelve-year-old boy who had obviously just entered the first stages of manhood. There is no shame in nudity within the spiritual realm, like mammals, birds, and all other creatures created on the earth, they are comfortable in their natural being. Before the two departed, Zebruel glanced through the windshield and said, "I see you demon. I know where you reside." With that said, his hair relaxed, his four sets of wings spread wide, and he and the boy were gone from sight.

Omeguel tilted his head and glared at Ellis' dangling body, inhaling the wind like a hound catching the scent, "I know you demon. Your scent is familiar to me, recent, within the century. How rare for one so newly cast in doom to escape its grasp."

Dickey shook in fear. Ellis' body appeared to be convulsing as Lloyd arrived on the scene. "Fear me not demon, I, by mission, am sent for another, but your sighting will be reported to the Dominions as is my duty."

Dickey and Omeguel watched as Lloyd, accompanied by the spirit of the middle-aged black man, crawled on the upward side of the SUV with a crowbar. Face to face, Jackie was completely focused on Lloyd, "Don't stop working on me Lloyd. Give me a shot in the heart, you haven't even tried the defibrillator yet."

Jackie's back was to the Principality. The angel placed his hand on Jackie's shoulder. When Jackie turned and saw the being he screamed, "Jesus Christ!"

The angel's hair stood on end from the words, his hand jerked back off the soul as if it were contaminated. Omeguel's bare chest broadened as he waited, "You call but ask of him nothing?" Returning as he was, he shook his head, "I am Omeguel, Jackson Luther Williams. I have been sent by the creator to prepare you for judgment. We have three days 'til the heavenly winds will retrieve you."

"Am I really dead?" Jackie asked.

"Your human form has ceased," the angel told him.

"Are you taking me to Heaven or Hell?" Jackie whined.

"I am not the Creator. That is for the Highest One to decide. I have authority over time and matter. Is there someone or some place you wish to see?"

Jackie, in fear, tried to flee Omeguel, but did not get far. The angel tackled the soul and pressed him to the earth, "Do not make me bind thee, Jackson Luther Williams."

"Police brutality! Police brutality!" Jackie screamed, "I mean angel brutality! Let me go! I have rights!"

Omeguel roared with laughter, something Dickey had never witnessed. "In the first dimension, man has freedoms no other creature in the universe shares. Freedoms that brought great divide among the heavenly realm. What good did you do with your freedoms, Jackson Luther Williams?"

"I am scared," Jackie cried out.

"From the dimness of your soul you should be. I suggest we return to a moment of unselfishness to help you prepare for your defense."

Jackie searched his memory, "I cannot think of any."

"It is why you are afraid of me. When I arrived, I saw not your guardian above. She has long left thee."

Dickey heard similar words as well and felt sympathy for the black man. The angel caught a whiff of Dickey's pity and looked over his shoulder at the dangling possessed man. Brought forward by the prying sounds of the crowbar made by Lloyd, Ellis shared consciousness with Dickey. "I am amazed that you emit such a scent. Has condemnation taught you compassion demon?"

The Principality returned his attention to Jackie, who saw his old friend at work, "I remember, I remember. Take me to the day Reagan was shot, Dixon High."

"That long ago? So be it." Omeguel clasped Jackie's shoulders like a hawk with its prey, spread his wings, and lifted his soul from the present to that day in 1981.

Prying the door open, Lloyd dropped his lean fit body into the interior, the cracking of the passenger window startled Ellis. "It's Lloyd Parker, Ellis, we're going to get you out of here. Are you hurting anywhere?"

"I've got one hell of a headache. I must have hit my head 'cause I've been hallucinating."

"Hallucinating?"

"Just saw an angel lifting a naked black man into Heaven."

Lloyd began the task of checking Ellis' vitals, when he saw Chief Lee staring down from the pried-open door. "How can I help, Parker?" the Chief asked.

"His pulse is steady, he may have a concussion. I'm going to need a pair of scissors and another man to secure him as I cut him loose."

"Is that you, Maxie?" Ellis asked.

"You know it," Maxie replied.

"Call Faith, let her know what's happened."

"I'm sure Charity already has," Max replied with scissors, a blanket and a harness to support Ellis. With everything in place, Lloyd lifted Ellis' torso as Max cut the belt. Ellis fell free and pressed Lloyd against the roof as he tried to hold him up. Standing, Max threw a blanket over the two as they prepared to break the front windshield. Dickey knew he had to make the leap to a new vessel now that the Principalities had spotted him. He sensed the presence of a Guardian, sword-bearing. They are more aggressive and temperamental than Principalities, always looking to merit that rare promotion. Dickey also realized the chances of him getting this unnaturally close to another man would be limited. "I remember watching Emergency, paramedics must have women falling all over them," the perverted spirit calculated, "he's in his 40s, but he obviously works out." The demon dug deep into Ellis' memories to find an Old Yeller kind of moment in the man. Located, Ellis started to cry.

Lloyd felt the man tremble, "Are you okay Ellis?" Lloyd asked looking up into the taller man's face. The tears struck home. Lloyd and Dickey were united. The smashing of the windshield covered up Dickey voicing, "What the fuck?" It was too late. He retreated from Lloyd's awareness so the paramedic could do his job. Once free of the vehicle, Dickey saw the heavenly being that stood watch over the body of Brandon John Howard. He quickly allowed Lloyd control of his own body.

The stretcher in place, Ellis was loaded into the back of the ambulance along with the hemophiliac. Lloyd stood staring at his dead friend. Dickey never had any black friends, of course his family had black folks that worked for them, some he even liked, but there was a line placed in his head from childhood he never considered crossing. He could not let Lloyd get emotional and even though there were still angels about, he had no interest in becoming a zombie. He took control, handed the body bag Lloyd held to a Yerby Twin, hopped into the ambulance with Charity and drove away.

"You seem a little nervous, you okay?"

Fuck, I didn't think this through, thought Dickey, *We're driving to a hospital filled with Guardians and Principalities. I'm a demon so new from Hell I still have the proverbial stench on me, damn right I'm nervous.* "I'm fine," Dickey lied.

"Hand me my phone will ya'? I've gotta' call Faith."

Dickey located the memory in Lloyd, opened the glove compartment and handed her the phone. "You sure have gained weight," Dickey said, thinking of the petite twelve-year-old girl he molested.

"Thanks a lot asshole! Ye who just moved back in with your mom. Have you told her? Why you split with Heather?"

"I don't want to talk about it," Dickey remarked.

"What's wrong with your voice?"

"Just a little emotional about Jackie, his mom was our maid. We played together as kids." Dickey delivered the thoughts Lloyd was having before he took possession of him.

After the Yerby twins placed Jackie in the body bag, they went and stood by Hector. Frank Payne was on the job, and he pulled the SUV up-right where the body of the twelve-year-old was revealed with a gasp from all spectators. Brandon's sweatshirt said Dixon Middle School, but his face was so bloodied and crushed that no one knew whose child he was. Hector hated this part of his job more than any other. He walked over to the backpack filled with library books. Written in a beautiful handwriting was the boy's full name, Brandon John Howard. He opened the bag and How the Grinch Stole Christmas fell out on to the pavement, only to be covered with the boy's blood. There were several sets of Howard families in Dixon. He called the school, but as his phone rang, he remembered that they were closed for the holidays. He called the library where the boy was obviously headed and got his address. The scene photographer continued to take pictures, "Make sure they clean him up as best as possible for identification," Hector told the twins.

Chapter Twenty-Six

Faith sat patiently in the dentist's office reading a Southern Living magazine when her cell phone rang. "Hi momma, Ellis told me, Charity is marrying that homeless guy. Isn't that good news? But that's not why I called. Faith sugar, we have a family emergency and I need you to come out to Lula May's old place tonight and bring Matthew and Hope with you."

"Why Matthew and Hope, momma? They have nothing to do with our sins and I don't want them learning that voodoo," Faith said.

"They have everything to do with our sins and get over it, knowledge is power," Bonnie replied.

"Well, what am I going to tell Oscar and Sally?" Faith asked.

"Tell them whatever you want to but leave them with Ellis."

"I got another call coming in momma, I'll call you right back."

"Hello," Faith answered.

"Faith, it's Charity, Ellis has been in a real bad auto accident, he's going to be okay. I'm arriving at the hospital with him right now. Parker, are you all right? Faith, I've got to go, something's wrong with my partner."

Faith called her mom back in short manner, "Momma, that was Charity. Ellis has been in a bad car accident. I'm heading down to the hospital. Can you come out to Dr. Stokes? Sally is in the middle of getting her teeth filled. Then go pick up the boys. I'm sure Hope is already walking to the hospital to see that Raul boy."

"I'll get Sally and the boys. I'll see you at the hospital," her mother said. Faith told the receptionist what was happening and left the office.

Dickey had just learned he could not hide inside his host, at least not from Principalities. And where there was death, there were Principalities. Hospitals were where people went to die. He felt he had already gotten too close to the infirmary. Dickey looked upward once he saw the hospital in the distance, he had not seen that many angels gathered in one place since he left Hell. The angels residing in Hell were there due to mankind, and they were not too happy about it. Dickey had a true respect for the creatures, from Satan, who he never met, on down, all nine orders could be accounted for within its realms. During his last days in hell, he encountered a damned Dominion whose violations of souls were legendary and went back to the days of Enoch, he proudly claimed. Many in Hell considered you a virgin to agony 'til you had been the subject of his abuses. He never did the same soul twice, not because he was a player or had become jaded to the souls' anguish, but because his tortures never ended 'til he possessed some fondness for his victim. Part of his damnation was once the blessing of love for a human spirit touched his heart, that soul would be removed from him forever.

For the next unlucky human spirit that happened to cross his path, the worst thing was when he accepted his assurance of abandonment. This certainty turned to anger, which he took out on this representative of mankind to hate and blame for his curse. Dickey was released, not by the angel's kindness, but unknowingly by his love for him. Dickey had been rescued by an unrighteous Guardian condemned to be a traitor to those he befriended and served. The Guardian moved Dickey across the realm as the Dominion searched for him. For days on end Dickey had heard the calls of his full name followed by wailing apologies and pleading by the Dominion for him to return. Dickey thought he had been found when he heard Faith's prayer and the small light appeared that landed him back on the terrestrial plane inside, of all things, the device that sent him to hell… fruitcake.

As Charity spoke to her sister at the light, she noticed how Lloyd was starting to shake, "Parker, are you all right? Faith, I've got to go, something's wrong with my partner."

"I'm too emotional to work right now. Jackie was family. I need to be alone," Dickey told Charity, opening the door and getting out of the vehicle. "I'll talk to you later," he said shutting the door. Looking down, so as not to give any angel access into the soul's den, he crossed the crosswalk in front of Charity heading away from the hospital. With patients in the back, she continued to the emergency entrance and secured an orderly to help safely remove them.

Ellis noticed Lloyd was missing as he was being removed. "Where's Lloyd, Charity, I wanted to thank him."

"Apparently the man that hit you was a close family friend of his."

"Dead?"

"Yes. I made him stop working on him and go work on you. I'm sure he was dead upon our arrival, no pulse, eyes dilated, unresponsive," Charity said wheeling the stretcher into the emergency room. "I called Faith, she's on her way."

"So Dickey," talking aloud as he walked down the sidewalk, "you're now sharing the body of a closet case living with his mother. The man has had over a half dozen relationships with women, five which were morbidly obese and the other downright ugly. No wonder he closed his eyes every time and fantasized about fucking men. You sure know how to choose 'em, Dickey," he said as he kicked a plastic water bottle down the way.

Damn it, I feel like I've possessed the damn Judge, Lloyd thought. Dickey reached Lloyd's mother's home and quietly went inside to the man's bedroom. The room hadn't changed since the early 80s. The first three Star Wars posters were tacked onto the wall, matching dresser and chest of drawers made of pressed wood with like nightstands holding panels of glass, a Billy Idol poster tacked to the back of the door. Looking into the mirror, Dickey searched through the mind of this man, "Gay?" He would never pick Lloyd off the street as gay. "When did men start going to the gym?" Following Lloyd's daily routine, Dickey found himself in the steam room at the local Y. "Oh, damn, shit, membership has its privileges. I now understand the song YMCA. No wonder you're gay."

Dickey had to dive deep, back into the late 70s, just as the man he possessed had reached puberty to find any images of attractive women. Playboys, Penthouses, Hustlers, all supplied by Jackie Williams. "Y'all boys go outside and play so I's can clean this house," every Saturday Jackie's mother would tell them, "It's too purty to be inside."

Out to the very back of the lot the two thirteen-year-olds went, straight into the two-level 'fort' Lloyd's uncle had built for him when he was eight. Once inside, the young black teen rolled up his jeans and removed the magazine held in place by his sock, a magazine that he had shoplifted from the drugstore sometime earlier that week. They placed the magazine on a tall stool that was between them, unzipped and they quickly went to whacking. It was during one of those Saturday rituals that Lloyd saw the first penis that was not his own.

"I see you looking at it," Jackie said.

"Looking at what?" Lloyd said in denial.

"My dick," Jackie said, "Go ahead, look." Jackie shook his erection before removing his hand. Lloyd looked. "Let me see your white dick," Jackie added. Lloyd showed him his engorged member.

"Damn Lloyd, you's a man. You got a big dick, but what happen?"

"What do you mean, what happen?"

"To your skin man," Jackie pulled on his foreskin, "all my brothers and cousins, we got skin."

"I'm circumcised," Lloyd said.

"Did it hurt?" Jackie asked.

"They do it in the hospital when you're born," he shook his head casually. "I don't remember, I'm sure it did."

"You want to touch it," Jackie asked, pausing, "my cousin Charley, he likes to touch it."

"You let him?"

"Shit yeah, it feels good," he smiled.

Lloyd went to touch him and drew back, "I'll touch yours, if you touch mine."

"At the count of three," Jackie said, "One, two, three."

"Not so tight," Lloyd snapped.

"Sorry man, you're a natural," Jackie realized. "That feels real good."

"Lloyd! Lloyd, are you home?" Dickey was grateful for the flashback interruption by the screeching woman that had to be Lloyd's mother. "You have a phone call. Charity McCrae is on the line. She told me about Jackie Williams. I know y'all were close growing up."

Dickey opened the door and Lloyd's mother handed him her cell. "Hi Parker," Charity said. "I tried to call your phone and realized you didn't have it when I heard it ring inside the cab. Are you okay?"

"Not really," Dickey answered honestly.

"The twins told me what happened in high school gym class. Let me take you out to Leo's for a beer. I'll be by after my shift."

"Okay," Dickey responded, bars were one of the few places he knew that angels feared to tread, unless someone is going to die, but otherwise, safe.

"I'll see you around four then, later."

"Bye," Dickey closed the phone and returned it to his mother.

"Do you want to talk about it?" his mother asked.

"Not really."

"Okay then," she said before reluctantly turning away.

After shutting the door, Dickey lay down and placed his hands behind his head, "So what happened during high school gym class, Lloyd?"

Will watched as Lula May and Hunter prepared the old shack for the exorcism that was to take place that night. He stood by the old wood stove, as it was the only source of heat in the early 20th century hovel. Bead-board wrapped the base of the room and dated old wallpaper peeled in places near its corners. A beveled wood plaque with a fading lacquered image of Franklin Roosevelt and a Last Supper print bought at a five-and-dime more than half a century ago hung on either side of a window centered on the wall. As he looked out the window over the sink, he could see waves in the window's original glass caused by decades of gravity. The home only had two more rooms and a bathroom on what was the back porch. When Lula May was growing up, she and her siblings all shared one room, all sleeping in the same bed until the boys reached that certain age and started sleeping on the floor. Her parents slept in the other bedroom 'til her father was lynched, she had explained to Will. Shortly thereafter her Granny moved in with them, in part to take care of the younger ones whilst her momma worked, the other part to ward off any who thought that because her daddy was gone that they could take advantage.

"All far and wide knew my Granny had powerful magic," Lula May said. "She's the one who taught me likes I'm teaching Hunter and Hope and ifs I lives long enough Mary Jane and young Oscar both possess the eye, just like Miss Bonnie and Miss Ethel do."

"You marrying into a long line of conjuring," Hunter added.

"How about Charity and her sisters?" Will asked.

"Let me see, what's the best way for you to understand it?" Lula May pondered. "They's extension cords, the power runs through them, and they can sting you, trust me, they's from a long line of practitioners, but the pure power, the ability to call on the spirit world usually, not always minds you, skips a generation," she said as she lit a batch of bound sage. "I'm afraid Miss Faith may be a prime example of it not, though she don't know it."

"Once you free the boy of the demon, how are you going to make sure he never comes back?" Will asked.

"We's going to trap him with a mirror," she said.

"Did you say mirror?"

"You's got good hearing Mr. Will."

"But why, they don't have their own body?

"Next time you look in a mirror, look into your own eye," Lula May instructed. "You'll find if you look deep enough, you can see your soul. Some's got old souls, others new. You've heard that's before, I know. Joe there is an old soul, or Jane there was born at forty, or even you wouldn't know old Tom there was sixty by the way he acts, souls age slower than the physical body. Your soul has its own reflection, it may be different than your shell, it may not."

"Do you know why?"

"Demons are vain creatures," Lula May warned. "Especially the one we're after. If there is a mirror in the room, a demon can't resist it for long. They's got to at least glance in it. Also now, I's just guessing, but I don't thinks there's any mirrors in Hell."

"How does the mirror capture him?"

"The mirror doesn't, it's bait. We's working the concoction that's going to hold him right now. The last ingredient Miss Ethel is bringing over shortly."

Hunter's cell phone rang, "Hello," he answered. "Yes, Ms. Bonnie, she's right here, her hands are full, you mind if I put you on speaker phone?" After he changed it over, Hunter placed his phone in the middle of the table. "Go ahead Miss Bonnie, we all can hear you."

"Miss Lula May, Ellis was in a car accident this morning. I don't know much, called Hector, he told me Ellis walked away from it but was hurt. He didn't know how badly. I'm on my way to Faith's to pick up the kids."

"You may run into Miss Ethel, she called me not too long ago and told me she was gonna' bring Hope over for lunch." Bonnie and Lula May laughed. "I guess I can fry up something. Be careful, don't upset him. We don't want him to catch on and move on. Keep me up to date, goodbye."

"So is Ms. Ethel bringing holy water?" Will asked.

"Oh no, Mr. Will, holy water, well the best way to put it is it's like a tetanus shot," she explained. "It can keep evil spirits from acting out likes they want, but booster shots are needed regularly, especially if a demon has made a visit."

"You can't watch a horror movie with Aunt Lula May," Hunter said. "cause she just laughs when they get it wrong."

"Most just religious propaganda, mind you," Lula May added. "But there's true spirits, all kinds, trust me. There was an album Miss Joy used to play over and over. Miss Joy used to listen to the craziest music growing up. One day, as I was tidying, I could smell she'd been smoking some weed."

"Nothing's changed there, girl, nothing. Miss Joy's always got the best weed in town." Hunter commented with flair, "Always."

"Anyways," she said, giving Hunter a look for interrupting her, "The song she was listenin' to kept on repeating 'as above so below, as above so below'," Lula May started moving, remembering the rhythm of the song. "The song had this intoxicating groove. I could tell why she liked it. But I ask her, do you's understand what that means? Too stoned to answer, I's told her the girl, what we do has outcomes, not just here, but everywhere. If you's smoking weed to have fun, to find some special meaning to life, so are those above, if you smoking weed to escape life and the duties it holds, the same holds true. Listen to what you're channeling, know the purpose of why you do what you do before you do it. Most importantly, know where and who it comes from, this is the evidence of what side you're on."

"And that's why she gets her weed from the sheriff," Hunter snapped his fingers.

Lula May slapped Hunter on back of the head, "Boy, what's I'm gonna do with you, not a serious bone in your body. I'm trying to teach Mr. Will here something. You's knows your ancestors are here watching you. Feels 'em? Capturing a demon is dangerous doings. You's don't wants them to pick another."

"I'm sorry Aunt Lula May, I just couldn't resist."

"And there lies your problem. Now go gets those pine beetles out the cabinet, we've got to roast them tills they completely dry. Mr. Will, you's add that to the list for Hunter there in the notebook." She handed Will the notebook that was in front of Hunter. Will opened the book to the last entry that is titled 'Demon Powder'.

"Demon Powder?" Will asked.

"That's the one," she said. "Add Dry Roasted Pine Beetle. They must be dry, ifs there is any goo it messes the whole jumble up."

Chapter Twenty-Seven

Sally's mouth was still numb from the Novocain. When she spoke, her words were extremely slurred, "Da ya tink my ma woo tide ta kill dat?"

"I don't understand you sugar," Hope said. "What'd you say?"

Sally repeated what she had said, but it came out no better and got the same response. She took out her cell phone and typed, "Do you think mom would try to kill dad?"

"No darling, why would you say that?"

"Biggest meanest fight, dad hurt mom," Sally wrote in her text box.

"Darling, couples fight all the time, sometimes they have knockdown, drag out, got to call the police fights. Your mom wouldn't had called me to bring y'all to the hospital if she tried to kill him."

"I'm still not sure," the girl typed. "Ask Oscar and Matthew, it was bad."

Hope and Ethel were walking out the door when Bonnie and Sally arrived just minutes after, "I'm glad I caught you. Ellis has been in a car accident. He's at County."

Hope went white, "Is he okay?"

"He walked away from the accident according to your uncle Hector. They are probably just running some tests to make sure his insides weren't damaged in anyway. Where are your brothers?"

"Oscar is playing video games, Matthew is up in his room."

"Sally, why don't you go with Hope and your Aunt Ethel to the hospital. I'll bring the boys."

Ethel hugged her sister, "Be careful, remember, that might be Dickey not Matthew, don't let him get too close, no matter what."

"I know sister, I'll be careful," Bonnie said as she went inside.

"Car full a wot?" Sally asked Ethel.

"Ask me again when the Novocain wears off darling," Ethel replied.

Bonnie went into the house and found Oscar still playing video games in his underwear. "Oscar, it's late morning and you're not dressed. You're no longer a boy. You got women around the house. Get upstairs and get dressed, your daddy's been in an accident and your mom wants me to bring you to the hospital. Where's Matthew?"

"Still in bed," Oscar replied.

"I know if your momma was here, your rear ends wouldn't be lounging, not when there is obvious work to do," Bonnie said. Bonnie saw housework that needed to be done everywhere she looked. "Stop playing that game and get your hiney upstairs and get dressed. Tell your brother what happened and to do the same." Bonnie picked up the cereal bowl and empty glass and placed them by the sink.

"He ain't coming."

"Oscar, is Matthew alright?"

"I don't think so, he's sitting up there reading his Bible right now."

"Let's go up there and talk to him, but listen to me Oscar, if I say run, you run, leave the house and you call your Aunt Ethel right away. She'll know what to do."

Bonnie took Oscar's hand, and they went up the stairs together. She knocked, "Matthew, it's your Bonnie Gram, can I come in?"

"Yes, mam'," Matthew replied. As they entered, they saw Matthew sitting on his pillow on the bed, his back against the wall and his Bible in hand.

"I'm glad to see you reading your Bible son. What's wrong, you can tell your Bonnie Gram."

"Everything's wrong," he pouted.

"Why don't you want to see your Dad?" Bonnie Gram asked.

"He's not my Dad."

"He may not be your biological father," Bonnie said, "but he is your dad. He didn't know you weren't his. I didn't know 'til I figured it out myself. You were too big to be premature. Don't hold your mother's shame against the man. Let's go to the hospital and see him."

"Y'all are just making this up, you want to put me in the State Hospital."

"Why would we do such a thing?" Bonnie Gram asked.

"I'm sure Oscar's told you everything," Matthew said.

"I haven't said a thing to anyone bro, swear to God," Oscar assured him.

"Told me what?"

"That I hear voices," he said. "Satan talks to me and through me."

"Is he talking to you right now?"

"Not since last night," Matthew appeared slightly reassured. "I've been quoting scripture and reading my Bible without sleep since Oscar went to bed." Bonnie asked what the last thing Satan said to him. "He told me that I wanted it. I thought I did, but I know now that I didn't."

"That wasn't Satan," Oscar scoffed. "That was Dad talking dirty to Mom. Couldn't you tell they were having some wild crazy sex last night? Those hot models from Aunt Iris' lingerie party just had the man horned to his breaking point. All those girls had turned you both into sex machines!" Oscar exclaimed. "Dad just came home and had mad sex with his wife, like you're supposed to do. It was holy matrimony sex, not demon sex like you had with those girls. You just don't want to face Mom after she caught you feeling that girl up in front of everybody there. I thought you were trying to start an orgy, which is cool."

"Oscar! Shame! Stop it now!" Bonnie exclaimed, "I would wash your mouth out with soap if I thought it would clean your mind. Now back up to the demon sex."

"Show her your back, Matthew," Oscar said, "His ass, I mean his behind, looks worse."

Matthew winced as he lifted his t-shirt. Oscar and Bonnie both gasped before their faces turned to looks of disgust. "Oh my, Matthew, your back is infected. I'm taking you to the hospital right now. Throw on a loose-fitting shirt, grab your coats, both of you, let's go," Bonnie demanded as she left the room. "Damn it, he's moved on to Ellis," she said.

As Bonnie pulled up into the hospital parking lot, Grace pulled up with Charlotte, Emily, and Anne. Grace and Charlotte were carrying Anne, whose face looked like it had acid thrown on it and had the same oozing pulsing movements as Matthew's back. A puss-like substance drained down her inner thighs. Charlotte's mouth was swollen shut with what appeared to be an overdose of Botox injections attacked by the worst case of herpes County Medical had ever seen. Emily's mouth looked almost as bad, but it did not compare to her fingers and hands that were so bloated, the only inclination that she had fingers were the tips of her nails. Because of this, her distended arms appeared to have become huge chicken legs. The girls' faces so disfigured Matthew could barely distinguish them. They sure recognized him and would have had a few choice words if their lips weren't swollen shut. What their mouths couldn't say their eyes did.

"Hi Aunt Grace," Oscar spouted. "That was some party last night."

"Yes, it was Oscar," Grace said. "Why are y'all here?"

"Two reasons, my dad was in a car accident, and Matthew's back looks like her face."

After they went inside and waited, Bonnie had Oscar dial Ethel first, "It's ringing." Oscar said handing his grandmother the phone.

"Ethel, where are you at?" She was with Faith and the girls in Ellis' room. They just took him to run some test.

"I'm the emergency room with Matthew," Bonnie said. "Grace is down here with three girls who look like they had their faces dipped in herpes. Matthew's back is so infected you can see the maggots crawling beneath his skin."

"Did you say maggots, momma?" Faith said having taken the phone from Ethel.

"Yes, darling," Bonnie said. "Those scratch marks down his back are oozing, and his back is as red as a brand-new Corvette."

"Lord have mercy," Faith said. "If this concussion doesn't kill Ellis. Where is Oscar?"

"Sitting right here next to me and Matthew. Honey, you stay up there with Ellis. I've been through more emergency room visits than I care to count with you girls. I'll call you once we're in seeing a doctor. Put Ethel back on, will you?"

Bonnie moved so she could speak to Ethel privately, "The demon's moved, he's no longer in Matthew. If what the boys said happened last night is true, it sounds like he's in Ellis.

"If it's in him, he's not behaving like it. You know what Lula May says about hospitals. The man was as cool as a cucumber."

"I haven't ever seen anything like Matthew's back, it's scaring me," Bonnies said. "looks like worms are crawling beneath his skin. You take Hope over to Lula May's right away."

Bonnie returned next to Oscar and asked where Matthew was, "Bathroom," he replied.

After the girls had been checked in, a nurse called for Matthew. "Is your brother still in the bathroom?" Bonnie asked. "Go check on him." Oscar called his brother's name when he entered, but there was no response, just a man standing at the urinal. He walked down by the stalls and saw the bottom of his brother's sneakers sticking out. He knocked, still again no response. He looked under the stall and screamed. Oscar ran back to the entrance. The Yerby twins, who had just delivered the bodies from the accident to the morgue, were making a pit stop.

"I think my brother's passed out," Oscar panted. "The stall is locked."

As one Yerby twin went out to get the necessary tools, the other brother looked under the stall to discern the situation. He quickly backed out, opened the other stall and vomited. "God Damn!" he said, wiping the back of his mouth. Stepping out of the stall, he looked at Oscar, "I understand son. If I didn't have to barf, I'd have screamed too."

When his brother returned, he said, "I'm going to get a stretcher and have the nurse call an urologist stat. And bro, before you open that door, I'm warning ya', it looks like he has a hundred cases of ringworm running around on his pecker all trying to find a way out. I've never seen anything like it."

Chapter Twenty-Eight

Omeguel and Jackie arrived on the fateful spring day that John Warnock Hinckley attempted to assassinate Ronald Reagan. The sky was blue as they watched the tenth grade PE class, unaware of the attempt, running laps in the back soccer field that was lined with privet bush. "See, that's me," Jackie said.

"I know which one is you. I can smell," Omeguel turned away. A path cut through the privet, which led to a ditch where guys went to piss rather than running back to the gym. Lloyd deliberately fell back to the 'tubs' and 'physical retards' as they were called, making sure the coach didn't see him cut through the hedge. After making a few laps and not seeing Lloyd return, Jackie dropped back into the pack and slipped through the hedge. The angel and soul followed. Once on the other side, he looked to his right and left, but no Lloyd. He heard mumbling blended with the rustling of leaves and followed the sound. He jumped over the ditch and followed a path that led into the woods. Not too deep into the woodland, behind a huge oak tree, he set his eyes on two seniors holding a bent over, bare ass Lloyd with his gym shorts around his ankles. Both were second-string rednecks on the football team. They had Lloyd's t-shirt tied around his mouth to gag him. The ash-haired brick shithouse pinned Lloyd's arms behind his back as the blonde forced a Coke bottle up Lloyd's anus with a spit and quick shove.

Lloyd's head threw back and with all that was in him, he tried to get away. The high school linebacker just laughed, shoving Lloyd's back horizontal with the ground, "Take it like a man, you pussy."

"Yeah, stop your whining, faggot, you know you like it, just getting you ready for the real thing." the blonde said rotating the bottle while singing the cola jingle, "Ain't nothing like the real thing baby, ain't nothing like the real thing."

Jackie saw a big stick on the ground, "I got your real thing," he said as he grabbed the stick and started running with all his might toward his friend. "You're the faggots, leave him alone!" he screamed at the top of his lungs before he whacked the startled blonde over the head. The ash-haired linebacker punched Jackie in the chest, sending the skinny teen flying into the briars. The blonde picked up the stick and was about to strike Jackie when they heard people coming in their direction. The rednecks ran, but not before they both kicked Lloyd in the nuts.

Coach Half arrived first with the young Yerby Twins right behind him and he quickly turned the twins around and stopped the others before they could get to the scene. "Don't say a word thing One and Two," as he called the lanky twins, "I'll kick your asses if you do."

"Get your butts back on school grounds!" Coach Half yelled at his class. "Hinson, tell Coach Boykin I need his assistance and need it now. Tell him to bring a first-aid kit." When the coach turned back around, he saw the bleeding black teen kneeling on the ground holding the white sobbing naked adolescent in his arms.

"It's gonna be alright Lloyd, nobody saw what happen but me. I won't tell if you don't want me to. But we won't catch the bastard unless you do," said the coach.

"What difference does it make if you catch them are not, he'll be marked as a fag for the rest of his life in this dinky little town if he tells what happened," looking the coach in the eyes, "and you know it. If there's one thing Dixon hates more than us niggers, it's fags. It will be in the papers. Lloyd here, in court against two white All-American football players, they'll be all lawyered-up by some booster club member if their daddies ain't rich enough to hire one. Get real Coach Half about what you're asking."

"You've gotta fight back, if not, they'll think they've gotten away with it and will do it again. You don't want another guy to go through this do you Parker?"

Wiping his tears away, "No, but I don't want to be called a fag all my life either."

"Tell me who they are so I can put an end to it, if they play football for us, I can make sure their careers end now." Seeing the blood run down the boy's thigh, "Lloyd, you need medical treatment, I'm sorry son, but you do. You boys have got to say some older men did this to you, say they were wearing ski masks, so you don't know who they were. Parker, I'll make sure it stays out of the paper. You have my word. Williams, you okay with this?"

"If Lloyd is okay with it, I'm okay with it."

Lloyd nodded yes as Coach Boykin called out, "Coach Half?"

"Over here, Tony. Tomorrow Williams, my office, point them out in the yearbook."

"Yes, Coach." As Coach Boykin rounded the corner, Lloyd stood up and covered himself with one hand and pulled his shorts up with the other. Coach Half nodded toward the Coke bottle and shook his head.

"You were not only brave and selfless toward your friend, you spoke truth to power," Omeguel said to Jackie.

"Did the Coach keep his word?"

"As I told you, you spoke truth to power. Remember what you said? If there's one thing Dixon hates more than us niggers, it's fags. Your coach called a member of the Klan, a friend of Lloyd Ronald Parker's father, Lloyd Thomas Parker, who made retribution. Your coach, Albert Benson Half secured your first employment."

"He was a good man."

"He is still, as to how good, the Creator will decide. Now Jackson Luther Williams, show me other good you have done."

"How much more do you need?" He asked.

"I need none, it is you who needs to defend your allotment of the gifts of time and place. We have but three days to gather your defense and two hours have been spent."

"Christmas eve, three years ago," Omeguel, as before, seized Jackie and took him to that time.

Dickey tried to catch that memory, but every time he achieved a foothold near the recollection Lloyd's body would knot up on its own, almost to the point of nausea. "Little pig, little pig, let me in," Dickey would say to his host. Dickey didn't know how long he would occupy this vessel; otherwise, with a huff and a puff he would just rip to shreds the barricade Lloyd had erected to this episode in his life. "He's twisted enough, no need to add injury." Dickey had not been one who wanted for much while in human form; instant gratification was an unspoken motto, and he didn't much care for the tedious work often needed for the best results. "Persevere Dickey, just a constant whisper while this vessel sleeps."

The human body doesn't like to be invaded, by a physical virus or a spiritual one.

Maintaining a host was hard work, any physical damage done during possession required great amounts of energy to cure. Throughout demonic inhabitation the human immune system must be suppressed in order to preserve corporal control, this altered the chemical make-up of bodily fluids much in the way certain chemotherapy treatments do. Because of the repression, when a demon vacates the body, it is vulnerable to various viruses, scratches or wounds of any sort could be deadly. A sulfuric stench augments from the injury if not healed, a tang that burns the nostrils of angels and humans alike. But for Archangels it's like throwing red meat to hounds, they know a demon is in their territory. An Archangel, not duty bound, liked nothing better than tracking a demon in their off time. Dickey had been careless, four possessions: Matthew, Anne, Ellis, and now Lloyd in twenty-four hours, not to mention the acidic nature of his seed seeped onto or ejaculated into three women: Emily, Charlotte, and Faith. It would be a miracle if poor little Anne survived both. But most of all Dickey worried about his son.

"I have a son, I have a son," he repeated. He got off the bed and paced, looked out the window before glancing in the mirror. "If I had a chance to tell my father before those bitches killed me, he would have snatched the boy up. I know he would have. Matthew wouldn't have been plagued by the neuroses these middle-class philistines plunked down in his head." He didn't want to stare at himself for too long. Playing with synapses within the brain, though entertaining, could lead to a number of psychoses making control of your host difficult to say the least.

Dickey went back to the window and watched the nine spiritual hemispheres rotate at their individual speeds. "I wonder if I would have believed or would I've just allowed some preacher or scientist to give these planes a label. If only I had listened to my ancestors when they came to me. But that would have been considered crazy heathenism by the religious and silly superstition by the scientific. How many cycles must humanity endure before Eden returns and the Creator's reality is understood by all His creations?"

"Lloyd," his mother said at his door. "I found your old Dixon High yearbook. I saw Jackie had signed it. I didn't know if you wanted to look at it or not."

Dickey was at the door. "I can't believe you still have this, thank you," Dickey said, taking the annual from Lloyd's mom.

"My yearbook still transports me back in time. At my age, sometimes you need to be reminded that you were young once, especially in today's world. Why in 1981 I still could shake my booty," the old woman laughed, trying to cheer her son up.

Dickey took the yearbook and played the distraught role of someone who a short time ago lost someone special in his life. "Thanks mom, I appreciate it, really," he said ahead of shutting the door. Dickey sat down on the bed, opened to the index, and found the pictures of Jackie Williams prior to exposing Lloyd to the time capsule of memories. Visual aids were underrated, their ability to trigger memories, even those best forgotten, was the foil to the best designed cover-ups.

"Through the hedges, there we go Lloyd, you've got to take a leak. Why that's Thad Goodwin and Neil Jones walking up to you, how nice, three boys taking a piss together, sort of reminds me of those communal urinals that were around when I was a kid. So, you looked, Lloyd, they knew you would. Well, well, I wasn't expecting that, you didn't draw your hand away. I prefer to shake the last drop out myself. A toke before heading back wouldn't hurt, they want to share more than a toke, I can tell. Why George and me used to smoke under that tree. I bet that tree is still there. I wouldn't suck their dicks either, good for you Lloyd. Oh damn, they… breath through your nose, you're making me dizzy, ah no, that's wrong, welcome to Hell 101 kid. Here comes your hero, Thad had some power behind him. Al Half, with his John Denver haircut, always thought he was some gift to the ladies. Your friend wasn't stupid, he knew his place in the world."

Dickey walks over to the mirror to talk to the man he possessed. "If it makes you feel any better Lloyd, Coach Half's brother, Bill Half, well he was a member of the Klan, and his brother called my father, who called Judge Schultz, well, let's just say the Judge was a huge man, in every way a huge hard man in those days. The Judge had asked if he could use the cabin for week or so, him and a few of his friends from out of town, he said. It didn't take much money to get those boys there under false pretenses. "Chicken to eat and playin' poker" the Judge laughed, he always laughed at his own jokes. Well, Thad and Neil, I don't think they knew they were the chicken, nor that they held one-eyed jacks for those gun-toting kings either. Seven-card stud and a royal flush had brand new meanings for those boys, and they knew why they were dealt the cards they were dealt by week's end too. I'd bet they'd piss themselves if they ran into you today. Now we're going to go meet your pal Charity for a drink."

Chapter Twenty-Nine

Ethel took Hope, Oscar, and Sally to Lula May's. As she waited, Faith gazed out the window at the scorched earth where the Dickson's mansion once stood, an emblem of the Old South when agriculture was king and the rich soil's goodness was drained to produce cotton and tobacco. She could see in the distance the textile mills that had shot up from the earth as fast and tall as the pines that surrounded them. They sat empty now, as hollow as the pines riddled by beetles. Across the road stood the old tobacco warehouse where farmers brought their fleshy leaves for auction. She remembered the waves of heat and humidity that weighed heavily upon the body during the last days of summer. The air around the building was once filled with a sweet smoky smell pooled with the perspiration of farmers and their workers. Due to the smoking ban on hospital grounds, Faith watched as men and women, pulling their IVs behind them, crossed the road and stood in front of the old building that formerly helped to supply their addiction. The South she knew as a child was dead. Its skeletal remains laid across the landscape like soldiers after a battle.

Grace walked into Ellis' hospital room. "Faith, how's Ellis doing?" she asked.

Faith, startled, turned around. Grace, even more so startled by what she saw, clasped her mouth.

"Oh my God! Faith, look in the mirror. I'm going to get a nurse." Before Grace could get to the nurse's station, she heard a scream reverberating out of Ellis' hospital room that made her hair stand on end. She was worried that some wild strain of herpes had descended upon her girls and that maybe Ellis had given it to her sister after sleeping with the new girl. Could she be the source of the contagion? She was a gypsy, after all.

While the nurses were running toward the continued screams of "I'm gonna' kill him!" Ellis was wheeled past Grace in a coma." While the doctors examined Faith, Grace stepped out into the hall to call Iris. Iris answered. "How are the girls?"

"Not good. Anne is in intensive care, they're running tests on all of them. Have you seen Nina, the exotic new girl today?"

"No. Why?"

"Faith has the same beginning markings around the mouth as the girls. Matthew's back is eaten up and his genitals have the same infestation as the girls. Ellis was just returned to his room in a coma. They just pulled down his sheets and are checking his genitals right now. I'm worried that the CDC is going to be called in and the finger will be pointing back at us. Find Nina fast, see if she's infected."

As Grace closed her cell phone, she saw her mother walking down the corridor.

They entered the room as two doctors stepped aside to discuss the situation. A tall nurse who did not shave her legs came to the women. Her nametag read Angelica Deville. Bonnie thought the nurse's parents had a great sense of humor, but the seriousness of the situation kept her from asking. Ladies, can you wait outside right now, the doctors are trying to assess the situation and may need to speak to you shortly.

Bonnie asked after Matthew and was told they had him across the hall from two of the girls Grace brought over to her house. "Are those girls… Did they give my poor boy a," Bonnie paused and whispered, "venereal disease?"

"I'm not sure momma," Grace said. "Only the doctors can tell. I'm waiting on a call from Iris, there was one more girl involved that night. She may have slept with Ellis."

"I can't talk to you," Bonnie bowed her head. "I'm so embarrassed, my own daughter, a madam, people are gonna' think I didn't bring you up right."

"Momma, I'm not a madam," Grace said. "I'm an accountant. I keep the books for a corporation that is registered with the state, the IRS, and pays taxes to both. I don't arrange dates or hire women out for prostitution."

"No, Iris runs that part of the business," Bonnie said sharply. "You just take in the money and write the checks. This is your momma you're talking to, not some Leave It to Beaver mom. I raised you girls by myself for most of your lives. I know you better than you know yourselves. You work for a business that sells sex, you're either a madam or a whore, maybe both. Don't try to whitewash what you do. 'I'm an accountant,'" she scoffed," well I'm Mother Teresa!"

Grace's phone rang and she stepped away from her mother and answered, "Well?"

"She's fine," Iris said. "No signs of anything wrong."

"Who did she sleep with?" Grace asked.

Iris asked Nina, "Did you sleep with Matthew and Ellis?"

"Only the old man, not the young one," Nina said in her Serbian accent.

"Only Ellis," Iris said.

"And you've checked her out, around the mouth and nothing down below."

"She's beautiful. I'm looking at her naked body right now. It's like looking at Isabella Rossellini in Blue Velvet. There is not a flaw anywhere."

"TMI, have fun," Grace said before hanging up and turning to her mother. "Momma, Nina is fine. If Ellis is infected, this means it came from somewhere else, not my girls, and it points to Matthew as the source. He's the only one who has had contact with all infected."

"Dickey," Bonnie said.

"Dickey Dickson?" Grace looked confused.

"Is there any other? Lula May is trying to figure it out."

The two doctors walked up to the women, "Hi, I'm Dr. Tim Gunnels and this is my colleague, Dr. Bianca Page."

"I'm Bonnie, this is my daughter Grace."

"Which one of you ladies brought in Matthew McCaskill and who brought in the three women, Emily Fisher, Anne King, and Charlotte Butcher?" Dr. Gunnels asked.

"I brought in the girls," Grace replied.

"I hope you don't mind, but we need to ask you both some questions," Dr. Page said.

An orderly, wearing protective clothing, arrived with a wheelchair. Grace watched as the nurse and orderly were trying to get Faith into the chair. Grace tapped her mother on the shoulder and motioned toward Faith. The nurse snapped on gloves, took out a syringe and injected the hysterical woman. "What are you doing with my daughter?" Bonnie reached out.

"We are placing your family and all three girls in quarantine," said Dr. Paige. "We would also like to run tests on you, if you don't mind, as well as any other family member that may have been in contact with the McCrae's and the Misses Butcher, Fisher, and King," Dr. Gunnels added.

"Quarantined?!" Bonnie exclaimed. "Are they contagious?"

"We'll know more after we get the tests back, Miss King, and both father and son are unconscious. Everywhere there has been an abrasion, infection has set, and we may have to take the senior Mr. McCaskill into surgery to relieve the pressure building on his brain. We have never seen anything like it. We are calling the CDC after we question you."

Bonnie took out her cell phone, still foreign to her and handed it to Grace, "What is all of this crap?" she said loudly in frustration. "Will you make this phone a phone, or just dial your Aunt Ethel"? Grace took the phone from her mom and dialed her aunt and handed it back to her when it started to ring. "Where are you at?" Bonnie asked.

"Lula May's."

"They have placed Matthew, Ellis and Faith in quarantine along with those girls Grace brought with her. They are calling the CDC, they want to test everyone who came in contact with them."

"Lula May knows what it is. Demon pox. It's deadly within two to three days if an antidote isn't administered. But she's missing an ingredient, something that personally belongs to him."

"Well, we'll dig him…" Bonnie started, "… It up." The doctors pretended not to be listening, but digging someone up obviously struck their interest. Grace noticed and put her arm around her mother and moved her away from the eavesdropping pair.

"Suggested that already," Aunt Ethel said. "It has to be something he personally touched, something that belonged to him."

Bonnie had gotten got rid of all his stuff the next year, and if she did have something, it's gone up in smoke. Alice took care of everything else. "That no good bastards getting his revenge. We have two days to find something that he touched that belonged to him. That's what Lula May said. Something that belonged to him and he touched. Maybe some of his clothes haven't decomposed."

"Momma, keep the doctors busy, I'm going to slide out of here. I know where something he touched and belonged to him is… Alice's." It was still a crime scene, but she planned on calling Hector as soon as she got to the door.

Bonnie returned to the doctors while Grace headed down the corridor, "Well doctors, I spoke to my sister, she has the youngest, but will go pick up the rest and bring them here for testing. Now what questions do you have for me?"

"Where is your daughter?" Dr. Page asked.

"Lady's room," she smiled.

"It's in the other direction," Dr. Page informed her suspiciously.

"When you got to go, you got to go. I'm sure she'll realize and be down this hall in a sec. Now Matthew has been back from Bob Jones for a couple of weeks, you don't think he may have brought it from there do you? A Godly education is important, don't you think? And well, Ellis is a lawyer, I can only imagine what kinds of low life he deals with day in and day out. That secretary of his, Tracey, was such a doll baby. I taught her during Sunday school. That daddy of hers was pure white trash, but her momma was a righteous woman, righteous I tell you. She had all four of her youngen's in the pew every Sunday, Sunday night and Wednesday night…" Bonnie rambled on talking about her family not giving the doctors a chance to ask any questions as Grace slipped out unnoticed.

Grace called Hector when she was driving out of the hospital parking lot. "Sakamoto," he answered. Grace told him he had to meet her at the Mayor's house. "I can't, I'm on my way to tell the parents of the boy crushed by Ellis' SUV their son is dead." She told Hector if she didn't get into their home Ellis, Faith, and Matthew will be dead in close to forty-eight hours. Lula May said and she's never wrong about illnesses. She went on to tell him all that have been quarantined and everyone who has come in contact with them they want to test. That means everyone who responded to the scene, including Hector. "Holy shit!" he said. "Call Joy, the keys are in my desk drawer. Don't disturb anything if you can help it, it's an ongoing investigation."

Chapter Thirty

The wind was whipping through the trees snatching the last few remaining leaves that clung to the oaks, hickories and willows. A relentless whistling drone mingled with the wind chimes that were hung throughout the neighborhood. The clamor from the blustery weather was thunderous and unsettling, occasionally rocking Grace's sports car as she waited on her oldest sister. When Joy arrived in her van, she jingled the keys to the music she was listening to before she opened her vehicle's door. Joy sprinted up to the entrance and had it opened by the time Grace arrived at the bottom of the red brick stoop of their step-aunt's home.

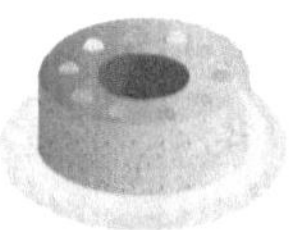

Chapter Thirty-One

Dickey loved driving when he was human. He noticed that nothing much had changed in Dixon since his death. Leo's had been a watering hole in Dixon for at least ten years before he met his untimely end. The parking lot still hadn't been paved. Lloyd's mother's car stirred up a sandy dust. As the dust settled, he put the Toyota into park and debated going in or waiting for Charity. A young large-busted brunette in a pair of tight jeans went inside after putting her cigarette out. Dickey was motivated and opened the Avalon's door. Watching the skies, he quickly went inside. The brunette was sitting at the bar. Other than a couple of waitresses sitting at a booth rolling silverware and Leo behind the bar, the place was empty.

"Hey Lloyd, your usual?" Leo asked.

"Sounds good," Dickey responded while thinking to himself, "Damn, you've gotten old Leo."

Leo sat a Grolsch in front of Lloyd, "Open a tab?"

"Yeah, and add this lady's drink to it for me," Dickey added.

"Thanks Lloyd, you didn't have to do that," the brunette said.

"My pleasure," pausing to find her name in Lloyd's head, "Martha."

"So, is the rumor true, have you moved back in with your mom?"

"For the time being, got to save up for a deposit. I left everything behind."

"Breakups are so messy and lonely," she said placing her hand on his knee.

Dickey looked at the girl's hand then back up to her eyes, "You don't say."

She sipped on the cocktail straw, "Not only lonely, but, well, you know."

Dickey was in charge of Lloyd's mind and body. What would have caused no response from Lloyd triggered a growth down his leg that didn't go unnoticed by Martha. "I've got to go to the john," Dickey said. He took Martha's hand off his knee and brushed it against the tube along his inner thigh. Martha's eyebrows rose. Dickey smiled and left his stool heading toward the back and waited. Martha finished her drink and followed Dickey back to the restrooms.

"Well, that's a first for Lloyd," Leo said to the waitresses as Martha disappeared out of site.

The two made out inside the cove by the water fountain before Dickey took her by the hand, pulling the buxom woman into the men's room and into a stall. Dickey tried to put his hands down her jeans but could not reach her clitoris due to the denim's tight design. Martha had no such problem and sat on the toilet and went to work on the firefighter. Dickey's hands went to her breasts and rotated his palms against her nipples 'til they were as stiff as his penis. He pinched them hard. She, in turn, took his nuts in her hands and drew them tight between her thumb and index finger with a tug that pushed the right buttons for Dickey Dickson. He lifted the woman up and turned her over. Yanking her jeans down and exposing her round tattooed ass, dribbling spit downtown, Dickey drove deep and fast. Martha was not the silent type, her muttering moans of pleasure pulsated with every slap of physical contact. Her groans escaped the stall, and bounced around the men's room, 'til Martha's climax crescendo, her wail penetrated the walls and reverberated out into the bar. The gossiping waitresses rolling silver went silent and looked back toward the restroom. Wide-eyed they turned around and glanced over at Leo and the kitchen staff before breaking into giggles.

"Who's that?" the cook asked Leo.

"Martha and Lloyd," Leo replied.

"Lloyd who?"

"Parker," Leo answered.

"The fireman? Damn, never thought Parker had it in him," the cook replied.

"Me neither," said Leo as Martha's whimpers began once again to climb.

With her hands on the floor and jeans and panties around Lloyd's neck, Martha said, "If we don't stop, I'm going to cum again, Lloyd. I'm even louder the second time."

"We're not done yet," Dickey railed and with relentless demon force he continued to pound the girl as she stared out from beneath the stall at the men's room echoing with a constant staccato, "Oh, Oh, Oh, Oh."

"Ramona," Leo said to one of the waitresses, "here's a fiver, go put some music on the jukebox."

"Should I try to match Martha's rhythm?" Ramona joked as she put in the money.

Charity was on the phone with her mother as she was driving to Leo's, "You've got to be joking, quarantined?"

"This is no joking matter. Everyone that has been in contact with Matthew, Ellis, Faith, or those three girls Grace brought into the emergency room. Depending on the results of the tests they are going to call CDC."

"Damn, that will be a first for Dixon."

"Look darling, I need to tell you more but can't, they want to draw my blood right now. Call your Aunt Ethel or Miss Lula May, they can tell you more."

"Okay momma, I'll call you later. I'm about to pull into Leo's to meet with Lloyd.

Love you."

Charity noticed Lloyd's mom's car as she arrived in the ambulance. "Good, he's here."

As Charity came into the bar and grill, Ramona's first selection, an old obscure Prince song began to play.

"Hi Charity, what can I get you?"

"A PBR will do," she said saddling up to the bar. "Where's Lloyd?"

"Men's room."

As "Take Me With U" faded a "Fuck yeah! Where you want it bitch?" bellowed forth from Dickey before the Stone's "She's So Cold" began to play.

Charity raised her eyebrow and looked at Leo who just shrugged his shoulders. *That can't be Lloyd?* she thought, *he wouldn't have sex with another guy in a straight bar or a gay bar for that matter.* She downed her PBR, "Give me another."

Marvin Gaye's "Got to Give It Up" came on the jukebox. Dickey came dancing out of the bathroom drunk on his orgasm, as sex demons are apt to be. All were stunned at how well Lloyd moved as no one had ever seen the reserved man ever tap his foot or bob his head to a rhythm, much less dance in such a provocative manner. Charity was amazed as he danced for Nancy, the other waitress in the booth, moving as if he were a Chippendale. A disheveled Martha strolled out of the restroom. She popped Lloyd on the ass as she passed him on her way to the bar. Charity's jaw dropped. She couldn't believe what she was witnessing. As Martha approached, her hair clung together, her lipstick was smeared, and one eye was bloodshot. She reached across the bar for a napkin and pen, wrote down her number, and gathered her purse before placing a twenty on the bar, "Keep the change Leo."

"Thanks Martha."

Martha strutted like a rock star over to Lloyd and stuck the cocktail napkin in his shirt pocket as he still danced. She departed with a kiss on Lloyd's mouth. Dickey followed the brunette as she pulled away from him and noticed Charity sitting at the bar.

"Sweet T," Dickey yelled over the music, "Come dance with me."

Charity went white. Only one person had ever called her 'Sweet T.' She nodded no and picking up her phone, called her mother. Bonnie couldn't answer as they were drawing blood. She then called Ethel who answered as Lloyd worked his way over to her, "I'll call you right back, Aunt Ethel."

Dickey could sense that something was wrong by the look on Charity's face, "What's up?" Dickey asked.

"Let's go sit down at a table," Charity said.

Ramona brought some menus over to them, "The usual?"

"Sounds good," Dickey replied. "So, what's up?"

"Back at ya."

"What? Martha? I needed to relieve some built up stress, it's not like I've never been with a woman before."

"In a public bathroom?" Charity asked.

"What, am I supposed to take her over to my mom's?" Dickey raised his eyebrows, "Your turn."

"Faith, Ellis, and Matthew along with three others have placed under quarantine. All those who have had contact with them are to report to the hospital for testing." Charity watched Lloyd go white. "They also want to know everyone we've been in contact with since this morning's accident. Here's your phone," Charity took the phone out of her breast pocket and placed it on the table. "Now that you're better, I'll let them know you'll be reporting in tomorrow. I'm going to go get this testing over with. They were testing mom when I arrived."

"I better go tell my mom, it will be a bit before we get there."

"Later then," Charity said leaving twenty on the table, "Enjoy the wings." Charity exited the bar and immediately called Ethel, "What's going on?"

"Dickey's free from Hell and is causing havoc with whoever he possesses. Lula May believes he first possessed Matthew and for some reason possessed Ellis."

"He's not in Ellis. He's in Lloyd."

"How do you know?"

"Lloyd was the one who worked on Ellis for one thing. Lloyd just had sex in a public bathroom at Leo's and Lloyd called me 'Sweet T' just like Dickey used to."

"Your sisters just arrived. Where are you?"

"Leaving Leo's," Charity said, "and headed toward the hospital."

"Don't leave your mother or sister's side. Dickey may try to kill your mom now that he's free."

"I won't," Charity promised. "Love you, Aunt Ethel."

"Love you too, Charity. Goodbye." Ethel turned as her nieces knocked on the door. "I have some important news."

"Oscar, let your aunts in will you please?" Lula May smiled. With the entrance of the two women, Lula May continued, "This room hasn't seen this many living souls since I was a child. Hunter, Mr. Will, where's your manners, there are ladies present."

Hunter got up and held out his seat. Will followed suit.

"Thank you," both women answered before taking their seat around the table.

"I just got off the phone with Charity," Ethel said. "Dickey has possessed Lloyd Parker."

"Dickey Dickson?" Joy asked still in disbelief. "How?"

"I's don't knows yet," Lula May replied for her, "but we's got to catch him or he is going to raise hell on earth. He's already infected six souls with demon pox, it's deadly in three days."

"So did you bring something that was his, that he held in his hands?" Ethel asked.

Grace lifted up the paper bag she had sat on the floor by her seat. She emptied the porn onto the table.

"What a pig," Ethel said as she dropped an old Playboy. A magazine hit the floor and opened to a spread of 'Girls of the SEC'. With so many women in the room, Oscar felt uncomfortable, but he crossed over to the table and picked the magazine off the linoleum striving to catch as much as he could before setting it back on the table.

"Thank you, Oscar," Grace said observing the teen's consumption of sexually stimulating imagery.

Ethel took the May 1984 Playboy with the cover story, "Older Women, Younger Men," Ethel turned the cover around to show Grace and Joy, "Are y'all old enough to remember her? She was one brazen hussy, had sex with her husband on the Capital's steps."

"I remember," Joy said. "But not all the details. I was just a teenager,"

"Can't remember the details, I wonder why?" Grace joked. "When did the term 'cougar' enter the lexicon to describe older women?" Grace asked.

"Who was she?" Oscar asked.

"Rita Jenrette, her husband was some congressman caught in a bribery scandal if I remember right," said Ethel.

"What does she do now?" Sally asked.

"The last time I saw her, she was some kind of journalist for Fox News," Ethel replied to her great niece, "but that was years ago. If she's still living, she is close to my age."

"All we'z needs is one," Lula May said. "Hunter, why don't you take Will and these chillen' over to's your place. Will, put these magazines back in the bag and takes them with you. Hides 'em from young Oscar here, his momma would skin us all alive if she knew that he'd even laid eyes on one."

Oscar displayed a face of denial, "Don't denies you wants to get your hands on um boy," Lula May said waving a rolled-up magazine at him, "I's cleans enough teenage boys bedrooms ins my days to know what's on their minds all the time. Sheets I's has to wash, trashcans filled with wadded up tissues, back in the 70s tube socks was always stuck together, and under every mattress one of these."

After Hunter, Will and the children left the old cabin and journeyed to Hunter's garage apartment next door, Lula May opened her book. "First step, I's got to create this potion for demon pox or a whole lots of peoples gonna' die," Lula May told the women sitting around the table. "We're gonna to have to make a large batch Chillen', I's a telling ya, Dickey Dickson is a full-fledged sex demon straight from the ninth ring of Hell, so we're gonna have lots of folks to heal. After we get Faith and her family healed were gonna' have to make a trap for that evil bastard. He knows ya, he can smell ya, and he eventually will be hunting us all if we don't catch him first. He's new to his demon nature. His hunger for sex is going to grow, that's his weakness. It took seven of us to send him to Hell the first time and it's gonna take all seven of us to send him back."

"Joy, darling, you have a feather in your hair," Ethel noticed.

Joy took the feather out and rotated the quill between her fingers. Lula May reached out and grabbed her hand. She gently removed the olive-colored plume from her fingers. The other women watched because Lula May seemed to be listening to people none could see. She pushed back her chair from the table and walked over to the window holding the feather up to the light. An aura of light encircled the feather, "I's heards of them, but in all my days I's haven't seen one 'til now. Where did you find this girl?"

"In J-Bird's house by a pool of blood that was dry when we arrived and wet when we left," Joy told her. "We thought it changed because of the rain," she continued.

"There was also a strange smell neither of us recognized," Grace added.

"It's an angel's wing, very rare. He may have left it for you," Lula May said returning the feather.

"It looks like a regular bird's wing to me. I thought all angel's wings were white," Joy replied.

"In Ecclesiastes it says a bird in the sky may carry our words and reports what we'z saying to the heavenly hosts. Angels are the messengers of God, and they take the shape of birds to spy and report on our doings. 'Til you see the nest hatch in the eaves, there is no telling if it's a real bird or a guardian angel," Lula May said on her soapbox. "Don't ignore your childhood feelings, your third eye is strongest then. Think about how many birds you noticed then in comparison to now."

"So, what do we need for the potion, Lula May?" Ethel asked.

"The essence of the demon," Lula May said, "which is on this here magazine, spurge, vervain, twitch grass, mandrake, horse mint, black bryony and a large Catawba bean."

Ethel and the girls went to the cabinet and took out the ingredients and returned to the table. Lula May retrieved a cast iron pot off the stove and set it in the middle of the table. She then filled a mason jar with water and held the jar to the four corners of the room. Walking in a spiral from the west corner to the container on the table, she chanted over and over, "cleans the mind, cleans the body, cleans the heart, cleans the soul," before pouring the water in the pot. "Shred the magazine and put it in the kettle." Lula May then reached for a wooden spoon she had tucked in her apron strings and measured out each ingredient.

Ethel's phone rang, "Hello."

"Ethel, it's me. Put me on speaker phone please," Bonnie requested.

"Grace, darling, I have some bad news. Your friend Anne died a few minutes ago and the one called Charlotte has taken a turn for the worse. They are searching the hospital for you now. Lula May, please hurry with the antidote. They have Matthew on a ventilator. Grace, when you come back to the hospital, bring Hope, Oscar and Sally. The hospital wants to test them as well. They are testing Charity and Hector right now."

"Hector?" Joy questioned, "why are the testing Hector?"

"They are testing everyone on the scene of this morning's accident, anyone and everyone who has had contact with any of the victims."

"Momma, please call Iris, let her know what's happened to Anne," Grace said.

"It's gonna' take over an hour to finish this here antidote," Lula May told all. "Tell 'em Grace has come to fetch the children. She can say she went to Faith's then to Joy's before she fount 'em. She'll bring the antidote along with Oscar and Sally and heads on backs to the hospital as soon as the cure is done. Bonnie sugar, I's gonna need Hope for the entrapment potion. I'll send Joy to the hospital with her shortly after. That asshole didn't get away with it all those years ago and he ain't getting' away with it now. Lula May is sending him and his lily-white ass straight back to hell where he belongs. You can count on that sugar, you can count on that!"

Chapter Thirty-Two

Dickey had no plans of going anywhere near that hospital. Having learned of his offspring, he was going to make sure that a last will and testament would place his family's fortune in their hands, with certain stipulations of course. With that in mind, he drove to Alice's home to write it out. *Possession has its advantages,* he thought. On the way he became aware that he had to be very careful as to how it was worded, or it would be considered a fake. "I wish I still was possessing that fat ass lawyer."

When he arrived, he went to the back of the house and let himself into the guest bedroom on the backside of the house with a crowbar. Once inside he went to J-Bird's office, he took a pen from the desk and wrote the will out in long hand. He began his will with "I, Richard Donald Dickson, of sound mind and body, am writing this Will and Testament on December 22nd, 1993." He confessed that he had impregnated his stepdaughters and was leaving the country rather than face prison. If his parents were to die before him, his share of the estate was to go to the children he sired with his wife Bonnie's daughters. Nothing was to go to a religious organization, church, charity, or university. If so, his lawyer and brother-in-law, James Weldon, was to place the money in a trust for his father's alma mater, the University of the South. He also stipulated that any relative of the Dickson's could use this trust to pay for their tuition. He sat aside a portion to maintain his parent's home and family cemetery. He signed it, placed it in an envelope, and sealed it. As he was leaving, he thought it would be wise to open it so it would look like someone read it and hid it. He did so, then opened J-Bird's desk drawer and slid the torn envelope to the very back.

Thirsty, Dickey went toward the kitchen but was thrown completely down the hall when he reached the kitchen door's threshold. "Damn," Dickey shouted. As he stood up, he could see J-Bird's ghost standing on the other side of the door looking down the hall. "J-Bird, why'd you do that?" Dickey asked the ghost.

"You can see me?" J-Bird asked.

"Yeah, I can see you," Dickey responded, "I see you've been imprisoned, decided not to face judgment, haven't you?"

"Who are you?"

"Oh, this is Lloyd Parker," Dickey referred to his body. "I'm your old pal, Dickey, Dickey Dickson. Remember?"

"So, are you dead too?"

"Well, sorta', kinda', you could say," Dickey shrugged. "Escaped from Hell, even possessed you for a while. Sorry I sent Alice over the edge."

"That was you inside my head?" J-Bird was dumbfounded.

"Yeah, remember, "Grudge Fuck, Grudge Fuck, Grudge Fuck! That was me all right."

"What stopped you from coming into the kitchen?"

"Same thing that keeps you from coming out. It's sort of a good thing actually.

Demons love to torture human spirits. The sad side is you are trapped for what will seem like an eternity. You'll go mad and your energy will show that anger, and the next inhabitants of your home will either leave or call for an exorcism. They can't get rid of you, but it will feel like acid being thrown on you," Dickey concluded casually.

"So, you're a demon?" J-Bird asked.

"Yep, any soul that escapes Hell is a demon," Dickey said.

"Why did you come here?"

"To write my last will and testament; who says you can't write one after your gone? I just did. Left everything to my boy. Looks like I'll have to go out the way I came in. Ciao, J-Bird."

"Goodbye Dickey," J-Bird said softly. "Feel free to visit anytime."

"Thanks for the offer, but I'll be spending my free time fucking." Pausing down the hallway Dickey turned around, "Tell me, are any of our old hangouts still jumping?"

"Group Therapy is still rocking from what I heard," J-Bird tilted his confused head.

"Group Therapy it is then, Lloyd," Dickey grinned an evil grin. "Time to teach you how to appreciate P-U-S-S-Y. What does that spell? Say it, Pussss-ay, and again, and again, and again. Gonna make a dog out of you yet, Lloyd Parker, gonna make a dog out of you yet."

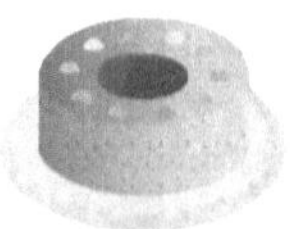

Chapter Thirty-Three

Nacha Gomez saw Bonnie, "Mrs. McRae-Dickson, I hope all is well."

"Mrs. Gomez, please call me Bonnie. How is Raul?"

"They are bringing him out of the induced coma tomorrow. I haven't seen Hope, is she alright?"

"Oh, Hope, she's fine," Bonnie informed her, "be here a little later this evening."

"She has been so attentive to Raul, this is the first day I arrived without her sitting by his side."

"She has been watching over her younger siblings. Her oldest brother and her mother and father are in the hospital. Both her brother and father are in comas," Bonnie added.

Charity came out of an elevator and made her way toward her mother. "Well, they told me I was clean, no signs of the virus."

"Virus?" Nacha asked.

"My family seems to have come down with some rare bug. We're still waiting to find out what it is," Bonnie explained.

"I will put you in my prayers," Nacha said, "say hello to Hope for me, Mrs.… I mean Bonnie."

"I'll do that, and we'll keep Raul in our prayers as well," Bonnie said as she saw Grace, Oscar, and Sally come off the elevator. Nacha waved at the children as she passed them in the hall.

"Hola La Señora Gómez," Sally responded in Spanish. "Raúl es hacerlo major," she said expressing her concern for Raul.

"Que lo de un coma mañana," Nacha said telling the girl about tomorrow's plans.

"Esa es una buena noticia. Dejaré que Hope conocer," glad to hear the good news, Sally informed Nacha she would let her sister know.

"Gracias," Nacha said with a smile, "Your Spanish is very good."

"As is your English, Mrs. Gomez," Nacha took the child's head in her hands and kissed her forehead.

"My prayers are with your family," she told the girl before continuing down the hall to Raul's room.

Grace greeted her mother with a hug and said, "I'm sorry it took me so long getting here, but I had to stop at the drug store and buy an eye dropper."

"They believe it is some new resistant strain of staphylococcus," Bonnie informed her daughter, "Well at least that is Dr. Gunnel's theory."

"Glad to see you made it back," Dr. Page said as she turned the corridor.

"Went to pick up the children," she said to the doctor.

"Oh, good, let's get you back down to the lab, so we can draw some blood," Dr. Page requested. "Do you know where that is located?" she questioned.

"Yes, should I take the children as well?" Grace asked.

"Who's their legal guardian?"

"I guess that would be me," Bonnie spoke up.

"Let me get some paperwork for you to sign. I'll be back with you shortly. Don't go away," Dr. Page added.

"Take my purse momma, everything is in there. I'll have Sally and Oscar distract them while you give Ellis and Matthew the antidote."

"How am I going to get in their room? They are in quarantine, remember," Bonnie exclaimed in as low of a whisper as possible and still be understood.

Watching Oscar and Sally stare into their father's room, Grace noticed a male orderly in protective gear remove his face mask as he exited Matthew and Ellis' room.

"Give me ten minutes and pray that he's not married or gay."

"What are you talking about? Grace Anne, what are you up to?" Bonnie asked.

"You don't want to know momma," Grace said bluntly.

Oscar and Sally walked up to them, "Are they going to be okay?" Sally asked.

"Yes, Darling," Bonnie reassured.

"But only if we can get your Bonnie Gram into their room to give them the antidote Lula May made for them," Grace told the girl.

"Oscar, I need you to make yourself scarce, so if the doctor returns before me, your Bonnie Gram can tell her you're afraid of needles and I've gone after you."

"Will do," Oscar said and walked down to the elevator.

"Sally, you stay with your Bonnie Gram for now. When I return with the key I need you to make a scene so your grandmother can get inside the room unnoticed, okay?"

"You can count on me," Sally said proudly, feeling included.

Grace went down the corridor in search of the orderly she saw earlier. Oscar took the elevator down to the floor below them. He wandered the corridors checking out the young nurses as they came and went on their rounds. *Wish they wore dresses like they did on old TV shows*, he thought. Oscar was extremely horny. Between the old porn magazines at Lula May's and the nurses that sparked his fantasies, he could feel the uncontrollable swelling in his groin. Usually, Oscar would have had masturbated twice by this time of day, but with Matthew reading Bible verses this morning and being sequestered at Lula May's amongst all those people, he had not had the opportunity to do so. He searched to find an off the beaten path restroom for a quick wank. He saw a men's room door that said, "Personnel Only." He looked both ways and quickly entered the room. Making his way down to the last stall he locked the stall door, dropped 'trou,' sat down and placed his feet up on the stall door so if anyone were to enter he'd go unnoticed. Getting as comfortable as he could, he took out his phone, and searched the web for some doctor-nurse porn. He knew his mom would kill him once she received the bill, but right now he was too horny to care.

Grace had found the testosterone driven orderly in the stairwell. The orderly's dark beard shown through his clean-shaven pale face, his thick black eyebrows sheltered his pale blue eyes and his chiseled jaw with a couple of battle scars took the man from being pretty to unusually rugged. She saw the Marine tattoo on his forearm and hoped for the best. *If he's not gay this might be easier than I thought*, she said to herself. "Hey, orderly," Grace called out.

The orderly looked over his shoulder at the beautiful red head and stopped in his tracks. "How can I help you?" he asked, staring at the woman as she descended the steps.

Grace could tell he was not gay by the way he stared at her, "I noticed your tattoo marine and wanted to thank you for your service."

"You're welcome," the thirty-something said to Grace.

"What's your name?" Grace asked.

"Geoff McDonnell, and yours?"

"You can call me Grace," she said. "So did you serve in Afghanistan or Iraq?"

"Both," he replied.

"Tours of duty?"

"Eight," he responded.

"Eight's a good size number, Geoff. An enlisted man I bet."

"Yes, mama," he responded.

"Service is so important. Don't you think Geoff?"

"Yes mam," he replied realizing where this was going.

Grace let her palm slide down the front of his scrubs before cupping the man's crotch with the full of her hand, "Would love to show my appreciation for your service with a bit a service."

"Here?" The young soldier asked.

"Got a better place?" she asked.

"Follow me," he said.

With his earplugs in, Oscar did not hear his aunt and the orderly enter at first. It was the slamming of the stall behind the couple that made the teen aware that he was no longer alone.

"God damn, you're one sexy woman," Geoff said to Grace as she undressed the former soldier.

"Thank you," Grace replied after she dropped his shirt on the stall floor along with the key card that was around his neck. She ran her fingers across the scars made by shrapnel and burns. "How'd you get this one?"

"The second Battle of Fallujah."

"And this," she said running her hand over the burn marks on his left side.

"Southern Afghanistan, our medevac was hit by an IED."

"Sexy," she said before kissing the soldier on the mouth.

Geoff drew Grace in tight and turned her around so she would be able to sit. Once seated, he lifted her blouse over her head and unhooked her bra. He took her breast in his hands and rotated. Her tits tickled his sweaty inner palm. They were as hard and erect as he was. Grace enjoyed a man that took control in the bedroom or bathroom for that matter. He pulled the drawstring of his scrubs as he kissed her and let them fall to his shoes. His boxers followed suit. He took Grace's hand and placed it on his throbbing erection, waiting for the moment when the sexy woman would realize he was missing his left leg.

When they broke the kiss, her eyes first fell to his handsome penis and unshaved testicles before she saw the glint of light made by his artificial metallic leg. She looked up at him, "Well at least they didn't get the leg that counts." She looked back down at his penis and with her index finger took the pre-cum from its tip, gazed up at him placing the finger in her mouth and said, "Yummy," before engulfing his member deep in her throat.

"Oh God, not many women can do that."

Grace knew when he said that it would not take long, and she was right, not five minutes into the blowjob, Geoff blew. She continued to work the head of his penis with his warm sticky fluids still in her mouth until he fell back against the stall door in a shiver. She stood up and spit his semen into the toilet before she knelt down and retrieved her bra, blouse and Geoff's door key, which she slid into her back jean's pocket. Standing before the completely exposed and still heavily breathing man, she quickly dressed. "Thanks again for your service," Grace said with a smile giving the once-over twice at what must have been a beautiful body that was now marred by war.

"Thank you for yours," he said with a wink, "most women of your caliber run."

"Caliber should not be judged upon appearance Geoff, if so, I would have been one of those women. I need to get back to my family before they notice I'm missing."

Geoff's head dropped, "I'm ashamed. Please, I was about to ask for your number, give me another chance."

"Let me think about it. I know your name and where you work. I need to go." Geoff stepped aside and Grace was out of the stall and men's room before the orderly could pull his boxers and scrubs up. Oscar had nutted during the loud gasps the former soldier had made. The evidence was splattered all before him. He wanted to leave but didn't want to get caught.

Geoff said, "Fuck," as he sat down on the toilet. "Don't do it Geoff, you're better than that."

Oscar heard the grown man cry. He never felt so awkward, until his phone rang.

"Hello," he whispered.

"Where are you?" Grace asked.

"In the bathroom."

"Well get back up here as soon as you can."

When Oscar hung up, he saw the bare-chested former soldier looking down into his stall as he stood on the neighboring john. Wiping his tears from his face, he started to chuckle, which turned into full-blown laughter as he saw the teenager sprawled half naked with the indication of his behavior clinging to his legs.

"I hope it was as good for you as it was for me boy," Geoff said returning to his stall to pick up his shirt. Not bothering to clean himself up, Oscar pulled up his jeans and bolted out of the room, but not before hearing, "Damn, where is it?" as the door shut behind him.

When Oscar had returned to the floor above, he heard Sally screaming, "Not before I see my mommy. I want my mommy," Sally continued. Grace was standing by the girl as he witnessed his Bonnie Gram exiting his father and brother's room. Bonnie stood outside of the room and watched through the window. Both men started going into convulsions, Bonnie watched the men, her hand over her mouth. All the bells and whistles went into overdrive and the staff left Sally and ran down to the room the two infected men occupied. With an injection, both men's seizures seceded. This gave Bonnie enough time to return to her daughter and the two remaining friends of Grace to give them the antidote. They too went into convulsions and the staff came to their rescue as quickly as they did for the men.

After Grace and the children were tested, they returned to look in on their parents. "How are they doing?" Grace asked her mother.

"It's miraculous," Bonnie replied. "Can you take the children home shortly? It will be getting dark soon. I'll come over there as soon as Joy arrives with Hope."

"Sure momma, I don't mind at all."

Dr. Gunnels found Bonnie, "I don't know what just happened, but your grandson's fever has broken. The antibiotics seem to be taking effect as well. It's amazing what modern medicine can do."

Bonnie made a sigh of relief, took the doctor's hands and thanked him while thinking, *Modern, my ass.*

Grace saw Geoff examine the floor as he walked down the hospital corridor. She made her way to the orderly and, as she passed him, said, "Follow me."

Once they were in the same stairwell where they met, she took out his key card from her purse. "Looking for this?" she asked.

"Thank you," he said.

"It got tangled up in my blouse somehow. I've got to get back," Grace started up the stairs when Geoff grabbed her arm, turned her around and kissed her.

Upon releasing her he said, "Please, let me take you out on a date?"

"Before I say yes there is something you've got to know. I'm the madam of the largest prostitution ring in this state. The girl that died today and the other two girls that came in with her are my employees. Knowing this, do you still want to date me?"

Geoff paused and thought about it briefly and nodded yes.

"What's your number?" she asked taking out her phone. He gave it to her. "What's the best time to call you tomorrow."

"Any time before fifteen hundred hours," Geoff replied. "I'm sorry, that's before three pm."

"My father was career military, I know what fifteen hundred hours means. I must go," Grace said before climbing the stairs. Reaching the landing she looked back down at the man, he grinned at her. She smiled back and watched him walk away with what she thought was a spring in his step, and then laughed at the reality of the metaphor.

Chapter Thirty-Four

Will gazed out the window watching the sun set on what he thought was a most peculiar day. Lula May had Will write all the procedures down earlier in her notebook, but the scraping of the lard off the 'sacrifice' made him more than a bit worried. That was because as Will watched the sun fall below the horizon, Lula May, Ethel, Hunter, and Joy stood around the table with old-fashioned razors in their hands, while on top of the table stood Hope, naked and greased down from head to toe in pure lard.

"Don't you look over this way Mr. Will," Lula May said in complete seriousness, "I'm trying to capture and rid the world of a sex demon, not create a new one."

The four, with razors in hand, shaved the 'lea's' as Lula May called it, off the girl. As the razors collected the lard, body hair and personal oils onto their single blades, they were drawn across the cast iron pot, producing what sounded like quick drags of fingernails across a chalkboard, which sent jolts down Will's spine with each deposit. "Well, y'all are saving me from the big, long shave. Raul will enjoy that, once he's out of his coma," Hope said trying not to laugh as the four removed the slick substance off her body. "Is that the same kettle y'all had used earlier to make the potion?"

"Yes, darling," Ethel said. "I washed it out after we had bottled everything. I remember Dickey when he was in human form. He even made a hit on me while Bonnie was putting the girls to bed one night."

"Married men bigger dogs than single men," Hunter directed to Ethel, "trust me on that."

"Be glad it's me and not your mother shaving you," Joy said, looking up at Hope. "She'd have surely cut you hearing that."

"Girl, you have a booty J-Lo would be envious of," Hunter said, scraping the area free.

"Ya think so, Hunter?"

"Your behind could bring on world peace, every straight man landing their eyes on your global hemispheres would find themselves saluting your fanny flag. Long may it wave, girl."

"Don't worry about that Hope," Joy said scraping the young woman's inner thigh. "Before you know it you'll be my age and find your fanny flag will be flapping in the wind."

"When you get my age, you'll find your bottom dragging the ground with old soldiers wondering if they should fold it and put it away or try to hoist it back up their poles," Ethel said.

"Ms. Ethel, girrrl," Hunter replied laughing with the others. "You just didn't say that."

The girls continued to scrape while Ethel informed them of the latest beauty shop gossip going around town. Once they had scraped all the grease off Hope, they wrapped her in a robe. "She's covered now," Joy told her future brother-in-law. "You can step away from the window if you like."

Lula May brought out of her cupboard four red candles and sat them on the table. She then went into the bedroom and retrieved an old box fan, which she plugged into the socket below the window. She took out her broom and swept the kitchen floor clean, collecting the dust in a dustpan. "Now listen to me, all of ya, and listen to me good, Ethel, I's needs you to lights these candles whens I's calls out to the spirits of the South. Mr. Will, when I calls on the spirits of the North, you turns on that fan for me. When I calls on the spirits of the East, Hunter you turn on the tap for me, and Joy, when I calls on the spirits of the West you toss the dust in this here pan into the air. But before that happens, Hunter hand me the box of cornstarch off the counter." Hunter does so and Lula

May poured the contents into the cast iron pot. "Will, do you remember the demon powder we made earlier today?"

"Yes mam'," Will said. "It's in the oven."

"Bring it to me."

"Joy, was Dickey a scotch man or a bourbon man?"

"Kentucky Bourbon," Joy said.

"Look under my bed, there is a box full of mini-bottles folks has given me over the ages. Find a bourbon and bring it here."

"Yes, mam'." Joy did so quickly and returned.

"Ethel, you were by him the night we ended that child molester's life. What were his last words?"

"What did you put in that God damn fruitcake?"

"Write it down on a piece of pure white paper for me," the voodoo priestess said.

"Hunter, bring me my church going hat, it's hangin' on my bed post," Lula May informed her nephew as she continued to stir the mixture in the pot. Holding her hat on his head, Hunter sauntered back into the room and with a tip of the hat, he presented his aunt with her hat. Lula May took the hatpin out of it and gave it to Ethel, "sterilize it with the lighter."

"Now Hope, the last thing that needs to be added will be three drops of your blood. When I ask for your hand give your left hand to me. I will prick the three middle fingers and squeeze each one till three drops of blood falls into the batch. After I draw her blood, everyone circle the table and clasp hands and repeat my words. Do not break hands 'til I let go. Only speak if I speak, no matter what happens. Does everyone understand?" They all nodded yes. "Now go to your places, Ethel take the lighter, go turn off the light and return to the table. I'll call on you first," Lula May instructed. "Our Lady of Mount Carmel, come to us on the winds of the South, help us light the fires of vengeance against one who takes advantage of the young." Once all the candles were lit, Lula May continued. "Our Lady of Czestochowa, come to us on the winds of the North, help us wipe out one who desecrates the body of women and children for his own violent pleasures." Will turned the box fan on high causing the lit candles' flames to soar, but they do not go out. Lula May saw the amazement on his face. "Our Lady of Lourdes, come to us on the winds of the East, wash clean and heal the hearts of young girls violated by an all-consuming evil spirit who feeds on innocents. Help protect those who seek revenge for those unduly harmed." Hunter turned on the water on key. Lula May declined her head in approval. "Our Lady of Prompt Succor, protector of sacred ground, come to us on the winds of the West, help us revenge those who threaten the hearth and home; protect the bonds of sisterhood from danger with quick justice." Joy wiped the dust out of the pan, which fell directly to the floor in a symmetrical pile. Lula May poured the bourbon into the kettle and stirred the batch in the cauldron. She then added the demon powder in with the other ingredients followed by Dickey's last words, which she lit above the flames of Our Lady of Mount Carmel before she tossed the paper into cast iron pot. Flames leaped up from the concoction.

"O kwa, o jibile," Lula May sang repeatedly in Creole, "Ou pa we m inosan?" Lula May then sang in English, "Oh, cross! Oh, jubilee!" she sang twice. "Don't you see I'm innocent? Baron La Croix, hear my plea for justice, hear of a soul who claims your swagger in death." A stream of blackness ascended high and formed the shape of a cross. The apparition appeared to vertically rest on the edge of the table. "Ayizan, hear me, a soul escaped your punishment, condemned for violating youth and wreaks havoc once again upon the earth taking an innocent life this very day. Come forth and secure our revenge." A puff of white smoke climbed forth from the pot and spread in the shape of a palm, descending like a feather to lie also on the opposite edge of the table. Lula May took a cigar out of her apron pocket and lit it puffing out rings of smoke. She blew the rings toward the other five individuals in the room. "Ke-ke-ke-ke-ke-ke-ke," Lula May chanted between exhales, 'til she saw the rings change into the shape of hearts as they floated toward Joy. "Before you Mamba Zila is a woman raped, her virginity and innocence as a girl taken by her mother's husband. Her sisters all ravaged and blemished in their hearts of trust. His cheating heart runs free from justice, help us garnish the justice due to us."

The heart-shaped ring of smoke descended and hung around Joy's neck like a wreath. Lula May nodded her head trying to assert calm over the woman, "Kalfou, lover of red, take this blood offering, come to this ancient crossroad and approve this conjure to bring justice given now denied," Lula May said before she picked up the hatpin from the table. Hope placed her youthful hand in the old wrinkled one and Lula May pricked each finger as she said she would. She motioned for all to come around the table, all locked hands as the voodoo priestess began to chant, "Baron La Croix, giver of justice, remove the cross we bear." They all repeated Lula May's call. "Ayizan, keeper of innocent children, right their wrongs, help us return the evil doer to his punishment in hell," Lula May joined in the answer chanting above those in her care. "Mamba Zila, protector of the bonds that bind marriage and family, return the blatant one to Hell who violated the marriage vow and ripped the virginal innocence from young girls. Kalfou, hear the validity of this spell, take the blood offering of his offspring, grant us your approval. Baron La Croix, Ayizan, Mamba Zila, search our hearts for the truth in our cause."

The smoke rose in the iron kettle and entered their nostrils. Their bodies convulsed as the three spirits moved one to the next. All were investigated, the smoky icons rose above the cauldron with a howl from a lone dog, the screech of an owl, and the pounding of a gavel. The mixture turned red then black before one more cloud of white smoke rose above the circle in the shape of a crescent moon. Will opened his mouth, but Lula May gave him a look and he quickly closed it. The four symbols took on their human form and danced a jig around the concoction resting on the table. As they moved faster around the brewing pot, the spirits joined hands and formed a cyclone. Lula May saw the spirit of her father and grandmother enter the room. They joined the four Ladies, bonding the mortals' hands as the winds lifted their feet off the floor. Having realized their dance would not break the bond of the priestess, they slowly reduced their velocity and size while staring into the sets of human eyes as they descended into the potion.

Lula May let go of Ethel and Hope's hands. She blew out the candles, cut off the water, then the fan. She gathered her broom and swept the dust up and emptied it into the trashcan. "The spirits are with us," she said, "thank the Ladies four, thank you ancestors for your added protection."

"Amen," Ethel added. "Amen."

"Joy, you need to get Hope to the hospital before visiting hours are over." The aunt and niece left the old shack.

"Did that just happen, Aunt Joy?"

"Never heard of joint hallucinations," Joy responded.

"That's not what momma says," Hope joked.

Joy laughed as she climbed into her van, "She would." As the women drove out onto the pavement, "If your momma had experienced that kind of magic she would be diving under Lula May's bed and digging into her stash right now. Me, I smoke, look in my purse, take out my billfold, and in the change purse you'll find pre-rolled joints. Take one out and light it for me will you?

As Hope opened Joy's purse, she saw the angel feather, which had an effervescent glow about it. She took it out and examined it. "Cool" she said.

"Is that the feather from J-Bird's house? What a difference seeing it in the dark makes," Joy said. Hope placed the feather in her aunt's hair before removing the billfold and procuring the weed. She lit the stogie up and passed it to her aunt.

"Taste familiar?" Joy asked. "It's the weed you were smoking the night of your car accident. I got it out of there before Hector and his deputies found it and saved you and Raul from facing possession charges. Your Dad was working to clear the other charges. As crazy as we are, you're lucky to be born into this family. Hector said any other girl would be sitting in jail facing vandalism charges at the very least. Lord knows the neighborhood you and Raul vandalized wants blood for destroying their Christmas. I fear one of the property owners will be going after Raul because of his ethnicity."

"I hate this small town," Hope said.

"I used to to, darling. Dixon is a beautiful town, aren't many like it, recreational lakes and rivers, parks, museums, history, stately architecture, and a classic downtown. Before 9/11, I used to say, there ain't nothing wrong with Dixon that a good case of anthrax wouldn't take care of."

Joy and Hope laughed together.

"Aunt Joy, why didn't anybody tell Matthew and me?"

"Because we murdered the man," Joy said. "A man that, because of the privilege of his birth, would have escaped justice."

"So, there is a license for the privileged class to escape justice," Hope asked, "to do as we please?"

"We have to answer to our own class," Joy told her. "But this is true of every class, not just the privileged. Look at the lower classes and how they shun each other based on their standards. They, too, ration out resources to those who govern their class, don't think that they don't. You are too young to remember the PTL Club. It was a religious TV show that made lots of money overselling time-share real estate. Once the scandal broke, the other televangelists were in the wings waiting to tear it apart. Greed is an ugly thing to watch in action. One just has to look at Enron." Hope yawned. "We'll talk about that later. Look through my CD case and play something you like," Joy said.

They drove listening to the Talking Head's *Remain in Light* 'til they reached the hospital. As they exited the van in the hospital parking lot, Joy felt a wave of negativity wash over her. *This weed has never had this kind of effect on me before*, she thought. When the two entered the elevator, Joy arched over. It felt as if she had taken a direct punch to the gut.

"Are you okay, Aunt Joy?"

"I'm not sure," she said as she righted herself.

When they exited off the elevator, Joy stopped in mid-stride and gushes of wind moved around her. She felt surrounded, but saw nothing. Hope kept walking 'til she became aware that her aunt was no longer by her side. When she turned around, she screamed. Joy's body was taking blow after blow as if she were in a boxing ring. She began howling in pain as the nurses and staff watched the display in disbelief. Taking a knockout punch, Joy fell to the floor. As a nurse walked toward her, but before she reached her, Joy's body started to move as if it were being kicked. Hector, who had been there for testing, ran to his wife and took her in his arms.

"Get a doctor, damn it!" he screamed.

Hector, Hope, Bonnie, and Charity waited outside the examination room as Dr. Gunnels examined Joy. When the doctor came out to talk to them, he shook his head. "I haven't ever seen anything like it since I interned in Atlanta. Mrs. Sakamoto has the same injuries as those of a gang member who had been in a fight and lost. She has a concussion, so we'd like to keep her overnight."

"Is that necessary?" Bonnie asked. Bonnie wasn't sure why her daughter was attacked by spirits or what kind of spirits they were, but she was sure that Joy was in danger from Hope's description.

"That is your call, but I don't recommend it."

"I know what to watch for Dr. Gunnels," Charity said. "Hector, take her home, I'll watch over her tonight. There is no need to make the kids worry any more than they already are with Matthew, Faith and Ellis in the hospital."

"Are you sure Charity?" Hector asked.

"Not a problem, tomorrow's my day off anyway," Charity replied.

"Well, since you're staying with Joy and Hector, and I'm staying at Faith's with the children, I'll call Ethel and let her and Lula May know that Joy is going to be okay and who you'll be staying with tonight. Hope, let's go home so Grace can get home before it gets much later."

"Okay, Aunt Charity, will you give this to Aunt Joy when she wakes up?" Hope handed Charity the olive-colored feather. "Miss Lula May said it was an angel's feather. It fell on the floor during the attack," she added.

"Let's go home sugar, your brother and sister are waiting on us," Bonnie said to her oldest granddaughter.

As Bonnie and Hope were leaving the room, Hope turned around and said, "Wait 'til you go outside, it glows in the dark."

Charity loaded her sister in the back of her ambulance. Joy was still out with the sedative that the doctor gave her. Charity took the feather that Hope had given her out of her pocket, "Damn, it does glisten in the dark." She placed it in her sister's auburn hair before she closed the door and began the drive to her sister home. Hector followed behind the ambulance and noticed a brief light emanate out the back doors. It dissipated and he thought no more of it.

Zachriel, in all his glory, sat next to the beauty stroking her hair. He was singing to her in a language she did not understand. With a bump in the road, Joy opened her eyes and saw what appeared to be a perfectly built twenty-something redheaded man cut out of cream cheese.

"You are the most beautiful creature I've ever seen, you tempt me so," which startled Joy, being that the angel was nude and had a full erection.

"Please don't hurt me," Joy whispered.

"I would never do that," Zachriel replied.

"Why are you naked?"

"Angels wear no clothes, only humans do," Zachriel replied.

"Am I dead?" Joy asked.

"No," the angel said inhaling deeply, delighting in the Anakite's scent.

"Where are your wings?"

"I'm in my human manifestation. I can shift physically into any creature the Creator has ever created within that dimension, but it has been commanded that we not take on our angelic form lest men might worship us. But I'll tell you a secret if you smile for me, in the rising and setting sun you can see our wings in our shadows, especially if we have them spread open. Few humans have seen this since we can smell you coming."

"Why do you have an erection?" She asked Zachriel.

"Your kind causes this to happen."

"My kind?"

"You and your family are all Anakites. I'm being called to duty. I must go. I will return," Zachriel said, before he vanished with a surge of light.

Joy was somewhat frightened by Zachriel's appearance. She was not sure if it was a dream or not. She pondered his words trying to fight her return to sleep but lost the battle.

Charity pulled into their drive, unloaded the ambulance with the help of Hector and put her sister to bed in their guest room. She checked her sister's temperature, blood pressure, and other vitals, then pulled the vanity chair over by the bed, sat down and brushed the hair out of Joy's eyes. "First Faith and now you, it seems my sisters are trying to escape witnessing the true miracle of the century, me, Charity McRae, marrying a man," she said to her sister with a chuckle. "Well, I'm not going to let that happen."

Charity propped up her feet on the foot of the bed and stared at her sister, "Do you remember singing this in your senior show? You were the sexiest Morgan Le Fay Dixon has even seen. I was so proud to have you as my sister. Stick around, will ya'?" she asked softly trying not to cry as she began to sing, "Far from day, far from night, Out of time, out of sight, In between earth and sea, We shall fly, follow me, Dry the rain, warm the snow, Where the winds never go, Follow me, follow me, Follow me…"

Chapter Thirty-Five

Lloyd had seen more vaginas, up close and personal, in the past two days than he had seen in his entire life. At one point he asked Dickey for a microphone so he could record his own *Vagina Monologues*, but the joke had completely gone over Dickey's head, apparently news of the play had not reached the inner sanctums of Hell. Dickey thought what good is it being a demon without tormenting someone and what better way to torture a gay man than to bring his consciousness forth in the middle of him devouring prime, honey-licking pussy.

Dickey eventually became tired of what seemed to him to be Lloyd's narcissism. Dickey had always enjoyed watching his performance, but his attention was drawn to the beauty of a woman's ass or the folds of warm pinky flesh engulfing his penis. Sharing Lloyd's consciousness made him aware of the male genitalia that he was using to provide his pleasure. He became more aware of the beauty and form of the male body than he ever wanted to be. Lloyd was as drawn to mirrors as much as his demon self, Dickey thought. Though Dickey was a handsome man in his day, he never lived in complete awareness of his appearance as Lloyd did. Getting down, dirty, and nasty and not giving a shit was what made living, living for Dickey, a part of the male gender's given rights that went way beyond just sex. Living with Lloyd was like living with a publicity agent, always prepared for the next photo-op.

Lloyd was complaining about needing to shower and shave. Dickey had to admit the body he occupied was getting a bit ripe. It was more the fact that women were losing their desire for a man whose clothes were more wrinkled than elephants' legs and whose body odor filled a room faster than Brut. A shower was needed Dickey conceded, more than giving into anything else that the fag desired. So away from the wanton wickedness that existed in every capitol city, a return to the provincial confines of the small town that was Dixon was in order.

"I hope I still have a job," Lloyd said to Dickey as they drove down the interstate.

"God, look at me," said Lloyd as he looked in the rearview mirror, "I'm a hot mess."

"Your testosterone is like a constant feed of opiates to me. I am so fucking horny," Dickey told Lloyd as he fumbled with his zipper.

"My dick is raw, leave it alone," Lloyd pleaded. "That girl with the mousey hair, snoopy-nose tits and hillbilly meth-mouth did a number on me."

"Don't worry, she'll pay for it," Dickey said.

"What do you mean? No, I don't want to know."

"That's fine, I'm still going to play with your, my, our dick," Dickey said as he released the penis from its confines. "So, have I converted you back to pussy?"

"Never stopped liking fish, just prefer beef," Lloyd thought. "As a matter of fact, I always order surf and turf at the Red Lobster when I can afford it. Just not many swingers in Dixon."

"There was in my day, hell, a little bitch swapping saved on gas and ass money my dad used to say. The old man said when the gas prices went up during the Arab oil embargo, private sex clubs sprung up in small towns across this great state. No need to spend extra money for city ass when country ass is not just as good, but even better from lack of constant abuse and tatter, cheaper too. It may turn out that the nation was saved by the Depression, he'd say. Save money son, wherever you can. My generation had their priorities straight, pay less, save more, especially on the extraneous pleasures of life. The cost of marriage is cheap in comparison to the yearly use of a whorehouse. Get married son, find you a good woman, he'd say. Every woman I married either died or tried to kill me, the last sending me straight to Hell, do not pass go, do not collect two hundred dollars."

"What's Hell like?" Lloyd asked.

"Everyone's different, look around you," Dickey said. "God is a very creative. For me, a mega-demon that's so in love with me he chased my ass around Hell."

"What's so bad about that?"

"One, he was a Virtue in the hierarchy of angels so he's twice my size and able to move the four elements at will, making him very hard to hide from. When he caught me, he raped me with that big-ass dick of his that's literally the size of an arm. This he called making love. In comparison to what followed when he got angry at me for running away and submitting to lesser demons for protection and shelter, the rape wasn't so bad."

"How did he find out?"

"He asked."

"Why didn't you lie?"

"There is no lying in the ninth realm, or vanity, or stealing, or gluttony, just sex attached to more types of pain than you can think of. When the pain traipses anywhere close to the realms of pleasure, that pleasure is lost in the most devastating of ways. There are different pains for every part of your body and soul. Your soul has only just enough rest to save you from oblivion, which is the only thing universally prayed for in Hell, but never granted."

"I thought Hell was fire and brimstone," Lloyd said.

"Those are only a couple of the tools used for your torture. They are in every realm of Hell, but are in constant use on the lazy and self-serving who brought souls into the world without working to support them. There are souls being exorcised in all the realms and various sub-realms of Hell, you never know where a door leads 'til you open it."

"How did you escape him?" Lloyd was horrified.

"After he tired of my torture, he went to take revenge on all those who gave me refuge." Lloyd asked if this monster had a name. "Of course," Dickey told him. "But I dare not say it or he'll come here and drag my ass back over there."

"Over, not down there?"

"Hell is a parallel realm, just like Heaven is. The only up and down are the same ones you know. Up can be just as torturous as down, just like in this world. Go too high, you freeze, too low, you incinerate, either way you burn." Dickey glanced down at Lloyd's limp penis, "You sure know how to kill a mood."

As they arrived at Lloyd's mother's home, she came to the door. Stepping out onto the porch she screamed, "Where have you been with my car? Why didn't you answer your phone? Aren't you aware that Jackie Williams' funeral is in a few hours and you're a pallbearer?"

"You deal with her," Dickey stated returning full control of Lloyd's body to him.

"Visiting friends, the battery died, and when did that happen?" Lloyd asked.

"Mrs. Williams called me and asked me if you could be one of the pallbearers yesterday. I said I thought you would be honored. Was I wrong?" She shrieked.

"No momma, you weren't wrong," Lloyd lowered his head. "Let me wash up. I'll be ready shortly."

"I have your good suit hanging on your closet door," his mother told him.

When Lloyd entered his bedroom, not only was the suit hanging on the closet door, a starched shirt and tie were hung on the doorknob, a fresh pair of ironed boxers, t-shirt, and socks were sitting on the bed. The man stripped and examined himself in the mirror. Dickey became mesmerized. "Time to jump in the shower," Lloyd said, breaking the trance.

Dickey preferred a cooler shower to a warmer one for obvious reasons. When Lloyd applied soap to his genitals, he winced. "Every pleasure has its price," Dickey said to him. Lloyd turned away from the water flow and continued to shower and shave. Once dried off, Lloyd examined his penis and said aloud, "Jesus Christ, that crack whore's mouth was made of shard glass."

Lloyd and his mother were among the half dozen white people in attendance. Lloyd recognized the aged Coach Half attending with his much younger wife, who Lloyd thought was his daughter. Jackie's former coach and mentor had also been asked by Jackie's mother to be a pallbearer. The coach still struck a handsome figure of a man dressed in khakis and a classic navy wool blazer he'd owned since the 80s. His hair was now white, his continued care for himself resulted in a face that didn't reveal his true age. The retired teacher nodded at Lloyd in appreciation of his presence. Dickey stayed buried deep in the sub-consciousness of Lloyd, he sensed the presence of angels before they reached the church's parking lot. He knew not that there would be more to fear than a few angels on duty, for not too far behind them, running late, was Lula May behind the wheel.

The church, still decorated for the Christmas season, was filled with most of Jackie's mother's congregation. Hunter removed his fedora that matched his pinstriped suit as he passed the threshold of the sanctuary. He held the door open for Lula May and Yvonne, who was dressed in classic black with matching wide-brimmed hat and veil. Women in white dresses were gathered near the front, they were all disturbed when they witnessed Lula May enter their house of worship. As whispering rose to a bellow of blustering contempt, many gave Lula May the evil-eye. There were not many in the African American community that didn't know that she was a voodoo priestess. Blame for many a hardship was laid at her feet, something which Lula May endured better than most scapegoats in small southern towns. Wearing a classic hounds-tooth overcoat over a half black and red dress, Lula May stood in the back of the building scouring the church seeking out Lloyd Parker, who was easy enough to find. As soon as they entered, Dickey could smell something familiar, he desperately wanted to seek it out, but he knew that with angels present, he'd best stay put. Any lack of decorum would bring him to their attention. Lula May sent Hunter to the far right rear corner of the church's pews, Yvonne to the far left rear corner, while she sat in the center aisle.

Omeguel's hair was out of control, "There is a blood offering in the church."

"My momma's church don't make no blood sacrifices, not in my whole life have I heard of any church in all of Dixon making such," Jackie told Omeguel. "Some snake handlin' deep in the country by some white Pentecostal rednecks, but I don't know of any church that makes animal sacrifices, much less human ones."

The funeral turned into a sermon. Lloyd's mom would fall asleep and leap to attention when the congregation would shout an Amen or

Hallelujah. The smell of the blood was making Dickey salivate. Lloyd's mom took a handkerchief from her purse and handed it to him, "Are you okay, Lloyd?"

Lloyd nodded yes. Finally, a young man went forward announcing in a loud voice, "I've sinned, I've sinned." As the pastor and the sinner sat on the front pew, the congregation sang "Come Down, Angels" while the young man made his confession, the gathered swayed back and forth, many with their hands raised high. Lloyd was in shock as he watched his mother participate.

I love to shout, I love to sing
Let God's saints come in
I love to pray my heav'nly King
Let God's saints come in

"I haven't heard this in years," Lloyd's mother leaned over and told him.

"My momma has soul," he thought as he watched his mother move and sing with the rest of the black congregation.

Come down, angels, trouble the waters
Come down, angels, trouble the waters
Come down, angels, trouble the waters
Let God's saints come in

Jackie was stunned by Omeguel's joy as he too sang with the congregation. All Jackie's experience had been stoical with the angel 'til this moment. "Rejoice Jackson Luther Williams, a soul is saved, Rejoice!" the angel said before he stood up in all his nude glory and began to dance. "Witness all the heavenly host present, Jackson Luther Williams, see how happy we are when one soul sees the error of his ways," the angel said before placing his hands over Jackie's eyes.

When he removed his hands, Jackie witnessed many angels present, singing, dancing—indeed rejoicing at the heart that was cleansed. He saw halos that encircled but a few heads amongst the congregation he grew up with and were happy to see the luminous ring surrounding his mother's head. He saw the sphere that surrounded his cousin's head intensify.

"Why does my cousin's halo grow brighter?" Jackie asked Omeguel.

"He's releasing the burden of sin with his confessions."

"Why doesn't Pastor Jones have one?"

Omeguel glanced above the preacher at the pastor's guardian angel who flew over to them. The two angels greeted each other with a kiss, staring into each other's eyes as they danced, the pastor's guardian angel dropped his head and sadness entered his eyes. Omeguel lifted the guardian's chin up and pointed to the halos present. "There is still hope," Omeguel told the lower ranked angel. A smile returned to the angel's face, and he returned to his post above the pastor.

"Leon Tabor Jones is a serial adulterer, thief, and glutton, his halo diminished eleven years, seven months and nineteen days ago. Why do you smile at such sadness, Jackson Luther Williams?"

"I always thought my mother was a saint, my heart is filled with joy knowing that she truly is and if I don't make it to paradise, she will."

"Then dance and sing, Jackson Luther Williams, celebrate goodness on earth one last time before the winds gather your soul and take you to face judgment before the Creator."

Jackie moved and clapped his hands and sang with the heavenly host feeling the joy of praising God as if he were once again a child. He noticed that Lloyd sat still as if he were horrified. "Why is my friend acting so stiff, he wasn't that way when I knew him?"

"He is possessed by a demon," Omeguel responded.

"Why don't you rid him of the demon?"

"A demon must leave voluntarily, to force him out could bond his soul to the soul of the one possessed. She," the angel pointed at Lula May, "is a witch." He stared at Lula May intently, "a very powerful witch, she has brought the blood offering. She is trying to lure the demon out."

I hope to meet my brother there
Let God's saints come in
That used to join with me in pray'r
Let God's saints come in...

Paster Jones rose from the pew, the congregation lowered their singing to just above a whisper. "Brothers and Sisters, we have a soul who has confessed to his sins and wants to rejoin our Lord, Praise Jesus." Hallelujahs and amens rang out from those gathered. The pastor announced to all the sins the young man was turning his back on. "No more drunkenness," the pastor said,"Hallelujah," they hollered. "No more fornication," was responded with "No, more, no more." "No more coveting of his neighbor," was followed by "Yes, brother, yes." "No more bearing false witness" the pastor rounded out, followed by the congregation responding with, "The Lord is great, Amen, Amen. And Jesus saves."

The congregation came down and surrounded the young man and sang the final verse in an elevation of emotions. The pastor stepped up into the pulpit, motioning for the congregation to sit and in the softest tone they sang.

Didn't Jesus tell you once before
Let God's saints come in
To go in peace and sin no more
Let God's saints come in

"Jackie Williams was a good man, always 'tentive' to his mother, not a Mother's Day went by where she didn't receive flowers. He was a hardworking man, provider for his family, there was always food on the table and the bills were paid. He was not perfect, you can ask any of his wives, all three are here. Not one of his children, no matter their mother, went without Christmas. He was present for all his friends, didn't matter if they were red, yellow, black, or white. No matter the task, whether it was to help them pack and move, or stand against gangsters wanting to inflict harm, Jackie was there. Jackie Williams is Heaven bound filled with good deeds. His children and family are the ones who are in pain. But know that the Lord will give you comfort, his angels will deliver massages of comfort to you. Let us pray."

Finally, the funeral came to an end, and one last viewing by close relatives. Lloyd walked up to the casket and glanced on his childhood friend. Dickey had to come out of the recesses of his mind, though he didn't want to, "Sorry Lloyd, but no tears, not now. Don't want to create a zombie now, do we?"

After the coffin was sealed the six pallbearers took their places next to the casket and rolled the coffin down the aisle. Dickey was on the opposite side of the aisle from Lula May, he recognized that she was where the scent originated. An evil grin came across his face, as he nodded no, "Well Lloyd, I'm going to release you, the question is who's next."

Jackie and Omeguel watched as the precession arrived at the century plus old burial grounds. Dickey scanned the crowd as they unloaded the casket at the city cemetery. His pickings were slim, half of those who gathered at the church did not follow the hearse to the graveyard, but Lula May did. They set the coffin on top of the straps that stretched above the pre-dug grave. Lula May, Hunter and Yvonne sat behind the wives and children, which meant they were four rows back. After the coffin was in place, the six men went and stood behind the folding chairs that had been placed under the funeral home's tent. Lula May watched Lloyd as he made his way to the back of the crowd. While waiting for the preacher to begin the service, Dickey noticed a young sixteen-year-old biracial boy who helped to unload the flowers that were set around the tomb after the final rights were said. The service started before the young man completed his tasked. He turned to finish the task, but the funeral director grabbed the boy by his coat sleeve and turned him around to stand behind the tomb.

Each of Jackie's three wives gave heartfelt testimonials about their late husband. Jackie watched in disbelief, "They sure as hell, I mean for heaven's sake they never said anything that nice about me when I was alive." A cousin told tales of childhood indiscretions. "Why'd you go tell everyone that one Charlie, my momma's here," Jackie said laughing.

Lloyd came before the gathering, Dickey retrieved just enough to give Lloyd emotional leeway, "For those of you who don't know me, my name is Lloyd Parker, I work for the Emergency Response Department here in Dixon. I knew Jackie from childhood. His mom came over every Saturday, and while she was cleaning our house, she would send Jackie and me out to play. We became the best of friends. What few people know is Jackie put his life on the line for me. I was being..." Lloyd paused and held back his tears, "I was being raped by two big bullies and Jackie, the skinny string-bean that he was back then, picked up a big stick and came running with a scream that could have woke the dead.

Coach Half can testify to his bravery. You can guess I really didn't want anyone to know this. Jackie kept my secret 'til the day he died. He was a good man and a good friend. I'm so sorry Mrs. Williams, I tried to save him. I truly did. I loved Jackie. He was the brother I never had."

The tears rolled from his eyes as did everyone else's by the graveside, Dickey turned Lloyd's back to the crowd, wiped the tears from his eyes and placed his wet hand on the hand of the teenager's, which rested on the stone. He looked at the sixteen-year-old, placed his hand on his face, and as Lloyd's knees gave out on him, he dropped, striking his head on the tombstone. Blurry eyed, he got back up, blood was running down his face. Dickey was gone. Mrs. Parker gasped as she saw the blood. Hunter, at the end of the aisle ran up to Lloyd, "you're bleeding bro, come over here and sit down in my chair," he said to the white man.

Jackie went and stood by his childhood friend, "It's good knowing you were loved," Jackie said to Omeguel.

"To bring love into the world erases a multitude of sins," Omeguel responded. "The winds approach, Jackson Luther Williams, it is time to meet the Creator."

Jackie looked over the crowd, at his children, his wives, his mother, and at Lloyd.

The preacher stood over his coffin. "Dust thou art, and unto dust thou shalt return," he began, "Let us pray, Heavenly Father that art in Heaven, hallowed be Thy name…"

Jackie gazed up at the sky, tubular clouds rolled in like a great tsunami, churning within the souls that had gathered from across the land. Their wails pre-heralded the Virtues' arrival upon all present in both dimensions with a gush of wind that sent shivers down the spine. Tears ran down Jackie's face, not from fear, but from the knowledge that he may never again see their faces. Two Virtues, one dark-skinned with wings of red, the other pale with wings of black and blue, descended to the cemetery grounds. They walked casually but with purpose directly to Omeguel and greeted their fellow angel with a kiss. They communicated without a word spoken between them. The Virtue with red wings held up his hand and a scroll appeared in it. The other held up his hand and a cardinal's quill appeared between his fingers. The scroll opened, the two wrote the testimony of Omeguel upon it while Omeguel returned to Jackie, "It is time." Jackie walked with Omeguel over to the Virtues, "Look after my momma, will you?"

"Her guardian knows your prayer."

Jackie looked back at his family and friends one last time. The Virtues handed the scroll to Omeguel. He examined what they had written, closed it, took the red feather, pricked his thumb, and placed his seal upon the scroll. He returned both to the Virtues, arms lifted, they returned them to the winds. They each took the crying Jackie under an arm and lifted his soul into the sky. Omeguel watched as they flew toward the rolling clouds. Jackie's tears fell like raindrops until he entered the horizontal cyclone as it continued eastward, toward Jerusalem. Omeguel turned toward the crowd that were saying their final farewells and spied the witch once more. He gazed at Lloyd, the demon wasn't there. He scanned the crowd searching for the demon, but Dickey was gone.

Dickey had passed the cemetery gates driving the delivery truck Shaddy, short for Shadrach, had used to transport the flowers from the church to the gravesite service. Demon possession mixed with the pure testosterone thrusting through Shaddy's veins caused a painful throbbing in his loins. "Nothing like an untainted natural high," he reflected. Dickey was drunker than a tick feasting on a dog's ass with the ever-increasing release of CHO compound from the teen. All women looked hot, young, old, and everything in between. If it was walking, he was looking. *It was good to share the mind of someone like-minded when it came to women. His posse took pleasure in partying, Shaddy worked for his cash. He was an all-around nice guy, a bit innocent, as a sixteen-year-old should be, basically untarnished, yet the youngster still looked to corrupt and be corrupted.* Dickey thought. "School's out, let's go find us some ass, Shaddy," Dickey turned on the radio, the only source of music in the commercial vehicle. As rap music began to blare, Dickey said, "We're not listening to this shit while I'm the one driving the ship." He tuned it to his old country radio station only to hear Colt Ford rapping, "Something about this generation just ain't right."

Chapter Thirty-Six

It was sometime after 10:00 am when Charity received a call from Sweet. She didn't recognize the number so she let it go to voice mail. It was not 'til three when she left work to relieve her sister's care from Mary Jane that she listened to the message. "Charity, please come get me, my parents have found out about us," she whispered. "They are going to…" Sweet said before Charity heard, "Who are you talking to girl? It better not be that bull dyke or I'm going to kill your ass, you hear me girl?" Sweet's father blasted in unmistakable anger before the phone went dead.

Charity called the number she had for Sweet, "Hello, can I speak to Sweet, please?"

"Can I ask who's calling?" the crackling voice of an adolescent boy asked.

"I'm Nancy Roberts," Charity lied, "Sweet's friend from Bob Jones U."

"Oh, okay, Sweet is in the hospital."

"Oh my, is she alright?"

"She got hit by a car, mom and dad are at the hospital with her right now."

"I'll pray for her, goodbye," Charity said. After Charity made a series of phone calls to her mother to let her know her whereabouts, and to Mary Jane to ask if she would explain her situation to her mother when she woke, she let the rubber of her ambulance hit the interstate. It wasn't long before she received a call from Hunter. He told her that Lloyd had been admitted to the hospital and that he, too, had demon pox and they needed her to administer the potion to him. "I'm an hour up the highway, can it wait 'til I get back from Greenville? Oh, and will you ask Aunt Ethel if she could make a pallet for Sweet? I'm bringing her back with me." She drove the ambulance into the parking lot of Greenville Memorial. If anyone had traumatic brain injuries, this is where they would have been delivered. She entered the hospital and asked the volunteer sitting at the desk what room Sweet Ride was in. The volunteer looked at her as if this was a joke. "God damn, what is Sweet's real name? I'm sorry, I forgot her real first name, she's been called Sweet since first grade. Her last name is Ride, she's nineteen and lives on West Carolina Avenue. I'm a friend of the family. I drove all the way from Dixon."

The volunteer looked up the last name, "We have a Geraldine Ride in intensive care. Only one person is allowed in the room to see her, but seeing that you're an EMT, and you drove so far, she is in room 455," the volunteer said.

When Charity arrived at the room, she saw that Sweet's parents were standing by her bed and holding each other next to their very bruised and battered daughter. The nurse was folding the top sheet just below her shoulders. She turned off the vitals machinery, "I'll leave you folks alone with her," the nurse said. Charity wanted to scream, but she stood there and watched her beloved's father clasp his hands together, lift them up and pray, "Dear Jesus, please don't send my daughter to Hell. She was led away by a jezebel spirit into sin. It was not her fault," the father cried.

Sweet's mother started beating her husband. It was a full-on assault, "Why! Why!

Why?" she screamed over and over with each blow pounding her husband. He secured her arms and she still screamed, "Why!" As the commotion grew louder, the medical team came running back down to the room. Sweet's father recognized Charity as the staff went around her.

"Jezebel!" he screamed as he lunged toward the door tripping over his wife. "Slay her, she is a demon from Hell," he stood up and tried to move past the orderlies. "My daughter is dead because of her!"

"She may be dead because of me, but you killed her," Charity told the man and all around him. She took out her cell phone and dialed 911.

"This is your 911 operator, how may I direct your call, ambulance, fire, or police?"

"Police please, I have evidence of a possible homicide," Charity said. As the phone rang, she walked to the opposite side of the bed and looked down on Sweet. "Hello, Sheriff, I'm Charity McRae, sister-in-law to Sheriff Hector Sakamoto, yes sir, down in Dixon. I believe I have evidence to the homicide of Geraldine Ride. Yes sir, it's a message on my cell phone. I believe you might find it disturbing. Here at Greenville Memorial, room 455."

Charity stood there looking at the battered face of Sweet 'til the police arrived. After she played the message for them, Sweet's mother moaned, fell to her knees and wept. Wiping her tears, she spotted the gun in the deputy's holster and went to draw it. The deputy grasped the desperate woman's hand and secured her on the floor.

"He killed her, he ran her over, he ran over my baby," she bawled.

"That wasn't our baby. She was demon spawn. She's the devil," the murderer said pointing his finger at Charity. "My baby's soul wasn't in her. She was dead in Christ! You made her a viper of lasciviousness, a fiend of Lilith, filled with unnatural desires and sinful lust. My baby is lost in Hell because of you!" Sweet's father screamed as the deputies handcuffed them and led them away.

"Can I have a few minutes with her?"

"Are you immediate family?" the nurse asked, obviously not approving of Charity's lifestyle.

"No."

"Then you need to leave," the nurse said touching her praying-hands pin on her collar. "Good, honest, God-fearing people trying to raise a descent family and your kind trying to turn God's way upside down. Our country is going to hell in a hand basket because of the likes of you," the nurse wailed.

Charity bent over and kissed Sweet on the mouth, very slowly, very gently, stealing the last bit of warmth that radiated from her body. The nurse screeched, "Get out now!" When Charity stood up, she held back her tears, glanced at her lover's battered face once more and stroked Sweet's honey colored hair one final time. She held everything back as she exited the building. Once inside the ambulance, she held back no longer, her yell rattled the windows. She too could only scream, "Why! Why! Why!"

After days of training the youth in the arts of carnal knowledge, Dickey was hanging with Shaddy's crew. Dickey enjoyed educating the young man, his enthusiasm was infectious. There were many girls and women that had their eyes on the young stud in his neighborhood, and Dickey took advantage of each and every one. Shaddy was developing the reputation of a player and his friends were amazed at how the once awkward young man was now such a smooth operator. As the bong was being passed around, girls were lap dancing to hip-hop that was beginning to get on Dickey's nerves. There was a knock on the door, and one of the girls dancing opened it. Shaddy's next-door neighbor, an obviously upset man, stood at the door. "Is Shaddy Carter here?" he asked.

The girl hollered, "Shaddy, there is some man here to see you."

The man shoved the girl aside and drew out his gun. "What the fuck skanky disease did you give my girl?" the man, said pointing the gun at Shaddy.

"I'm clean Mr. Caldwell. I didn't give Delores any disease."

"That's not what Delores said along with Tammy Smothers, Kim Hinson, Janet Hayes, Laura and Gina Timmons, and Brenda Ensley. All of them are in quarantine and they all say they were with you."

"Brenda Ensley?" one of Shaddy's crew asked. "Dog! You fucked my mom?"

Dickey was eyeing the door. He knew it was time to run. "You ain't going nowhere boy, but straight to hell," Mr. Caldwell informed him.

One of Shaddy's friends sprung from a chair and tackled the distraught man. The gun went off striking Dickey in the shoulder. "Fuck me!" Dickey screamed.

His heroic friend continued to pound Mr. Caldwell's hand to the floor 'til he released the gun. Another dude from Shaddy's crew picked it up.

"Don't point that gun at me," the heroic friend said.

"Then get off of him. I've got him covered."

Releasing Mr. Caldwell with a kick to the gut, the hero said, "What do we do now?"

"Get me to a hospital!" Dickey screamed. When Shaddy's friends looked his way, Mr. Caldwell ran out of the house.

When they arrived at the hospital with gunshot wounds, the Sheriff was called immediately. His pals were waiting in the emergency room when Shaddy's mother arrived. As round as she was tall, she was a doting mother and frantic when she arrived. She smacked Shaddy's friends with her purse before she asked any question. The boys explained what happened to her son, at which point she hugged and kiss them both. When the nurse told her Shaddy was out of x-ray and that his life was not in danger from the bullet wound, a resounding "Praise Jesus!" was heard loud and clear.

Zachriel followed the screaming mother clutching her two-year-old boy into the emergency room. The boy had swallowed an object from his older sister's board game and had stopped breathing. When the boy died Zachriel lifted the child's spirit into his own arms. He turned toward the emergency room doors when he smelled the residual scent of Joy on Hector. He watched where Hector went and, holding the hand of the toddler, followed.

The Sheriff spoke to a nurse and passed through the triage doors when he overheard, "The bullet cleanly penetrated his shoulder," the x-ray technician told the Doctor, "I saw no residual shrapnel. No surgery should be required."

"That's good news, is it okay to question the patient, Doctor?" the Sheriff asked.

"He's a minor, but his mother is in there with him." the doctor replied. "I need you to put on this face mask," he added as he lifted his up onto his face.

Zachriel smelled the demon behind the curtains. He followed the Sheriff and doctor. Shaddy in the hospital gown and his mother in a chair, the doctor introduced himself, "I've got some good news and some bad news, which would you like first?"

"Good news," the woman said.

"The good news, Mrs. Carter, is that the bullet cleanly penetrated Shadrach's shoulder. There will be no need for surgery."

Mrs. Carter clutches Shaddy's hand, "Yes, Jesus. So, what's the bad news?"

"Shaddy tested positive for a virus and we need to place him in quarantine."

"What kind of virus?"

"The only thing we know is that it is usually sexually transmitted."

Mrs. Carter took her purse and started whacking her son with it, "What kind of trash have you been fornicating with son? I didn't take you to church every time the doors were open for you to be following the devil."

"Mrs. Carter, Mrs. Carter, please!" the doctor yelled. "I'm not finished." Mrs. Carter stopped in mid-whack, "It's deadly, we have only had one death here in Dixon, but there have been several in the capital. We have four in intensive care that are connected by having sexual intercourse with your son. After the Sheriff finishes his questions, we will be moving Shadrach into quarantine. We also will need to test you as we have had one transmission non-sexually related."

"Dear God," Mrs. Carter said stunned.

"Mrs. Carter, is it okay for me to question your son?"

"Yes, Sheriff."

Dickey had no intention of going into quarantine. He let the fear of death germinate in the boy, which led to streams of tears. After telling the Sheriff about the incident with Mr. Caldwell, he simply wiped his tears before shaking Hector's hand after being questioned. As Hector stood to leave, he turned and Dickey smiled at Zachriel. Zachriel's immediate thoughts went to Joy. He took the cherubesque boy into his arms and departed.

I'm now the Sheriff of Dixon, I'm married to the delicious Joy McRae and my sister owns a brothel. This rivals my first life, Dickey thought as he quickly exited the building.

Chapter Thirty-Seven

Dickey's first line of business was to kill the man that shot him. Robert Caldwell was smart enough not to return to his home. Dickey had found only his two younger sons at the house, the younger one had the features of his sister. Using Shaddy, he had fucked Delores Caldwell in the bathroom at a party the night of Jackie's funeral. Both watched in the mirror when she swallowed the whole of his excitement. She was delightful, Dickey remembered as he thought of her young tender breast swinging to greet their image in the mirror. Soon, he reached Shaddy and his crew's crib.

The wonderful aspect of being a demon is the heightened sense of smell. He picked up Robert Caldwell's scent and followed it to the curb, where he found a brown paper bag that surrounded a tall Colt 45 malt liquor can. The receipt pointed to Lucy's, the corner market where members of the black community, which were of a certain maturity, could be found.

Got him, he said to himself, *but I can't kill him in front of witnesses.* Dickey drove back to the station and procured the Mustang for the stakeout.

Zachriel appeared in physical form to Joy, who was napping in bed with Kind by her side. With the angel was the aspiration of the boy whose spirit was in his care. Joy woke as the Dominion stroked her hair.

Startled to see an erection staring at her, which was obviously not her husband's, she gasped while sitting up in the bed pulling the covers up to her chin.

"Fear not," the angel said.

"Please don't tell me for, behold, I bring you good tidings of great joy. I'm too old for a miraculous conception," Joy told the angel. "I see you brought a cherub with you this time."

"He is no cherub, but a boy who has died in this past hour."

"So, you are an angel of death?" she asked.

"It is but one of many duties," Zachriel said.

"You are not here for my son?"

"No, I am here to warn you, your husband has been possessed by an incubus, to have any sexual relations with him could lead to your death," Zachriel paused, "I do not want that. Please leave and hide from him, do not let him do you any harm. Take your daughter with you. He has no boundaries. He knows not, but he collects souls for the Destroyer. But this knowledge would not stop the beast within him. He has slain many."

"Why do you tell me, and not warn the others?"

"I should not feel shame, but I do. I have encountered Anakites over many a millennia, all who I have been able to repel out of hatred for the base addiction they have caused to my brothers. That is until now. I love you, my excitement is true. I nary will lay with you, lest I be cast down to hell and become an incubus like the one I've warned you against, but you tempt me like none since my creation. Only my love for the Creator is stronger than my love for you."

"What are Anakites?"

"Mutant humans that produce a scent that transforms angels into sexual beings."

"So that is why," she pointed at the wetness that oozed from his maleness.

"Yes," he said, "The feather you possess belongs to me, if you are in danger, hold the feather towards Jerusalem say my name, Zachriel, and touch the feather to your forehead. I will come as soon as I can."

"Zachriel, which way is Jerusalem from here?"

"East, by south-east. I must take this child to comfort his mother. She is in need of feeling his presence. Take my heed, leave this place. He knew you once years ago, he wants to know you again."

He left as before, with a flash of light. Joy pondered the last thing the angel told her. *He knew me once years ago,* she thought. "Dickey has possessed Hector. Damn it. Mary Jane, Herb, pack your suitcases," she hollered, "We're going to visit Lula May for a few days."

Dickey waited most of the day for Robert Caldwell to return to Lucy's. From experience he knew that most of the men that drank malt liquor were alcoholics. Having just shot a man, his need would intensify. It was no surprise to Dickey that it was shortly after nightfall that he got his first strong whiff of Caldwell. He watched the man exit his car and enter the establishment. When he left, he had a case in his hand. Dickey followed the man leaving the town as he drove toward the lake. Dickey was pleased that he didn't stop at the old motel. Instead Caldwell drove out to the north side of the lake where many folks had lakeside cabins.

The fugitive noticed that he had been followed since he left town. "The police would have already turned their lights on by now. Stop being paranoid Rob," he said to himself.

Dickey backed off a bit, placing a good bit of distance between the cars. With the lack of streetlights, he could see the radiance of the old Chrysler's taillights a mile back. It was not long before Caldwell turned off the main road. Dickey followed 'til he saw the old beat up '84 Laser by an old lake house. He kept on driving checking to see if anyone was occupying any of the homes that were usually used as vacation cabins. All the homes on Canty Lane were black, Dickey could not believe his luck. He came back down to where the Laser was parked and turned on his lights. Caldwell saw Hector stepping out of his car, gun drawn. There was no use fighting or trying to escape. Caldwell exited his car.

"Put your hands on top of the car," Hector commanded. Caldwell did as he was ordered. Hector frisked him, found some weed and put it in his pocket. Hector placed his left hand on top of Caldwell's head and said, "You should never shoot a demon, they'll hunt your ass down and kill ya. Yep, they can send you straight to Hell as easy as this," he uttered before quickly placing his right hand under his chin and, with a twist, Dickey snapped the neck of Robert Caldwell. Abraxos, the Dominion, stood with the spirit of Robert Neil Caldwell and watched as Dickey dragged the deceased's body to the pier and dumped him into the cold December waters.

"These are your sins demon, recorded for the nether regions you have never seen. Rest not, I know a demon, once Virtue, who has asked for your whereabouts," Abraxos told Dickey. "Your returning hour is nigh."

Dickey made his way past the two spirits, opened the Mustang's door, and glared at the angel, "I have fed both Heaven and Hell, and they are still hungry. As long as I nourish them equally, there will be no jealousy. I am but another chef of disease and pestilence who serves up the sexually deviant and occasionally a side dish of murderous hearts. You are but a waiter that works for tips that never come. Bother me no more with your paltry poultry threats," Dickey joked toward the feathered one. He entered his car and made his way toward Joy. All this work made him horny.

Joy, with her car full of children, pulled up to Lula May's. Yvonne opened the door, "It's Joy, Aunt Lula May, and she has all her children with her." Yvonne kept the door open 'til Joy and her family entered. Lula May, Ethel and Hunter sat around the table.

"Lordy be," Lula May said, "I wish you'd called and lets me know you're coming. I'd cooked up these chillen' something good to eat."

"I would have but I don't want Dickey to know where I am. Hunter, do you mind if my brood watches TV over at your place."

"Not at all, Will is over there and the door is unlocked," he said.

"Yvonne, why don't you go over there with them, if a demon's seeking them out theys might needs protection," Lula May said.

"What's your name, little man?" Yvonne asked.

"Herb," he replied.

"My boys about your age, he's over at his Uncle Hunter's playing video games. I bet you'd like to play Madden NFL with him." Yvonne and the children left the house and crossed the yard to Hunter's detached apartment.

Joy sat down and said, "I know y'all are going to think I've been smoking weed when I tell you this, but I was visited by an angel who led me to believe Dickey had possessed Hector. He came to warn me, told me to leave or Dickey could possibly kill me."

"We knows where he is and we needs to catch him fast. But we needs to set a good trap for him. Hunter, call Grace and that Ho she works with. Ask her if theys have a room of mirrors?"

"We need to hide you, all of you and me too. Holding all the authority of a sheriff and all the power of a demon, he can kill us all and no one would know the better."

"But where?"

"Zachriel would know, "Joy said, "He said if I was in danger that I was to call him with his feather, and he'd come as fast as he could."

"Well call him," Ethel said.

"Which way is East by south-east?"

"My phone has a compass." Hunter said pulling it out and locating the direction.

Joy followed his instructions, pointing the feather East by south-east, calling his name, and touching her forehead. All were looking in the direction that she pointed the feather.

"Girl, you sure you weren't smoking weed?" Hunter asked.

There was a click on the kitchen window, followed by another. Joy looked out the window and Zachriel was standing by the old oak tree that rose between the house and the garage. "That's the first time I've seen him without an erection," Joy said.

"He must not want to talk to all of us. Joy you best go out there to him," Ethel said, "we'll wait inside." Hunter, Lula May, and Ethel watched the beautiful nude angel standing under the tree. "He's perfect, not a single flaw," Ethel said.

"I hope she invites him in, must be cold out there with no clothes," Lula May said.

As Joy approached the angel, Zachriel's affection for her showed itself. "Oh, my," Hunter said, "Wish that was my undercover angel."

"Why don't you come inside?" Joy asked.

"I can't, a witch resides there."

"It is white magic," Joy assured.

"Not always, I see things you cannot."

Joy looks back at the house. She looks up into his eyes, "We need to know where we can hide, where Dickey cannot enter?"

"Dickey?"

"He is the spirit that possessed my husband."

"Was that his human name?"

"His nickname."

"You must call him by his full name, no matter the length. Tell that to the witch."

"I will."

"Return to where you found my feather. A soul that refused judgment is bound there. He is bound to the room in which he breathed his last breath 'til the last day. In that room and that room only, you are safe. No demon can penetrate it physically. There is no physical structure that cannot be destroyed. If he sets fire to it, you are all lost. Do not let him know where you are." He disappeared with the flash of light that Joy has now grown accustomed to, but the three who watched from the window saw spots before their eyes for minutes.

All seven women that took part in the demise of Dickey Dickson sat around the table. Bonnie brought Faith directly from the hospital, all signs of the demon pox were gone. Lula May sat at the end of the table, the same as where Alice had killed J-Bird. Ethel and Bonnie sat across from each other next to Lula May. Joy sat across from Grace, and Faith from Charity.

Joy's phone rang, "It's Dickey."

"Answer it," Lula May said.

"Where you at?" Dickey asked through Hector.

"Hanging with the girls, they let Faith, Ellis, and Matthew out of the hospital today. Momma wants us girls to have some alone time. Ellis is watching the kids. Not sure when we'll be home."

"It's been a long time since I had the house alone. I think I'm going to go visit Iris to see what I can do to help her get ready for her New Year's bash. Have my own family night out. Is that cool with you?"

"Have fun."

"Love you." Dickey said, listening for Joy's tenor.

"Love you too, Hector, kisses," Joy said as usual before hanging up.

"Well done," Bonnie told her daughter.

"Now let's review all of our roles. Joy, you are the bait," Lula May said. "Grace, your room of mirrors is the trap."

"Make sure it is lined with curtains," Grace said.

"Charity, you must physically bind him," Lula May said.

"Make sure I bring something that inflicts pain," Charity grinned.

"You don't want to hurt Hector too bad, you just need to make him cry."

"Faith, you must capture his soul, his tears must land in the compact."

"Once three drops fall, set it on the floor and step back," Faith said.

"All of you," she said, "do not, whatever you do, touch him with your bare hands. Do not let any tears touch you. I watched Lloyd when he was possessed, after he broke down in tears, Dickey was gone. I don't know who touched them first, but they had to be the host that infected Hector."

"Ethel, Bonnie, you must repeat what I say. Bonnie you first, Ethel you follow."

"We must capture his soul before we can send him back to Hell."

"Oh, Zachriel said you must use his full name," Joy added.

"Who's Zachriel?" Charity asked.

"An angel with the hots for your sister," Ethel told all.

"Ah huh," Lula May nodded.

"What is his full name?" Joy asked, trying to detour the conversation away from her personal friend.

"Richard Donald Dickson," Bonnie said and repeated, "Richard Donald Dickson."

Bonnie look at Lula May, "How can you tell he has the hots for Joy?"

"The same as any naked man around a woman, but bigger, much bigger."

"He's just a friend." Joy said. "Don't worry momma, I'll explain it to you later."

"Why you?"

"Momma, not now, it's embarrassing."

"That's a first," Faith said. They all laughed.

All of Iris' girls were in top form. At Grace's insistence all the girls had to create their own modern version of Holly Golightly, which meant they were to wear gloves. Each girl had brought a flower to lay at the shine that Iris had created for Anne. Iris reminded them that there would be children present, as well as law enforcement figures, and if any transaction took place the utmost discretion was required. Penelope and Frank were dressed as the famous Capote characters, Penelope's beehive dragged the trailer's ceiling, which caused the couple to laugh. Not since Christmas had the whole family been together. Hope had Raul and his parents as her guests. Matthew and Charity, both dressed as George Peppard toasted Sweet. Lula May examined Iris and her home with a discriminating eye, "You're no Patricia Neal, Ho! But you got style, can't believe I's inside a trailer."

Dickey had arrived late. He had forced himself on a female prisoner, who became more than willing when the evidence was lost. All became a bit stiffer when the Sheriff arrived as Holly Golightly's Asian neighbor but relaxed as Dickey smiled revealing the character's buck teeth. Joy, also in a Holly Golightly gown, held Hector back. Kissing her gloved fingers and, touching his lips, Dickey took her fingers in his mouth.

"Not 'til after the family photo," Joy said, "I don't want to mess up my make-up."

The party was rocking, people were coming and going and Iris was documenting it all with her cameras. Because of the children and Ellis never leaving, Dickey didn't notice as his sisters-in-law, mother-in-law, or even Lula May left. Also, all the women moving and brushing against him was intoxicating. Slowly, each woman who had gathered the night before slipped outside. Grace nodded to Joy when all were in place. As Grace left, Joy went to Hector and smiled, "Want to go play before the ball drops?" Joy asked Hector.

"Damn right I do," Dickey replied.

"Grace said the blue-striped trailer on Ft. Sumter Lane was empty." As Joy and Hector entered the trailer Joy shut the door behind them. Dickey made his moves, copping her buttock and breast. "Not so fast," Joy said, "Grace said this trailer was special."

That was Grace's clue, "Hi Hector," Grace said sticking her head from behind the curtain, "Joy and I thought that we'd thank you for your service with our sister dance."

"Happy New Year Honey," Joy said. Grace began the music moving Hector to the center of the room. As she and Joy danced, they yanked down the black curtains revealing the mirrors that were behind them.

"It's getting hot in here," Dickey said to the sisters. He began taking off his clothes. When Grace and Joy got to the last curtain, Dickey was entranced with his own image, his shirt off, posing, flexing his muscles. Joy moved in closer, turning Dickey in her direction as she moved. When Dickey's back was to Grace, she removed the last curtain where

Charity and Faith stood. Charity, in one swift run, lunged at Dickey and tackled him flat binding his hands with zip ties.

"Ah, the McCrae sisters, do you really think you can hurt me?" Hector's face began to transform into Dickey's. Charity lifted the spasmodic demon and handcuffed him to the stripper pole. "He's secure!" Charity bellowed.

Lula May, Bonnie, and Ethel came down the hall, each holding a candle. After entering the room of mirrors, the women lit another candle each at the altar that was hidden behind the last curtain before blowing the one they held out. Lula May then circled the demon and began to chant. "Ayizan, keeper of innocent children, right their wrong, help us return the evil doer to his punishment in Hell." Bonnie repeated followed by Ethel. All three stomped once simultaneously then shook a rattle. "Oh, cross! Oh, jubilee! Don't you see I'm innocent? Baron La Croix, hear my plea for justice, hear of a soul who claims your swagger in death," said once, then twice, then a third time in complete corresponding correctness. All three stomped twice together, lifted the crucifixes hanging around their necks and kissed them.

"Mamba Zila, protector of the bonds that bind marriage and family, help return the blatant one to Hell who violated the marriage vow and ripped the virginal innocence from young girls." Dickey began to laugh out loud trying to disrupt the chanting. All three women in white stomped simultaneously three times before reaching in their pockets and tossing red rose petals in the air.

"Kalfou, hear the validity of this bond, take the blood offering of his offspring, grant us your approval," Lula May, Bonnie and Ethel concurrently stomped four times before removing the gavels held by silver braided cords around their waist and pounded the iron pole that secured Dickey seven times. "Baron La Croix, Ayizan, Mamba Zila, Kalfou search our hearts for the truth in our cause." Faith opened the compact and the four spirits called forth rose out of it and examined the eyes of all seven women before ascending to hover near the ceiling. The spirits locked their arms and began to circle above Dickey. Charity quickly took an onion and knife out of her pocket and cut it below Dickey's eyes.

"Not fair," Dickey screamed, "not fair!"

"When were you ever fair Richard Donald Dickson? When were you ever fair?" Charity asked, cutting the onion once more as Dickey clinked, clanged, and banged against the stripper's pole. Grace grabbed hold of his body and Joy clinched his hair, pulling his head back as Charity cut the onion once again. The tears were building in his eyes, and she too began to cry, but the large woman laughed right through it as she told the demon, "You're going back to Hell, Richard Donald Dickson, straight back to Hell."

The tears rolled down Hector's cheeks. Faith, wearing latex gloves, held the compact below his face as they rolled downward into the compact. She counted aloud as they hit the dried caked powder, "one, two, three." Faith stepped away, nodding at Lula May.

"Baron La Croix, Ayizan, Mamba Zila, Kalfou, seal Richard Donald Dickson to the blood of our sacrifice." The circling spirits stared into the eyes of the demon. "Chain his soul with this blood sacrifice of his own child 'til the great Damballah claims him." Bonnie and Ethel complete the chant. Ayizan hooked his fingers into his nostrils, Baron La Croix reached in and seized his heart as Mamba Zila clutched Dickie's genitals. Kalfou circled to the back of the demon and with one hand cinched Dickey's hair and with the other hand his tailbone, and with a nod of his head the four removed the squirming demon from Hector's body. Faith sat the opened compact on the floor as all watched in amazement as the five spirits diminished in size. In their minuscule state they tossed Dickey onto the caked powder. Three identical apparitions of Hope, covered in blood, rose up, clutched him and sank down in the compact as if they were standing in quicksand. The four spirits called forth were drawn up with the wisps of smoke from the candles lit at the altar. Fearing Dickey may try to escape with them, Ethel quickly blew them out.

Lula May walked over to Faith and closed the compact and slid it in her pocket. Joy kissed Hector as Charity unlocked her brother-in-law. They all hugged each other in congratulations and after Lula May, Bonnie, and Ethel changed back into their costumes, they all returned to the party singing "Auld Lang Syne."

"All is good in the world once again," Ethel said.

"We got a wedding to plan, that's when all will be right with the world," Bonnie said looking at Lula May.

"You remember what you said girl?" Lula May said to Charity.

"Yes mam, I'm eating my words, I know" she said wrapping her arm around Lula May.

"How about a Christmas in July wedding?" Charity asked.

"It's your wedding," Grace said, "You can have whatever type of wedding you like."

"Celebrating Jesus," Faith said, "I think that's a lovely idea."

"With an angel choir," Joy added thinking of Zachriel.

"Hallelujah," Hector said, "Hallelujah."

Chapter Thirty-Eight

"It's my honor to present Mr. And Mrs. William Zemp," the Good Rev. Doctor Three Names said to the applause of the crowd and whooping firefighters. Ethel stepped up to the pulpit and announced, "Please join the bride and groom in the fellowship hall for the reception."

"That's my signal," Lula May said to the void next to her, "You oughta' come, it ain't like you ain't family." Many around Lula May thought she suffered from dementia, but the White sisters knew differently. Lula May knew a short cut to the basement where the fellowship hall was located. It appeared as if she were trying to trick a dog inside a fence. Lula May went against the flow of the crowd to the left-side door beside the pulpit. Lula May knew this hidden path for long ago she cleaned the church building to help her nieces go to college. A chill was felt by those who stepped by Lula May, which caused many to try to find the source.

"I wonder what brand of air-conditioning they have?" a woman said looking to the ceiling for a vent that was not there. As Ethel looked over her shoulder, she too got shivers for she could see the spirit of Dickey Dickson, chain bound, following Lula May through the door.

"I've got to serve the groom's cake, Dickey, you'll never guess what kind it is."

"Fruitcake," Dickey's haunted voice said sounding as if it had originated from a deep well.

"You's ain't been spying on me has ya'?" Lula May teased the ghost. Bonnie and Ethel entered the alcove and, joining Lula May, they began to circle the demon counterclockwise. "You knows Dickey, many a person from all walks of life has come to me for a poisonous potion to killz someone. And no matter the money they offered I's always turns um down. People come to me for poison the same reason Bonnie did and I's turns um down. You's rapes them girls and that's enough reason, anyone would tell ya'. But I's the one who killed ya' and it ain't why you think. It alls goes back to your daddy killing his own blood. I's remembers the day like it was yesterday. Mama cluchin' us chillen' under the pines next to the old pecan grove on cedar hill. You sees it don't ya'? Your daddy out there with the rest of that cracker trash, beaten 'em, kickin' 'em just like a stray dog. Yous there, I's saws ya'. Your's Daddy was killin' my daddy because he was his brother and your grandpappy did right and left my daddy a little wee bit of land. My daddy didn't haft to work for your daddy no more and he told him so. The lies, the lies your daddy told on my daddy. And when those people lifted my daddy up on that mule and tossed that there rope into that pecan tree, I's broke loose from my mama and was screaming, 'Don't kill my daddy! Please, don't kill my daddy' and my brother Jim chased after me and tackled me to the ground. He puts his hand over my mouth, and I struggled and wrestled with him in the tall high grass. And I heard your daddy say 'Yous going to Hell, niggar!' And I's looked up and he slapped the mule and my daddy was left there hangin'. His body was jerking like a worm on a hook. He struggled so hard that pecans rained down on you crackers. They was all silent but you. I sees you standing there, pointing your finger and laughin' and thens they all starts to laugh. And when his body was still, them white cracker ass bitches started picking up the pecans off the ground and puttin' them in their aprons. And I bit my brother's hand and he let loose, nothing could stop me from howlin'. I's never felt any pain that could tear your gut apart as much. Tears running down my face, I stood there. My brother holdin' onto my ankles so I's wouldn't run. Your daddy saws me, and just picked up a couple of nuts, looked at me and cracked them. Then with pride theys all stood by my daddy's dangling body and took a picture. You laughed and did cart wheels 'til the storm clouds showed their face. And I swore

I would kill you then, all of you. When y'all was gone, my brothers climbed that tree and cut my daddy down. We took him home, and I's clean all the blood from his face, and we buried him knowing there was nothin' we could do here in Dixon."

Both Bonnie and Ethel had tears in their eyes hearing the story for the first time. Coming to a complete understanding of the tragedy the woman who cared for them contained inside her since before their births. Lula May, after the third circle around Dickey, stopped to stare at the spirit before she reversed the flow to clockwise.

"The next day though, mama and me took salt and spread it all under that tree. My granny came and started teaching me the art of plants and which spirits to call on. One by one, them crackers died. Not all at once. Mama cursed your Mama first, 'cause she confirmed your daddy's lie and that got the Klan all riled up. Many died by God's hands, if not by the German's. 'Til all that was left was you chillen' and I kills everyones of you and I watched your momma and daddy suffer like we did on that day, one by one, over and over again, 'til all that was left from those that lynched my daddy was you and your sufferin' daddy and momma, and they suffered 'til the day they died by your own sister's hand. I made sure of it. But I's killed ya' Dickey Dickson, knows that. And I's the one who's sending ya' back to Hell."

Dickey's spirit laughed aloud at Lula May just as if he were a child once more. Ending the third clockwise circle the sisters departed Lula May. At the bottom of the stairwell stood Bonnie and at the top stood Ethel. The two sisters placed silver chokers around their necks, white veils over their heads and chanted, "Damballah, who lives in the tree, Damballah, a soul has escaped thee." Lula May began to whistle a tune that ended with the hiss of a snake. Her body moved with serpentine grace. Her wrist with silver charms chimed. "Damballah, who lives in the tree, Damballah, a soul has escaped thee," the sisters chanted twice more.

The spirit of Damballah appeared before them. His face appeared as if it had been painted in white lead. His garments moved as if snakes writhed underneath. Once amongst the three women and the ghost of Dickey Dickson, snakes crawled out of his ears and eye sockets. Sensing the silver, the snakes recoiled from the women. But Dickey Dickson had no silver. Damballah's snake fingers extended and coiled around the spirit of Dickey Dickson. "No, please, no," Dickey's spirit cried out.

A massive snake struck from Damballah's mouth and swallowed Dickey's spirit whole. His body-like form writhed inside the now enlarged snake. His muffled screams reverberated through the stairwell, and as quick as the Voodoo spirit's snake tongue struck, it returned into Damballah's mouth. Lula May and Damballah danced together, the mouth's snake slipped over the spirit's pale lips and lapped the tears of joy streaming down the old woman's face. Damballah kissed Lula May on the cheek with his cold scaly mouth before he dissipated leaving the smell of sulfur behind.

"I hope his ass rotisseries gold in Hell," Bonnie said.

The two sisters hugged Lula May and kissed her on the cheek. "We've got a weddin' to celebrate my babies, all evil is gone from this place," Lula May said, returning their kisses.

Lula May, Bonnie, and Ethel went into the crowded fellowship hall all smiles as if nothing had happened. Ethel found the MC slash DJ and got the music started. Bonnie went and stood by Charity and greeted the guests, and Lula May stood behind the groom's cake.

"Fruitcake y'all? Have some fruitcake, it's me and my sisters' blue ribbon winning recipe, the county's best. This ain't no Claxton or missionary fruitcake made by some tipsy nuns or jolly ole priests. No sir, nothing bitter in it, not too sweet, flavored with the right amount of spirits, just likes me. I knows, I's made it myself," Lula May said with pride.

The End

About the Author

MARK DANIEL COMPTON was born and raised in South Carolina. He spent his early years going to weddings, funerals, church and family reunions. His grandparents spoiled him with the beauty of the Carolina low country and its culture. He has a BA in Theatre and Speech from the USC Columbia, an MA in Cross-Cultural Tourism Development and a MFA with a focus on Time-Based Media and Graphic Design from ETSU. He has written, produced, acted and directed on both stage and screen. His photographic works have been shown at the Reese Museum. In 2007, he began teaching various humanities courses in higher education, including Cinema for the Tennessee Consortium for International Study in Edinburgh, Scotland and English for AB Tech at Craggy Rock Prison in Asheville, NC. Mark has traveled and lived from Miami to Seattle, and many places in between; currently he lives with his partner in Columbia, SC.